SHADOWSWORD

SHADOWSWORD

GUY HALEY

BLACK LIBRARY

A BLACK LIBRARY PUBLICATION

First published in 2016.
This edition published in Great Britain in 2017 by
Black Library,
Games Workshop Ltd.,
Willow Road,
Nottingham, NG7 2WS, UK.

10 9 8 7 6 5 4 3 2 1

Produced by Games Workshop in Nottingham.
Cover illustration by Adam Tooby.

A CIP record for this book is available from the British Library.

ISBN 13: 978 1 78496 610 2

See Black Library on the internet at

blacklibrary.com

Find out more about Games Workshop
and the world of Warhammer 40,000 at

games-workshop.com

Printed and bound by CPI Group (UK) Ltd, Croydon, CR0 4YY.

It is the 41st millennium. For more than a hundred centuries the Emperor has sat immobile on the Golden Throne of Earth. He is the Master of Mankind by the will of the gods, and master of a million worlds by the might of his inexhaustible armies. He is a rotting carcass writhing invisibly with power from the Dark Age of Technology. He is the Carrion Lord of the Imperium for whom a thousand souls are sacrificed every day, so that he may never truly die.

Yet even in his deathless state, the Emperor continues his eternal vigilance. Mighty battlefleets cross the daemon-infested miasma of the warp, the only route between distant stars, their way lit by the Astronomican, the psychic manifestation of the Emperor's will. Vast armies give battle in His name on uncounted worlds. Greatest amongst his soldiers are the Adeptus Astartes, the Space Marines, bioengineered super-warriors. Their comrades in arms are legion: the Astra Militarum and countless planetary defence forces, the ever-vigilant Inquisition and the tech-priests of the Adeptus Mechanicus to name only a few. But for all their multitudes, they are barely enough to hold off the ever-present threat from aliens, heretics, mutants – and worse.

To be a man in such times is to be one amongst untold billions. It is to live in the cruellest and most bloody regime imaginable. These are the tales of those times. Forget the power of technology and science, for so much has been forgotten, never to be re-learned. Forget the promise of progress and understanding, for in the grim dark future there is only war. There is no peace amongst the stars, only an eternity of carnage and slaughter, and the laughter of thirsting gods.

DRAMATIS PERSONAE

The Paragonian Seventh Super-Heavy Tank Company

The crew of the Baneblade *Cortein's Honour*

COLARON VOR ARTEM LO BANNICK	Honoured Lieutenant
EPPERALIANT	Second Lieutenant Commsman
KARLOK SHOAM	Driver
MEGGEN	First Gunner
JAMERON LO KALLIGEN	Second Gunner
DEMIS LEONATES	Third Gunner
HUWAR LO GANLICK	Third Loader
DOTRIAN VASKIGEN	First Loader
GOLLPH	Second Loader
MOS KOLIOS	Tech-Adept Aspirant

The crew of the Shadowsword *Lux Imperator*

HURNIGEN	Honoured Lieutenant
VREMONT JINEREEN	Second Lieutenant Commsman
UDOLPHO LO KRAST	Driver
VANDO HASTILLEEN	First gunner

| Rastomar Kalligen | Third gunner |
| Starstan | Enginseer Tech-Adept |

Some of the crew of the Baneblade *Artemen Ultrus*

| Marteken | Honoured Lieutenant |
| Cholo | Second Lieutenant Commsman |

Some of the crew of the command Hellhammer *Ostrakhan's Rebirth*

Kandar Vor Ostrakhan Lo Hannick	Honoured Captain
Cholken	Second Lieutenant Commsman
Rosdosigen	First Gunner
Primus Brasslock	Enginseer
Chensormen	Commissar

The 477th Paragonian Foot

Lubin Lo Santelligen	Captain
Mazdaran	Lieutenant
Jonas Artem Lo Bannick	Lieutenant
Bosarain	Ensign
Suliban	Commissar
Lin Coass Lo Turneric	Medicae

MICZ	Special Weapons Veteran Trooper
CARIUS KILLEK	Trooper
ANDERICK	Commsman

The Eighth Paragonian Super-Heavy Tank Company (Assault), 'The Lucky Eights'

| ARDOMAN KOSIGIAN LO PARRIGAR | Honoured Captain |
| GULINAR | Second Lieutenant Commsman |

The Black Templars, Adeptus Astartes

MEODRIC	Chaplain
BASTOIGNE	Emperor's Champion
ADELARD	Sword Brother

The court of Magor's Seat

MISSRINE HURATAL I	Governatrice
DOSTAIN HURATAL	Heir the Second
POLLEIN HURATAL	Heir the Third
ORAVAN	Captain, Magorian Yellow Guard

The servants of Chaos

| LORD DAMIEN TRASTOON | Emperor's Children Traitor Legion |

DIB   Herald of the Dark
                           Prince

Others

BANNICK VARDAMON VOR   Lord Colonel
ANSELM LO BANNICK

CHAPTER ONE
THE DEVIL'S CHOICE

IMPERIAL GOVERNOR'S PALACE, MAGOR'S SEAT
GERATOMRO
0458394.M41

They came always to the droning of priests. The rapturous, augmitter-amplified singing of a hundred Adeptus Ministorum clerics penetrated the doors to the Grand Hall of Magor with ease. A hundred yards away, on the other side of thick wood clad in bronze reliefs, and still Governatrice Missrine Huratal could hear them. They did not stop singing when the gong of audience, hung outside the Hall of Magor, sounded the customary four times to request admittance. They did not stop while Huratal made them wait.

Oravan, captain of Magor's Yellow Guard, looked to her for permission to open the way to the delegation. She ignored him and bent down to fuss over her canids, her corpulent body shifting painfully in a throne that would once have swallowed her four times over with room to spare. The gong sounded again. Four sonorous notes. She ignored it. The canids yapped.

'My lady!' cried Oravan from the gates, hesitant in his concern that she leave the emissaries of the Emperor waiting so long. 'The adepts demand admittance.'

From the floating crib behind Huratal, Heir the First Missrine II set up her squalling.

'Stop your bellowing, foolish man,' said Missrine, making her chins wobble. 'You disturb our daughter.' The rest of the court, arrayed in all their finery, stood in silence.

'Mother, mother! The noise!' squawked the vat-born infant. 'It scares me so.' Wet nurses scurried to the Heir the First's bed, crooning and fussing over the thing within to no avail.

Many in the court looked to the floating crib from the corners of their eyes, their revulsion showing behind masks of deference.

Missrine II continued with her gurgling, half-human cries. Huratal gave her clone-daughter's nurses a glower. With panicked faces they shushed harder, until Missrine II finally quieted.

The audience gong resonated to a third set of four notes.

The mistress of Geratomro plucked up Mikki, her favourite canid, from the barking mass at her feet. She kissed and petted it. 'Shall we let them in, dear one?' she said. 'Shall we?'

Mikki yapped piercingly. Her sisters joined in.

'My lady...' said Oravan.

'Oh, let them in,' said Missrine with a slow wave.

Oravan saluted crisply and turned on his heel. At his command the gates were swung wide by the yellow-cloaked guard. A wave of blue incense smoke roiled through the door, thick and sudden as a sea fog. Thus shrouded, the Departmento Munitorum mission entered the heart of her domain. They strode up the aisle between the crowds of silent courtiers to the throne dais, expressions severe, as bold as if they owned the world. *Her* world. She curled her lip at their presumption.

There was a crowd large enough to intimidate a lesser soul than she. For all this show of strength, in reality there were only two – Borowik and Querol – who mattered out of the lot of them. Missrine kept her mind fixed on that. She had decided not to be cowed long since.

Borowik and Querol were opposites in every regard. Senior Assessor Borowik behaved like a conquering general and not the pen-pushing parasite among a billion similar creatures that he was. A low-gravity upbringing was apparent decades after he had been taken from his home. He was tall and thin to the point of cadaverousness. Callipers hissed on his arms and legs, supporting his delicate frame against Geratomro's entirely average pull. Typical of the Imperium, to send one such as he here rather than to a low-density world or orbital habitat to which he might be better suited, thought Missrine. The Imperium was unthinking, unfeeling, a mess of illogicality and inefficiency. They treated her the same way, but there was no sense of kinship at her and Borowik's shared misfortunes; Huratal thought only of her own power. Her jaw set harder. Thoughts like that were good. They steeled her resolve at what she must do. Heir the Second Dostain had laid it all out to her in impressive detail. She hated to listen to the boy. He was weak-willed and feeble. But in this matter he was right; there was no other choice.

Tithemaster Querol was short, tubby and relatively young to Borowik's emaciated antiquity. Where Borowik carried a metal shako loosely under his arm, Querol clutched a data-slate as tightly as a child holds a comfort blanket. He hurried along beside his master, taking two steps to his every one. Where Borowik kept his gaze fixed on Huratal, Querol's went everywhere but the Governatrice, most often lighting on Borowik in an obvious need for the older man's approval. Borowik studiously ignored him.

An army of black-armoured guards, modified savants, robed functionaries and servitor automata followed them – and the damn priests, of course: a clanking, mumbling, wailing parade of Imperial power. The score of middle-ranking Adeptus Administratum bureaucrats that afflicted her planet skulked in the centre of the crowd in a pathetic bid for anonymity, for it was they who had summoned the assessor, an act of craven treachery which she had been powerless to punish. She recited their names to herself. She would forget not a single one.

Borowik and Querol continued their mismatched march down the aisle of the Hall of Magor, the former stalking like a bird, the latter scampering in the manner of a rodent between the massed assemblage of Huratal's court. The nobility and officers of her government were numerous, and resplendent in their plumes and breastplates, dresses and lofty headgear, most of them large, for weight was a sign of status upon Geratomro. To them Borowik gave no attention, while Querol stole furtive, nervy glances at their well-fleshed faces.

The parade stopped with a crescendo, the hymns, chants and proclamations ceasing in perfect time with Borowik's last footfall. The delegation arrayed themselves at the foot of the stairs leading up to Huratal's throne with practised precision. Servitor power plants puttered in the uneasy silence. Servo-skulls whined overhead, sweeping the chamber and its occupants with wide-spread augur beams for who knew what purpose. A measurement of hats? A survey of powder usage? A cross referencing of tooth size? Mikki yelped as Huratal's hands tightened around her. The demands of the Adeptus Administratum for pointless information was one of the many things the Governatrice would not miss.

The court herald stepped forwards to the foot of the dais steps, his round head lost in the layered ruffs and lace-trimmed lapels of his yellow uniform.

'Senior Assessor Borowik!' he proclaimed. 'Tithemaster Querol! Arrived this day from the deeps of space and the peril of the warp, here to treat with our most blessed and wise lady, Governatrice Missrine Huratal, of the House of Magor, of the line of Magor, planetary governor of Geratomro, mistress of all human souls within the bounds of the system of Gerat by holy fiat of the God-Emperor of mankind. Queen under the sun. Our queen.'

Trumpets blew. The herald rolled his parchment and bowed so low to his lady that the yellow plumes of his helmet brushed the floor. He stood and waited to be dismissed with a look of nervous adoration. She nodded, generously she thought, to show that he had done well.

Borowik waited with stony patience for the herald to finish, his unblinking, deep-set eyes not leaving Huratal's face once. Such impertinence from any other man would be met with blinding. But not he! No, Borowik thought himself above her. He would learn.

'Lady Governatrice, your tithe is overdue!' Borowik said. His powerful voice contrasted with his weak body, and Huratal's determination wavered. With the Imperial authorities, it was always what you could not see that was important, and Borowik's voice was an uncomfortable reminder of that. 'You flout the primary and only rule of planetary governership. You refuse the tithe. Release the military assets owed or pay the consequences. This is your only warning.'

Silence but for the scratch and whir of the autoscribe embedded in the torso of Borowik's Keeper of Records, and the whisper of creamy paper folding onto the floor, every word recorded. Huratal's misgivings burned up in the fire of her anger. The autoscribe caught up and fell quiet. How dare he, this ink-stained drone, threaten her? Huratal made a dismissive noise in her throat. She levered her huge bulk forwards to better glare at her challengers, dislodging Mikki and several cushions. Gripping the armrests with her chubby hands, she spoke, her chins rippling with her anger.

'In the wilds of Geratomro, in the mountains near this palace, in fact,' she said, 'there is said to dwell a puckish creature no taller than a child and covered in hair.'

A servitor piped a shrill whistle for silence. Ordering her, in her own throne room.

'I fail to see the relevance,' said Borowik. 'I come with but one command – obey the High Lords, or the light of the Emperor will turn from your world.'

'They call it the Devil-in-the-bush,' she continued. Borowik's fingers curled around his hat and his eyes narrowed, but he held his peace. 'Not a thing of this world or any other, but perhaps from somewhere else. It is dangerous, as such uncanny things can be, but not to the body. Rarely is it seen by day. Sometimes at night. But almost always by dusk or dawn. It dances, they say, on the line of the night and the day.

'The story goes that those who meet this fiend are offered a choice between two seemingly unconnected things,' she continued. 'Single words only, usually. Such things as "heartfelt or stones" it might say. "Money or eggs", "time or deliverance". It has deep brown eyes wiser than those of any human, and a grin of delight plays across its face throughout every encounter. In the legends – they are all the same, since such beings always have the wiles to force the unwary to undergo the prescribed course of the story – one cannot look away from those eyes until one chooses. They seem to grow bigger and bigger until they swallow up the world, and the victim – make no mistake, lord senior assessor, those that the Devil-in-the-bush meets are its victims in every way – feels they will be lost inside, and blurts out a choice to avoid that fate. At which point the Devil-in-the-bush laughs, skips away along the line between the night and the day, and vanishes. "Spice or lace", "Earth or sea", "Matter or vapour".'

'Heresy!' muttered a priest. Episcope Chulux, caught in an unenviable position between his Planetary Governor and outraged Imperial authority, shushed him and gave Huratal a queasy smile.

'And what is your meaning in reciting this charming, if possibly heretical, folk tale, my lady?' asked Borowik.

'A myth, that is all,' said Huratal with deadly sweetness. 'A story as likely to be found on this world as on any other, and meaningless.'

Borowik opened his mouth. Huratal held up her hand.

'We have not finished! Pray let us conclude our argument. Inscrutable though they sound, the choices the Devil-in-the-bush offers most definitely have a bearing on the chooser. Their life will be changed, they can be assured of that. For but a few, a very fortunate few, one of these choices will precipitate a cascade of events that bring great reward twined inextricably with unbearable loss. The other might simply see the chooser dead. Either way, the chooser is doomed to sorrow from the outset. The outcome of neither choice offered is predictable, and very rarely desirable. To we of Geratomro, the legend gives the aphorism of "the devil's choice". Can you guess what that might mean to us, my lord assessor?'

'Enlighten me,' said Borowik tightly.

'To be given the devil's choice is to be given a pair of options which cannot be chosen between in any good conscience. You see, we face the devil's choice today. A choice you give us.' She sat back and stared imperiously at the representatives of the Adeptus Administratum. At the bottom of the dais' twenty-seven steps they seemed small and insignificant. She was set high over them by birth and circumstance, a planetary governor, whereas they were merely functionaries of a remote, half-dead god. They were surrounded by her officials, her officers and family, who glittered in their finery brighter than the stars of any firmament. The various lords-superior of her council and the minor lords-civil were useless to her in this choice. But they outnumbered the delegation several times over, and that counted for something. The local Administratum functionaries, uncomfortable looking in the group, were the delegation's only allies, and unreliable ones at that.

However distant the Imperium, however small its agents seemed, its reach was great. Huratal held a planet by her birth; these men, these scribblers, could put her off her throne with the stroke of a pen. She was gambling everything. A devil's choice indeed.

'We do not have the men,' she said. 'We cannot comply.' Three hundred noble faces looked from her to the visiting adepts.

'You proclaim open rebellion. To withhold men from the tithe of the Departmento Munitorum is gross treason, Governatrice,' said Borowik.

'How many times do we have to say it?' she said. Her face flushed. 'We relayed this information to you via astropath. Again by direct hololith whilst you were still in orbit. We have been visited by the recruitment fleets of the Departmento Munitorum eight times in the last seven years. Every one of those eight times, we have complied quickly and to the letter. You already have every able-bodied man we can spare. This ninth time, we say no! We do not have the men,' she said, enunciating her words very carefully. 'Can you comprehend what we are saying?'

Querol stepped forwards. 'If... if I may?' he said apologetically. Borowik nodded. 'What of your planetary garrison?' Querol said. He licked his lips and consulted his data-slate. 'Our records indicate you have thirteen regiments under arms.' He was a small, sweaty man, with a small, sweaty man's stridulating voice.

'Had, Tithemaster Querol, had. Do you note our use of the past tense there? Had! You have had your one-tenth of men, and then another, and another, and another. We have fewer than five hundred thousand men under arms to defend this world and all its dependencies in our system. Our factories are empty. The husbands of our wives are missing. The fathers of our children,' she opened one pudgy hand quickly, 'gone.'

'If you have men, then you must give them, and freely,' said Borowik. 'Or you shall suffer the consequences.'

'No,' she said. 'It is not enough. It never will be enough for you.'

Querol licked his fat, purple lips and tried a conciliatory smile. 'This is but a little misunderstanding, senior assessor. I am sure our lady can spare them for the greater glory of the Imperium. The Lord Solar Macharius requires more troops if he is to conclude his glorious conquests.'

With great effort, Huratal heaved herself from her throne. Scattering cup-sized canids before her, she descended the steps, forcing aside the gaggle of minor heirs she had to attend on her, and came to a halt only three steps from the bottom. Shock at her descent whispered around the court like wind through reeds.

'No! You do not hear, though you have ears. We say again, we cannot spare them. The Lord Solar's crusade has bled this planet dry. All systems in this subsector report increased incidences of xenos raids. Five months ago, our outermost outposts were attacked. They will be attacked again. The enemies of mankind smell blood in the water. If we are weak, then we will perish.'

'Then raise more troops,' said Borowik.

'From where? Who will man our factories and our fields?' she said, her voice trembling with anger. 'If we give my men to you, we will not be able to pay the due exacta, a tithe as important as yours, as so many other parasites like you impress upon us. On the one hand, we have the Departmento Exacta, on the other, the Departmento Munitorum. Who shall go without?'

'Then put your women to work, your children,' said Borowik. 'You have a population of one point five billion on this world alone. Four times that much in the Gerat star system. Cogitator simulation suggests you can rearrange your workforce sufficiently to provide Terra's due with a drop-off of a few tenths of a per cent and fulfil the requirements of the Astra Militarum immediately. I am sure my colleagues of the Departmento Exacta will be merciful.'

Huratal laughed, sending her pulse skyrocketing and her chins jiggling. 'Mercy? Your kind knows nothing of mercy. You have ink in your veins. What happens when you return again for more men?' she said. 'Who do we give you? Our babes? Our livestock? This then, is the devil's choice we have. Give you what you demand, and risk disappointing another coterie of bureaucrats. Neither branch of your organisation is tolerant of failure. What would you have us do?'

A nervous titter sounded from somewhere in the court. She silenced it with a glare that swept out over her relatives and vassals like a las-beam.

'Local governance is not our concern,' said Borowik. 'The fulfilment of the tithe is. Every problem must be overcome individually. This matter at hand can be addressed immediately. You choose not to do so. Other issues that arise may be dealt with as they emerge. Dozens of worlds fall to the Lord Solar Macharius. The Imperium expands on your doorstep. Your system stands to benefit much from the increase in trade and shipping passing through this subsector from the new territories.'

'Pain now, plenty tomorrow?' she snorted. 'We have heard that too many times from the mouths of Imperial officials. What do I tell my people when the xenos come and burn their cities? We have heard the reports from nearby systems. We are not the only ones to refuse. Genthus has declined.'

'Ah, well. Genthus has been retaken, and its governor replaced,' said Querol gently.

'Yes. But if we decline, and then another world and another, can you retake them all? This level of recruitment is unsustainable. The subsector strains under your demands. We cannot bear it. We will not. We refuse. Others will follow.'

'I ask you one more time for the Imperial record, Governatrice, are you denying us our due?' Borowik looked down his nose, nostrils arched at the smell of stale perfume and sweat coming off her.

'Listen to us, you foolish man!' she bellowed. 'We are denying you. The line has to be drawn here, before we run out of sand to mark.'

Borowik looked around the court, its high ceilings of marble, the glittering chandeliers, the gold and statuary and other trappings of Huratal's wealth.

'Do you see this, Querol? Such riches. All this glory is not yours, Governatrice. This belongs to the Emperor of Mankind. You belong to Him. We all do. To deny our request is to defy His Will. I say one final time, comply with the tithe. I will give you no more chances to redeem yourself.'

Huratal smiled, an expression made up of sorrow, bitterness and despair. 'We are sure we can come to an accommodation to prevent any unpleasantness. Give Geratomro a few more years.'

'We cannot,' said Borowik. 'The data says you can pay, so pay you shall.'

'The data is wrong,' said Huratal, vainly attempting to hide the plea in her words.

'Nevertheless, it says you can pay. There is no negotiation.'

'Then so be it!' she said. She exhaled with relief. There was no backing out now. 'Our ancestor, Magor, settled this world seven thousand years ago. For long periods we have known no Imperial interference. We have fared well enough. This is our world by right. Take your empty threats away.'

'They are not empty. Think you that we shall cut ties and let you drift, to return with the world on its knees once you have tasted the poisonous fruits of liberty? Geratomro is of too high value to be allowed to secede. You will be invaded,' said Borowik unpleasantly, as if he savoured the prospect.

'There is no force in this part of the segmentum big enough to take a planet like Geratomro, unless you divert fleets and men from the crusade. Withdraw your demand, understand our position. Leave us be, and you will be short fifty thousand men. If you do not, the deficit will be ever so much greater.

'My lady, we cannot. There is no space for discretion in the workings of the Departmento Munitorum. If our orders say fifty thousand men, then fifty thousand men you must provide. You court censure already with that thing you have bred,' he said, looking to Missrine II's crib.

'Succession must be assured,' she said. 'Another duty.'

'Not in that manner. But it shall be overlooked, if you comply.'

'Now you threaten our daughter. No and no again. It is our final answer.'

Borowik bowed. 'Then you know what will occur now.' Borowik's guards aimed their guns at Huratal. The court babbled in fear. Huratal raised her hand. The crowds seethed as yellow-robed warriors pushed their way out, and raised their own weapons. Along the galleries of the hall, others emerged from auspex-shielded positions and pointed their guns down at the delegation.

'Unwise,' said Borowik.

The Departmento Munitorum's soldiery opened fire. A fraction of a second later, so did Huratal's men.

Ruby beams of las-light snapped around the chamber, sending the court scattering. Obese nobles fled in all directions in an explosion of yellow and gold. Dozens of them were cut down in the cross-fire, but fewer than might be expected, for the soldiers in black were gunning only for Huratal.

She stood in the heart of destruction, a score of las-beams striking at her. Her conversion field flared brightly with every shot, absorbing and re-emitting the energy of the weapons as blinding light. Behind her, Missrine II's crib wobbled as its in-built field did the same. Through the field glare she saw men topple, cut down by her personal guard's merciless shots. Most of Borowik's entourage were unarmed. Priests died with prayers on their lips. Cyborgs bled blood and oil. Querol ducked behind his gaunt master, only to be taken by a shot from behind. His data-slate, that instrument of Terran tyranny, shattered upon the floor. More than any amount of spilt blood, that gave her satisfaction.

The last of the black-clad guards died. Hopeless defiance. They never stood a chance. Never advance into enemy territory when your enemy holds a superior firing position. Huratal had learned that at her father's knee.

'Cease firing!' bellowed Oravan.

The Yellow Guard rounded up the few survivors. Huratal's conversion field sparkled and went out. She breathed in deeply, tired by her exertions. Behind her, her monstrous child wailed in its crib, but her wet nurses were all dead and she went uncomforted. Picking her way through the corpses of her minor heirs Huratal huffed her way up the twenty-seven stairs and settled herself back into her cushions. She plucked one up that smoked with multiple las-burns and tossed it aside. Canids lapped at bloody puddles.

'My lady Governatrice,' said Oravan. 'Our artillery is ranged against the Adeptus Arbites precinct house. The ordnance of the polar defence fortress is locked upon Borowik's ship. Both await your command to fire.'

'It is given,' she said. 'Obliterate them. Geratomro stands apart.'

'My lady Governatrice,' said Oravan, and bowed. He made to go. Huratal halted him.

'Beware guilt, captain. Their protestations of common cause hid that they were trespassers, for all their writs and parchments that said otherwise,' said Huratal. 'Find us the Lord-At-Peace. Tell him he is relieved of duty while hostilities continue. Bring us the Lord-At-War. He is needed now.'

'Yes, my lady Governatrice,' said Oravan.

The surviving members of the court crept out from their hiding places, aghast at the carnage wrought upon their fellows. Huratal did not mourn the court's thinning; it had been getting unmanageable.

'And find us Heir the Second Dostain,' she said. 'We must tell him he was right.'

CHAPTER TWO
VISIONS

THE *EXCELLENT*, BLACK TEMPLARS
STRIKE CRUISER
THE WARP
010398.M41

Black plasteel boots rang on deck-plating. Chaplain Meodric strode through the dark corridors of the strike cruiser *Excellent*, two brothers of the Reclusiam marching after him. The hour was late, if only according to ship time. They were deep in the warp. There was no temporal law which affected that dread realm, no turning of worlds to bring day and night, nor spinning atoms to count the passing of seconds. The least of its insanities, Meodric thought, but still he regarded himself as safe, even in the heart of the enemy's territory. The Geller field cocooned the plasteel skin of the ship the same way that his faith protected his ceramite-armoured body. To know that dread powers were all around and they could not touch him was proof of the Emperor's might.

Further evidence of this was that he had been called out

during the last watch. The Emperor was reaching out to the Michaelus Crusade, and he had to respond.

The spinal corridor of the *Excellent* was quiet at that hour. A sole brother on penitent's patrol stepped smartly past, clashing his fist against his chest armour in salute. In dark rooms servitors performed mindless maintenance routines. A Chapter cenobite hurried across a transverse corridor, head and arms engulfed in his habit. The unaltered man was tiny, emaciated by fasting, but Meodric touched the forehead of his skull helm out of respect to his holiness.

The Sanctum was the lesser of the cruiser's two chapels, yet it was still vast, occupying a space three decks deep. Its spires and towers extended into the void either side of the spinal way. The thoroughfare split either side of a steep stair that plunged down towards the Sanctum's doors. Meodric and his guard descended past trophies from ancient crusades half-hidden in niches, or encysted in time-yellowed bubbles of protective plastek resins. The guard-of-the-watch had two sentries stationed at the chapel door at all times. These warriors saluted their spiritual leader, and pushed the gates inwards. Meodric went through without breaking stride, his footsteps echoing from the high chapel vaulting. Starlight shone through tall armourglass windows trapped in traceries of pure adamantium. Forests of candles in heavy stands flickered in the draught from his passing. The Sanctum's nave was deserted but for a handful of red-robed cenobites, these bound to tend to the chapel and never depart its precincts.

Adelard waited for Meodric by the archway to the confessional. He was dressed in the bone-white-and-black robes of the order, emblazoned with a red gothic cross.

In the gloom he blended into the heavy curtains blocking the archway.

'My lord Chaplain,' Adelard said. 'I thank you for breaking your rest.'

'I am at the Emperor's call. I come when He commands.' Meodric's voice was harsh from his vox-emitters. 'It has happened again?'

'Yes, my lord,' said Adelard. 'Bastoigne woke me an hour ago in a state of agitation.'

'And Brother Poldus has already seen him?'

'Yes, my lord. The apothecarion report that he is healthy, and that no biochemical imbalance is present.'

'Then rejoice, brother, for it is likely Brother Bastoigne has the favour of the Emperor.'

'Praise be,' murmured Adelard.

'You are concerned for his welfare?'

'He was my neophyte once. The bond never truly goes.'

'Then put your trust in the Emperor, brother. All will be well, for whatever the cause, it is in the Emperor's plan. He who seeth clearly, seeth far. And none sees so far or so clearly as the Lord of Man.'

Meodric thrust aside the curtains and went inside. His warriors took up station side by side, blocking the archway. Adelard opened his hand, then let it drop and went to pray before the great effigy of the Emperor Vengeful that dominated the forward wall of the chapel.

Bastoigne looked up at Meodric's entrance. Sound baffles kept the room isolated to preserve the shame of the brothers within from those who might be listening without. Black Templars confessed their failings in squad groups, and so the room was circular, set around with a bench big enough to accommodate a dozen or more of the giant, transhuman warriors. That night Bastoigne was alone. Like Adelard, he was garbed in the loose bone habit and black tabard the Black Templars wore when not in armour.

'Lord Chaplain,' Bastoigne said, and fell to his knees. He bowed his head, oiled hair falling forwards to obscure his face.

Meodric held up his crozius over the younger warrior's head. The disruption field ignited with a crack, filling the cell with the smell of ozone.

'You swear all that you speak to me in here shall be the truth?'

'I do, my lord,' said Bastoigne.

Meodric thumbed off the field and touched Bastoigne's shoulders with his crozius. 'Then the blessing of the Emperor be upon you. Rise.'

Bastoigne did so hesitantly. Sweat gleamed in the stubble of the shaved sides of his head.

'Sit and be at ease, my brother,' said Meodric, 'and speak unto me, for I am the priest of the Emperor.'

The Space Marines sat at opposite sides of the room. Meodric's helm lenses glowed, highlighting the bones cast into his armour in wicked red.

'I have had another vision, my lord. I... I am sorry to seek your guidance at this hour, I...'

'Do not apologise,' said Meodric sternly. 'Tell me of your vision.'

'I was in battle. There was a fire that burned no material, but that seared the soul. From a doorway of flesh many beings came. I...'

'Go on, my brother.'

'They were, they were creatures. Fell beings.'

'Xenos?'

'Not xenos, no, Chaplain, but something else. I do not know what they were. They were...' He searched for a word to fit. 'Hellish.'

'Describe them to me.'

'They were humanoid, lithe as eldar, swift, of mixed gender, neither male nor female. They had claws in place of their hands, and black, soulless eyes.'

'And they came through a gate, you say?'

'A gate made of flesh, with arms and legs.'

Meodric made a low noise. Bastoigne was yet of the Outer Third Circle, and was not privy to certain truths. Meodric knew what the warrior spoke of.

'Where did this happen?'

'In a square, by a palace, on a world where the sky was black.'

'Did you recognise it?'

'No. But I *knew* it.' Bastoigne's face was changed by doubt. 'How can this be, lord Chaplain?'

'The Emperor works through us in strange and unpredictable ways. Do not be afraid. Continue.'

Bastoigne swallowed and nodded. 'In my dream, in the vision, I knew it as the world we sail to. Geratomro. I knew that as soon as I saw it. Is this blasphemy? I am but twenty years in the order.'

'That depends.'

'A black sword appeared to me, my lord. Wreathed in a pure light that the creatures shrank from. I am not worthy to bear it. Why do I see it in my sleep... I–'

Meodric held up his hand. 'It is for others to decide your worth, brother. Was there anything more?'

'Yes. Yes!' Bastoigne's eyes rose, and he looked into

Meodric's helm lenses. 'A voice!'

'And what did it say?'

'It said, "Seek my light, so that it might banish the darkness." Then I saw myself clawed down and laid open, and I died, but not before the most glorious light struck across the sky and slew the creatures, and threw apart their gateway, and they all fell to ruin.'

'The end was in our favour?'

'Assuredly yes. Victory, though I perished. What does it mean?' His voice dropped to a whisper, not daring not contemplate the possibility. 'Have I been touched by the Emperor? Can it be true?'

Meodric stared at him a moment. 'That remains to be seen, brother. Wait here. When summoned, return to your cell immediately and pray until your duties recommence at first watch. Do not speak with anyone else of these dreams.'

'There will be no penitence? Perhaps I am prideful, and dream myself better than I am.'

'True vision and dreams are hard to tease apart. That is my task. Do not concern yourself over it. I will discuss matters with Sword Brother Adelard.'

Meodric was glad of his impassive helm. He had always been poor at hiding his emotions, especially regarding matters of faith, and now the light of revelation was upon him. He pushed his way back through the heavy curtains, letting them and the sound baffle fall back across the confessional chamber.

'Well?' said Adelard.

'Leave us,' said Meodric to his guard. They departed without comment. 'It could be. Bastoigne shows no pride.'

'Praise be!' said Adelard.

'You know of his visions?'

'He dreams of the war we sail to, the rebellion on Geratomro. A possible incursion there.'

'You have given no instruction yet as to the nature of this most great of enemies?'

'No, of course not, and I would not until he is admitted to the Inner Circle, or must face this enemy in battle,' said Adelard.

'Then it is more likely that he is genuine. He dreams of the sword, Adelard.'

Adelard drew in a sharp breath.

'He has heard the voice of the Emperor. He must be tested.'

'Praise, praise, praise!' said Adelard. He paused. 'We should warn army group high command. As of yet, there is nothing untoward about this uprising. It is one of many, but if Bastoigne's visions are true, we may be heading for disaster.'

'We shall not speak of this,' said Meodric firmly. 'We shall tell Marshal Michaelus. Let the choice be his. My counsel to him will be to remain silent. If we inform high command, we shall expose them to the details of the unspeakable truth and bring many complications upon them. Furthermore, if we are believed, then the planet will likely be subject to exterminatus at great loss of life.'

'But if it could be stopped sooner–'

'Brother, this is meant to be.' Meodric waited for Adelard to relax. 'The Emperor demands we face the dark upon Geratomro blade to blade. This is His will. It is plain to me that He commands this threat must be met with steel and ceramite, not orbital bombardment.'

'If the Emperor wills it,' Adelard said.

'There are preparations to be made. Tests. Bastoigne has many travails ahead of him before he can claim the Black Sword.'

'I have every faith in him.'

'Speak to no one of this. The invasion must go ahead as planned. Silence, brother. Let that be our watchword. Ave Imperator.'

'Praise be.'

APPENDED NOTATION: GERATOMRAN RECONQUEST

+++ADEPTUS TERRA SYSTEM CLASSIFICATION+++

Gerat System

Segmentum Tempestus

Chiros Sector

Agritha Subsector, f 2.723.2.444

STELLAR BODY: 'Gerat'. Single Type L-V main sequence
orange dwarf star [stable]

ORBITING BODIES:

Gerat I – Orbital distance: 0.2 AU. 0.01 Terramass.
Moons: 3

Gerat II – Orbital distance: 0.8 AU. 0.8 Terramass.
Moons: n/a.

Gerat III [ref. Geratomro, Gerat Prime]

Gerat IV – Orbital distance: 5.33 AU. Gas Giant; 1,000
Terramass. Moons: 46. Population 897,146 Lunar
testing grounds. Mining platform. Gas extraction. Trade
Guild post. Guild Captains freeport. House Ynnyg
rogue trader concession.

Gerat V – Orbital distance: 6.88 AU. Gas Giant; 426
Terramass. Moons: 39. Population 2,001,765. Sublunar
agricolae. Mining platform. Gas extraction. Fleet base.
Marshalling grounds.

Gerat VI and *VII* – Orbital distance: 9 AU. Double
planetary subsystem. Anomalous rocky super-worlds;
321 Combined Terramass. Toxic atmosphere.

Req. world: *Gerat III [Geratomro, System Mundo Primus]*
Orbital Distance: 0.9–1.0 AU.

Equatorial Temp.: 7–31c

1 G

1.1 Terramass.

Planetary Grade: Industrial world
DESIGNATED SYSTEM CAPITAL
Aestimare: Exactus secundus, optimare prime
Geography: Grade III temperate world [subclasses:
arboreal, tundra, steppe, oceanic]
Imperial Planetary Commander: Missrine Huratal
[traitora]
Status: Rebellion

*Thought for the day: Turn not your back upon the Emperor,
lest His light burn you when you seek to return.*

CHAPTER THREE
COMBAT DROP

'Emperor, lord of all mankind, protector of Terra, master of humanity, look upon me now,' said Second Lieutenant Epperaliant.

At the sound of the prayer Honoured Lieutenant Colaron Artem Lo Bannick stopped his tests and deactivated his tac screens. The cessation of their irritating whine was a relief. He leaned back, closed his eyes. In the left emitter of his headset the calm exchanges of the deck officers and drop-ship pilots kept him informed of their deployment status. He focused on the human sound of Epperaliant's prayer, trying to ignore the vox-dehumanised chatter of the men outside his tank.

'Emperor, guiding light of mankind, protector of all, master of the stars, protect me now.'

At the long operations desk that took up most of the command deck's left side, Epperaliant whispered his prayer.

With the twinned emblems of Emperor and Omnissiah grasped in his left hand, he rocked to the rhythm of his words. All the ten-strong crew of the Baneblade prepared for battle according to their own habit. For most, that meant prayer. Epperaliant's was a Paragonian standard. Only a year ago every man in earshot would have joined in, but the days when their comrades in *Cortein's Honour* were all from home were gone. The crew were chosen by the tank's machine-spirit, its will divined mysteriously by the members of the Adeptus Mechanicus attached to their company, and so there were representatives of four worlds under Bannick's command.

In his enginseer's pit, Kolios attended to the soul of their tank. Not so long ago he had been a simple trooper. Selected by ritual and extensive testing, he had been inducted into the most rudimentary mysteries of the Omnissiah by the army group's Adeptus Mechanicus contingent. He took his charge seriously, muttering machine cant as he tested each of the tank's systems one by one, taking them through their rituals of awakening and stabilisation. It was not unknown for men like him to petition to join the Adeptus Mechanicus formally. They were rarely accepted.

Third Gunner Leonates and Third Loader Huwar Lo Ganlick checked over their own stations, responding to the short questions Kolios directed at them. While they were the lowliest of the gunnery crew, their equipment was nevertheless the most sophisticated: remote controls for the weaponry of the tank's two sponsons. Consequently it was the most likely to malfunction. Ganlick muttered along with Epperaliant's prayer. He was of Paragon, brought in from the regular tankers of the 42nd. Leonates was a transfer from the Atraxian 18th super-heavies. Despite their differing cultures they worked well together.

Bannick let his attention drift. There was plenty of time before the drop. He was in two minds if that was good or bad. The longer they had to wait, the longer he had to live. On the other hand, he wanted to get it over with. The thoughts chased themselves around his head. His eyes snapped open. He couldn't wait passively like this. He sighed and undid his restraint harness.

The snap of Bannick's clasps had Epperaliant looking up. His prayer stopped. Kolios looked at him then returned to his pre-battle checks.

'Honoured lieutenant?'

'Go back to your prayer, Epperaliant. I need to stretch my legs.' Bannick smiled at his own joke. The tank was incredibly cramped. It was impossible to stand upright save in two places – under the turret ring, and halfway down the ladder leading to the lower deck. In that regard Bannick missed *Mars Triumphant* the most. An older, more sophisticated vehicle built on the Red Planet itself to the most ancient of patterns, its systems were more advanced and so had taken up less internal space, giving more to the crew.

Bannick patted Epperaliant on the shoulder. Along with himself and Meggen, they were the only survivors of *Mars Triumphant*'s destruction on Kalidar. Ganlick, Vorkosigen, Marsello, Ralt, Radden and Cortein himself, were all dead. Even five inches of plasteel and a platoon's firepower were not enough to keep a man alive in the crucible of war.

'More regiments of Paragon will be joining us on the surface,' he said encouragingly. 'Including the Lucky Eights. Six super-heavies from Paragon. Nothing can stand against us!' He spoke with an optimism he did not feel. His stomach knotted inside him.

'Sir,' said Epperaliant. He ran his amulets through his fingers, his mind elsewhere.

'It'll be good to see some fresh faces. There's the Four Hundred and Seventy-Seventh Foot too, raised a year after us.'

'Maybe they have some news?' said Ganlick.

'No news is good news, we say on Atraxia,' said Leonates. His accent was lilting and soft; pleasant, Bannick often thought.

'Cheerful lot, you Atraxians,' said Ganlick.

Bannick went below. The ladder foot opened up not far from the left sponson. The sound of its auto-loaders and servos whirred from the other side of the track unit as it was tested. Bannick made his way down to the corridor running the length of the tank, awkwardly placing his feet in the narrow width between the sled tracks leading from the magazine to the secondary armament – a demolisher cannon – mounted on the front.

He went aft first, passing the tank's shrine to the Emperor and wall of honour next to it. *Cortein's Honour* was new, forged on the fleet's Ark Mechanicus only months previously, and so there was only one brass plaque on the wall bearing a name, and that name was his. For luck, he touched the plaque and the fresh scripts of blessing affixed to the wall beneath. Raw parchment from the army priests, deep red from the tech-adepts. The creeds of Omnissiah and Emperor were intertwined on a tank like *Cortein's Honour*. It was no wonder so many super-heavy tank regiments were raised on Paragon, where both cults held equal sway.

The tank interior was always hot, but there, at the rear, so close to the ever grumbling reactor, it was hottest of all. His fingers marred the softened wax of the seals when he touched them. He wiped his hands on his trousers, pulled his medallions from under his vest, bowed his head before the shrine and kissed them both.

He went into the magazine. First Loader Dotrian Vaskigen was sat on an ammo case, playing cards with Gollph, the Bosovar savage.

'Sir,' said Vaskigen.

'We play cards. Make Vaskigen less scared,' said Gollph with a grin.

'Your Gothic is improving, Gollph,' said Bannick.

'Hell, honoured lieutenant, there's nothing much else for him to do round here,' said Vaskigen. They had had their differences, these two, but were now fast friends. Bannick was glad for it.

'You are both ready?'

'Sure. Lift's in good order.' Vaskigen nodded backwards at the shell lift that carried the main armament's huge rounds up to the turret. 'Gollph's ready too, aren't you?'

'Sure thing, sir,' said Gollph. 'I am very ready.'

'Never thought I'd say it, but he's a fine loader. Gets that shell sled up and down the gangway real quick, sir,' said Vaskigen.

'I learn quick,' said Gollph fiercely, slapping his hand to his chest.

Like everyone on the tank, they were stripped to their vests. Sweat ran down their skin freely. Gollph's pinker flesh was not as wet as Vaskigen's.

'Yes. Well. Drop soon. Stow those ammo crates. Get into your harnesses.'

'Sure thing, sir. I winning anyway.' Gollph laid his cards down. Vaskigen cursed as Gollph scooped up a pile of liquor ration chits.

Bannick nodded. Feeling like he was intruding, he left.

Down to the front, head bowed, hands careful of the sharp metal clips holding in the miles of looped power cable running in the coign of ceiling and wall at both sides of the cramped corridor. He popped his head into the second gunner's station, Kalligen's little room behind the demolisher.

'Sir,' said Kalligen around a tarabac stick.

'How are you?'

'Soiling myself,' he said, honestly. He blew out a cloud of aromatic smoke. 'I'll get over it.'

'And how is he?' said Bannick, looking meaningfully down and lowering his voice.

'Chem-Dog does what a Chem-Dog does. Not helpful intel for you, I know, but he's not tried to steal anything off me for three watches, so I'm happy, so long as he stays on his nitrochem and off my gear,' said Kalligen, loud enough for the driver to hear. Bannick's attention strayed to the bottle of rough alcohol stashed in the webbing at Kalligen's side.

Bannick withdrew. Kalligen ducked down and looked out. 'Can you tell Kolios to tell Brasslock that the demolisher's still pulling to the right? I told him after the last test but he hasn't done anything about it. The tracking is off, I swear.'

'I will. Have you tried asking it not to?'

'Yeah. All that machine-spirit stuff. Prayers, oil, being nice to it, all that. I'd rather someone who knew what they were doing asked with a spanner in his hand, though.'

'Can you climb out a moment? I want a word with Shoam.'

Kalligen unbuckled himself and slid out of the second gunner's seat.

Bannick took a deep breath of the fuggy air. Climbing in and over the gunner's chair he poked his head into the driver's station. It smelt bad in there. Shoam practically lived in his seat. Ganlick, the driver of *Mars Triumphant*, had been the same before he died, and that was not the only similarity the two men had shared, thought Bannick, as he saw Shoam's nitrochem inhaler hanging by its straps from the wall. He remembered Ganlick's fondness for gleece.

'Why, if it isn't our little lord of Paragon. Hello, sir.' Karlok Shoam's eyes glinted in the dark, lit by the pict screens and instrument panels. A slot of brighter light shone in through the viewing block. Shoam hunched below it.

'Shoam. I thought I'd check on everyone,' said Bannick. He rebuked himself. Why did he always feel he had to explain himself to the Savlar?

'Got the frights? That normal,' said Shoam. 'We all gonna shake before a fight like this. Combat drop. Big risk. Never know if you's gonna make it.' He took up his respirator mask, hanging as ever from a strap at his neck, and pressed it to his face. There was a click and a hiss of gas from the bottle strapped to the wall. Shoam inhaled deeply.

'Yes, well. If you need anything, let me know.'

'Get me away from this? Nice quiet place, nice wife? No more fighting, no more killing?'

'I'm afraid not,' said Bannick.

'Then I got all you could give in any case,' said Shoam.

'Better driving big brute like this than little Salamander I used to have. Safer in here.'

'Right.' Bannick paused, his eyes fixed on the bottle. 'You'll need to be sharp once we're out.'

Shoam stroked his nitrochem mask. 'This keep me sharp. If we die, it not be the fault of mine, nor the nitro, bossman.'

'Don't overdo it.' Bannick had considered confiscating the mask and the Savlar's chem supply, until he'd read about the horrifying side effects of withdrawal. Savlar had been known to go insane if deprived of their narcotic, and would attack anyone who came close. Honoured Captain Hannick had protested strongly at Shoam's selection as the driver of *Cortein's Honour*. His words had fallen on deaf augmetics. The machine-spirit had chosen him, said the machine priests, so Shoam had stayed. While Bannick had come to respect the Savlar's skill as a driver, he doubted he would ever trust him. But then, Ganlick had been hooked on gleece, and Kalligen was going the same way. War left no man's mind untouched. He knew he was prejudiced against the Savlar; he could not stop himself. He resolved to do better.

Back on the command deck Bannick paused a moment to listen more closely to the chatter of the deck crew. Orders were going to and fro for the landers to prepare for final checks. No signs of imminent departure forthcoming, Bannick climbed up the ladder to the turret.

Though large, much of the turret was taken up by the breech block of the massive main cannon. First Gunner Meggen sat to the right of it. The ladder came up in such a way that Bannick's nose brushed metal slick with condensation and grease as he clambered inside. The shell lift was set right behind the breech, the top lumpy with auto-loading mechanisms. Meggen's seat was hemmed in by two racks, one for more shells and another for spent casings. To the rear was a viewing cupola, another seat crammed into its base – Bannick's secondary command post. Despite all the mass of machinery around him, Meggen had the most space of any of them.

'Hey, Bannick,' said Meggen. 'Bored?'

'I don't like waiting,' said Bannick. 'You?'

'Just fine as wine, Colaron,' said Meggen. He and Bannick had become closer since Agritha, and the honoured lieutenant did not pick him up on addressing him by his given name. 'We're in a metal box, inside another metal box, in a third metal box, waiting to be dropped into a firefight. What more could I possibly wish for?' He caught Bannick's expression. 'Don't worry, won't be long,' he said.

'That's a relief.'

'Then again, the longest I've had to wait for deployment like this was forty-eight hours,' said Meggen. 'So don't get your hopes up. My arse was fit to burst, I needed to go so bad.'

'How's the wound?' asked Bannick. On Meggen's shoulder was a livid purple scar, the veins around it traced out in a dark red – the legacy of their engagement with eldar on Agritha.

Meggen rotated his shoulder. 'It's all right. Damn thing only hurts when I'm cold or trying to sleep sometimes. First don't matter much in here, it's always hot, but the other I could do without.'

'Well, I'll–'

'Don't say you'll do what you can. I appreciate the sentiment, but I've had every sawbones on this transport poking at me. There's nothing they can do, and seeing as all you can do is ask them, there's nothing you can do either. Nothing they give me works so well as this. I'd kill for a bottle of decent gleece, but we live on, eh?'

A sharp noise burst in Bannick's ear. Vox override brought the voice of the ship's deckmaster. *'All troops prepare for deployment. All troops prepare for deployment.'*

From outside, the muffled wail of a klaxon sang. The low conversation of the crew in the tank ceased. A tense hush fell. A metallic bang sounded. Bannick felt *Cortein's Honour's* machine-spirit stir in expectation.

Meggen glanced up at the hatch above him.

'Looks like we're going in. Good luck, sir. Let's hope we don't get shot down before we land.'

Bannick slid down the turret well ladder with his feet either side of the rails. He nimbly slipped around Epperaliant into the press of his instruments and back into his chair. Without his vox-piece to remind him that an outside world existed, he might have succumbed to claustrophobia. *Cortein's Honour* was enclosing at the best of times, but it seemed ten times worse while the tank was held in the lander. Box in a box in a box. Meggen had that right.

'Are we ready, men?' he asked. A chorus of 'Aye, sirs' responded. Epperaliant had finished praying and was on the vox, communicating with his opposite numbers aboard the Seventh Paragonian Super-Heavy Tank Company's second Baneblade, command Hellhammer and Shadowsword.

'I've the honoured captain on the horn, sir,' said Epperaliant.

'Patch him through to the internal hailers. He'll want to speak to the men.'

Hannick always addressed his tankers before combat. He

often didn't say much, and that was as good for morale as the fact he spoke at all, but the effect was rather spoilt by a fit of hacking coughing that went on for ten seconds before he began.

'*Damn Kalidar!*' he spat. '*Get a breathful of that place, it never leaves you.*' The men laughed dutifully. '*Are we all ready?*'

'*Marteken ready. Artemen Ultrus prepared for combat,*' said the commander of the company's other Baneblade.

'*Us too, captain,*' said Hurnigen of the Shadowsword, *Lux Imperator.*

'Aye aye, sir. Ready for drop,' said Bannick.

'*Good. In three minutes, or less, probably less, our company will be shot from the relative comfort of these fine Imperial Navy vessels right into the heart of battle. For those of you who have not done a combat drop before, it's exhilarating. I expect every man to pull his weight,*' he said, and the crew of *Cortein's Honour* mouthed the words along with him. Hannick was a good man, but had a set of stock phrases. '*For all elements of society operating optimally in their proper place is the Paragonian way.*' And then he added, unexpectedly, '*I realise a lot of you are not from the planet which this regiment hails, but the same applies to you. May the Emperor watch over all. See you when we've taken the spaceport. Hannick out.*'

The vox cut out. Clanks sounded outside, conveyed from somewhere in the giant landing craft through the metal of the Baneblade's hull. *Cortein's Honour* vibrated, taking on the thrum of the drop-craft's engines as they spooled up to bear the immense strain of delivering such a large amount of mass to the bottom of a gravity well.

A new voice crackled over the internal vox. '*Flight crew*

report we are cleared for launch. All crews, prepare for drop. Marking on fifteen. Three, two, one, fifteen. Mark.'

A third voice sounded in the room, taking up the countdown. *'Fourteen,'* it intoned, with all the interest of a man set to counting a mountain of beans.

'Vox-sets up and on,' said Epperaliant, scooting up and down his long desk on the rails that held his chair.

'Sound off, crew,' said Bannick. 'Affirm restraints fixed.'

'Aye aye,' said Meggen.

'Tighter than they need to be,' said Vaskigen.

'Yes, sir!' said Gollph.

'Affirmative, bossman,' said Shoam.

'We're in correctly, sir,' said Leonates, tugging at his and Huwar Lo Ganlick's harnesses.

'Bindings set,' said Kolios. Both he and Epperaliant were now engaged in a complicated series of tasks, ensuring that their part of the datanet linking the four behemoths of the Seventh would survive the drop. Peak operational performance was demanded by Astra Militarum diktat. Bannick would settle for being able to talk to their commanding officer and get every other word. The engine noise outside built.

'Restraints tight and cosy,' said Bannick, checking his belts for the sixth time. It wouldn't do to arrive in battle dead from a sloppily fastened seat belt.

'Six,' continued the dull voice. *'Five.'*

Better a dull deck crew than a staff of hotheads, thought Bannick.

The tank shook. Equipment rattled in its webbing. A quiet alarm beeped. Kolios shut it off.

'By the Throneworld,' said Ganlick. His smile was false, a brave face for his comrades.

'The shaking will become significantly worse,' said Kolios. Ganlick blanched. Most of them, Bannick included, had never performed a combat drop. To descend the turbulent ladder of a planet's gravity into the teeth of enemy fire was a costly exercise in men and machines. They were all scared.

'Don't listen to him, Huw,' said Meggen. 'Hold on tight.'

Klaxons blared outside, signalling the opening of the great docking bay doors and the disengagement of the integrity fields on the flight deck apertures. The atmosphere was vented into the void, and the clamour of the klaxon became muted, travelling only through direct material contact.

'Four, three.'

The engines howled. Bannick felt suddenly light as the grav-plating in the embarkation deck was disengaged.

'Two. One. Countdown complete. The Emperor protects.'

'He better be basdacking watching today,' grumbled Meggen.

The tank shifted in its own restraints as the giant landing craft lifted off and blasted out into the cold depths of space.

Creaks and rumbles, the groans of tortured metal fighting mass, velocity and pressure, the grumble of engines pushing them off fast from the assault fleet – these were the only signs of their traversal through the void. Bannick was blind to the outside, at the mercy of the Navy crews piloting the lander. He couldn't hear anything beyond the company, he couldn't see anything beyond the dark hold. Men prayed again, more fervently this time than before. He hated this feeling of powerlessness. On the battlefield the peril was orders of magnitude greater, but he could respond, he could formulate plans. If there were to be disasters they were his to deal with. Here he was nothing, a lump of meat to be conveyed in an expensive sealed can. If the pilots made an error, there was nothing he could do. Death by mistake was prevalent in the Imperial Guard. The Departmento Munitorum's only virtue was unbending rigidity, but orders could be worked around, solutions figured out. At no other time but landing did Bannick feel what he truly was – one fighting man among trillions, a resource to be expended. To the adepts, his loss during transit was of no more consequence than the wastage incurred by a spoiled tin of fruit.

Hot in the tank. A box in a box in a box. A box in a box in a box. The phrase went round and round his head. He realised he was saying it under his breath.

The gravity of Geratomro tugged at Bannick's mass, and he was pulled into his chair, uncomfortably at odds with the force of the lander's acceleration.

The tank jiggled violently. Items strapped up on the walls rasped and rattled. Epperaliant swore as his caffeine mug, overlooked in the intense preparations for the landing, walked off the edge of his desk and bounced on the floor. The building howl of atmospheric re-entry growled at them, growing louder and louder, the roar of a hostile planet. Gollph shrieked in terror below. There were some things he had not assimilated yet, probably never would. Above, Meggen swore over and over again.

Now came the significant worsening Kolios had spoken of. The crew shook so hard their vision blurred. Bannick clamped his jaw shut to stop his teeth smashing into each other or biting his tongue. He wrapped his arms over his restraints to hug them closer to his body. He gripped the left strap with his left hand. His right hand sought out his medallions and clutched them tightly.

'The Emperor protects, the Emperor protects,' he said through his clenched teeth. He was not alone in repeating the mantra, but he may as well have been. Every noise was drowned by the deafening roar of air blasting against the landing craft. Metal shrieked and sang as they plunged down.

And then, a terrifying lurch. The ship pitched sideways to an alarming degree, bringing cries from the lips of every man aboard *Cortein's Honour*, that ice-cold basdack Shoam included. Bannick tensed, terrified, awaiting a fiery death as the landing craft came apart. The ship levelled. Distant bangs were, perhaps, projectiles contacting the hull. Maybe one of the other craft had been hit. His own tactical analysis prior to the battle, crude though it was, suggested at least a twenty per cent loss among the landing craft.

He thanked the Emperor they lived.

They were flying forwards now, prow down, G-force pressing him painfully back as the landing craft raced to the surface and away from murderous ship-killing fire. A short hoot on a siren was the only warning they got that the craft was going to level out. Regulations called for Bannick to direct his crew to brace at that moment, but he had no inclination to do so, and he could not have opened his mouth if he had.

For a moment, he felt weightless again as the ship abruptly changed direction to fall bellyside down. Another roaring, a second beast come to fight the first. Retro jets blasted downwards, arresting the descent, he told himself.

His restraints bit into his shoulders, his head filled with blood. They slowed rapidly. The terrible pressure on his body lessened. Another klaxon.

'We're down!' he managed. But they were not. The signal came early, and the spine-shortening impact, when it came a half-second later, took them all by surprise. The ungentle kiss of Geratomro boomed through the ship, and suddenly they were still.

'Sound off!' called Bannick.

'Turret ready!' said Meggen.

'Secondary weapons ready,' said Kalligen.

'Tertiary weapons team ready,' said Leonates.

'First and second loaders ready,' said Vaskigen.

'Reactor primed, online and ready for war, all praise the Omnissiah,' said Tech-Aspirant Kolios. He began to chant as he and Epperaliant worked together to rouse the machine-spirit of *Cortein's Honour.*

His efforts were unnecessary. The tank was eager for battle. The reactor rumbled throatily.

'Reactor online. Visual systems activated. All signum codes inputted and weapons released,' said Epperaliant, sliding up and down the rail before his long operations desk. 'Weapons live, don't shoot them in here.'

Leonates and Ganlick shared a grin as their twitch sticks jerked into life. Meggen muttered something uncouth about dropping his cheroots out of reach. Bannick heard them all through the vox. He heard the Savlar take a long draw on his nitrochem. Kalligen sounded pained. New noises took the place of the old. The drum beat of heavy fire rattled on the ship's hull.

'*Prepare for disembarkation,*' the anonymous flight crew informed them. '*You have two minutes before we're away. If you ground pounders are not out of this craft by then, you can explain it to high command on the ship.'*

'Bring up the engine to full power. Engage drive units. Easy now,' said Bannick.

The vox burst into life again and Hannick spoke.

'Normal spread, two by two. Artemen Ultrus will take the left. Ostrakhan's Rebirth close in behind. Bannick, lead out Lux Imperator on the right. We have our intelligence – let's see what we're dealing with before we do anything rash. Targets are those of opportunity. Anything from the defences that survived orbital bombardment. Clear the way to the spaceport for the Atraxians and Genthus Reclamation Force. The landing fields must be taken intact.'

'Land ramp deploying,' advised the ship's crew, men Bannick had never seen and never would. *'Retracting tank restraints.'* A series of clunks sounded as mechanical claws relaxed their grip. Pistons eased them back into the walls.

A tremendous boom came from outside. They all flinched.

'Throne, they've got some heavy ordnance here,' muttered the pilot. *'Ramp down in three, two...'*

'Activate full sensorium. Give me eyes on the outside, Epperaliant,' said Bannick.

A dark picture, punctuated only by running lights, took shape on the multiple screens around Bannick's command station. The chartdesk built into the front of the console fizzed with the random motes of an undirected hololith. The ship moaned like an animal giving birth, giant pistons pumped on wheels by the ramp, and a thin sliver of blinding light filled Bannick's screens and poured in through the cowled, armoured windows set around the command deck. It took a moment for the tank's augur eyes to readjust and the screens to dim.

Then the ramp was lowered, and the day's battle took shape outside.

'*Ramp down, ramp down!*' shouted the flight crew, and immediately the lander's engines began their rising song. '*Away! Away!*'

'*Go! Go! Go!*' bellowed Hannick.

'Kolios, engage transmission! Shoam, get us into it!' said Bannick. Fear was gone, anticipation of battle taking its place. He may very well not survive the coming fight, but he would not be at the mercy of others. Bannick was his own master again, and when one commanded a super-heavy tank, that meant something. Would there be cheering outside? Would the soldiers see the tanks roaring out of their lair and punch the air? Once, he would have believed that, for that was the vision he had of life in service before he joined. He had seen too much suffering, had too much experience of the intense exhaustion war inflicted on men to believe it any more. He only hoped they could do some good.

The Savlar responded by revving the engine and sending the giant tank forwards, one clanking link at a time. Slowly at first, then with the implacability of an avalanche, *Cortein's Honour* picked up speed and rolled from the belly of the heavy lander into a firestorm.

Battlegroup Geratomro, 398.M41

Astra Militarum
->Battlegroup Geratomro [note, initial reclamation force. Much depleted. Reinforced]
Commanding officer General Jonatan Hern
415th Cadian (foot) [@18%]
754th Cadian (armoured) [@28%]
89th Cadian (support) [@76%]
Fourth Jupian Ironlords (foot) [note, low technological base, supplies inadequate. Petition #100003427328905, filed 976.M40, unresolved] [@17%]
36th Ogryn Auxilia [@63%]
First Drani New-Pledged (foot) [@56%]
Second Drani New-Pledged (rough riders) [@72%]
->->Battlegroup Kalidar
(cross ref. Dentares Wargroup of the Indranis Campaign sheet #71, Cc/ref Eldar attach. 391-394M41]
Commanding officer, Captain-General Iskhandrian [advised, Grand Captain Olgau. Cc/ref Atraxian command protocols, *Sibellius' Guide to Imperial Guard Regiments of Segmentum Tempestus*]
23rd Paragon (foot) [@50%]
322nd Paragonian Armoured Veterans (armoured) [@29%]
62nd and 84th Mechanised Infantry/Infantry Paragonian (merged, Mech. Inf.) [@83%] Vet./ Non-national officers (cross ref sheet#2066; *Lost Regiments of the Dentares Suppression*)
Seventh Super-Heavy Paragonian (multiple role) [@full]
18th Atraxian Super-Heavy Tank Company (generalised) [@full]

12th Savlar (light infantry; toxic environment specialists) [@72%]

13th Savlar (light Infantry; toxic environment specialists) [@57%]

121st Atraxian Mechanised (heavy infantry) [@37%]

122nd Atraxian Artillery (support) [@90%]

Atraxian Guard Paramount (heavy infantry) [note, Tempestus Scions]

Reinforcements, Battlegroup Kalidar [raised Paragon VI, 6, {Primus, Moon} "Paragon", Paragon System, 395. M41]

63rd Paragonian Mechanised [@26%]

42nd Paragonian Armoured (number reassigned, 42nd disbanded regiment – cross ref Appendix 101, Emperor's Gift Grants to veterans, Segmentum Pacificus, 4th century, M41). [@54%]

Reinforcements, Battlegroup Kalidar [raised Artemis V {Primus}, "Bosovar", Artemis System, 396. M41]

31st, 32nd, 33rd and 34th Bosovar Levies [@99%, 100%, 100% respec.] (cross ref. feral world troopers of Artemis Subsector +++document missing+++)

ADDITIONAL

Command assets incl. Leviathan-class command vehicle, *Magnificence* [undeployed?query?]

->->Second Gulem Recovery Force
Commanding officer, General Maden Heldor Lo Basteen

Eighth Paragonian Super-Heavy Tank Company (assault)

477th Paragonian (foot) [note, double-size raising]
Tempestus Scions 'Black Suns'
84th Paragonian (armoured)
109th Paragonian Artillery (support)

Beginning of Departmento Munitorum listing of Astra Militarum assets present on Geratomro. In total three merged battlegroups were present with an overall strength estimated at five million men.

CHAPTER FOUR
LANDING

MATUA SUPERIOR
GERATOMRO
082398.M41

Cortein's Honour emerged from the shadow of the lander's protruding nose into torrential rain, the green and tan of its new camouflage darkening abruptly as it was wetted. The black sky churned with lance strikes and atmospheric disturbance brought on by the massed landing. The ground was a quagmire, cratered and stripped of life by orbital bombardment. The splintered sticks of native fauna stuck out of a sea of pale mud sticky with corpse flesh. Many men had died here during the first attempt to take back the world. The stink of their smashed bodies was so great Bannick engaged the atmospheric filters.

The city of Matua Superior was ahead. The plan had been to take it intact along with the spaceport, but it would not emerge unscathed. Fires burned everywhere even in the pouring rain, the result of stray rounds and misdirected lance bursts. It was not a large city and

appeared well ordered to Bannick's eye. What had surrounded it – farm, forest or chemical wasteland – was
impossible to tell. Where it had not been smashed to
pieces, the whole hinterland of the city was filled with a
defensive cordon of bastions linked by a minimal trench
system, islands now lapped by a sea of mud. The intention was of defence in depth, isolated forts and towers
ranging in size from rockcrete gun nests to macrocannon emplacements. Formidable, but not against a merged
battlegroup of their size.

Bannick quickly took in the situation on his chartdesk.
Spinning a wheel, he zoomed the hololith out to a view
that encompassed the whole of the attack. To the west,
pre-existing Imperial forces were abandoning their siege
lines and pushing into the city suburbs. To the north
west, the Atraxians were landing en masse to snatch the
northern landing fields before they could be sabotaged.
The assault of the south side of the city and the southern port fields fell to men of Paragon, albeit regiments
from two different battlegroups. The southern port group
was drawn from Paragonians in the Genthus Reclamation
Force, one of the three battlegroups that had gathered over
Geratomro. The role of the Seventh super-heavies was to
neutralise the remaining defences blocking access to the
city south, before driving on to reinforce the soldiers at
the port. It was strange to think of seeing new Paragonian faces. Bannick wondered if he would know anyone
in their ranks.

The pillared lightning of orbital fire stabbed downwards
ahead, obliterating a tower and sending the pulverised
bodies of men flying out on its wave-front. Artificial
thunder boomed, vying with the relentless pounding of

artillery. Electrical discharge spidered through the clouds. The sky was water and fire, lightning, lances, rain and fury, streaked with the trails of burning landing craft and duelling air superiority fighters.

For all the devastation being wrought and the length of the siege preceding the attack, Matua Superior was not going down without a fight. Tracer fire streaked from its interior, chasing Navy craft around the sky. Irregularly, the sky flashed ruby as the remnants of the area's orbital defence grid spat defiance at the fleet in orbit.

As ordered, *Cortein's Honour* ploughed through the mud to take up the right. *Artemen Ultrus* spread out to take the left. *Lux Imperator* rolled down the ramp and sheltered behind Bannick's vehicle. The tanks paused, awaiting their commander. To the rear, more heavy landing craft roared out of the sky, ramps cranking open the moment they hit the ground. Lighter ships came down with their bay doors open, spilling floods of men and machines into the mud.

'I've high command on the vox, sir,' said Epperaliant.

'Put them through. My vox-feed only,' said Bannick.

'*Seventh Paragonian. You have halted. Proceed to your objective, then rendezvous with the Eighth at the port,*' came a sharp voice.

'*Ostrakhan's Rebirth* is yet to emerge. Awaiting arrival of commanding officer and adoption of correct formation, please advise,' replied Bannick. Even with the crackle of weapon-born interference, the vox was clear here, so different to the howl of Kalidar's tortured magnetosphere.

'*Where's Hannick?*' said Marteken over the company vox.

Hannick responded. 'The basdacking landing claw has not retracted. We're locked in place, we cannot disembark, we...' Hannick began to cough again. 'Go forwards!' he gasped. 'We will join you. Attack.'

'You heard the captain,' said Shoam. The Baneblade's engine grumbled, and the tank set into motion. Bannick stabbed the button for private communication with the driver. 'Hold for my command in future,' he said, and re-engaged tank-wide comms. 'Roll out! All forwards. Kolios, keep an eye on the transmission. This mud's thick.'

Cortein's Honour rolled towards the defence line in formation with *Artemen Ultrus* and *Lux Imperator*, the men and lesser machines of the Kalidar Army Group following in their wake. The tank shook with shell impacts as the enemy redirected some of their fire away from the attack to the east and onto the landing zone at the south. Very slow, thought Bannick. Either their militia's not up to much or they're not falling for the trick.

From towers piercing the mangled battlefield, heavy macrocannons flashed, the bark of their discharge sounding a second later, the impact of their shells a second after that. Pillars of earth roared upwards, sending men wheeling high, scattering their limbs all about. *Cortein's Honour* rocked, but it was calm inside the tank. They were aboard a strong ship in a storm while others drowned in the raging surf.

'*Bannick, Hurnigen here,*' voxed the honoured lieutenant of the *Lux Imperator*. '*I have alpha-priority target request upon those turrets. Stand cover while we charge.*'

'Affirmative,' said Bannick. From the foremost part of the defence line, heavy calibre stubber fire clattered on the tank's glacis, no more harm to the Baneblade than gravel tossed at sheet metal. Outside, men danced to the jerky tune of death.

'Epperaliant, get me a fix on the origin of that fire.'

'Hold-outs, sir – a platoon of Geratomran defence forces. The rest of the first line is clear.'

So it should be, thought Bannick, taking in the steaming mess left by the pre-landing bombardment. Targeting information flashed up around a cracked bunker, half buried in mud.

'*Bannick?*' voxed Marteken from *Artemen Ultrus*. '*You see that?*'

'We've got it. Have *Artemen Ultrus* cover your side. This is our quadrant, you hear me?' Bannick said.

'*Loud and clear. You just keep your hands off our targets.*'

'You have a deal. Shoam, twenty degree right. Tertiary weapons, prepare to open fire. Take out that gun nest.'

'Got it, honoured lieutenant. Target locked in, preparing to fire,' said Leonates.

'It's time we did some good here. Meggen, get a range on those macrocannons.'

'It's a distance, sir,' said Meggen.

'Give them something to think about then! Kalligen, flatten that razor wire at forty degrees tank front. We can't do anything about this mud, but we can make things a little easier for our comrades.'

'Aye aye, sir,' both men said in turn. All at once, the Baneblade's weapons fired. The twin boom of demolisher and battle cannon rocked *Cortein's Honour* backwards. The noise of the discharge inside would have deafened the men had they not been wearing their vox-sets.

Hundreds of small explosions raked the gun nest, pockmarking the rockcrete as the bolts buried themselves within and detonated. Of the men in the defences, nothing could be seen, but the weapons fell silent. Meggen swore as his shots hit the macrocannon towers but exploded without doing any harm. The giant guns continued to fire, hurling ordnance into the mass of men and machinery landing behind the Baneblade.

'*We've come down too close to those macrocannons,*' voxed Marteken. '*This is a bad landing zone.*'

'Distance ain't going to make any difference to guns that big,' muttered Meggen on the internal vox.

'Marteken's fears are not your concern, first gunner,' said Bannick to Meggen. 'Hurnigen?'

'*We've flipped the switch. Transmission is off and volcano cannon charging. Twenty seconds until capacitor is energised,*' responded the other.

'Get me Hannick, Epperaliant. Boost the signal, I can't hear him on the company vox.'

'Aye, sir!'

'Hannick? Honoured Captain Hannick, what are your orders?' Bannick voxed his commander, stepping into an argument between the captain and the flight crew.

'*We leave in ten seconds,*' the pilot was saying.

'*You do not!*' Hannick shouted. '*Belay that. Get me off this ship and with my men. This is a Navy failing. You will remain grounded until–*'

'*My orders are clear,*' said the pilot. Bannick heard him click off his vox.

'*The basdacks are taking off!*' said Hannick.

The ship rose up from the ground, eight engine pods flash-drying the quagmire, ramp closing as it rose into the air.

'*Nine seconds to volcano cannon charge,*' came the voice of Hastilleen, Hurnigen's chief gunner.

The drop-ship turned in the air, pods rotating to carry it

forwards and upwards to join the steady stream of empty ships climbing back into orbit.

The macrocannons fired again.

A shot blasted into the side of the drop-ship, holing the hull. A half-second later a massive explosion tore out the sides of the transport compartment. The lander dropped out of the air, hitting the ground before the debris flung from its wreck could fall back to earth. The engines burned erratically then blew up. When the fireball cleared, the ship was blazing fiercely, forcing the men streaming past it to give it a wide berth lest they burn.

'We've lost Hannick!' said Bannick.

'*Basdack!*' replied Marteken. '*Hang on! I've a target request. Ninety-eight degrees front. I'm pulling away to deal with it.*'

'*Volcano cannon ready, opening fire,*' said Hurnigen.

A beam of blinding light surged from the long barrel of the Shadowsword, its firing making the air boom and adding to the artificial thunder of the bombardment. One of the macrocannon towers was decapitated, the giant gun on top disintegrating as it fell forwards.

'Sir, I've had notification that high command judge force concentration to be high enough to commence the full assault. The Navy are ceasing fire in three, two, one...' said Epperaliant.

The stabbing blades of lance fire cut out. A final shell hurtled down from orbit and exploded somewhere deep within the city.

The sky rumbled and flashed. The maelstrom in the clouds quietened.

'*All units, advance,*' came the command. The shouted response of the men amassing on the plain could be heard inside *Cortein's Honour*.

'Marteken, come in. Marteken,' voxed Bannick.

'*He's busy, sir,*' said Cholo, *Artemen Ultrus*' commsman.

'Ask him to return to formation. He's got to take command!' said Bannick.

There was a pause.

'*He says we'll follow your lead,*' said Cholo.

Bannick clasped his head. 'Is that you saying that, or Marteken?' said Bannick.

'*Marteken here. Look, I've got my hands full here. You're in command,*' Marteken said, sounding unusually clipped and officious.

'You have seniority, Marteken. It'd be a breach of command protocol. What are your orders?'

The vox clicked as Marteken engaged privacy. '*For the love of Terra, Colaron, I can't. Just do it,*' he said in an urgent whisper.

Bannick sat back. He glanced at his men, who were unaware of what was occurring. 'Very well.' He keyed the company vox broadcast switch. 'This is Colaron Artem Lo Bannick to the Seventh. I am assuming command with Marteken's permission. We move out now. Hurnigen, recharge your weapon. Those macrocannons have to go.'

'*Aye aye.*'

The tanks moved forwards, rolling down the slope towards the flatter ground before Matua Superior. Infantry transports fell in behind, flanked by the Leman Russ battle tanks of the 322nd Armoured Veterans and the remnants of Bannick's old regiment, the 42nd Armoured.

A roar came from behind. Fire billowed skywards, illuminating the gloomy day with violent orange. A large section of burning hull fell outwards from the wrecked lander. Pushing its way out came the Hellhammer *Ostrakhan's*

Rebirth, paint scorched, patches of burning fuel all over its hull, but very much in one piece.

'*Hannick here!*' shouted the honoured captain over the vox-net. '*Gentlemen, I apologise for my tardiness. Bannick, stand down. What were you about to do with my company?*'

'*Good to see you, sir!*' voxed Marteken with all too evident relief.

'Sir,' said Bannick. 'We're commanded to deal with these targets, clear the way for the infantry and proceed on to the port.' He sent a packet over the company datanet. 'The Lucky Eights and the Four Hundred and Seventy-Seventh Foot of the Second Genthus Reclamation Force are coming down.'

'Their forward elements are already requesting assistance,' said Epperaliant.

'*I know the ord–*' The captain's entrance was ruined by a round of awful coughing. He drew in a ragged breath.

'The macrocannons, sir,' said Hurnigen.

'Lux Imperator, *deal with them,*' said Hannick.

'*I'm getting a weapons malfunction. Capacitors charged, but the energies won't release. Enginseer Starstan says there's a problem with the refractor array,*' said Hurnigen.

'Baneblades, then. Cortein, Ultrus, *to the fore. Destroy them, then we move on,*' said Hannick breathlessly. '*For the Emperor! For Terra! For Paragon!*'

The Seventh grumbled on through the mud, all weapon's blazing as they drove. *Lux Imperator* hung back while *Cortein's Honour* and *Artemen Ultrus* pounded the leftmost macrocannon turret with their battle cannons, which, though inaccurate at range, could cast their shells several miles. Meggen and *Ultrus'* primary gunner, Rosdosigen, zeroed in on the turret shot by shot, until their rounds pounded it directly. The macrocannons continued to lob shells at a rate of one every thirty seconds. Three sailed overhead, crashing into the landing fields and causing carnage there. An entire platoon was vaporised as it emerged from its lander. A pair of light landing craft were broken by one shot, their shattered wrecks spinning into the men around them and killing dozens. In desperation, Colonel Sholana of the 42nd called in a lance strike, but it missed, sending up a column of steam five hundred feet high wide of the mark. The Baneblade shook as the main gun was discharged, rocket gases venting from the barrel exhausts on the muzzle in bright white streamers. The shell lift rattled constantly through the command deck, bearing fresh rounds into the turret.

'Damn Navy,' growled Meggen. His last round hit the side of the tower, knocking free a rush of broken rockcrete. 'Good job we're here.'

Rosdosigen hit also, and the Baneblades finally toppled the tower. The remaining macrocannon kept up a much lower rate of fire, leading Bannick to believe it was damaged or under-crewed. Still it fired, impacting the ground not far from the Seventh's position.

'They're getting the message. They're targeting us.'

'Not for long,' said Meggen.

More shells from the battle cannons slammed into it. The turret remained standing, but fell silent.

'*Get me an augur reading of that tower,*' Hannick ordered.

'Must have got the crew,' said Ganlick. 'Save some for me, eh, Meggen? I'm out of range with this shotgun.'

'The better man gets the better toys,' said Meggen.

'*Command report zero life signs,*' said Cholo.

'*That's it, move on,*' said Hannick. '*All enemy alpha-class defence turrets accounted for. You may sound the general advance, General Lo Verkerigen. Advise: send a squad to check the turret is clear.*'

Bannick heard only this, and not the responses Hannick would undoubtedly have. Commanding a company of tanks like the Baneblade was a world away from directing the efforts of one.

At the general's order, the Seventh cut diagonally across the front, running roughly parallel to the city outskirts towards the landing fields of the port. They crunched over shattered rockcrete and ferrocrete fortifications, flattening razor wire, uprooting tank traps with their awesome weight, churning the bodies of the dead to slurry under their tracks. Ahead the drop-ships of the Gulem Recovery Force were coming down in numbers.

'Basdacks have it easy,' said Meggen. 'We took the brunt.'

Bannick thought twice about rebuking Meggen. But he was right. The smaller Paragonian force was coming down into a far friendlier environment. Most of the anti-aircraft and anti-orbital weaponry of the rebels was so much scrap.

We could have waited, thought Bannick. We could have come down after the weapons were gone. Perhaps, tactically, it made sense, drawing fire off the Imperial forces already on-world, but Bannick suspected nothing more than rivalry and a rush for glory. Generals Lo Verkerigen and Basteen of Paragon had been chafing under the leadership of the Atraxian Captain-General Iskhandrian. This was a race to the surface, a matter of national pride resolved with the needless expenditure of lives.

In neat columns men, lighter tanks and armoured

personnel carriers broke away from the Seventh's wake. Troopers fanned out to tackle remaining pockets of resistance. Lines of Chimeras headed by Leman Russ main battle tanks headed off towards the city. The enemy were not beaten yet. The interior of *Cortein's Honour* flashed as a tank outside exploded half a kilometre away, its magazine detonated by a concealed lascannon.

'Basdacks know what they're doing,' said Meggen.

'Provide moving fire curtain,' ordered Hannick.

The turrets of *Artemen Ultrus, Ostrakhan's Rebirth* and *Cortein's Honour* swung out perpendicularly to the line of the tanks' advance and commenced hurling shells.

'Defence in depth. Every point a fortress, every one needing to be broken on its own,' said Epperaliant. 'This victory is going to cost us dearly.'

'Show me a victory that doesn't!' shouted Kalligen between two thunderous booms of the tank's secondary cannon.

'We serve,' said Leonates, so quietly he probably hadn't intended to speak aloud, but his words carried over the vox and rebuked the Paragonians even if he had not wished them to. Talk stopped as the men became engrossed in the efforts of war.

The Seventh rumbled onwards, approaching the Gulem group's landing zone. Enemy fire, for several minutes quiet, intensified. The hull rattled.

'We're taking a lot of hits, sir,' said Ganlick nervously.

'All light stuff,' said Bannick. 'Keep up your fire.'

A tocsin beeped its alarm. Kolios deactivated it. 'Lascannon hit, right trackguard.'

'It's not that light,' said Kalligen.

'You'll learn soon enough that one of the privileges of

being on a Baneblade is attracting the enemy's fire,' said Bannick. 'Now, we've another target.' He was busy with the tac display. A new main objective had flashed into being and was creeping line by shaking line into view on his small chartdesk – a large, six-pointed star fort at the edge of the spaceport, four turrets atop it, all firing on trajectories towards the Gulem force. An angled roof of thick rockcrete and plasteel sheltered a firing deck whose slits covered every angle of the approach.

'We should attack,' said Shoam, speaking for the first time in a while. His cold voice had the others on the command deck glancing at each other; it sent ice water running down their spines.

'Negative,' said Epperaliant. 'We'd breach the walls, but we lack the manpower to overrun it.'

'And that's why we're babysitting the Lucky Eights. No wonder they're so basdacking lucky if they've got the likes of us to shelter them from the enemy.'

'Meggen,' warned Bannick.

'Yeah, sure, sir,' grumbled Meggen. The first gunner blasted a shell at the fort. Bannick watched it glance off the roof and explode in the air.

'Huh,' Meggen said. 'It's not going to be that easy.'

'And the Eights aren't that lucky today,' said Epperaliant. 'They're drawing fire from the turrets.'

'Concentrate on light targets for now,' said Bannick. 'Ignore the fort.'

Another las-blast connected with the tank. This time they heard the bang, and thin smoke curled through the light of the vision blocks.

'Light fire. Right,' said Meggen.

'Nearly there,' said Bannick. Blinking green icons indicated the approach of the Eighth Paragonian Super-Heavy Tank Company.

'Sir, I've got one of the Lucky Eights on the vox. He's signalling Hannick. The captain is requesting you listen in.'

'Patch it through to me, private channel.'

'It's done, sir.'

An exterior feed opened, fainter than the internal tank's comms. Bannick dialled down the feeds from his men to better listen.

'*This is Honoured Captain Hannick of the Seventh,*' said Hannick. '*Good afternoon, gentlemen.*' There was a strain in his voice, Bannick thought. He's holding back his cough.

'*Fine day for a stroll,*' said a clipped, aristocratic voice.

'*I hear the accent of the harvester clans. You are a Parrigar?*' asked Hannick.

'*Quite. Ardoman Kosigian Lo Parrigar, honoured captain.*' A large boom sounded from his end of the connection. '*We are being fired upon.*'

'*We are proceeding to meet with you.*'

'*Damn the orders, we're taking a lot of fire from those turrets. We are above them currently, but elevation dips three hundred metres out. With our backs exposed, we risk the infantry we're carrying, without whom this endeavour will fail.*'

'*Damn the orders?*'

'*Modify the orders, and in so doing, damn them, yes,*' said Parrigar.

'*Agreed,*' said Hannick. '*Lux Imperator, halt and come about. Knock out those turrets.* Artemen Ultrus, Cortein's Honour, *take lead, inverse arrowhead,* Ostrakhan's Rebirth *at the rear. Can you find a little shelter, honoured captain?*'

'*From those guns, not likely.*'

'*Then cut obliquely towards us. We'll meet midway between*' *our position and the rendezvous,'* said Hannick. The mission marker shifted on Bannick's chartdesk. *'The rendezvous point looks difficult. Enough mud to bog us down.'* A hint of suggestion crept into Hannick's voice.

'Doesn't it?' said Parrigar. *'We cannot risk being immobilised. Suggestion heard and accepted. Parrigar out.'*

The feed cut out. Hannick began his wracking cough. The feed to his tank cut out also. Bannick was glad his men hadn't heard that.

'All done, Epperaliant.'

'Comms reset, sir. Hails coming in from *Emperor's Lambent Glory,* sir. High command. Cholo is requesting we take it.'

Bannick sighed through his teeth. 'Put it through.'

'Seventh, you have deviated from planned course, please advise.'

'Battlefield adjustment. The Eighth are taking heavy fire, the enemy has correctly identified them as the major threat.'

'Then seek support. Stick to the general's plan. Where is Hannick?'

'Indisposed. This is a broad front. Support is too far. We will proceed on our current course.'

'Negative. Resume course.'

Bannick's temper flared. 'We are in the situation, high command. Original plan is inadvisable under the current circumstances.'

'Irrelevant. The plan calculated to yield the most...'

'I'm sorry, I didn't catch that. Please repeat,' said Bannick.

'Orders are to be followed. This order is being reissued, forcefully.'

'Still not getting it. We're losing you,' said Bannick. 'We shall proceed as situation dictates.'

'*We hear you fine. Did you get our last? Respond please.*'

'Sorry, only hearing one in three words. Suspected malfunction. Please repeat we're–' He depressed the vox button and cut them off. 'Basdacking kree bird fools,' he said.

'*What did they say?*' said Hannick hoarsely. '*For some reason I couldn't catch that.*'

'I have no idea, sir,' said Bannick.

The Seventh continued on. *Lux Imperator* fell out of line. Tracks spinning opposite ways, it turned neatly on the spot to bring its volcano cannon to bear on the fort while the others headed on to meet with the Eighth. The tank crews held their breaths as Hurnigen reported the cannon charging, wondering if the tank would deign to fire, but two shots blasted out, atomising two of the turrets, leaving craters of molten rockcrete marring the fort. The remaining two turrets swivelled to fire upon the Shadowsword. Shells rained down all around it while the volcano cannon charged a third time, and duly a third turret exploded. The remainder of the Seventh kept up their suppressive fire, deterring reinforcements from approaching the fort.

The tank's augur eyes projected a live pict-feed onto Bannick's tac screens. Three Stormlord tanks approached them. Sister designs to the Baneblade drawn from the same STC family, they were nevertheless different in many respects. Squat and square turretless infantry transporters, the twin, short muzzles of vulcan mega-bolters projecting from the front of command decks that sheltered open fighting decks behind.

'*Parrigar, fall in behind us,*' said Hannick.

'*One turret remains,*' said Parrigar.

'*It'll be dealt with.*'

Now the companies had met, the Seventh halted and turned to face the fort head on. *Artemen Ultrus* and *Cortein's Honour* nosed forwards, so that *Ostrakhan's Rebirth* could retake its trailing position between them. The Eighth manoeuvred to take shelter between the Seventh's tanks. A final muzzle flash from the remaining turret preceded its annihilation by *Lux Imperator*. The shell flew true, slamming into the lead Stormlord. It exploded with no ill effect, and the mighty tank continued its repositioning as fires guttered out on its glacis.

'I see why they call them the Lucky Eights,' said Epperaliant.

'*Tanks of Paragon, forwards.* Lux Imperator, *prepare to open up the wall,*' ordered Hannick.

'*We're having problems again here, sir,*' replied Hurnigen. '*Cannon's not charging now.*'

'Another malfunction?' said Hannick.

'*A problem?*' voxed Parrigar.

'*Nothing we can't handle,*' said Hannick. '*Baneblades, open fire on the fort to my coordinates. Make the Four Hundred and Seventy-Seventh a breach to exploit.*'

'Aye, sir,' said Marteken.

'Direct all fire forwards. Follow Hannick's mark,' said Bannick. The chartdesk flickered, and the view of the general landscape was replaced by a close-in view of the wall. A rotating red reticule appeared at the joint between two of the spines of the star.

'Transmitting mark to gunnery stations,' said Epperaliant. 'Mark transmitted.'

'Open fire,' said Bannick and Marteken almost simultaneously. *Cortein's Honour* bucked as it flung a shell at the fort.

'*Eleven hundred yards and closing,*' said Hannick.

'*Marteken, we're closing in too tight. Take* Artemen Ultrus *out ten yards.*'

'*Affirmative. Repositioning.*'

The tanks drove at the fort. The buildings and huge hangars of the spaceport resolved themselves from the rain. Artillery deployed from orbit had arranged itself by now, and the edge of the city was a rolling field of fire. The charms hanging from the ceiling of *Cortein's Honour* tinkled with the vibration. On the far side of Matua Superior, the fleet commenced its barrage again. For what purpose was unclear; there were no fortifications that way. Enemy reinforcements coming in from the north, perhaps.

'We're coming within range of their weaponry. It'll be light fire, but brace,' said Bannick.

The tanks rumbled their way through increasingly thick mud, slowing as they climbed up and over the torn earth of Geratomro. All the while the tanks' automatic tracking systems, beseeched correctly by their tech-adept aspirants, kept the gun barrels level. The thunder of the primary weapons played over the rattle of the shell lift as it hoisted more munitions up from the magazine.

'*Hurnigen, get me that cannon back online. The battle cannons are barely scratching the fort,*' commanded Hannick.

'*We're doing all we can, sir! Starstan says the machine is disquieted. He says its spirit must be placated or we'll have more problems.*'

'Artemen, Cortein, *keep up the barrage,*' said Hannick, not bothering to hide his frustration.

'Coming into range of their weapons. I'm reading various power spikes, sir,' said Epperaliant.

'Hold steady, men,' said Bannick. 'This is going to be a bumpy transit.'

Seconds later, missiles and lascannon bolts spat forth from the fort's firing slits. The weapons the rebels held had a much longer range than the one thousand yards the super-heavies were at, but refraction reduced the efficacy of lascannons on full-atmosphere worlds, while the effectiveness of both projectile and energy weapons was dictated entirely by the skills of the men handling them, which, Bannick noted with relief, were not very high.

'Emperor's teeth!' said Kalligen as missiles and auto-cannon rounds belted off the forward facing of the tank.

'We'll make it,' said Bannick. The racket of impacts on the hull nearly drowned him out, even through the internal vox.

'With all due respect, sir, you could say that after sitting down here at the front.'

'Bolters at optimal range, sir,' said Epperaliant.

'Tertiary weapons, open fire. Target the slits. Drive them back. How much longer to demolisher range?'

The muted rattle of the heavy bolters struck up.

'Another hundred yards, sir,' said Epperaliant.

'Prepare. A couple of rounds should deal with the problem.'

As Bannick gave the order, an uneasy feeling swam beneath his elation at battle. This was not like fighting xenos; these were men he was slaughtering. Tuparillio's dying face flashed in his mind, the cousin he had killed back on Paragon in a duel. An event that had led him, step by step, to where he was now. He compartmentalised his emotions, shutting down his objections.

'Not now,' he murmured to himself.

'Intensifying fire,' said Leonates. 'They are not responding to our polite requests to cease fire.'

'More fool them,' said Bannick.

'*I'm coming forwards,*' said Hannick. '*Demolisher cannons ready. All primary and secondary weapons systems hold to fire on my command.'*

'Prepare demolisher,' Bannick passed on.

'Demolisher ready!' shouted Kalligen.

'Secondary weapon in range,' said Epperaliant.

'We're in range,' reported Cholo on Marteken's behalf.

'Primaries and secondaries, open fire, my mark. Three, two, one. Fire,' said Hannick.

Marteken and Hannick repeated Hannick's order for their crews. A wall of fire blasted from six assorted cannon muzzles as the super-heavies fired together. The rounds blasted into the wall within milliseconds of one another. Flames burst out of the firing slits on two arms of the star. When the smoke and fire cleared, a cleft had opened up in the wall.

'Breach open,' said Hannick. *'Parrigar, you're clear to attack.'*

Hurnigen's voice crackled over the vox again. *'Sir, Lux Imperator is listening to us again. Volcano cannon charging.'*

'Need a second breach?' asked Hannick. He stifled a cough.

'By all means,' said Parrigar.

'Lux, fire on the joint two down from the initial breach. Sending targeting data now. Tanks of the Seventh, spread and fall back. Allow the Eighth through.'

'Affirmative,' said Bannick. 'Shoam, full reverse, bear right. All weapons keep up fire.' He waited for the next double boom of battle cannon and demolisher cannon to sound. 'Parrigar, sir, please be wary. We could not do much to discourage the enemy from the slits.'

'We'll see about that,' said Parrigar. *'Lucky Eights, prepare vulcans to fire on my command.'*

Artemen Ultrus and *Cortein's Honour* rolled back. From the rear a brilliant las-beam smashed into a section of the fortress a way along the wall from the first breach, bursting the rockcrete, sending molten gobs and fragments out in a lethal burst.

The three tanks of the Lucky Eights pushed between their sisters, heading with impressive speed directly for the fort. After the respite bought by the breaching, enemy fire started up again, less intense than before, but still worrisome. As Parrigar's command tank rumbled between *Cortein's Honour* and *Ostrakhan's Rebirth*, Bannick caught a glimpse of an entire platoon of men, pressed into the lee of the command deck to shelter against the enemy's wrath.

Bannick felt pity for them. Then the vulcan mega-bolters opened fire, and his pity shifted to the enemy.

He had never heard anything like it. Thousands of bolt-rounds going off together, the distinctive twin-reports of barrel ejection and propellant ignition joined into a cacophony as penetrating as a million firecrackers set off at once. He tore his headset off, seeking refuge in the din of his own tank, and stood, pressing his face against one of the observation windows. Through the accretion of dust and grease on the armourglass, he saw whole sections of the firing slits crumble under the barrage, widening from narrow, perfect rectangles to lopsided holes like the empty mouths of crones. The vulcans ceased firing. Pulverised rockcrete rose as dust into the air.

The Stormlords rolled on untroubled. They ran themselves right up to the breaches in between the star's arms, one at the first breach, two at the one opened up by *Lux Imperator*.

'Cease firing,' ordered Hannick.

The Seventh's weapons fell quiet.

'Second lieutenant, you have command,' said Bannick.

He slid out of his chair, snagged his greatcoat from the back of the seat and clambered up into the turret. Meggen watched him go to the command cupola and open the hatch.

'Fancy a look, Meggen?'

'Sure,' said the gunner. 'I ain't got nothing better to do.' He picked up his tarabac cheroots.

Together the two men poked themselves up out of the hatches of the tank. The rain had stopped and it was warmer than Bannick expected. He dropped his coat back inside. The contrast between the fuggy interior of the tank and the warm breeze blowing over the plains prickled his skin, but he welcomed it. As always when he emerged from the Baneblade, he felt dirty. The triangle of sweat soaking the back of his vest chilled rapidly. Meggen lit a cheroot next to him. He offered one. Bannick declined.

The 477th were leaping up over the command decks of the Stormlords. Platoon standards waved as the men hurled grenades in through the ragged firing slits and the breaches, then poured inside.

The dark apertures of the fort flashed with las-fire, very brief. Resistance collapsed. A few minutes later, the standard of the 477th's Eighth Company was held aloft atop one of the shattered stumps of the artillery turrets.

'Honoured Captain Parrigar reports objective rho-sigma twenty-three secure, sir,' voxed Epperaliant from below.

'We've still got to go into the port,' said Meggen.

'Orders, Hannick?'

'I've heard from high command. The Atraxians have encountered only light resistance to the north. This fort was the southern strongpoint. The enemy are surrendering. The spaceport is in our hands. Stand down, gentlemen.'

'It's over,' said Bannick.

'Just like that, all done,' said Meggen, flicking ash from his cheroot.

Bannick pulled his vox-set off, letting the air refresh his sweating head. 'Paragon be blessed, but I hate the way these things make my ears so damn hot.'

'I can think of worse,' said Meggen.

All around was a scene of utter devastation, but now the fighting was done, Bannick thought he could guess at the area's peacetime use. 'Fields. This was fields,' he said.

'It's a basdacking mess now,' said Meggen dourly.

Artillery still boomed in the distance, the crumping of shells a background noise that had become as natural as avian song to Bannick. Black smoke stretched to the sky from the city. The sound of small arms fire from a mile or so away crackled and popped. The stench coming off the mud was nauseating.

'Still, the sun's coming out,' said Bannick. The dark clouds were parting. They were high, unnaturally so, the product of such massive atmospheric interference caused by planetfall, and all around the horizon the sky was the colour of beaten gold.

'Boring place,' said Meggen dismissively. 'Very flat. Still, better than the last two dreckholes we've been.' He withdrew inside and clanged his hatch shut.

Bannick remained out top, the pleasure of victory bringing a great calm to his soul. It would pass, then the nightmares would begin. In the past it was the shame of outliving his comrades. Here, with the enemy so very close to home, he expected his shame to be of a far worse kind.

Even so, a morbid curiosity led him to put one pad of his vox-set to his ear.

'Epperaliant, signal Hannick.'

'I have him, sir.'

'Switch me to private comms.'

A click informed him Epperaliant had done so.

'Sir, perhaps I should go to Honoured Captain Parrigar and offer my congratulations.'

'*It should be me,*' said Hannick, his breath laboured. '*But you know...*'

'*I understand,*' said Bannick. '*I'll come up with a plausible excuse.*'

'*Thank you, Bannick,*' said Hannick gratefully.

Bannick went below to fetch his uniform jacket, greatcoat and weapons. Properly dressed and standing tall in the turret, he ordered *Cortein's Honour* to the fort.

CHAPTER FIVE
A MEETING OF COUSINS

MATUA SUPERIOR
GERATOMRO
083398.M41

Bannick jumped down from the front of *Cortein's Honour* and made his way to the lead Stormlord. He clambered up the access ladder at the back, and went across the fighting deck. Discarded canteens and packs were scattered against the parapets. He knocked on the armoured door leading into the command deck.

The slam of bolts being disengaged came a moment later. The door opened a crack, and the muzzle of a laspistol emerged, charge indicator on full, followed by a suspicious face.

'Who the Throne are you, knocking on the basdacking door?' said the man.

'Honoured Lieutenant Bannick, of the Baneblade *Cortein's Honour*, Seventh Paragonian Super-Heavy Tank Company,' he said crisply, flashing his lieutenant's pips at the man. 'I am here on behalf of Honoured Captain

Hannick to congratulate Honoured Captain Parrigar on our victory.'

'Right,' said the man, still suspicious. He opened the door. Behind him was a gloomy command deck radically different to Bannick's own, so dominated by the mechanism of the mega-bolter that the crews stations were arranged around it. Other details he could not see, for the contrast between the light outside and the dark within was too pronounced.

Bannick looked down at the gun in the man's hand, now pointed firmly at him.

'Did you open the door so that we might converse more easily, or to allow you to cover me properly?' asked Bannick.

The man gave him a level stare. 'The Lucky Eights didn't get that name by being careless. We don't take kindly to strangers trespassing on the *Righteous Vengeance*.'

'My apologies. And you are?'

'Second Lieutenant Gulinar, SIC to the honoured captain.'

Bannick held out his hand. 'A pleasure.'

Reluctantly, Gulinar took it.

'Parrigar's not here. He's inside with Captain Dolisto of the Four Hundred and Seventy-Seventh.'

'Where?' said Bannick, peering past him into the tank.

'Inside,' said Gulinar, pointing up, in the general direction of the breach in the fort. 'That's where you'll find him.'

He stepped back inside and shut the door behind him.

'Charming,' said Bannick. He clambered up the ladder at the side of the door and walked down the tank to the breach. The climb inside was harder than the infantry had made it look, a tight squeeze through a gap made dangerous by sharp edges and jagged reinforcement bars.

Inside was a scene of carnage. The star point was a single gallery with firing slits either side. Dead men lay where they had fallen. Some were shredded with shrapnel, especially near the breach. Further away most appeared to have died from bludgeoning overpressure. Vitae trickled from noses, ears and mouth. Eyes were red with ruptured blood vessels. Bannick picked his way through their tangled limbs, his heart sinking. The men were of a type similar to Paragonians. A little darker, perhaps, a preponderance of premature grey hair, but any one of them would have blended into the population of his home world without drawing remark.

Further on, the corpses were las-burned, many in the back. Among them he counted a handful of Paragonian dead. Most were Geratomran.

He went into the centre of the fort. Part of the hall had been cleared of corpses, and a medicae team worked on the wounded, Paragonian and Geratomran alike. He approached one.

'I'm looking for Honoured Captain Parrigar and Captain Dolisto,' he said.

'In the central command hall, sir,' said the medicae without looking up.

Bannick walked down a line of wounded waiting for attention. A hand grabbed at his ankle. He looked down to see a young Geratomran soldier, one eye swelled shut, a nasty wound in his forearm, leaning back against the wall, legs sprawled out in front of him.

'Water, please,' he croaked.

Bannick knelt by his side. He should hate this man for his treachery, but he could not. All he felt was pity. It was not the decision of common soldiers to secede. Bannick's hand went to his canteen and he pulled it from his belt, unscrewed the top and handed it to him.

'I'm sorry, it is warm.'

'You came in those tanks?' said the man. Bannick figured he couldn't be more than nineteen or twenty Terran standard years.

Bannick nodded.

'I always wanted to see a Baneblade in action.'

'Why did you rebel?' Bannick asked.

'Because I was told to,' said the boy. 'Isn't that the way it works in the Astra Militarum?'

'It is. But why did your governor turn traitor?'

'The tithe.'

'It was a question of economics?'

The soldier shook his head. 'Not the exacta, the other one, the Munitorum Tithe. All of my brothers, my cousins, my father, my uncles. Gone. Drafted into the Astra Militarum. This planet is empty of men. The Munitorum came back for an ninth tithe in as many years. Our planetary commander told them what they could do with their requisition papers. What else could she do? There's no one in the agricolae, no one mans the fabricators in the manufactoria. They said make women work. Our women work anyway. Now our children do too, youngsters who should be in the scholum. This planet's dying, and the Emperor is the one who sucked it dry. If you're going to ask me if I went along with my orders gladly, no, I didn't. I'm a traitor. Do you know how that feels? But you know what? I don't really think we had a choice, so here's to the Governatrice.'

He raised the canteen in ironic salute and gulped from it thirstily.

Bannick stood up quickly.

The boy held out his canteen. 'Thank you for the drink,' he said.

'Keep it,' said Bannick coldly. He left shaken that someone could turn against the Emperor and talk about it so calmly.

He made his way around the fort hub by the circular corridor. There was only one door, and when he passed through it he found himself in the command centre. A group of Geratomran officers sat in the corner, their hands on their heads, guarded by a bunch of hard-bitten Paragonian infantry with unfamiliar regimental flashes. Burned-out stations lined the walls, their gel screens cracked and dribbling liquid. An honoured captain he assumed to be Parrigar was in deep, quiet consultation with another officer in the uniform of a Paragonian infantry captain; Dolisto, he guessed.

Sentries on the door saluted Bannick as he passed through. Parrigar looked up, and Bannick saluted.

'Honoured Lieutenant Colaron Artem Lo Bannick, sir,' he said. 'Commander of the Baneblade *Cortein's Honour*, Seventh Paragonian Super-Heavy Tank Company.' He saluted Dolisto next.

'Stand easy. Good to meet you.' They shook hands Paragonian style, palm to palm. 'This is Captain Dolisto.'

Parrigar was old Paragonian aristocracy, older than Bannick by twenty years at least, tall, thin faced, long fingers. Patrician was the word Bannick immediately settled on. Dolisto was younger than Bannick, but carried himself similarly to Parrigar. A man of a different generation, but with the same thoughts and feelings and prejudices.

'What can we do for you?' said Dolisto.

'I came to get my eyes on the situation, get a breath of air and offer my congratulations on an engagement well fought.'

'A breath of air,' said Dolisto. 'Must get stuffy in those tanks. Safe though,' he said, and he did not mean it disparagingly, but spoke it as a jest between comrades. 'Thank you for your congratulations. They did not put up as much of a fight as we expected. We lost seven men, I think.' Dolisto looked over at the Geratomran officers. All but one, who glared ferociously, looked shamefacedly at the ground.

'How many of theirs?' asked Bannick guardedly.

'In total? Two hundred, give or take,' said Dolisto. 'Most were dead already thanks to you. They didn't stand a chance.'

'Local defence militia. Not up to much,' agreed Parrigar.

'They still managed to frag all cogitators before we got in here, so that's one success we won't be able to report,' said Dolisto. 'But our primary mission objective, the securing of the spaceport, has been achieved. It would have been much harder without your company. Please pass my thanks on to your commanding officer.'

'We were following orders given by better men than I, sir,' said Bannick. He meant it lightly, but the memory of the boy in the corridor returned to haunt him as soon as the words were out of his mouth. Somehow it got mixed up with Tuparillio's face in his head, and his smile froze.

'Nevertheless, thanks are due, honoured lieutenant.'

Bannick bowed and departed.

On the way to the breach he heard panicked shouting, and a sudden fusillade of shots. He ran towards them, tugging out his own pistol from its holster and thumbing the battery coupling to engage. He arrived pointing it directly at the impossibly clean uniform of an Imperial commissar. At his feet slumped the bodies of the Geratomrans the medicae had been treating, smoking las-holes burned in their foreheads. The boy he'd spoken to lay staring lifelessly, mouth open, water glugging from Bannick's canteen onto the floor. A pair of solemn Adeptus Ministorum deacons moved down the line of dead, drawing the sign of the aquila on bloody faces in scented oil and muttering the benediction of the dead.

'Good afternoon, lieutenant. You appear to be holding a gun on me.' The commissar's face was surprisingly young under the shining peak of his cap, but his eyes were so piercing they were impossible to hold. Bannick holstered his weapon.

'I... I am sorry, sir. I heard shouting, and gunfire. I feared a hidden unit of the enemy.'

'Then you are to be commended for you initiative, if not your reaction.'

'You executed them?'

'Of course,' said the commissar. 'Is that not the appropriate action when dealing with traitors?'

He stepped in too close. Bannick tensed and held his ground.

'We show mercy to the civilians. This is not their war. But there will be no mercy to men under arms who fight against the rightful rule of the Imperium.'

The commissar dabbed at a spot of blood on the white front of his greatcoat with a handkerchief, succeeding only in smearing it.

Bannick stared at him. The handkerchief smelt of flowers. The commissar frowned and tutted at the mark.

'They were under orders. These men would have fought for us.' Bannick doubted his own words. Maybe they were all as embittered as the young man had been, but this wholesale slaughter was not right.

'They might have said they would,' said the commissar. 'And perhaps many of them would have held to their word. But tell me, how would you winnow the genuine traitor from the contrite soldier? If you have a solution, I would dearly like to have it. I dislike the waste of loyal blood as much as any man.'

'Hey, Suliban, what's going on here?' An exhausted lieutenant in a mud-spattered uniform pushed his way past the priests.

'I was just telling Honoured Lieutenant...?'

Commissar Suliban directed a quizzical look at Bannick.

Bannick stood to attention. 'Honoured Lieutenant Colaron Artem Lo Bann–'

He never finished. The lieutenant's face crumpled with rage, and without warning he slammed his fist into Bannick's stomach.

Bannick collapsed, the wind driven from him. Gasping for air, he scrabbled for his gun. Suliban nodded one of the men over, and a foot descended on Bannick's wrist, pinning it in place. The lieutenant moved in, fists clenched, but Suliban stopped him with a palm to the chest.

'Do you mind telling me what this is about?' he said to Bannick's assailant. 'I could shoot you, here and now, for striking a fellow officer.'

A flicker of fear passed over the lieutenant's face, but anger overcame it. 'This is him. This is the man that ruined my thrice-cursed life, with his pride and his duelling, and his desire to please himself! This,' he shouted, trembling with rage, pointing a dirty finger at Bannick, 'is my Throne-abhorred cousin.'

Suliban looked from man to man, his amusement plain to see. Bannick gaped, more in shock than from his winding. He recognised the man now. Last time he had seen him, he had been little more than a boy, the son of his mother's sister.

'J-Jonas?' he gasped.

'Yes, Jonas, you basdack.' Jonas pushed against Suliban's palm. Suliban shook his head with quiet authority.

'Don't make me restrain you. Do not make me discipline you. We have fought together, you and I, but I will not let that come in the way of my duty. I could and I will shoot you without compunction, and I would do so knowing the Emperor approved. Is that clear?'

Jonas Artem Lo Bannick tensed. Suliban pushed him back.

'Away, Jonas. As this is that cousin, about whom I have heard so much, I shall overlook this incident. I am not a martinet. But just this once. Do you understand?'

Jonas stared at Suliban, but none could hold the man's reptile gaze for long, and he turned on his heel and stormed away.

Suliban bent down and helped Bannick to his feet. He brushed Bannick down in a manner that was part sympathy, part condescension.

'I can tell you think these executions harsh, honoured lieutenant, but justice cannot be gentle in so cruel a galaxy as ours. Brutality is a weapon that is too useful to put aside. Like all terrible weapons it must be used sparingly.' He looked Bannick up and down, straightened his collars and stepped back. 'There, that's better. I would watch out for your cousin. He is very unhappy with you.' He patted Bannick twice and departed, his guard casting derisory glances back at Bannick, standing numbly amid the slaughtered men, the mumbling of priests in his ears.

I'll give you a choice, said the Devil-in-the-bush,
A choice between night and day.
I'll give you a puzzle, said the Devil-in-the-bush,
A game you must assuredly play.
Choose life, choose love,
Choose the sun or the moon,
Choose from what I might give.
Choose to be a king,
Or choose to be wise,
Simply choose, or you shall not live.

– Part of the *'Lay of Magor'*,
Geratomran chant-epic

CHAPTER SIX
DANCING ON THE LINE OF THE NIGHT AND THE DAY

MAGOR'S PEAK
GERATOMRO
082498.M41

'This is a waste of time.' Heir the Second Dostain stopped and set his fists on his hips. 'I'm dripping. This is no way for a lord of Geratomro to travel. Why couldn't we take a cutter? We could have flown up here in minutes.'

Pollein cocked her head to one side. 'Shhh! Can you hear that?'

'What, the rumble of the guns? I hear it all the time.'

'And can you see that there?' She pointed away to the south, where the dark sky was cut over by crisscrossing contrails.

'From the fighter craft of the Imperial Navy. Why are you asking such stupid questions? I'm not an idiot.'

'Aren't you? You're the one who had a dream that we should tell the Adeptus Administratum to go away, only they didn't, did they?'

GUY HALEY

Dostain's eyes narrowed. 'Aunt Missrine never listens
to me!'

'But she did, and now we have guns and ships with
guns.'

'Is that why we are walking rather than flying?'

'It's a reason for walking I thought you might accept.
I'm walking because I like it. Are you sure you're not an
idiot, dearest nephew?'

'You shouldn't call me that,' he said. He hated his petulance. Pollein always brought it out of him. She made
him needy. 'I'm older than you. You're only third in line.
I am Heir the First.'

'You keep getting that wrong! Not first any more, not
since my sister paid that outrageous sum to have Missrine II cooked up in a vat.'

'Second then!' he snapped. 'I still outrank you.'

'Second, third, whatever.' Pollein shrugged. 'I am your
aunt, like it or not.' Unlike her sister, Pollein was lithe
limbed and tanned. Her skin did not shine so luminously
in the light of Geratomro's two small moons as Dostain's
did. She smiled, even teeth pearly. She was beautiful, and
unobtainable, and tormented Dostain because of it. 'Think
what sister would say, we two up here all alone!' She giggled. 'This is exciting, isn't it? I've never had company
before, Dostain.'

Dostain squirmed under her gaze. Sometimes when she
looked at him, it was like he could feel her fingers in his
head, squishing through his brain as though it were warm
butter. 'You spend too much time out under the sun. It is
unseemly for one of your rank.'

'Not as unseemly as sweating like a swine running after
sweetbobs!' she mocked.

Dostain's unreciprocated infatuation turned again to anger. 'What is it exactly you want to show me?'

'The dance! The dance between the line of the night and the day. What else?'

She turned and plunged on up the slope, shaking showers of water from the broad-leafed undergrowth.

'Nonsense. Myths. Stupid little girl,' he said. A treacherous voice responded inside his head, *If that's the case, why are you following her?*

He concentrated on his annoyance to the expense of his disquiet, and pushed on.

She was quicker than he, nimble as a caprid on the slopes of the mountains. He reckoned they'd come two thousand feet already since leaving the palace late the previous evening. Pollein's silly games irked him, dressing as urchins and sneaking from the laundries under the west wing, but he would do anything to be near her. There were two reasons he went along with it, if he were honest with himself. The first was obvious. A marriage to his aunt would secure his position within Geratomro's aristocracy, as his other aunt the Governatrice had so often hinted. The second embarrassed him in the way that only affection for someone you feel will laugh in your face for it can. He desired her. Already she was in the first flush of womanhood. Her majority was a month away. He did not much care for the idea of marrying her; all that dynastic nonsense demeaned his love for her. But having her... That was a different thought entirely. His palms sweated.

When they were married, he'd stop these little excursions, that was for sure. It wasn't right to prance around the mountains like a common herder.

He shoved his way through the band of palmleaf trees,

their hand-like foliage waving idiotically at him as he passed inwards into a small wood. Once away from the edge, the palmleaves grew tall, spear-thin trunks supporting crowns of five big leaves, all waving in the wind so they looked like a crowd at a game saluting the players. Their spread obscured the stars, and the dark thickened. The withered brown hands of dead palmleaves crunched underfoot, louder than plastek wrapping. His neck prickled. He turned suddenly, certain of eyes on his back, but there was nothing there.

'Pollein!' he whispered, not daring to shout. 'Pollein!'

Leaves crackled ahead. He caught sight of movement and ran as fast as his flabby legs would carry him.

'Wait!' he called. 'Wait for me!'

Eyes flashed, followed by the glint of a disdainful smile. She was on the other side of the stand of trees, shoving her way out through the lesser plants that guarded its borders. In sudden panic at losing her, Dostain flung himself after, bursting out of the wood hot and flustered.

An acclivity of bare rock leaned up away from him. The angle was difficult to judge, and it tricked him into thinking it flatter than it was until he caught sight of his aunt, seemingly hovering in the air high up. She pointed west.

'Look! The sun is coming! Better get a move on, fat little nephew, or we'll miss it!' She turned and sprang on upwards, hopping from rock to rock. Dostain stumbled on the first boulder, skinning his knee. He swore. By the Emperor, he'd whip that attitude out of her. Shadow turned from black to grey at the approach of the sun. He glanced back. The lights of Magor's Seat glowed like gridded jewels at the foot of the mountain, the palace spires rising five hundred feet from its centre. Beyond stretched the expanse of the Norta Great Plain. Towns revealed by similar grids of light receded into the distance. At the far edge the horizon was a sabre-blade of orange.

Dostain pushed himself hard. For the time being, what favour Pollein showed him was dependent on his efforts, not his whim. Besides, it would be irritating in the extreme to come all this way to miss whatever it was she wanted to show him. She would only laugh at him, and he hated it when she laughed at him.

Dostain made it to the crest of the rise as Geratomro's quick dawn spilled over the horizon. A band of light raced across the farms and little towns of the Great Plain towards Magor's Seat, lifting night like a curtain.

Pollein gestured frantically at him to join her behind a large boulder. There were a number of similar large, tired-looking rocks scattered about a small meadow of tough furze-grass on a shelf on the mountain. The peak, invisible from where Dostain stood, was some five thousand feet higher still.

The largest boulder was set almost dead centre to the meadow, a stone needle that appeared to be more obelisk than natural formation. As the dawn flashed across the sunward side of the mountain and hit the top of the stone, it threw out a hard, black shadow towards the cliff, hiding the further slopes of the mountain.

'How ugly,' said Dostain, who preferred the order of the manufactorum over an untamed landscape. More importantly, he knew Pollein loved such sights and he desired to hurt her. Petty, but he was tired, and his legs hurt. He had never sweated so much in his life. 'What is it, then, that I am here to see?'

'The Devil-in-the-bush!' she whispered.

'What? I thought you were joking!' He looked around the rocky meadow, making a real effort to show his disinterest. 'We're over the treeline. I don't see any bushes, only rocks.'

'Silly! That's not his real name. That's just what people call him.'

'I see,' he said, unconvinced.

The sun burst up over the edge of the slope, flooding the little meadow with gold. Pollein closed her eyes and shuddered at its touch. Dostain swallowed. She was even more beautiful in that light. He imagined her in all the finery of the court, not rude rags, fattened, made up exquisitely, skin pale away from the outdoors, inside where she belonged. He steadied himself. The thought of it made him giddy. Or was it that strange effect she had on his brain again? She was still shuddering, making little noises. He thought he saw a blue light flash under her eyelids. It dizzied him.

Her eyes snapped open. 'He's coming!' she said.

Dostain blinked black spots away from his eyes.

'Get down!' Her hand closed about his wrist and yanked him towards the floor. 'He doesn't know you're coming. You'll scare him off. He's very skittish.'

The strange feeling left him at her touch. He looked at her face, but saw nothing amiss. He supposed he could have imagined the light. She did strange things to him for perfectly normal if shameful reasons, and he *was* short of breath.

'There!' she said, pointing excitedly.

Dostain blinked. The stone needle appeared to have acquired a door in its base. Not a square cut thing, but a crude gash in the stone. To his complete amazement a small, hairy head emerged from it. He slapped his own hand over his mouth to stifle a squeal and made to run off, but Pollein had him firmly and would not release him.

The thing peered about until satisfied it was alone. It stepped out from its crack in the rock and went to where the new morning was cut into a stark line between light and shadow. It smiled. It had a big smile, clear to Dostain from fifty yards away. The funny thing, he thought afterwards, was that he should not have been able to see it, but he could. Rubbing its hands together, the creature put one hairy foot either side of this miniature terminator of day and night, closed its eyes, and began to prance back and forth over the line in a clumsy but joyful caper.

Dostain's bladder clenched. He had the overwhelming urge to soil himself.

'The Devil-in-the-bush, dancing on the line between the night and the day,' Pollein whispered, exhibiting none of the terror he felt. 'Not a myth. Would you like to meet him?'

'Are you mad? The thing's a curse! We should run away and never come back!'

'No! Of course not, silly. He's harmless! He and I have become quite good friends, actually. Come on. He's really not very scary.'

Before Dostain could voice his strong objection, his aunt had got to her feet and shouted, 'Hallo! Little man in the bush! I am here.'

The creature spun on the spot, crouched low, teeth bared. For an instant it looked daemoniacal. But its smile chased savagery away when it saw that it was Pollein calling. She ran to the creature. They clasped hands, and together they danced round and round over the boundary of shadow and light, laughing like children until they collapsed, giggling madly.

Dostain straightened, unable to take his eyes off the thing. He'd seen animals from a hundred worlds. He'd seen examples of sentient xenos, some of them even alive. He had never seen anything like the Devil-in-the-bush. It was about the size of a seven-year-old child, but more powerfully built. Knotted muscles moved under skin covered with a sparse coat of wiry hair too thin to be called fur. Only its feet, face and hands were free of it. It thickened on top of its head into an unkempt mop full of twigs and dirt. The simian, lipless mouth protruded our far. It would have looked ridiculous, were it not for the eyes being as exactly as legend had it – deep and brown and full of wild power.

'Ah!' it cried in a rough little voice. 'You have a friend! How lovely.'

Pollein snatched up the creature's hand and dragged it towards Dostain. 'This is my nephew, though he's a year older than me, aren't you, Dostain? He is nearly nineteen. He was my elder brother's son, but he sadly died, and so my sister became Governatrice.'

'He-hello,' said Dostain.

'He-hello,' mocked the being with a broad smile. 'Hey, didn't your mother assassinate his father?' said the Devil-in-the-bush to Pollein.

Pollein became grave. 'We don't talk about that. Don't be mean. Mother has an awful temper.'

'She must have, to kill her own brother,' said the thing, its face crinkling merrily. Dostain had the bizarre vision of it as a friendly uncle, teasing children with the promise of vast gifts on Ascension Day, and not some abhuman monster idly discussing murder. 'And aren't you the fellow who told his aunt to dismiss the Departmento Munitorum? Very brave, or very foolish.'

'I had a dream! How was I to know she'd kill them all? I only wanted to do some good.'

'No good comes from following your dreams, boy, everyone knows that.'

'Shut up! It's not my fault! What by the Throne are you?' said Dostain.

The thing winced. 'Oof! Such language!' it said. It did a little bow. 'I am the Devil-in-the-bush, though I'm not so bad as all that.'

'I've never seen anything like you.'

The thing leaned closer, baring flat yellow teeth in a horrible grin. 'And why should you have? There is only one of me.'

'You look like a degenerate, a mutant.'

'Ah. You mean the face?' It circled its finger around its face. 'A conceit I wear in memory of certain pilgrims.'

'From where?'

The thing smiled back. 'That's for me to know.' The sun felt cold on Dostain's back. 'So, good sir, I assume you have heard the tales?'

'They didn't mention anything about the chit-chat,' said Dostain.

'Oh! He is a dry one, he is. You're dry! I like you. Well. The stories then. They are tales. But broadly true. Five months ago, I met your lovely, lovely aunt. A fine young lady, very fine.' It looked over Pollein's curves with a lascivious gaze that she seemed not to see, nor did she catch the broad wink at her behind it gave. Dostain trembled at seeing such a lustful look on so ape-like a face. 'Do you know what I do?'

'You give choices that bring no comfort to the chooser.'

The thing pursed its lips admonishingly. 'Come, come. That's harsh. The trick with the choices I offer is what you do with them. Any misfortune that may befall you can be evaded, if you are nimble. No prize is worth it without a challenge, don't you think? Failure is the fault of the chooser, not the choice-giver.'

Dostain, who had enjoyed many advantages in life at minimal outlay in personal effort, did not agree. From the thing's leer, he supposed the creature knew what he was thinking.

'You sound like a sensible lad, when your aunt talks about you. You did advise the Governatrice to turn away the mission of the Adeptus Administratum. And maybe it wasn't such a bad idea. I mean, the alternative isn't that much worse. You never know, you might even win!'

Dostain scowled. He didn't like the way the thing was stroking Pollein's wrist with its leathery hands. 'I wanted to help. There was no other way. I examined the problem from every angle. We could not give them yet more men. Dreadful business. We had no choice.'

'And getting more dreadful by the day!' said the thing, cupping its hand over its ear in the direction of the distant guns. 'But there's always a choice. Which brings me to yours!' It clenched its fists in glee and hopped from foot to foot in excitement. Then stopped, assuming a posture like a soldier to attention. It looked at Dostain side on, chinless jaw jutting out. 'Power,' it pronounced solemnly. 'Or slavery?'

'Do I have to choose?'

'What happens to those that don't? In the stories.'

The stories. In the stories those who tried to get away were never seen again. Not in one piece, anyway, or with their sanity. But those were only stories. Dostain's palms sweated. His fear slid out and took a hold of his limbs. His body began to shake.

'Power or slavery? That's a suspiciously straightforward choice,' said Dostain, in a small voice.

'You are a lord, my lord! High station brings privilege.' It bowed again.

'Power, then,' said Dostain in confusion. 'Isn't it obvious?'

'The choice is always obvious, but is it always right? Your choice in goading your aunt to secede.'

'I didn't goad!'

'I know what you did. You opposed her. You made her angry and she acts rashly when she is angry. It was your fault, because you hoped she would be removed and that you would be installed in her place. That was an obvious choice, wasn't it? Keep your hands clean, but get the throne.'

'I... I never did!' Dostain coloured, appalled that Pollein had heard the truth, but she was giggling and did not seem to mind.

'Be careful of your choices as much as your dreams,' went the hairy man. 'You never know where they will take you.' The Devil-in-the-bush grabbed Pollein's arm again and pressed a long finger against her wrist. She giggled with delight.

'Ooh, it's tingly!' she said.

'Tis done, in part,' said the thing.

'I didn't choose! I was only thinking aloud.'

'Loud thoughts lead to rash actions, such as provoking the enmity of the Imperium of the corpse-god,' said the thing in a low, menacing voice. 'Wasn't that your thought? You wanted power, you couldn't get it yourself, so I give you power. You chose it. Remember me when you are enthroned.'

'Power,' said Dostain. The thought of it was intoxicating, and dulled his fear at the unnatural being.

'Indubitably. Fate bends its attention to you. Make yourself heard.'

Dostain looked at his aunt.

'How do I know this is not a trick, like in all the stories?'

'Stories are stories, as you have implied. This is real, my lord. If you are nimble, if you are willing, fortune will be yours. Didn't I already say that? I did!'

'If I am not, um, nimble?'

The thing released Dostain's aunt and rubbed its hands together. With mounting horror, Dostain thought it had grown, at least by an inch. 'Either way, my lord, you will see me again!' It looked skywards. 'Full day comes. I must depart! Events run away from you. Soon the armies of the Corpse Lord will be knocking on the palace gates,' it said, miming a rapping on a door, 'bringing with them rope and fire for the traitors of Geratomro. If you wish to avoid this fate, heed my words. You do want power over slavery, don't you? I can, this once, change it, if you wish.'

'I will not be a slave,' said Dostain with fresh resolve. The sensation of Pollein's hand slipping into his only strengthened it.

'Very well then,' said the thing. Without another word, it scampered away, hurling itself at the base of the rock, where it vanished with a bang. Pollein clapped. Dostain ran after it and threw himself at the base of the obe-lisk, much like the thing had. He landed in dewy, spiky furze-grass.

He placed his hands on the cool stone in wonder. There was nothing there. No crack, not even a shadow to sug-gest one. He looked up. The stone looked more like an obelisk than ever, pitted with hollows that might, once, have been carvings. He shook his head. They were just hollows. It was just a *stone*.

What had happened could not possibly have happened. Already it felt like a dream.

His aunt called him. Her pretty brow was creased, and her skin had gone a little grey.

'Let's go home,' she said tiredly.

CHAPTER SEVEN
THE SURRENDER OF MATUA SUPERIOR

MATUA SUPERIOR
GERATOMRO
082998.M41

Seven hours after the spaceport fell, Matua Superior's lord-civil sued for peace and offered unconditional surrender.

The next day the army entered the city arrayed for the maximum show of strength. The tanks of the Seventh Paragonian Super-Heavy Tank Company went in first, followed by those of the Atraxian 18th. Lesser tanks and armoured fighting vehicles came in column behind them, their commanders standing sternly in full dress uniform in their turrets. Every tank had been washed and had pennants affixed to their antennae. Over them swarms of servo-skulls darted, blasting out martial music and messages intended to calm the population, all short and to the point:

'Rejoice, for the Emperor embraces you!'

'Yield the traitor unto justice, and live illuminated by the light of Terra!'

'Clean minds have nothing to fear.'

'Clemency is offered to the man who turns his weapon on the traitor.'

Among this aerial swarm of skulls there were other, more sinister devices. Scout and augur cybernetic constructs scoured the buildings either side of the city's main way with their sensoria. Squads of Atraxian Guard Paramount patrolled the rooftops. Sniper teams lurked on the ledges of tall buildings. All was unnecessary. Matua Superior had been cowed.

Flights of landers roared into the spaceport, bringing more men down to speed the reconquest of the world. Among them came a Titan coffin ship, its arrival timed to coincide with the parade.

From outside, Matua Superior had seemed to suffer during the assault, but much of the city appeared untouched, the damage being restricted to certain areas. Many windows had been blown out, and as the tanks rolled past block after block of whole buildings, they would suddenly come across a toppled edifice, reduced to a pile of broken rockcrete and fused glass, or a perfectly round crater punched into the ground by a lance strike. In such places, the roads had been bulldozed clear. The population lined the streets, dirty and thin from months of siege, but waving their flags and shouting enthusiastically in what seemed to be a genuine show of gratitude. Bannick kept his eyes forwards, but he could not prevent the occasional sorrowful face from catching his eye. Bereaved mothers, or men who knew they would be called up to fight far away from home, never to return, now the Imperium was tightening its grip on Geratomro once again.

The weak, orange sun was warm, and the plasteel of

Cortein's Honour soaked up the heat and reflected it back. It was a pleasant heat, not like the broil of the Baneblade's interior. The sight tapped Bannick's guilt, and it flowed freely. He was clean and warm and well fed, and though the food he ate was little better than swill, and he was weary to the bone, his situation was far better than these wretches on the pavements of the city, cheering him on like dumb farmers welcoming sho-beasts into the pens of their cattle.

They couldn't all be traitors. He expected the truth was complex and sad, that they would do whatever they were told, and that their opinions might flip back and forth no matter how strongly held. The black-and-white truths he had been taught as a child – truths that he had never had the wit to question – were anything but as stark as he had once thought. All was grey. His brief time with the mutants on Kalidar had helped crystallise this conception, although the change had begun earlier, he suspected. He wondered if he had killed any of these people's kin that so desperately cheered for him. Almost certainly, he thought. If it weren't for his first-hand experience of the greater threats facing mankind in the stars, he would have been ashamed. But he hardened his heart as his upbringing had intended it to be hard. Behind the broken remains of one toppled set of certainties, he saw the truth – the real truth – and the horror of it exceeded the injustice meted out to individual men millions of times over. The truth of the Imperium was not about oppression, or conformity, or a will to dominate the minds of every human being for the sake of it, but to do so to prevent extinction. Every time the guilt at killing his fellow man threatened to overwhelm him, he imagined the skies of Geratomro full of the drop-ships of orks.

The further they proceeded into the city, the lesser the damage. The centrum was free of it. Office and administration buildings stood untouched. The emblems of Imperial Adepta were on many. Soon they would begin the work of administering this city for the benefit of mankind again.

At the very centre of Matua Superior was a vast square, dominated by a basilica to the Emperor. A stage had been set up in front of the cathedral gates, covered in bright cloth and lined with the standards of the regiments fighting upon Geratomro. Of the dozen or so there, only half were familiar to Bannick, those of Paragon, Savlar, Atraxia and the new raisings from Bosovar. With three differing army groups merging in orbit around Geratomro, it was to be expected that the others would be exotic to him. A lectern carved in the shape of the aquila, wings outspread, sat in the centre. Two iron gibbets stood a safe distance away from the stage, their doors open. Wood was piled high around their bases. A ladder led up to each.

The tanks of the Seventh drove down the centre of the square, their column stopping fifty feet to the left of the centre of the stage. The tanks of the Atraxian 18th pulled up alongside. Engines roared and revved, then fell quiet. Behind, the Leman Russ battle tanks of the victory parade drove out to the edges of the square, shattering paving slabs under their heavy treads, and forming a hollow square around the plaza. Then men marched in to fill that square, representatives of every regiment. Savlar Chem-Dogs stood to attention next to proud Atraxians in their bulky carapace armour. Paragonians lined up behind pink-skinned Bosovar in rag-tag uniforms. There were others Bannick had no idea were even present in the system, including strange warriors with crested helms and archaic looking armour, ranks of female soldiers, disciplined units of Cadia, and a cohort of fearsome ogryns, who meekly followed their commissar officers to the front.

A fraction of the forces in the system, but representative of their bewildering variety.

When the square was full, half the swooping servo-skulls sailed off down the streets leading from the four sides of the plaza. There were no Geratomrans in the square, only the warriors of the Imperium. Bannick had no idea if the locals had private pict screens or vox-casters, but the skulls would ensure what occurred there would be shared by all in the city.

The sun passed behind the basilica's twin towers, putting them all into shadow, and Bannick shivered. As if this obscuring of the light were a signal, the cathedral doors creaked open. From within strode Captain-General Iskhandrian himself, accompanied by a large entourage of priests, Adeptus Mechanicus, fleet personnel, Departmento Munitorum and assorted other functionaries. Behind them, escorted by members of the Atraxian's elite Guard Paramount, were a number of others, all Geratomran. Ten of them were led to the front of the stage, where they knelt facing outwards in the position of the penitent, a Guard Paramount behind each. Two others – an overweight noble and a second, thinner man in the uniform of the local defence militia – walked grim-faced to the podium. The nobleman stood tall with proud bearing despite his corpulence. The military man produced a sheet of paper and spectacles, and began to read.

'I, Colonel Maden of the Geratomran Planetary Defence Militia, do hereby announce the surrender of the city of Matua Superior to the forces of the Imperium of Man.

We have erred from the path, and regret our actions. Not for the fate that will befall us, but for the sorrow we have caused the Lord of Mankind. We are but insolent children ignorant of the Emperor's wisdom. May He find it in Himself to forgive us, and show mercy to our people for the cowardice of we, their ruling classes, who abandoned our duty to further the reach of the Imperium for our own ends, so imperilling the world and its population. On behalf of the people of this city and region, we renounce the rule of our traitorous planetary governor, Governatrice Missrine Huratal, and her court of serpents. A man has but one duty in life, and that is to the Most Holy Emperor. To ignore one's conscience and obey the orders of the traitor for fear of reprisal is as great an act of treachery as any other.'

Then he handed his paper and spectacles over, and unbuckled his weapons. These too were taken by the Atraxians. He knelt down, as did the lord-civil of Matua Superior. Together they prayed, heads bowed, while priests blessed them, too quietly to be heard in the ranks. The soldiers were silent. Gusts of wind cracked the tanks' pennants. The square was a graveyard, full of bodies bereft of animation.

Bannick was saddened to see this act of prayer used in such a flagrantly manipulative way. Servo-skulls with pict capture devices imaged it from every angle. The moment before death when a man asks for the Emperor's benediction should be private. But Bannick had been ordered to watch it all, so that when images of the surrender were disseminated across the subsector, the planet could see the weight of the assembled armies' disapproval, and he looked ahead unflinchingly.

The men finished. They were taken to the foot of the ladders leading to the gibbets, into which they climbed willingly. The heavy cage fronts were locked closed. For all his dignity, the lord-civil of Matua Superior was too fat to be comfortably accommodated. The ogryns showed their amusement at his flesh pressing out through the lattice with rumbling bass laughs, silenced by hard words from their commissars.

'In these cages, those who defied the orders of the traitor Governatrice were burned alive,' said High Chaplain Moktarn, the Kalidar army group's spiritual leader. 'Into these cages these men go now for a higher treason: they turned their back on the Emperor of Man, and so they shall face the same fate. But even in this moment of painful death, they can rest assured that their transgressions will be forgiven by our Lord, who sorrows to see any man turn away from the light of holy Terra.'

Grim-faced soldiers thrust lit torches into the stacked wood at the bases of the gibbets' iron poles. Stacked faggots burst into violent fire, sped on by accelerant. Flames whooshed up. The face of the lord-civil squirmed as they licked at his feet.

He started screaming a moment later. Colonel Maden held his silence for half a minute, but even he could not bear such pain, and he too began to cry, awful, shrill shrieks of agony that went on far too long. The wood burned clean; there was no smoke to choke them. Only when black matter bubbled from their burning lips did they stop writhing and fall silent.

Bannick watched as the fire consumed the traitors, keeping his face impassive as expected, though he was horrified by what he saw. Maden had named himself and the lord-civil cowards. Bannick thought that a spiteful calumny forced on them by the victors. On the contrary, to surrender and accept such a fate, the lord-civil and the city commander must have been very brave men indeed.

CHAPTER EIGHT
LEAVE

MATUA SUPERIOR
GERATOMRO
083298.M41

Cities are robust organisms, unconcerned with the lives of
the teeming creatures that make up their constituent parts.
What is it to a city if one man dies, or ten thousand? The
city persists. By the time night fell, the siege was already
fading from Matua Superior's forgetful memory. Busi-
nesses opened their doors wide to their conquerors, their
owners hungry for trade, though they had little to sell. So
it was that the crew of *Cortein's Honour* found themselves
wandering through the pleasure district of Matua Superior along with five thousand other men on short leave.
The Departmento Munitorum had a system for rest and
relaxation of its troops, as it had systems for everything.
There were nearly a million men marshalling at the spaceport for the conquest of the world. Not all of them could
take leave. Not all of them were worthy, by any means,
and that was the first filter. Seventy thousand men had

taken part in the landing. More filters were applied. Specialists and middle-ranking officers were denied leave, as were regimental arbitrators. Any man with a negative mark against his record was restricted to the port. Those with less than a year's service were ineligible, ruling out the newest regiments, including all of Gollph's countrymen.

The twenty-seven thousand men who were permitted rest were allotted two hours, thirty-six minutes of free time each, to be taken in groups according to strict rotation. Twenty minutes of this was taken up by a religious service, attendance compulsory, or remaining leave was to be forfeited. As soon as this was done, the men naturally headed out in search of bars and bawdy houses. There are few other things of interest to soldiers other than quick pleasures, especially to those who measure their lifespan in days.

To the Atraxian Leonates, the pleasure district was a shocking place. To the Paragonians it was disappointingly tame. Gollph – whom Bannick had ordered to accompany the others to get around his lack of leave – took it all in with amazement. For him, everything was equally strange and wonderful.

Kolios remained to pray to the tank. Bannick had an invitation to dine with his uncle, and the Savlar Shoam had gone off on his own. That left seven of them. Conquering heroes wandered the conquered city. Tensions between native and Militarum were lessening by the hour. The personal wealth of an average Astra Militarum trooper was small, but multiplied by their numbers, considerable sums of money were changing hands. The tankers were not challenged, only enticed by barkers with eager smiles shouting out the virtues of vice. Nor did they see much in the way of violence towards the fabric of the city or its inhabitants on the invaders' part. To these veterans of the appalling fighting on Kalidar, the relative peacefulness of Matua Superior was surreal.

The streets were narrow, the evening sky a light-polluted orange bar crowded by soaring hab-blocks. Tavernae and refectoria occupied the ground floors of the buildings.

A churning ventilation fan pumped out the oily smoke of cooking flesh, and Ganlick made a face.

'Ooh, that turns my stomach. I can still smell burned meat,' he said.

'You couldn't smell nothing!' said Meggen.

'I could too – the air filter's bust in the tertiary gunnery station intake. I could smell them. I smelt those lords burn.' He stuck out his tongue. 'I can still taste it.' Then he burst out laughing cruelly. 'Best way for traitors to go. Gives them time to think about what they did. Did you see the fat one jig?'

'You smelt nothing, Ganlick,' said Leonates grimly. 'You are a crass man.'

'Better to be crass than crisp,' said Ganlick. Much of his morbidity was a defence mechanism; he was not cruel but he was already drunk. They had expected Kalligen to be the first to go, but he was a more hardened drinker than his comrade, swigging often from his bottle of liquor without any apparent effect.

'And don't go pulling any more tricks like what got you that booze,' said Meggen. 'Or you'll end up on the end of a rope.'

'This was a donation.'

'There are better ways of getting your booze than thieving,' said Kalligen.

'You'd know,' said Ganlick. 'Anyway, it wasn't thieving!'

'You practically snatched it out of his hand,' said Epperaliant, breaking his silence. 'Be careful, Ganlick.' He pointed up.

The crew of *Cortein's Honour* came to a halt before a pair of Savlar Chem-Dogs strung up on opposite sides of the street from lumen posts. Signs hung around their necks.

'Looooters,' read Gollph arduously. 'They steal?'

'Mm huh,' said Kalligen, who took little notice of the corpses and was instead checking over the local tavernae. They had come upon a run of them, each one blinking neon signs to tempt in customers.

'Commissars do it,' said Meggen. 'I don't hold with stealing from the civilians, but fighting's hard, men need an outlet. Sometimes they overstep the mark. A little flexibility's needed.'

'Something I'm sure Shoam would agree with,' said Vaskigen.

'They can't help themselves, those Savlar,' said Meggen. 'You shouldn't punish a loyal man for what he is. They fought hard on Kalidar, those boys, even if they are scum. Nobody's perfect.'

'Where is that slippery basdack Shoam anyway?' said Vaskigen.

'Your guess is as good as mine,' said Ganlick. He shivered. 'Come on, Kalligen, choose somewhere to drink for the sake of the Throne, I'm dying here. It's freezing. Why is this planet so cold?'

'Don't you remember the long winter back home? This place is tropical, if you ask me,' said Vaskigen.

'I ain't asking you. The sun was warm today, and I don't have my heat vest or anything other to wear than this flimsy basdacking Militarum jacket, do I?'

'That one,' said Kalligen. 'Says "soldiers of the Imperium welcome"'.

'And they'd be fools not to put a sign like that up even if they would rather cut our throats in our sleep than water us,' said Leonates. 'This is no place for celebration. We should go back to barracks. I don't like it here.'

'You're buttoned up, you are,' said Ganlick.

'And you're drunk,' said Leonates.

'Guilty!' said Ganlick, and giggled.

'We can commend ourselves for being sensible if we go in there,' said Kalligen.

'You fine with that one,' said Meggen. 'Epperaliant, you're ranking officer.'

'I'm easy,' said Epperaliant.

'You're quiet,' said Ganlick.

'Don't pay that any mind,' said Meggen. 'Just his way. He spends all the time in the tank shouting, so he likes to keep his lips buttoned tight outside. Isn't that right, sir?'

'Something like that,' said Epperaliant.

The group strung itself out as Kalligen led the way to the bar and passed through its greasy glass doors. Discordant music thumped out.

Gollph remained staring seriously at the hanged men.

'Come on,' said Vaskigen. 'Don't look too long. Don't think about it. Be glad it's not you.'

'But... but it could be. On Bosovar, it is custom to take possessions of defeated enemy.'

'Yeah well, sometimes it is with us too, but not now. The high-ups want this planet to fall back in line as quickly as possible. They can't do that if we trash everything. They put those men here because they know most of those on leave will end up coming down this street. Don't be worried by it.'

'I don't understand.'

'You'll get it,' said Vaskigen. 'Just understand this – if you see a commissar, Gollph – the men in black, yeah? – you stay away from him. They're nothing but trouble.'

Vaskigen had to gently lead Gollph into the bar, for the feral-worlder could not stop staring at the results of Imperial justice.

They found a table, though the place was full. Epperaliant's lieutenant's badge scared away a group of field engineers from a large booth in the corner. Leonates protested that it was not fair on the men, but the Paragonians took their seats with clear consciences. As far as they were concerned, the seats were Epperaliant's due as an officer and as a nobleman.

They had limited time, and began the serious business of getting properly drunk. They ordered local ale that was hard on the palate but possessed of a pleasing aftertaste, and a spirit that was harsh as promethium all the way down to the gullet. They drank it anyway, grateful to be out of the tank and the war.

Meggen drank quicker than the rest, and set to grumbling.

Vaskigen jibed him for it. 'Don't you ever quit complaining?'

'Do you ever start? You don't stick up for yourselves enough,' said Meggen.

'Maybe,' said Vaskigen. 'But the reason me and Gollph here don't moan so much as you, Meggen, is that we're too basdacking busy working the shells to have the breath to spare. Why don't you save all our ears and quit your whining when we're in the fight?'

Gollph chuckled.

'What are you laughing at, you pink-skinned midget?' growled Meggen.

Gollph's laugh turned instantly to a scowl. 'You do not speaking with me that way, Meggen.'

'Yeah, don't,' warned Vaskigen genially, whose own relationship with the feral-worlder had got off to a rough start. He'd regularly meted out beatings to the smaller man, until Bannick had told Gollph it was all right to fight back. Once Gollph had floored Vaskigen, they got on just fine.

'I'll say what I want, Vaskigen. You ore grubbers always think you know best. See what I mean, Leonates? There's a bit of clan rivalry for you right there.'

'I do know best. He'll put you on your back and break your arm if you don't watch it,' said Vaskigen.

'Man's as weedy as a slowtail after the long winter,' said Meggen doubtfully. 'He might be able to best a sissy like you, Vask, but I doubt you'd get one over on me.'

Gollph grinned wickedly. 'Not strength. Fighting skill. You got it? Gol... I have,' said Gollph, correcting himself.

'Yeah, yeah, I'll bet you have.' Meggen raised his glass. Gollph looked at him in confusion.

'You knock glasses together? Yeah?' said Kalligen, and knocked his against Vaskigen's genteelly. 'Cheers,' he said. 'See? Now you do it.'

Gollph looked doubtful. 'On Bosovar, this is big insult. You must not knock another man's drink unless you want to fight.'

'Not on Paragon, you pink pipsqueak. Cheers,' said Meggen.

'Now you insult me again!'

'It's called banter where we're from,' laughed Kalligen.

'All right.' Gollph brought his glass up, then snatched it back with a scowl. 'You sure you not mock me – stupid man from feral world, haha, let us laugh hard at the savage?' he said. 'You nasty. Maybe I teach a lesson, Bos-ovar way?'

He said this with such vehemence, Meggen's mouth hung open. 'Hang on a minute, I'm only teasing you, little man. We're all friends here–'

Gollph laughed uproariously. 'Ha! Now I mock yo, big grox man! Cheers!' He clanged his glass hard into Meggen's. Everyone laughed, and the two downed their drinks, slapped the table and grimaced.

'How, by the Throne, do they make this stuff?' said Meggen.

'It does have the distinct whiff of ablutorial cleanser about it,' said Kalligen.

'Ladidada! Look at him, getting all Lo on us. Prefer a nice gleece, your lordship?' said Ganlick.

'As a matter of fact I do,' said Kalligen, affecting an upper-class accent. That made them all laugh.

'I'm a Lo, and I'll drink it,' Ganlick slurred and sniffed his. 'I don't give a damn.'

'I do not understand you people. All this lo that, and vor this,' said Leonates. 'Does it matter?'

'Yes,' said Kalligen.

'Simple,' said Ganlick. 'You got Paragon right? You have a given name, a mother name, and a clan name. If you've any noble blood in you–'

'Which Ganlick has greatly diluted with this piss,' Meggen interjected.

Ganlick persisted. 'Any noble blood at all, then you're entitled to use "Lo" before your clan name. If you don't, you're just a filthy commoner.'

'You're as common as me and Vaskigen,' said Meggen. 'Born and bred to the manufactorum floor.'

'I don't think so. These lovely hands of mine did not a jot of manual labour. Scribing, that's what the family did, and proud of it too,' said Ganlick.

'Lo doesn't mean anything any more,' said Meggen.

'I admit,' said Kalligen, 'there has been talk of abolishing it. Some on the unified clan council say it's devalued. Too many nobles putting themselves about. They've only themselves to blame.'

The Paragonians fell quiet. All of them were suddenly reminded of their home, uncrossable light years distant.

'This is so divisive,' said Leonates. 'Why carry it with you into the Astra Militarum? It means nothing.'

Meggen gave the Atraxian a grave look through the bottom of his empty glass. 'It means everything.'

'I still don't understand,' said Gollph.

'On Bosovar, you got your elders, yeah?' said Kalligen. Gollph nodded. 'Well back home, we've got the high bigwigs in their glass palaces, and then there's the rest of us living in the stink and noise of whatever our clan specialises in.'

'But you, and him... Meggen says you live in stink too,' said Gollph.

'Reminding others you got noble blood is a way to make yourself feel better,' said Kalligen.

'I do not understand either, friend Gollph. It is alien to me also. On Atraxia, all men are born equal,' said Leonates. 'We are tested throughout our lives to find the most suitable role for us in life. Birth is no guarantee of a man's quality.'

'Yes it is important!' said Meggen. 'How in Terra's name do you know who you are if you can't count on your roots?'

'But you said that the elders are bad to you,' said Gollph.

'It is the way of men from society where birth is important, Gollph,' said Leonates. 'They decry their situation, but will defend the system to the hilt. Fair testing is the only real alternative. In this way, we can be sure of serving the Emperor to the best of our ability.'

'You must have scored low then,' said Kalligen.

'How so?' blustered Leonates. 'I scored very highly!'

'Did you? Then why did they send you to join the Astra Militarum then?'

'Here you go, little Leo, these scores sure are good. Honest,' said Meggen in the sort of voice a mother soothes a babe with. 'We've a lovely lasgun and a small bunk for you on the other side of the galaxy where you'll be out of the way of the serious boys.'

'Step this way!' said Kalligen.

'What?' cried Gollph in mock outrage. 'This is exactly what happen to me on Bosovar!'

All of them laughed. Even Epperaliant, lost in his own thoughts, smiled.

'What's all this about then?' A bearded fellow with violence in his eyes spoke.

The tank crew's mirth subsided as shadows fell upon them. A ring of Atraxians surrounded their table.

'Nothing that concerns you, friend,' said Meggen. He finished his drink with an exaggerated gasp, and set the glass down hard. He pulled out a soft packet of tarabac cheroots and lit one. He offered them round, pointedly ignoring the Atraxians. Vaskigen and Kalligen took one each.

'Hey, you. I'm talking to you.' The Atraxian slapped Meggen's beefy shoulder.

'Don't do that, friend.'

'Then, "friend", tell us what the joke is. Laughter concerns us all. Tell us the joke. You, you are Atraxian. Are you with these men?' he said to Leonates.

'I am. These are my comrades, as they are yours.'

'And what about that?' said their leader, pointing towards Gollph. Gollph stared back. His old nerves returned suddenly, and he shrank into himself, unsure of what he should do.

'That's right, cringer. You cringe,' said the Atraxian leader. 'He shouldn't be out.'

'That,' said Meggen with deadly amity, 'is also our comrade.' He stood up, the chair scraping back on the stone flags with bar-silencing volume. Chatter died away as he looked down at the Atraxian. 'A member of the Seventh Paragonian Super-Heavy Tank Company, as we all are here. Brothers in arms. What, by the Emperor's chamber pot, are you?'

The Atraxian leaned in, breathing alcohol fumes into Meggen's face.

'I am a man in mourning for his friends, his brothers and his kinfolk, slaughtered when these cowardly subhumans broke and ran.' He pointed to Gollph. 'Let me prevent the same happening to you. We will deal with him, then you can have a civilised man in your crew instead, not this savage. The lumen posts outside are not yet all decorated.'

The other tankers stood to face outwards at their ring of challengers. The other Paragonians and Atraxians in the bar eyed each other. Hands closed on bottles.

'Two to one,' said Meggen to Vaskigen. 'What do you reckon?'

'Unfair odds. For them.' He cracked his knuckles. 'Gollph,'

said Vaskigen, 'The elders say it's permitted to kick the dung out of these basdacks.'

'Sir?' asked Gollph of Epperaliant.

'Fine by me. If they want a beating, you are permitted to provide it.'

'Pink runt like that couldn't kick a ball,' said the leader. 'Out in the north the lot of them broke. Ferals have no place on a battlefield.' The Atraxians closed in.

'We're not starting anything,' said Epperaliant. 'But if you do not stand down, we'll finish it, and I'll have you up on charges.'

'You can't tell me to do anything.' The Atraxian tapped the lieutenant's badge on his shoulder.

'You heard Epperaliant, boys,' said Meggen. 'No fighting.'

Gollph dropped into a low stance. His demeanour changed so radically the men facing him took a step back.

'Give us the feral, and you'll have no trouble.'

'This feral ain't your feral. He's our feral,' said Vaskigen.

Meggen took a long, slow drag on his cheroot and blew the smoke in the Atraxian leader's face.

'You're not taking him anywhere.'

'Who's going to stop us? You tankers? You haven't got our edge. We've been walking everywhere for the last six years, not sitting on our padded behinds.'

'Hear that, Vaskigen? He thinks we're soft.'

'Yep,' said Vaskigen, grinding out his own smoke on the heel of his hand. 'I suppose years of hauling basdacking heavy shells about don't count.'

'Just give him up, or suffer the consequences,' said the Atraxian lieutenant.

Meggen sighed, cast his eyes heavenwards and landed a punch of such power on the Atraxian's nose he flew back, face spouting blood, bearing two of his comrades to the floor with him.

The bar erupted into violence.

Atraxians took military training from a young age. Martial artistry was beaten into them. Individually, they were capable bare-hand fighters, but they were better together, and they fought as a group, for that was the Atraxian way.

In this first regard, the Paragonians were at a disadvantage. There was no comparable fighting art on Paragon to that employed by the Atraxians, but the Paragonians were more heavily built. The majority of them had performed punishing physical labour from childhood into early adulthood. The gravity was heavier there, and so they were stronger.

Meggen and Vaskigen made good account of themselves, their bodies further hardened by years of manhandling the Baneblade's heavy shells. Vaskigen took a flurry of punches from a smaller man, then picked him up and bodily heaved him through the air.

In the second regard, that of fellowship, they were the equal of the Atraxians. As tankers they lived in a state of intimate proximity that exceeded even that of a common foot-soldier. They fought back to back. Epperaliant went down with a broken rib. Ganlick was hopelessly drunk, and for all his ferocity, was tackled to the floor, where an Atraxian commenced frantically punching him in the face. Leonates faced off three of his countrymen, his facility with Atraxian open-hand combat greater than theirs, though their number prevented him from incapacitating any. Kalligen wrestled with a short Atraxian.

But it was Gollph who surprised everyone but Vaskigen, who had fought the feral himself. The little man tumbled and weaved his way through the melee, jabbing the points of his fingers into various vulnerable nerve clusters, dropping surprised men wherever he went. The Atraxian fighting style focused on dealing gross damage; Gollph's was subtler and therefore more potent.

The man fighting Kalligen wrapped his hand around Kalligen's face, fingers searching for his eyes. Kalligen bit deep into the webbing between the man's forefingers and thumb. Leonates finally dealt with one of his opponents, and began to press hard on the remaining two. Ganlick was out cold, face swollen. Epperaliant curled up in a ball, hands wrapped around his head to protect himself from the kicks raining down on him. Gollph slid up, caught a kicker's foot and snapped his ankle with a savage twist, overbalancing him and shoving him into his fellows. Meggen and Vaskigen roared, backs pressed together, weathering blows that would have seen to the smaller tankers, and responding with bludgeoning fists hard as plasteel.

Men of four worlds piled out of the bar to escape the fight. Those who remained inside were drawn into it. Glass shattered. The floor became a sticky minefield of sharp slivers and spilt drinks.

Meggen charged out of the scrum of men, bowling combatants from both sides over, catching an Atraxian about the midriff and slamming him through a table, then out the window. The taverna's front broke outwards, and the Atraxian landed badly on the pavement.

Meggen turned back to the fight to find the leader pulling out his bayonet from inside his jacket.

'They'll shoot you for having that off out of the camp.'

'You should have given me the pinkskin,' he said, and

lunged. Meggen threw out an arm to protect himself. The blade cut a line of red into his skin.

'Basdack's got a knife!' he roared, blood pouring from him.

Gollph was there a second later, coming in at Meggen's head height with his feet extended in a double flying kick. He smacked into the Atraxian's head and used his face as a springboard to push off and somersault backwards. The Atraxian screamed to have his broken nose hit again, but came at Gollph, swinging wildly through the pain. Gollph sidestepped, took the man's arm at the hand and elbow, and neatly broke it.

'Stupid man,' said Gollph.

Meggen staggered back against the wall, blood dribbling through his fingers.

'Basdack!' he swore. 'That's my good arm!'

Whistles sounded outside, then shots: the weird crack and whistle of webguns, the flat whump of baton rounds.

'Nobody move! Peacekeepers, peacekeepers! Halt!'

The melee separated itself. There were many bloody faces around. Paragonian military arbitrators flooded into the taverna, face masks on, shock mauls crackling.

The Atraxians faced the Paragonians with naked loathing. The Atraxian leader stood, cradling his broken arm. He spat blood.

'Let me revise what I was saying. You want Gollph, you try and get him, my friend,' said Meggen.

'This isn't over,' said the lieutenant.

'No, brother of my world,' said Leonates sadly. 'But it will be when they hang you.'

If you don't take it, a rich man will.

– Paragonian proverb

CHAPTER NINE
AN UNCLE'S CONCERNS

MATUA SUPERIOR
GERATOMRO
083298.M41

Unsurprisingly, Bannick's uncle had secured himself a fine house in the city's richest area as his billet. Bannick walked up the broad street to it with his senses alert, but no attack came. There were no partisans launching reprisals, no rioting mobs of common civilians. Matua Superior had rolled over and given up without a fight. The street was quiet. Many houses were shuttered and lightless, excepting those commandeered by the Astra Militarum commanders. The rich had fled. Such was always the way. There wasn't so much as a las-scorch on the stucco fronts of the mansions. Not one leaf was out of place in their expansive gardens. It was pristine, like war had never come here.

Still, he went cautiously. He was an obvious target in his dress uniform, bright red jacket, white-and-purple sash and his medal for his actions on Kalidar prominent on his chest. All his death required was one fanatic and an unguarded moment. He told himself to be calm. Without a hab-sized tank and five inches of plasteel to protect him, he felt vulnerable. He was getting soft.

He stopped before the biggest house on the street. Gates swung open at his approach, leading to a block-paved driveway lined with inset yellow lumens and crowded with civilian groundcars and small Militarum transports. Local insect analogues chirruped in the bushes. Far off, a group of people laughed and shouted, but there was no one about in the grounds of the house fronting the road. At the rear of the house glass broke, and there was more laughter. A short flight of semi-circular steps led up to the porch, poorly lit by low-quality lumens. He stood in the pool of light, feeling more vulnerable than before. The back of his neck crawled in expectation of a sniper's bullet.

He pulled the bell rope. A ponderous chime sounded inside. The door was opened instantly by a man in a sergeant's uniform crossed by a sash in the Bannick livery. The higher officers of Paragon always seemed to have servants, wherever they went. Light spilt onto the house steps and conversation, laughter, music and the clink of glasses pushed out into the night, but the sergeant was as forbidding as a bastion.

'Yes?' said the sergeant. People moved behind him, viewed through the door as if through a pict screen. Another servant whisked past, bearing a silver plate laden with delicacies. Bannick, hungry, involuntarily followed it with his eyes.

'I am Honoured Lieutenant Colaron Vor Artem Lo Bannick, here to see Lord Colonel Bannick Vardamon Vor Anselm Lo Bannick.'

The sergeant gave him an unfriendly stare.

'Papers?' he said. Bannick kept his face neutral. What a farce. He pushed his chest out a little further so his medal took the light, made a show of adjusting the hilt of the power sword given to him by Captain-General Iskhandrian himself. The sergeant retained his expression of studied scorn.

Bannick pulled out his identity papers and handed them over. The servant examined them minutely, turning over every page in the book. He squinted at the pict-ID, bringing it closer to his face, then held it at arm's length, eyes flicking from Bannick's pict to his face and back again.

'I assure you it is me, sergeant.'

The sergeant handed back his identity pass, and his face changed completely, going from disdainful to servile in an eye-blink. Not touching on apologetic as it did so, Bannick noted.

'This way, honoured lieutenant. Your uncle is expecting you.' The sergeant stepped back, arms wide and welcoming.

Of course he is, thought Bannick. With a curt nod, he went through the door and into a world he'd never thought to visit again.

Vardamon had done his best to recreate Paragon high society in his stolen mansion. Most of the people there were Paragonian officers, brightly clad in dress uniform. The others were Imperial officials, fleet officers, Departmento Munitorum divisio heads. There were plenty of women there, nearly all of them local, flirting and drinking with their conquerors. Bannick spotted a few other officers from other worlds, but no Atraxians. He wondered at that.

'This way, sir,' said the sergeant, gesturing to a showpiece staircase heavy with bronze. Bannick followed the sergeant upstairs. A pair of liveried footmen who appeared to have no formal connection with the military opened doors. He was shown in to a small antechamber. Inside were six chairs in two facing rows of three, a low table decorated with dried flowers, a bookcase, a clock and Jonas Artem Lo Bannick.

'Good evening,' said Bannick.

'Hello, Colaron,' said Jonas neutrally. He was sprawled untidily in the chair, legs thrust out in front of him.

Bannick took a seat opposite his cousin.

'You look like a shelled crustacean without your tank,' Jonas said. 'You're even the right colour tonight.' He took a swig of his drink.

Jonas meant to rile him. Bannick had earlier decided if they came across each other again, he would not respond.

'Funny thing that, I was just thinking the same before I got here,' Bannick said.

'Really?'

'Really. It changes your perspective, riding about in one of the most powerful assets on a battlefield. Do you have a long association with the Lucky Eights?'

'I do. Get to ride them all the time. My platoon's permanently attached.'

'Then you know what I mean, then.'

Jonas shrugged. 'Maybe.'

'Not one of the Eighth's Stormlords has taken significant damage in twenty-five years. I hear the oldest is over four thousand years old. That's impressive, for assault tanks.'

'Isn't it just?' said Jonas. 'That's why they call them lucky. Thing is, they have an unusually high casualty rate for the men they carry. Pretty much every time they go out, one of the platoons boards the one-way to the Emperor's side. It takes a day or two to slop out the gore from the fighting deck. Trust me, I know. So maybe I don't know what you're talking about, riding around in your giant fortress on tracks.'

'Tankers die too,' said Bannick

'We all do eventually,' said Jonas. 'It's a little easier to stay alive behind half a foot of armour.'

'Yes, it is,' said Bannick.

Jonas narrowed his eyes, wrong-footed by Bannick's unwillingness to fight.

'This uncle of yours, what's he like?' said Jonas. 'I've heard of him. Never seen him.'

'He left Paragon when I was very young. I met him again before I joined up. Once since – he was fighting on a different part of the front on Kalidar, and was transported on a different barge. He was promoted while I was fighting on Agritha. I can't give you a full answer.'

'Then give me a partial one.'

'He doesn't suffer fools gladly.'

Jonas snorted.

The door opened.

'Lord Colonel Bannick Vardamon Vor Anselm Lo Bannick,' announced one of the doormen.

'A doubled clan name?' said Jonas as he and Bannick got up. 'I didn't know he was so important. We're in trouble then.'

Vardamon came into the room in an evident hurry, wiping his hands on a cloth. He passed it to the servant, who withdrew. The younger Bannicks saluted.

'Uncle,' said Colaron Bannick.

'Kinsman,' said Jonas Bannick.

Vardamon scowled at them. 'You two are in a lot of hot water right now. Come with me.'

Whoever's study it was that Vardamon had appropriated had appalling taste. The walls were covered in flock wallpaper of violently clashing colours. The desk was similarly decorated, a distressed white base colour decorated in complicated designs of blue and orange that looked like they had been thrown on. Vardamon frowned deeply at it as he waved his relatives into the room.

'Sit! Sit, the pair of you. I'll get us drinks.'

He went to an occasional table that matched the desk, where a decanter of gleece waited. He poured generous measures for all three of them.

'Sit, go on!' he said. There were two chairs in front of the desk, right next to each other. Jonas and Bannick eyed each other warily before taking them.

Vardamon went round the back of the desk.

'Look at the size of this chair!' he said. 'You know, on this world, gluttony is respected as a sign of nobility. All their ruling classes are huge basdacks. No wonder they're losing. Excess is the enemy of discipline.'

He plonked the glasses of gleece down before his kinsmen and sat down. Good living had rounded the colonel out, but he was lost in the chair. He laced his hands together and looked at them sternly for a couple of seconds apiece, the focusing lens of his augmetic eye whirring as it changed focus. He was greyer and heavier than when last he and Bannick had met, and had grown a thick moustache. 'I'll get to the point quickly,' he said. 'There are many far more important people than you downstairs, and I should be talking with them, not you.'

Jonas took up his glass. He sipped it appreciatively. Bannick followed suit. The gleece was exceptional. He had not had anything near this quality since they'd shipped out three years ago.

'Verkerigen's throwing his weight about now Iskhandrian is no longer de facto commander-in-chief. Command's been devolved,' said Vardamon. 'What with the fleets and group coming in from Genthus and the previous force here, the army's grown too big. There are too many equally qualified generals barking about their right to command for even Iskhandrian to shout them all down. This is a delicate time for everybody.'

'Do you think he should stand down?'

'I'm doing the talking here, Colaron, but if you must know I think Iskhandrian should stay in charge. I know he's not from home but he's a better general than Verkerigen ever will be, and far more dynamic than that fossil the Atraxians defer to when they're not sure.'

'Grand Captain Olgau?' said Bannick.

'That's him. Ceremonial post, mostly, but I hear once an Atraxian Captain-General begins to lose authority, they call in the old men, and that we do not need.'

Vardamon slurped his gleece. 'And I do not need this enmity,' he said, looking pointedly between Jonas and Colaron Bannick. 'I am caught in a delicate position. Verkerigen expects me to support him in his goal of securing higher office. I do not want that either. Your altercation is a distraction and an embarrassment that undermines my reputation. What were you thinking? The pair of you, members of the finest stems of the Bannick Optics clan, raised to be gentlemen, having punch-ups at the scene of an execution? Where's your damn respect?'

'I threw no punches, uncle,' said Bannick.

'Quiet, Colaron. We all know from your history that you are perfectly capable of provoking people into rash actions. And you, I don't know you personally, Jonas. Your mother is his aunt, correct?'

'That is so, sir,' said Jonas.

'Never met her. That makes you more kin to him than me. Not enough to make me care for you on its own, but enough to embarrass me badly if you make a hash of things. That's a bad spot to put me in.'

'Yes, sir,' said Jonas.

'Care to tell me why you punched your cousin, a fellow officer, in the guts in front of a Throne-blessed commissar?'

Jonas rolled his glass around in his hands, warming the gleece. He met Vardamon's eyes defiantly.

'All my life, I've wished to be a tank commander. To follow in the glorious footsteps of our ancestors as an officer of armour, as is our custom and my right.'

'I see. You wear the uniform of foot, however. How did this make you assault Colaron here?'

'You know of his disgrace at home,' said Jonas. 'I hear it was you that secured the annulment of his draft exemption.'

'That is so, as a favour to my blood.'

'Well, because of your actions, if I may be so bold, *sir*, Bannick did not marry into the Turranigen clan, and because he did not marry, the proposed alliance between their clan and our own collapsed. Very acrimoniously. We lost hundreds of thousands of Paragonian dira. Someone had to take the blame. Of course, Colaron's father's family was judged blameless. The weakness flows in female blood, isn't that what they say? So all we Artem Lo Bannicks were thrown into disgrace. It was a close-run thing anyway. The entire financial stem suffered, but my branch of the stem, oh, we suffered the most. The vors of our branch were stripped of that title. I was denied the honour of mechanised command. It could have been worse. Some of the lesser clansmen were sent to the foundries, including some I was close to.'

'What?' said Bannick. The colour drained from his face. 'Jonas... I... I am so sorry–'

'Save your apologies. I am trying to think.' Vardamon sighed. He drummed his fingers on the table. 'All this is regrettable.'

'Fine words,' said Jonas.

'Oh do get hold of yourself! What is done is done. It can't be helped by belting people.'

'It made me feel better,' said Jonas mildly.

'How you didn't get shot on the spot...' said Vardamon.

'Suliban and I are friends, sir,'

'Commissars don't have friends, you stupid little arse!' Vardaman's fist thumped into the table. 'You are my clansmen and my close kinsmen. Under clan law, you are my responsibility. I want to hear that this affair is over. Colaron?'

'Yes, uncle,' said Bannick. 'Over.'

'Jonas?'

Jonas nodded after a moment's thought. 'Very well.'

Bannick stood. 'Jonas Artem Lo Bannick, cousin. Please accept my most sincere apologies. I never wanted to fight Tuparillio with sharps, I did not intend to, and throughout the duel I kept my blade dull. I certainly did not want to kill him, and if I had known the deeper repercussions I would never have accepted his challenge, no matter the dishonour it would have caused me. As it is, I should have done more to set it right once I... Once I killed him.'

'You could have shot yourself,' said Jonas.

'I probably would have. I do not deny my responsibility. I behaved less than honourably towards Kaithalar Lo Turranigen. That I did not know Tuparillio was in love with her until it was too late does not lessen my crime there in the slightest.'

This reply made Jonas pause. He stood too, and extended his hand. 'Apology accepted then.' They shook hands. 'You know, you are annoyingly hard to be angry at. I've spent most of the last couple of years fulminating against the injustice of my suffering for your actions. I expected to find an insufferable plank of a man but you seem... Upright.'

'My regret hounds me still,' said Bannick. 'I'll never be free of it. If I could take one moment back in my life and relive it, it would be the moment Tuparillio died.'

'Well then. Well,' said Vardamon in relief. 'That's settled. Jonas, as we're so close in blood ties, you may call me uncle also.'

'Thank you... uncle.'

'Well, go on. That's it. Go and enjoy this party. The pair of you are beginning to be noticed. If you are careful, more careful than you have been, a glorious career awaits.'

'Sir, uncle. Might I beg your indulgence?' said Jonas.

'Be brief.' Vardamon stood and adjusted his sash and medals.

'I do not quite comprehend why they sent so many of us here. I mean, this place is a walkover. One of the army groups could have dealt with it, surely? We retook Genthus with a tenth of the men. From what I hear there were half as many men on Kalidar to fight the orks, and here we're only fighting the militia.'

'I can trust you not to repeat anything I say outside of these walls?'

'You can,' said Jonas. Bannick nodded.

'This is a show of force, clansmen. We are here beating out brushfires sparked off by the need to supply Macharius' crusade, and have damn near started one ourselves. A smaller force could triumph, naturally. But with greater collateral damage. In face of our arrival, already three other cities have surrendered. There are four responses to widespread rebellion – a show of force, exterminatus, neglect, or planetary bombardment.

'As for the second, this world needs to be working for the Imperium, not scorched to ash. There are not so many planets in all of human space that we can afford to cast them aside lightly. Neglect is often effective, over the centennial scale. The industry of Geratomro is only modest, but waiting for the system to beg to come back to us would be slow and the planet would likely deteriorate. Furthermore, abandonment would encourage the others. We could bomb the place into submission, but Geratomro would be severely downgraded, not to mention the human cost. So, a show of force. By showing this subsector, where unrest simmers dangerously, that the Imperium is capable of assembling a major fighting force even while the greatest crusade since the Emperor walked the stars is under way, it will discourage discontent turning to outright rebellion elsewhere.'

Bannick remembered Cortein giving him a similar speech, but he had gone further, talking about individual lives. Vardamon's reasoning reminded Bannick that there were powerful men in the Imperium who would think nothing of destroying a world. He shifted uneasily in his seat.

'Take heart, my boys. We are winning this war, and in doing so preventing a host of others. In the human body there are trillions of cells – all it takes is for one to turn cancerous to threaten the whole. So here also, this city is but one among many billions. We have restored it to proper function, and prevented it from threatening the body entire. If the amount of force seems disproportionate, then consider the alternatives and be thankful. Now, I have pressing business downstairs. You are dismissed. Next time we meet, it better be under better auspices.'

Jonas and Bannick spent little time in the party. There were too many captains and colonels for them to feel at ease. They spoke briefly with Hannick, whose skin looked paler than ever against the bright red of his uniform. He had come to rely on a stick, and stifled his coughs with a handkerchief. Their conversation became awkward, and so Jonas and Colaron took their leave and went to stand at the edge of the party, by the buffet.

'Look at this lot, scheming away,' said Jonas quietly.

'That's the way of command in such a large, mixed army, I suppose,' said Bannick. 'Our regiments have to fight for their corner. I thought I'd be getting away from all this, from Paragon's intrigue, but it looks like Paragon has followed me.'

'I had heard you had got maudlin and self-obsessed, but you're quite something. Very stiff, aren't you?' said Jonas.

'What do you mean by that?'

'It's all about you, is what I mean. Look again, what do you think they are talking about? It's not whether Verkerigen can become the next grade of general.'

Bannick dipped in and out of the talk.

'They're discussing settlement rights, don't you see?' said Jonas. 'All these men are high nobility back home, higher than me and you. They want to rule – these people always do. Half of them have enough years under their belts to take the Emperor's gift. Who do you think is going to run this place once the incumbent ruling class have been purged? That stuff "uncle" was saying in there was half the truth. The other half will be "if we bomb this planet to pieces, we won't be able to take it over for our personal benefit". Mark my words, he's wondering how grand "Planetary Governor Bannick" would sound.' He looked around the room distastefully. 'I've been on the sharp end of clan politics. I can smell it on the air. "Human cost" indeed. Monetary cost, is what he meant. The more reasonable someone with a fine rationale sounds for lining their own pockets, the more you have to be cautious. Welcome, dear cousin, to New Paragon.'

'I... I hadn't thought...'

'You know, you've got a reputation for that too.' He thumped Bannick on the back. 'Come on, Colaron, I need some air. Do you smoke?'

'No.'

'I do. I know you drink.' He pulled a bottle partway out of his sash. 'I pocketed this from the bar. Gleece, a good one too, not this Geratomran promethium water. Care to share?'

'All right then,' said Bannick.

Jonas thrust it back into his sash. 'Good man.'

They went out of doors onto a wide patio where a number of people now congregated. Most were lower-rankers like themselves, uninterested or too unimportant to be involved in clan politics. They were, however, very interested in the local women, and as they vied for their attention they dispelled the uneasy quiet of the earlier evening.

'How easily they accept their new lords,' muttered Jonas. 'Come on, this will do.' He pointed out a bench at the top of a sloped lawn away from the building. He dropped into it and groaned. 'These boots kill my feet.'

Bannick sat next to him. Jonas took a drink then passed him the flask and lit a cheroot. Bannick swigged. The gleece was rougher than his uncle's, but still welcome after months of inferior spirit.

'You like that? Tastes like home, eh? I'd have thought we'd have run out of it. There must be a whole fleet tender dedicated to the stuff. I'd like to know which one.'

'Someone must be distilling it,' said Bannick.

'From what though?' said Jonas. 'Where are they going to get the glest? I've not seen any glest trees on board my ship, don't know about yours.'

'Treeless,' said Bannick.

Jonas sat forwards. 'You know a woman runs this world. What do you think of that? Reminds me of Kaithalar. She got married, you know – to Gedling Lo Basteen of the Engine Clans. She's become a very rich lady.'

A sharp twinge twisted in Bannick's guts. Was she happy? His cheeks coloured for the shame he had brought to her. He had accepted betrothal to her and then he had rejected her and her clan.

'What other news do you have from home?' said Bannick, keen to change the subject.

'Nothing new, not heard anything at all since I left.'

'Your news is a year fresher than mine.'

'Well,' said Jonas, considering, 'let me see. A few months

before I went, Lord Commander Materiak was finally forced to disown his brother. He was found guilty of fraud by the Unified Clan Council. He didn't dare veto another judgement.'

'About time,' said Bannick.

'I think that his brother was caught in bed with the head of the Clan Council's daughter, already promised to someone else, mind you, helped cinch that. Materiak exiled him before he could be lynched.'

They talked a little while, Jonas filling Bannick in on the affairs of their families. Bannick enjoyed it at first, but as Jonas went on, a painful numbness enveloped his heart. He had put his cousins and siblings out of his mind. Hearing of the struggle his father had in finding a successor was particularly hard. He'd lost his first heir to accident, and his second to self-destructiveness then the Astra Militarum. Shame Bannick had largely managed to lock away crept out from its prison anew.

The approach of a member of the Adeptus Arbites attached to Paragonian command stopped their conversation. Bannick was almost glad to see him, though arbitrators of any kind were only ever the bearers of bad news.

'What does he want?' said Jonas quietly.

The arbitrator came to stand in front of them. 'Lieutenant Bannick?' he said.

'Yes?' both men replied.

'Honoured Lieutenant Colaron Lo Bannick, that's who I'm looking for.'

'What is it?' said Bannick.

'You're to come with me.'

'Why?' said Jonas.

'There's been an altercation involving the honoured lieutenant's men.'

'No rest for the wicked,' said Jonas. 'See you around.'

Bannick stood and saluted his cousin. 'There's no rest for anyone.'

CHAPTER TEN
JUSTICE

LANDING FIELDS, MATUA SUPERIOR
GERATOMRO
083398.M41

The Adeptus Arbites precinct fortress had been destroyed the moment Missrine Huratal had made her stand against the tithe, and so the arbitrator took Bannick by ground-car to a commandeered building that had once belonged to a free captain. Situated on the edge of the spaceport, it was heavily fortified to guard expensive off-world cargoes against theft. The Free Captain was away on a voyage, the arbitrator said, or he would have been dead along with everyone else who'd had off-world connections.

The arbitrator led Bannick through an armoured door into a vast, reconfigurable warehouse space. On one side of it the stalls had been raised to form makeshift cells. Nearly all of them were full of soldiers.

'Why aren't they in the regimental gaol? Why not let the regimental peacekeepers take care of this?' said Bannick.

'Civil justice must be seen to take precedence,' said

the arbitrator. The new army badge issued to all the forces on Geratomro – a blue star on a white lozenge – gleamed on his shoulder. 'A return to normality is desired.'

'This is normal?'

'Most of the Adeptus Arbites were killed in defence of the planetary precinct house, but a lot of the local arbitrators managed to go into hiding. We've nearly a fully functioning justice force here. Missrine targeted them for liquidation also, which makes our job of deciding who is loyal and who is not easier. They all hate her.'

'You'll be moving on with the fleet then?'

'Maybe, maybe not. I go where the Emperor's justice demands, and at this moment that is here.'

He took Bannick to a cell. It was crammed with men, including his own. He looked in dismay at their wounds.

'What by Terra happened to you?'

'I've had worse,' said Meggen, flexing the hand of his injured arm.

They looked shamefaced as the arbitrator read out their charges from a pad.

'Disorderly on leave,' he said, 'destruction of civilian property, brawling. Injury of fellow soldiers of the Emperor. Right. They're all yours.'

'They'll not face civil charges? You said a return to normality.'

'In appearance only. The law courts are not functioning. And whose law would we use? Military, Paragonian, Geratomran and standard Imperial are all applicable. We've processed them, that's enough to keep up appearances. Please get them out of my gaol.'

'So now military law takes over?'

'Yes. If it sounds like a waste of time, it is. But orders, you understand those, yes? We'll let the military arbitrators catch the few others that have escaped the net. Military law, as defined under cross-planetary force statutes, is to be applied, which I suppose means you do whatever you do on your planet when men get into brawls. Their officers will punish them, not the civil authorities,' he said meaningfully. 'That means you. I'll need your mark here, here and here.' He handed Bannick a stylus, and he imprinted the flimsies presented to him with smudgy carbon black. The arbitrator peeled a carbon copy flimsy off his pad and pushed it into Bannick's chest. 'That's that. I'll leave this with you. I'll fetch the gaoler.'

The arbitrator left.

The men crowded towards the bars, pushing the other prisoners in the cell out of the way.

'What happened?' said Bannick.

'Throne-cursed Atraxians tried to take Gollph. They wanted to string him up,' said Meggen.

'Why?'

'They lost some buddies because the Bosovar supporting them broke and ran,' said Ganlick. 'So they say, anyway. Some of the men in here say it's true.'

'Did you start it?' said Bannick.

'Definitely not,' said Epperaliant. The left side of his face was bruised purple and black, and his jaw was swollen closed. 'They did.'

Bannick tightened his grip on his sword hilt. 'Have you had someone look at that face?'

'No, they brought us straight here. To tell you the truth, sir, I don't feel so great.'

'And your arm?' said Bannick to Meggen.

'Atraxian pulled his bayonet on me.'

'They were arrested also?'

'Damn right they were, most anyways. The one with the knife got away. He was drunk, but not so drunk he forgot they'd hang for that. Especially seeing as Leonates here reminded him of it,' said Meggen. 'Listen, it wasn't us that started it, but you're going to have to do something. You heard the adept.'

'I'll not have you punished for something you didn't begin,' said Bannick.

'We gave as good as we got. A couple of theirs are nursing broken bones. One got a cracked skull. I tell you, Gollph is a combat monster. We'll be charged. You know we will. We've decided we'll plead. I'll invoke the right of one. I'll take the stripes.'

'That we didn't agree, Meggen! We're all in it together. We'll get five or ten lashes each – you take them all yourself, it'll be too much,' said Epperaliant.

'I'll do it. I can handle a flogging. No sense all of us getting punished.' He shrugged.

'Don't be ridiculous, Meggen, you're in no fit state.'

'Better than us all getting flogged,' said Meggen.

'It's my decision, Meggen,' said Bannick.

'I know Col, but think on it. And sorry and all for speaking out of turn, but you have us all beaten, it's not going to go down well with the rest of the Paragonians. The Atraxians are going to need an example.'

'What you mean, you take it, Meggen?' said Gollph.

'On Paragon, in a joint enterprise like this, one can suffer the punishment on behalf of all,' said Epperaliant.

'Then I will take it,' said Gollph pushing his way to the front.

'You're not Paragonian,' said Meggen.

'I am in Paragonian regiment now. These rules, they apply to me, yes?'

Bannick nodded.

'Then I take pain for all. These men, my friends. They stopped me from death. If they not there, I would be gone to the Sky Emperor now. It is not good that they should suffer for me.'

'I don't know, Gollph...' said Bannick.

'Listen!' said the little man. 'I not Paragonian, not Atraxian. I Bosovar. The men of Paragon will not be caring about me, the men of Atraxia will be satis... satis...'

'Satisfied, Gollph,' said Meggen, resting his head against the bars wearily.

'Satisfied. This means happy, yes?'

'It'll hurt, man. You're the smallest of us,' said Meggen.

Gollph stood tall. 'To become a warrior of my people, I am bitten thirty-four time by spider-rat. It makes a poison that causes great pain for three days and terrible visions.' He looked at Bannick. 'So what if man hit me with stick?'

They all looked at one another.

'He's speaking a lot of sense,' said Epperaliant.

'It's not you going to get beaten, sir,' said Vaskigen.

'I know it's not!' said Epperaliant. Bannick had never seen him so dejected. 'But it still makes sense.'

Gollph looked at Bannick determinedly.

'So be it,' said Bannick. The gaoler arrived and opened the door. 'But I don't want this to ever happen again, do you hear?'

A vast camp of tents bounded by prefabricated walls had been set up on one of the landing fields. The crew of *Cortein's Honour* stood at the edge of its castra principia under dawn skies the colour of lemons. In silence, Gollph was led to a frame at the centre of the courtyard and tied up by his wrists. A peacekeeper with a whip waited five yards behind Gollph. The Atraxian brawlers waited, pale-faced, for their turns at the frame.

Representatives of several regiments lined the edge of the square, present to witness justice being carried out. Sound from elsewhere in the camp carried easily on the wind, but the principia was silent, the fabric of the tents around it rippling audibly. Bannick was reminded of the scene in the city the day before yesterday, when the governors of Matua Superior were burned alive. There was a certain cruel predictability to Imperial justice, no matter the gloss put on it by local custom.

Colonel Sholana of the 42nd acted as magistrate. He faced the east, awaiting the sun. As soon as a sliver of its disc rose over the wall, he unrolled a parchment heavy with seals and broke the silence with a clear voice.

'Second Loader Gollph Bosovar of the Seventh Paragonian Super-Heavy Tank Company will allow himself to suffer thirty-five lashes for his own crimes and those of his comrades in inciting violence. May his pain earn the forgiveness of the Emperor for them all. Begin.'

It was a ridiculous charge. Bannick did not doubt the truthfulness of his men. But the Atraxians had told a different story to that of his crew, and witness accounts were predictably split along national lines. The Paragonians supported the tank crew, the Atraxians their infantry.

'What a basdacking mess,' he breathed.

Two men came forwards, gave Gollph a drink from a canteen and set a wooden bit between his teeth.

Sholana nodded. The peacekeeper let his coiled whip drop.

'One,' he called out, sending the lash hissing through the air. With a deceptively light smack it kissed the bared flesh of Gollph's back. When it flicked back, a fine line of blood sprayed off onto the sand. A tightening around Gollph's eyes was the sole display of discomfort.

'Two,' said the peacekeeper. The whip sang again. Gollph stared forwards and spat out the bit.

The men of *Cortein's Honour* stood to attention, watching the punishment solemnly. A movement to Bannick's side had him glance over. Karlok Shoam appeared next to him.

'Where by the Throne have you been, Shoam?'

Shoam shrugged. His kit was unkempt, hung with non-regulation additions, and his face was seamed with oil. Unlike all the others, he had not taken advantage of the lull in fighting to get clean. 'I been around, bossman. Doing my own thing. Gotta do right by my crew buddies.' A sickly, sweet smell came off him that Bannick had come to recognise as the odour of nitrochem addiction.

Bannick looked over the punishment ground at the Atraxian infantrymen. Their crime had been deemed the greater, and they were facing ten lashes apiece. Their ringleader had escaped justice, so far.

'The Atraxian. Lieutenant Prazexes. Shame he not here to suffer with little Gollph,' said Shoam. He spoke very quietly, barely moving his lips.

'You know the one who started the fight?' said Bannick, staring ahead. 'You weren't there.'

'Man can find anything out if he wants to bad enough. It weren't hard.'

'Shoam, do you know where Prazexes is?'

Shoam looked sidelong at Bannick with bloodshot eyes. 'Why would I know that?'

'They looked for him all day. They couldn't find him,' said Bannick.

'They never will, man like that, knows he's got the death penalty over him,' said Shoam. 'A pity. When he mess with my crew, he messes with me. I could do things to him that make him wish he never born. Superior, those Atraxians. They say they all the same, and that make them think they better than everyone else. Irony, I say. Is no one better when they in the mud and blood than a Savlar born.'

'What did you do to him?'

'Why you ask that? You accuse me, sir? Murder serious crime. Carries death penalty, don't it?'

'They'd have to catch the murderer,' said Bannick.

'They would. They never gonna. This place warzone.'

'You could find him,' said Bannick.

'Maybe. Like I say, man can find out anything he want, if he wants bad enough.'

'Did you kill him?'

Shoam stared off at Gollph.

'I cannot condone murder!' hissed Bannick.

'We're all murderers. You gonna tell me you not, boss-man sir. You gonna say you never kill a man?'

Bannick set his jaw.

'Twenty-six!' called out the peacekeeper. The whip hissed through the air. Sweat and blood dripped off Gollph's pink skin, but he made no noise.

'But some murderers, they be heroes,' said Shoam. 'Best honour men like that, eh, boss? Best stick by them and do what's right by them. You never know when you might need them help you.'

Bannick had no reply, and they stood in silence until the last lash landed on Gollph's skin.

'The punishment is concluded. The crew of *Cortein's Honour* have paid their due.' Sholana beckoned. The men ran to Gollph and unlooped his wrists. Shoam remained by Bannick's side, watching with his dead, red eyes. Gollph took a step, then staggered. Seven pairs of hands grabbed him gently. Meggen and Vaskigen looped his arms around their necks. The others gave him water, poured it on his wounds, prepared bandages. Bearing the sagging Gollph between them, they rushed him from the square.

'Get the medicae!' Meggen said urgently. Epperaliant ran ahead towards the surgeon's tents.

Shoam gave Bannick a lazy salute and sauntered after them. 'Be seeing you, sir,' he said.

Bannick remained where he was. This was his men's moment, not his. Let them bond over Gollph's punishment. It sounded callous even to him, but there was benefit to this misfortune.

Gollph would come back to the tank a hero. Whatever residual prejudices there were against him would have been eradicated. He had already proven himself up to the role of loader; now he had proved he was an excellent fighter, and had shown self-sacrifice for his fellows.

As the first Atraxian was strung up to receive his flogging, Bannick couldn't prevent satisfaction taking the place of disgust at Gollph's beating. This mongrel crew that had given him so much cause for concern was becoming the kind of group one needed to run a Baneblade effectively. Maybe there was something in what the Adeptus Mechanicus did in allowing the tank to choose its own. A cocktail of emotions overwhelmed him: guilt at having doubted the intentions of the Emperor-Omnissiah as expressed by *Cortein's Honour*; guilt at turning Gollph's undeserved punishment to his advantage; relief it had all been dealt with; grim satisfaction at Shoam's murderousness. He was, he realised now, no different to the other nobles scheming for position on Paragon; if anything he was worse, because it had taken him longer to realise it.

The Atraxian moaned piteously as the first lash landed. Bannick left the principia.

As he was walking along the via principalis to the porta dextra, a runner caught up with him.

'Honoured Lieutenant Bannick! I have orders for you from General Lo Verkerigen.' He saluted and handed over a sealed orders tube.

Bannick snapped the metal twist seal and drew out a flimsy. He scanned it quickly. The defence of the planet was collapsing, but outside the capital Magor's Seat, there were a number of isolated pockets of resistance that needed tackling. The Seventh were being sent north. He rolled up the orders and handed the tube back to the runner.

'Report orders received and understood,' said Bannick.

CHAPTER ELEVEN
A DANGEROUS OFFER

IMPERIAL GOVERNOR'S PALACE, MAGOR'S SEAT
GERATOMRO
085198.M41

Governor Dostain was planetary governor, master of all he surveyed. The lords and ladies of Geratomro bowed their heads and fell to their knees.

'Lord Dostain! Saviour of Geratomro! Lord Dostain the Great!' cried the herald. Never had the man seemed so sincere in his blandishments.

Dostain raised his chin proudly. Not the three he possessed in reality, but a square jaw on a handsome face. It was still his face, but it was idealised, improved, altered. A face on a head full of wild ideas, a head upon a body that rippled with muscle under its pleasing coat of fat. A heady perfume filled his nostrils. His senses were alive with the pleasure of power. He felt full of confidence. No man could challenge his judgement without their arguments dying on their lips. He was wise beyond compare, immeasurably clever. A feast of unbelievable size was piled high on the creaking tables that ran the length of Magor's Hall. Around him were arrayed his twenty wives, the finest females the world had to offer, and they looked to him adoringly. Chief among them was Pollein, lovely, loving Pollein. She held a brimming goblet of purple wine to his mouth. He sipped it and smiled at her. She dropped her head coyly. There was nothing they would not do for him, a devotion he would take full advantage of every night.

Dostain moaned in his sleep.

Still it was not enough! He had all he wanted and now he wanted more. There was a hollowness inside him, a vacuum that demanded it be filled with more power, more sensation. A tremor of fear thrilled in him.

'I can give you everything,' said Pollein. She looked up shyly, and he flinched in surprise. Her eyes were not her own – not perfect grey, but depthless brown. He knew those eyes. He pulled his head back, knocking the wine from her hands all over his rich clothes. She smiled as another girl sponged it away with lingering strokes of her soft hands. He could not break eye contact with those brown eyes. An ancient part of him, bred on Terra in forgotten antiquity, recognised them for a predator's eyes. The eyes of a great cat.

Sweat beaded on his perfect upper lip. There was no excess that could fill the abyss he saw in the eyes, not in all the galaxy. Wailing, he fell into them.

'Time to wake up, little boy,' said a harsh voice.

He plummeted towards a place he had thought of as Elysium. As he neared it, he knew it for Hades.

'Dostain! Dostain!' A sweet whisper pierced Dostain's dreams.

Screaming, he could hear screaming.

'Dostain!' Gentle hands shook him, setting up a quiver in his belly that was not all in his fat.

The Heir the Second came awake, pouring sweat. He patted his bed sheets, peered nervously into the dark corners of his ceiling. Already the terrifying finale to his dream faded. He was left with the taste of incomparable wine in his mouth. Fear was replaced by the longing to taste it again.

'Are you all right?' Pollein's face came into view.

'Pollein?' he croaked.

'Indeed, nephew!'

She hopped astride him, intending in her innocence to tickle him awake, but Dostain was far from innocent himself, and he sat up quickly and shoved her off. He pulled the covers to his chin. She frowned at him, hurt.

'Yes, it's me, dummy. No need to fight.'

'Sorry. What are you doing here?' he said.

'I've something to show you. Get up.'

Dostain's heart, still pumping with adrenaline, had its own ideas about what he would like to see. His cheeks burned. 'What is it?' he said. He brought his legs up, half curling into a ball. 'Throne of the Emperor, Pollein, what is the time?'

'Very late! Very, very late,' she whispered. She leaned in close. Her perfumed breath stirred his wispy beard. He shivered. 'He's here!'

'Who?'

'Him,' she said.

She took his hand and yanked on it. Dostain barely had time to rearrange his nightshirt before she'd hauled him out of bed. She was unbelievably strong for her size. Or maybe he was just fat and weak.

'This way,' she said. 'He's in my chambers.'

Their feet padded on rich rugs down long corridors. The heirs were quartered apart from each other to discourage assassination. Yellow-robed sentries guarded the passages leading from the heirs' quarters into the palace, but there were ways between their domiciles. Assassination was supposed to be difficult, not impossible. It served as a useful way of keeping the succession manageable, and ensuring only the cunning survived.

They ducked out of a small window and down a low wall. Pollein led Dostain across the cold courtyard that separated their halls, their bare feet leaving prints in the frost, then through a door that was supposed to be locked but never was, and through a secret passage hidden behind a statue of their ancestor, Magor. Dostain knew the route well. He'd often used it to go to Pollein's quarters. He'd stand outside, ear to the door, convinced he could hear her breathing, longing to go in and take her in his arms. A greater heir might have done that whether she were willing or not, then forced her into marriage or killed her. She was next in line and might very well do the same thing to him. But he did not know how to cheat the locks on her doors. She might even have been planning to kill him right then. He was too hopelessly ensnared by his infatuation to do anything about it if she were.

She peered out of the secret tunnel exit and led him into the corridor that led to her rooms.

'Shhh!' she said in that girlish way that set Dostain aflame. 'I want this to be a surprise for him.'

He nodded dumbly, excruciatingly aware of how sweaty his hand was in hers.

They went to her room. The door's simple machine-spirit

recognised her scent and opened inwards, inches of plasteel swinging noiselessly back. It reminded him that she had got into his room somehow, and he hadn't questioned it.

'I better go back,' he said, suddenly afraid. Maybe he should act first, crush her pretty neck in his hands, but she was so strong, and he didn't think he could bring himself to do it.

'Don't be silly!' she said. 'Listen, he's in there now. He wants to see you.'

Dostain calmed enough to listen. Someone was singing tunelessly over a running cascade. Pollein tugged his hand and they went into her chambers. They were so charmingly feminine and disarrayed. He expected there would be bits of twig in her bed, she spent so much time outdoors.

The singing grew louder. The door to Pollein's ablutorial was open. Steam came from inside tinged golden with lumen glow. The cascade shut off. The singing ceased a few bars later.

'Dib?' called Pollein. She clapped her hands in delight. She seemed to sparkle when she was happy. Dostain looked away then looked again, like a clown in the comedia, unable to believe his eyes. She *was* sparkling, a burst of firefly lights that fizzed out around her head. That strange feeling he'd had upon the mountain returned. Once he could dismiss it. Twice he could not. He moved back from his aunt, but she kept a tight hold of his hand.

Dostain expected the strange hairy man of the mountain, but instead a smooth-skinned youth came out, a towel wrapped around his waist. He appeared to be a little older than Dostain, but different in every other respect. In place of Dostain's noble flab, he had a torso as sculpted as a statue's, and flawless skin that was tanned a light colour, almost gold. His hair was also gold, and his face was beautiful enough to drive Dostain's desire for Pollein back a moment.

But the eyes, they were the same. If anything, they were worse. Dostain averted his gaze before it could be captured.

'Hello, Dostain. What a pleasure to see you.'

'Who are you?'

'You know who I am.'

'The Devil-in-the-bush,' said Dostain, risking a glance. The youth gave him an admonishing look.

'You know that's not my name. Why don't you call me Dib, like your lovely aunt. That's fitting, isn't it? Halfway between a name that is not mine, and one I will not tell you.'

'What happened to you?'

'That awful wiry pelt?' Dib brushed at his shoulder. A hank of matted hair drifted to the floor. 'Gone, thanks to your aunt here. She's not just a pretty face. She has magic in her.'

Pollein squealed in delight. 'He says I'm talented. Can you believe? Me, talented! And I haven't done anything!'

'Oh yes you have. You are key, my dear, to a world of wonderful delight.' He slid an easy arm around her waist. Pollein released Dostain's hand finally. Dostain was at once relieved and furiously jealous. Dib gave Dostain an outrageous grin, then sat on the bed, dragging Pollein down with him. He patted the sheets the other side of himself and said, 'Come sit with me. We have much to discuss.'

'I'd rather go back to my bed,' said Dostain miserably.

'Very well. Then you may sleep in your bed for another twenty-seven nights, before the Imperial forces march into this palace and drag you from it, and send you away to labour as a slave for the rest of your life.'

'What do you mean?' said Dostain.

'Again you profess ignorance!' said Dib, throwing up his hands. 'If you are going to be obtuse, then I will spell it out for you. Matua Superior fell three weeks ago. Your armies crumble before their advance. The only reason they have not levelled this place from the void is that they wish to take the world as intact as possible.'

'We are a prize, I suppose,' said Dostain glumly.

'Don't be so stupid,' said Dib, and there was the sting of venom in his words. 'Their general, Iskhandrian of the planet Atraxia, is a canny man. A dozen systems in this sector teeter on the edge of rebellion, and have refused demands like your Aunt Missrine. Teeter, totter, teeter!' he said, his smile perfect and white and full of malice. 'If they are too heavy-handed, the others will most likely rebel out of fear. Being merciful to the populace not only keeps Geratomro working and in minimal need of reconstruction, it undermines the efforts of rebellious lords to foment dissent in their own populations. While treating the ruling class with utter ruthlessness discourages other Planetary Governors from taking that final step. I hear they are burning the lords-civil of the defeated cities alive,' said Dib. 'Fancy that! That could be you.'

Dostain clutched at his night gown.

'Don't be disheartened. Do you know why they are doing this?' asked Dib.

'Because the Emperor is merciful in His wisdom?'

'No!' snarled Dib, his face twisting into something

inhuman. He recovered his smile and his smooth manner. 'Because they are weak. At any other time they would bomb every major settlement on this dreary mudball into pieces. But they can't, because if they do and push the others into rebellion they will be unable to bring them to heel. They lack the souls under arms. The other worlds will fight harder because they will have nothing to lose. The Imperium will lose this whole subsector, perhaps forever. They do not want that.'

'They'll burn me because of what my aunt did.' Dostain was close to tears.

'No, they'll probably just mutilate you with cybernetic implants and enslave you, so that'll be all right, won't it?'

Dostain whimpered.

Pollein sat next to Dib and took his hand.

'There is another way, you know. One that can bring you to power. You will be planetary governor. You will be king! That's what you've wanted all along.'

'How? How can you do that?'

'Dear little Dostain, I am not a little hairy legend, not really. And I'm not a scheming fat boy like you, who has bitten off more than he can eat. I am... Well, I suppose I am a kind of herald for a great and powerful master. I am sent out to find those worthy, those who might rally to our cause. For the few I find that accept me, there are allies I can call. And then there are more allies after them,' said Dib, making an apologetic face. 'They're not very nice but they are very powerful. They can be on your side, but it all depends how willing you are to...' Dib trailed off.

'Willing to do what?'

'To make a show of commitment,' he said. 'These allies I have, they will not come for a quaking milksop. But they will come for a man who can show them his quality, his *resolve*. Do you want me to tell you what you have to do?'

Dostain looked to Pollein. She smiled at him and nodded encouragingly. Dostain's heart melted. He ignored the fact that she was leaning into Dib, her fingers interlaced with his. Dib inclined is head towards her. 'You want her too? She can be yours,' his face seemed to be saying.

A sudden strength suffused Dostain, a light strong and pure. For a moment, the Emperor had His eyes upon him, he was sure.

'No,' said Dostain. 'I do not want to know.'

He fled the room, the laughter of Pollein and Dib ringing in his ears. He did not stop until he had reached the palace chapel and locked the door behind him.

CHAPTER TWELVE
THE ROAD NORTH

RASTOR TERRITORY
GERATOMRO
086898.M41

Five Atlas recovery tanks roared together, straining to drag *Ostrakhan's Rebirth* out of the ditch. Adeptus Mechanicus machine priests on hovering thrones or stilted mecha-legs picked their way around the mud, rebuking the men of the Imperial Guard for their lack of proper reverence. Tow cables creaked against a massive drag beam. The recovery tanks were five monstrous oxen tethered to an unmovable plough, like the legend of Tiw's Acre from back home on Paragon, re-enacted by giant metal machines. Tank tracks churned in the mud. The Hellhammer didn't move, and the Atlases burrowed deeper into the mud. They strained and strained, until a tow cable suddenly gave, upsetting the balance of the bar. The tanks skidded forwards, scattering men.

Horns blared. Enginseers and higher ranking priests blasted orders from vox-emitters turned up to maximum gain. They yelled Gothic and binaric and lingua-technis and forge world pidgin, but it all amounted to the same thing – 'Stop!'

The lesser priests slogged their way through the torn-up ground on foot. Hard words were exchanged between the Astra Militarum and Adeptus Mechanicus. Disputes were resolved. The arguments died away. Servitors adapted for auto-worship were brought forwards. Censers wafted scented smoke over the tank's glacis while machine adepts splattered the hull with holy oils in an attempt to placate its angry soul. Honoured Captain Hannick watched on from the cupola hatch, his arms folded. Bannick caught his eye. The captain raised his arms in an exaggerated shrug at the chaos going on around his command. Bannick grinned and touched the brim of his cap, and went to find Meggen and Kolios.

Fires blazed all around the Seventh's position. The shattered shells of enemy Leman Russ battle tanks burned, pumping out masses of oil-black smoke. Teams of men lugged dead Geratomrans in yellow uniforms to the back of flatbed trucks and tossed them aboard. The trucks trundled along paths in the muck marked out with red flags. Men and adepts with minesweeping gear walked slowly about the battlefield followed by vigilant servo-skulls, hunting out explosives.

'Stand clear!' shouted a team. Bannick winced as the mine detonated. He walked up a low hill, its yellow grasses and pale lilac flowers untouched by war. *Lux Imperator* loomed over them, as if protecting the blooms.

By the time he had mounted the ladder of *Lux Imperator*, more chains and cables had been attached to the stricken Hellhammer, and the recovery tanks were taking the strain again. He paused a moment to survey the battlefield. The enemy had chosen their spot well, using augur-detectable mines to direct *Ostrakhan's Rebirth* into the deep ditch where it still languished. *Cortein's Honour* stood side by side with *Artemen Ultrus*. The second Baneblade's right-hand track lay flopped on the grass, three mangled road wheels and a shattered track skirt where the cannon had hit it. That had raised the Baneblades' fury. The Leman Russ that had fired the immobilising shot was a black crater studded with metal shards, its platoon mates silent masses of metal, giant holes punched through their armour. An engine grumbled a few hundred yards away as another Atlas outfitted with a dozer blade pushed heaps of yellow-clad bodies into a mass grave, intermingling them with the earth.

Bannick took a deep, thoughtful breath. Seven tanks had ambushed four super-heavies. Suicide, but effective. Three out of four of the Seventh's tanks were out of action.

He made the sign of the aquila on his forehead at the engine block shrine of the Shadowsword, climbed aboard and went down through its hatch.

'Officer on deck!' shouted Udolpho Lo Krast, the driver. Men stopped their work and saluted.

The Shadowsword was in a sorry state. The lights were blown, illumination provided by red emergency lumens. Bannick held a handkerchief up to his mouth to stifle the smell of scorched flesh permeating the command deck. The body of First Gunner Vando Hastilleen had been removed, but patches of his burned skin still adhered to his station. Menial-grade tech-adepts infested its innards. There did not seem to be a housing panel left unopened. Miles of wires and tubing spilled from the tank onto the deck-plating. Enginseer Starstan, the machine's permanently attached enginseer, fussed around his subordinates, anxious burbles emanating from his metal face.

Meggen was on the lower deck, in the thick of it, a servo-skull bobbing close by his head, his arms buried up to the shoulder in the guts of the volcano cannon's power feed. There was no space aboard. Every gangway had be traversed sideways. All was dominated by the cannon's enormous capacitors.

'How is it going?' asked Bannick.

'It's an Emperor-forsaken, basdack-damned mess!' said Meggen, heaving aside a hopeless tangle of power cabling. An hour after the battle, and acrid smoke was still curling from somewhere deep inside the *Lux Imperator*'s primary weapon's array.

Starstan poked his head down through the command floor ladder well. 'Be respectful!' he shouted in metallic Gothic.

The skull rotated, the eye piece whining as it focused on Meggen. 'Treat *Lux Imperator* with more respect. Its spirit is already disturbed, you risk angering it.' Brasslock was outside helping with the recovery of *Ostrakhan's Rebirth*, but he had enough processing capacity to spare to oversee the efforts aboard *Lux Imperator* simultaneously.

'Yeah, whatever,' said Meggen, pushing heavy plastek piping that refused to stay put. He kissed his machina opus nonetheless. 'Sorry,' he said.

'What is the problem? Why did the tank not fire?'

'Beats me,' said Meggen. 'I've some experience with these energy weapons, but shells is where I'm at.'

'You're the most experienced gunner in the company after Hastilleen. After Hastilleen was,' Bannick corrected himself. 'You've done the acclimatisation training, and plenty of drills. You're too modest.'

Meggen rubbed furiously at his nose with his forearm to scratch an itch. His hands were covered in lubricant and white, sticky conductive media. 'Still doesn't mean I know how the damn thing works.' He lowered his voice. 'I'm pretty sure the Adeptus Mechanicus haven't got a basdacking idea either.'

'It just wouldn't fire,' said Commsman Vremont, stepping down the ladder. 'Starstan primed the capacitors, but when Vando opened up the main conduit it wouldn't fire, then it blew up right in his face.'

A Shadowsword carried a crew complement of six, one of whom had been killed and two others wounded by the explosion. Vremont's broken arm was bound up in a sling. Hurnigen had taken a lump of shrapnel to the thigh. Third Gunner Rastomar Kalligen had been knocked unconscious.

'How are the others, sir?' asked Vremont.

'Rastomar's just woken up,' said Bannick. 'Hurnigen's been swearing fit to make the Emperor's ears burn, but he'll be all right.'

Vremont nodded gratefully. 'Too many crew out. We are seriously compromised,' he said. 'The power surge from the capacitors went everywhere but the cannon. My desk is fragged. Hurnigen's chart table cracked.' He gestured with his good arm at the command chair. A pool of Hurnigen's blood shone on the floor. 'Our main cogitator bank is offline – the logic engine luckily started up again. I don't understand it.'

Brasslock's servo-skull flew up into Bannick's eyeline.

'It is the machine's spirit,' said the magos.

'Yes,' said Starstan. He too descended to the lower deck. It became intolerably crowded, and Bannick wanted to get out.

Starstan's hands, both incongruously flesh on a body that was mostly of metal, wrung. 'Since the orks on Kalidar, it has not recovered from the humiliation heaped upon its sacred shell. It feels guilt for what it was made to do. There is trauma in its logic centres. It will take time to exorcise.'

'The tank is traumatised?' said Bannick incredulously.

'Why are you surprised?' said Brasslock. 'You have seen the power of these machines' spirits. You wear the machina opus beside your aquila. Do you have no faith?'

'I am sorry,' said Bannick. 'The miraculous is hard to believe, even when it is before your eyes.'

'Guilt, fury, anger, shame, joy – these and all emotions the spirit of the machine feels, for their souls are born from the crackling energies of the motive force, just as yours.'

'Can you not have a quiet word with it?' said Meggen.

'It is not so simple. The shame that *Lux Imperator* feels can only be truly purged in battle. It is a machine of war. Only by performing its function as intended can its spirit reach equilibrium again. That is why it is behaving erratically.'

'Oh, so until it feels better it can go on refusing to open fire and killing its crew by spectacularly malfunctioning in combat?' said Meggen.

Bannick held up a hand to silence his gunner. 'Enough, Meggen! Starstan, we need *Lux Imperator* to be fully functional. The Yellow Guard of Magor are no amateurs, and they defend the capital. What might be done, magos?'

'We can perform the rituals as demanded, but there is only one sure remedy. The one I have stated,' said Starstan. '*Lux Imperator* must regain its confidence through battle, or it will never function correctly again.'

'I'll let Hannick know. He won't be happy but it could have been worse,' said Bannick.

Bannick's vox-set peeped. '*Sir, Epperaliant. I've a man here from the Sixteenth Company of the Four Hundred and Seventy-Seventh. Says he has a request order from Colonel Edel Lo Dostigern.*'

'Tell Hannick,' said Bannick.

'*Hannick told me to tell you. They need a super-heavy. Ours is the only one operational.*'

'I'll be right back. Bannick out. Meggen, come with me,' he said to his gunner. 'We're leaving.'

'Duty calls,' said Meggen to Brasslock's skull.

Starstan sang something out in binaric.

'My esteemed frater wished to know if you might spare Tech-Aspirant Kolios for the placation of *Lux Imperator's* spirit.'

'No,' said Bannick mounting the ladder out. 'We're going into combat. I need him where he is.'

The day was pelting with rain by the time *Cortein's Honour* rolled out to relieve the 477th.

The tree-lined road they followed was not wide enough to accommodate the massive bulk of the tank, and so Bannick ordered it to slog through the fields alongside. Had there been space, the road would still have been hard going, being choked with men heading both ways. The Salamander detailed to come and fetch them followed the lead of *Cortein's Honour*, driving off the road, over the ditch and into the crops. Bannick stood in the cupola, the tank's great height enabling him to see far over the flat terrain and its many agricolae. Farming on Geratomro seemed to function at a lower technological level than the industry in the cities, relying on manpower and draught beasts to do the jobs performed by machines elsewhere. The fields were large, arranged as segments of a circle radiating from a round central farmyard housing the main buildings of the agricolum. For all its chilliness, Geratomro supported a wide variety of crops, including orchards, vegetables of various kinds and grains. The Baneblade crushed them all under its treads without showing preference to any, grinding food to feed hundreds into a cold soup that seeped into the mud. The touch of war was everywhere. Draught beasts lay piled in red puddles alongside their masters. More than one farm complex had been sacked, the walls over the windows and doors streaked with soot. The further they proceeded, the more scars marred the land, until they drove through fields whose crops had been burned to the ground, and buildings reduced to shells in crater-pocked fields.

Progress was slow. The Baneblade was not the most agile of vehicles, its top speed of twenty miles an hour reduced to a grinding fifteen off-road. When the heavens opened, the mud was waiting and the driving worsened.

Bannick stayed up top through the rainstorm. Some vagary of the local meteorology generated drops that were widely spaced but unusually large and that splashed mightily in soaking bursts on the tank. His hat and the upturned collar of his coat kept him dry enough for a while, and the warmth of the tank heated his legs. The crew would be glad of the sharp fresh air the rain brought.

The situation on the road was getting worse. Many men were heading away from the front, walking wounded and field ambulances pushing against the flow onwards to Magor's Seat. The Baneblade rumbled past an altercation at a crossroads, where a Chimera had thrown a track, blocking the way. Bannick watched men in rain ponchos shouting at each other, calling for recovery vehicles to clear the way. He imagined the exchange, their words lost to the thrumming of the Baneblade's reactor and the drum of the rain.

Five hours passed. The Salamander commander voxed in to inform Bannick that they were close to forward head-quarters, and turned sharply towards a large agricolum hub.

'Forty-five degrees left!' Bannick ordered. The left track spun backwards at Shoam's direction, and *Cortein's Honour* swivelled towards their goal.

They rolled over an outlying fence into a muddy pen. The Baneblade could not enter the mean complex of stone and corrugated plasteel buildings without demolishing it. Bannick called the Salamander over so that he could jump in and avoid the sucking mess under the tank's tracks. Straw and dung were mixed equally into the mud.

The agricolum probably had a name that meant some-thing to someone, but to the invaders it was just a cross on a map, and they occupied it as though it had no more significance than that, rudely altering it to meet their tran-sient needs. The farmer and his family were dead and propped up against the wall of their home, the word 'trai-tors' scrawled above them in their own blood.

'What happened there?' said Bannick.

'They opened fire when we said we were going to

commandeer the agricolum,' said the Salamander's commander. 'We lost four men.' He looked at Bannick accusingly. His eyes were hollow with exhaustion. 'You don't approve? Not all these basdacking natives are happy to see us. Those men that died were my friends.'

Bannick turned away. There were seven corpses. Five were children.

The scout tank stopped suddenly.

'The captain's this way,' the sergeant said.

They jumped down into a yard ripe with the smell of animal waste. A large, hemicylindrical, open-fronted barn housed the forward headquarters. Bannick followed the sergeant into a large area lit by portable lumen trees where vox-operators worked at makeshift desks covered in maps. A single, lobotomised tacticus cognosavant shouted pearls of military wisdom at weary soldiers. A malfunctioning chartdesk fizzled in the centre. The floor was thick with mud and smelt strongly of livestock.

The sergeant saluted a bare-headed man bent over a map. 'Captain, this is the tanker,' he said, and walked away.

The officer looked up from his desk, revealing a heavily scarred face missing a portion of the upper lip, exposing the teeth in a permanent sneer. 'Captain Lubin Lo Santelligen, Four Hundred and Seventy-Seventh Paragon Foot, Sixteenth Company,' he said.

'Honoured Lieutenant Colaron Artem Lo Bannick, *Cortein's Honour*, Baneblade, Seventh Paragonian Super-Heavy Tank Company.' Bannick saluted.

'Right, Jonas' cousin. I thought I might get you.'

'Is that a problem, sir?'

'It would have been, had he not told me recently you

aren't half the basdack he was expecting. Whatever, it doesn't matter. Whoever you are, I need your help. If you were the dread Horus himself, I'd have to take it.'

He beckoned Bannick to the table and tapped at a map printed on plastek draped over the desk. 'There's a cohort of Huratal's Yellow Guard dug in here, on this ridge – hundreds of them, backed by artillery. There's no air support available in the sector, fleet's too far off tangent to offer direct bombardment, and my artillery company got hit two days back and is scattered in bits up the Matua road. Their heavy guns are taking pot-shots at the road and my troops filtering north to the rendezvous. You saw the wounded heading back?'

'Yes, sir.'

'All down to those yellow basdacks. We can't bypass them, it'll leave our flank exposed. Until they're gone, the advance on this front is stalled. This road here,' he tapped the paper near their location, 'leads to the main Drava highway and gives access to the south-western districts of Magor's Seat. Our job was to secure it and allow the rest of our regiment, supported by the Savlar Thirteenth, to push on to the capital here and here, meeting towards the centre.'

Bannick nodded. The Seventh's orders had been to reinforce the push to the south.

'So now I've got men from five different regiments all trying to get past dug-in artillery where they're sitting ducks. I've had them backing up the road and I'm running out of space and it won't stop raining.' He nodded to an aide who depressed a button on a blocky autoscribe assemblage. Five armatures dipped their quills into integrated ink pots, thrust forwards like daggers and began to scratch out a copy of the map onto rough paper.

'I've my own men at these locations. We've tried to take the ridge three times, and been driven back every time. We tried an armoured assault twice. The first time, I lost all my APCs.'

'A Baneblade should make short work of it, sir,' said Bannick.

'I was hoping for your whole company, or two super-heavies at least.' Santelligen produced a battered pack of lho-sticks, a smoker's choice Bannick had rarely seen. Santelligen offered him one. Bannick shook his head. 'Good, these things are murderously expensive. Got a taste for them way back. Cheroots just aren't the same once you've tasted lho.'

'Lascannons, autocannons, they won't tax *Cortein's Honour* so much.'

'Cocky, aren't you? There's something bigger up there than that. Something with real punch. We've not got eyes on it yet, but you want to steer clear of it.' Santelligen's aide lit the stick for him. The captain puffed at it until the tip glowed and a generous cloud of smoke wreathed his head. 'We tried the second attack with half a platoon of Leman Russes to back us up. They're all gone too.'

'You need to be cautious,' put in Santelligen's aide. 'If *Cortein's Honour* is lost in this venture, you will have difficulties from the Departmento and the Adeptus Mechanicus.'

'So you think I should let them range in on our boys and then bomb the life out of them, is that it, Mazdaran?' said Santelligen.

'No, sir. I am only thinking aloud. Perhaps we could wait for the rest of the honoured lieutenant's company?'

'Can we wait?' Santelligen looked at Bannick for an answer.

'It'll be three days at least before the others are repaired, sir. *Ostrakhan's Rebirth* was caught in a pit trap. *Lux Imperator* is suffering serious technical difficulties, and *Artemen Ultrus* lost its right track and suffered damage to its road wheels that can't be remedied simply by swapping them out.'

'If we wait–' began Mazdaran.

Santelligen looked sharply up. 'Incoming!' he shouted over the whistle of shells. All of them dived to ground, and lay in the filth with their hands clasped over their heads. A trio of closely spaced detonations banged outside. Bannick stood to see the agricolum's main dwelling on fire, the dead family obliterated. A man screamed for help.

'That's that then,' said Santelligen. 'They've got our range. There's no time. You're attacking now.'

The rain did not let up, becoming stronger as *Cortein's Honour* ground its ponderous way to the ridge-line three miles distant from the 477th's forward headquarters. Night was falling. The chaos on the road was absolute. Paragonian peacekeepers in rain ponchos were directing traffic off the rough road right where the Baneblade was headed. Headlight beams were filled with streaking raindrops like tracer fire. Bannick looked in dismay at the mess of men blocking his path. A massive, twenty-wheeled heavy hauler was half on the road, half off, its flatbed stacked high with supply crates.

'Get that transport out of my way!' shouted Bannick from the cupola.

'You! Move that Chimera to the side!' shouted Meggen from the gunner's hatch.

'We're doing our best, sir! It's stuck.'

'You want this road clear, then we need to get to that ridge!' said Bannick, who was in very poor humour. He was soaked, the enormous raindrops of Geratomro having battered their way past the protection of his clothes. A warm, unpleasant mist rose from the line of march. The evening stank of promethium exhaust, fouled mud and wet, unwashed men. The peacekeepers blew whistles and waved lit batons, guiding a squadron of Chimeras off the road and parting the men. These tracked vehicles fared well, but the hauler resolutely refused to move. Massive tyres spun round, spraying men with mud. The hauler lifted forwards a few feet, then sank up to its axles.

'Emperor's teeth!' shouted Bannick in frustration.

'Try the other side, sir!' shouted a peacekeeper. 'Drive over the road and go past that way.'

'Aye to that,' said Bannick. He pressed his vox pick-up to his mouth. 'Shoam, ninety degrees right. Watch out for the men, they're everywhere.'

There was a note of petulance to *Cortein's Honour*'s engines as it turned laboriously to face the road. Peacekeepers shouted and blew their whistles. Men trudged wearily through the trees lining the way to clear a space.

'Shoam! Forwards.'

The Baneblade rumbled like a displeased god and shoved its way onto the road. Tree trunks cracked into splinters as it crushed them under its massive hull.

Four distant bangs sounded. Light flashed in the sky over the ridge.

'Incoming! Incoming!' Shouting men fled in all directions, tripping over one another as they scattered and threw themselves into the mud.

Screaming shells hurtled downwards. The first raised

a spout of filthy water a hundred feet high ninety yards south of the road, but the next was closer. Meggen ducked below and slammed his hatch. Bannick was about to follow him when he saw men lying in the ruined ground, sheltering from the shells right in the path of the tank.

'Get out of the way! Move! Move! Shoam, three degrees left. Men on the ground, men on the ground!'

The soldiers who had their wits about them rolled out of the way.

'Move!' screamed Bannick. 'We'll crush you!'

Too late, a man looked up, right into Bannick's eyes.

'Move!'

The tank rolled right over him.

'I... I... Shoam, Throne curse you! More care!'

'I cannot see, bossman. The rain is thick,' voxed Shoam back, coolly factual, unworried by the man's death.

'Move!' yelled Bannick at others. These heeded him, and scuttled out of the path of the tank, heads down.

On the ridge, the guns fired again.

Shells banged into the ground, blasting the infantry. One screamed down dead on the cab of the hauler tractor. The vehicle exploded, lifted four feet off the ground and slammed back to earth. Bannick reeled from the shock wave. Mud and flesh slapped down all over the tank. Shrapnel pinged from his raised turret, and he dropped into an instinctive crouch.

More shells fell further down the road, bringing forth mushrooms of fire where they impacted vehicles. Then they were silent. Bannick stood.

The column had been hit hard. Craters smoked all around them. The peacekeepers were dead. Pale flesh was luminous in dark mud in the last light of the day.

Men were shouting and screaming in pain, but the way was clear.

'Sir, if we stop we can drag that hauler off the road,' said Epperaliant.

'No. We can't do anything here. Forwards, Shoam. The best service we can provide these men is to take out those guns.'

To protect the line of Magor,
So we swear.
To be the guardians of Geratomro,
So we swear.
To forbear no enemy to live,
So we swear.
To hold the Emperor dearer than life,
So we swear.

CHAPTER THIRTEEN
THE YELLOW GUARD

HILL SEVEN-BETA, RASTOR TERRITORY
GERATOMRO
087198.M41

Full dark waited for them at the hill. Their masked head-lights fell suddenly on filthy Paragonians cowering in foxholes filling with cold water. An officer came out to meet them. Bannick ordered the Baneblade to a halt and poked his head out into the downpour.

'Are you in charge here?' He had to shout. The guns on the crest were booming repetitively, the hilltop flashing with their discharge in the rain. The pop of detonating shells sounded from the distant road.

'I am,' shouted the man back. 'Captain Kenrick. I am very glad to see you. Perhaps you can resolve this little situa-tion for me, and we can get on with finishing this war?'

'Come up, sir!' called Bannick. 'Get out of the rain for a moment.'

The captain nodded and clambered up the Baneblade's access ladder. Bannick took the man's freezing hand and hauled him up onto the turret. Seconds later, they were by Bannick's chartdesk.

'Throne,' said the captain, shivering heavily. 'It's warm in here. I don't want to get back out.'

'Trust me, it's too hot most of the time. What have we got here then?'

The captain pulled out a data-slate from his satchel and keyed it to transmit to Bannick's chartdesk. Bannick moved aside the map Captain Santelligen had given him. A hololith of the area sprang into being from the desk.

'Right,' said Kenrick. 'We've designated this hill as seven-beta. It looks solitary, but past here the land bunches up and there are a series of shallow valleys with higher ridges beyond, then the moors. Just here is the Drava – doesn't look like much, but it becomes a sizeable river within twenty miles of its source. We think this is the last enemy concentration in this sector. At least, I hope they're concentrated here and nowhere else, because taking this one hill has been the Emperor's own task. There's a trench complex atop it. From it, their artillery battery has clear sights over the road to the west. As you can hear, they've started their bombardment in earnest. My men are stuck here, here and here.' The captain pointed out troughs round the bottom of the ridge, which was wrinkled by numerous rills and scarps along its flanks. 'Within minimum distance of their big guns, but we're suffering from small arms and man-portable heavy fire.'

'Where did you try the assault before?'

'There, and there,' said the captain, pointing out two smoother portions of slope that led up to the hill crest. 'This one to the south is five hundred yards from here. The other lies opposite, to the north. The cliffs give out in both places, so the hill is a bit of a saddle, and these approaches are almost as good as roads. Both times, we went in simultaneously on two fronts. The rest of the ridge is too steep to run up easily. Everywhere else it is fronted with escarpments like these.' He poked the hololith with his finger. 'So they know that too, right? There are heavy bolter and autocannon emplacements covering all angles on both approaches, lascannons and missile launchers too. All teams, I think, not armour mounted. But these men, they're Yellow Guard, fanatics.'

'Yes. We ran across some of them earlier today.'

'The Geratomran militia melts like cheese on the griddle, if they don't just surrender. The Yellow Guard are something else. Huratal's elite, the match of anyone we have, and they're dug in well. This is a permanent position. Whoever planned it knew their strategy.'

'Santelligen told me they have some sort of potent anti-tank here.'

'I was coming to that. There is at least one self-propelled piece up there, mounting an energy beam weapon. I've not seen the like before, but I checked my Tactica Imperium.' He tapped the screen of his slate. 'I think, and I'm sorry to tell you this, that they have a Destroyer, or something very like one.'

'Where did they get that?' said Bannick. Destroyers were tank hunters based on the Leman Russ chassis: no turret, but a single, mighty laser cannon mounted directly into the hull. Few forge worlds had the knowledge to produce the cannon; they were relics.

'Throne knows, but they have one. It's horrible. Cored the Leman Russes with one shot apiece, those it didn't blast to fragments.'

'And that covers the two approaches?'

'It did last time. They've got it set up at the top where it can redeploy to shoot down both slopes. There's not a clear line of sight from any one position, but they're pretty quick with it. Crew's good.'

Bannick studied the map a moment. 'Then we can't go directly up either of these ways.'

'Not even in this?'

'This is a big tank, sir, but a Destroyer's made for punching through any amount of plasteel.'

The captain sagged. 'But when the rest of your company–'

'Not coming, we're it. I told you, we ran into Yellow Guard this morning. Look, we can attack, but we'll have to take a different approach. If we start here,' he said, his finger disturbing the hololith at the edge of the nearest of the previous assault vectors, 'we can lob a few shells into them, stir them up a bit and get them anticipating an attack from that direction. We'll be vulnerable – they'll know we're here soon enough because we're pretty damn hard to miss. As soon as that Destroyer has a bead on us they'll start firing, so we'll get off two, maybe three rounds before we'll have to retreat behind this slope. Then we'll move from there to here, below where the cliffs are tallest at the western edge, here over the Drava Valley. Their weapon won't be able to draw a line on us there. You commence your assault here,' he said, pointing at the southern slope, 'while we drive up to the foot of the crags, then around the other side. We attack from the rear. We'll have cover along here for most of the way. If we can catch the Destroyer before it gets us, we can take out the rest of their anti-tank teams, then we'll be among them, and the havoc we'll cause will see this all over quickly.'

'The Russes couldn't do that. They said the slope was too steep.'

'It was, for them. Their centre of gravity's too high. If they turned on that slope or swung their turrets about too quickly, they would have toppled. Our mass is held a lot lower, we're broader and I have the best driver in this army group. We'll not have the same problem.'

'How long will it take you to make the ascent and go around?'

'On this ground, ten or twelve minutes.'

'Twelve minutes is a long time to leave my men in a las-storm.'

'Take cover by the wrecks of your APCs – it's better than nothing. But we need a diversion. On our own, we can put out as much firepower as a platoon. If we allow them to concentrate all their fire on us in one place, then we'll all be knocked out and you'll be left sat here in the mud.'

'I'm going lose a lot of men.'

'I know,' said Bannick. He hated the coldness that came into his voice. 'But it's better than delaying the conclusion of this war. That artillery hasn't stopped firing since we left the road, and it is crammed with men. There can be no advance in this sector until the guns are silenced. Who knows how much ammunition they have up there? And believe me, sir, the greatest risk will be ours.'

The captain looked at his data-slate. He pulled out a stylus, made a few marks on the screen and frowned at them.

'I suppose you're right. Give us half an hour to get organised. We need to get this done before they figure out you're down here.'

'Thirty minutes then.'

* * *

Whistles signalled the mortars to open up, and they peppered the hillside with explosions. With a roar of 'For Paragon!' the men of the 477th ran forwards. In response, flares blasted up from the top of the hill, lighting up the hillside with a hard glare. Las-bolts and heavy bolter rounds blasted out from hidden positions, raking the lead elements of the Paragonians. Men dropped. Those caught by bolt-rounds exploded.

Epperaliant examined the augur feeds of the tank. 'I've got them – fifteen positions, here, here and here.'

'Forwards!' shouted Bannick from the cupola. 'Fire on the move. Meggen, get as many rounds off as you can. Epperaliant, transmit targeting data.'

'Aye, sir!' shouted Meggen from beneath his feet. Epperaliant's more muted reply came via vox.

Shoam rammed both sticks forwards, and *Cortein's Honour* burst through the small wood it had been sheltering behind, crushing those trees that hadn't already been shattered by battle, and rose up and over a neck of land protruding from the hill. Bannick put his magnoculars to his eyes. The top of the ridge blazed with weapons fire as thick as the rain. Kenrick's men were running up the shallowest slope, making for the burned-out hulks of a dozen armoured personnel carriers littering the approach.

'Main gun has sight and ready!' shouted Meggen.

'Forty degree right. Target that concentration of fire dead centre.'

Fire and white gases spurted from the exhaust vents on the main cannon's muzzle. The shell streaked across the sky, its subsidiary rocket flaring. A ball of fire and a resounding boom marked its detonation. The fire coming down at Kenrick's men slackened.

'Keep on going up, Shoam. Get ready to drive down the side of this ridge. Meggen, fire at will.'

The nose of the Baneblade climbed steeply. Bannick braced himself against the hatch ring and flicked his magnocular view to thermal imaging.

'Epperaliant, do you see the enemy AT?'

'Negative, sir,' Epperaliant replied. 'Augurs aren't getting anything.'

The turret swung around to track the enemy weapons as the Baneblade drove up the steep slope. The cannon boomed again. Bannick's magnocular screens were dazzled by the discharge and he lowered them from his eyes. Again a pillar of fire and earth rose from the summit of the hill. In the light of falling flares he saw movement up there, and put his glasses back to his eyes.

Thermal imaging revealed the blocky, turretless shape of a Destroyer. As a thermal image it was a confusing shape obscured by the glare of weapons, without definition, but there was no mistaking the powerful cannon protruding from its hull. This long snout swung slowly to point at them, and the tank's body glowed white with the heat of working generators.

'Shoam, down the other side! Now, now, now!'

The Baneblade lurched on the hillside, turning thirty degrees to the left and running down the far side of the ridge in the slope. Again Bannick's magnoculars flared, this time from the discharge of the Destroyer cannon, so bright he winced. A beam of collimated light seared the sky feet over the turret of the Baneblade. It impacted half a mile away then snapped off, the site of its connection with the earth glowing red.

'Missed! Keep low. Follow the downside of this ridge.

Head for the crag. Meggen, there's a change in contour one hundred yards ahead. We'll have a shot at the top again. Take it. Secondary and tertiary weapons prepare to engage targets at will. Let's make them keep their heads down, if nothing else.'

Shots came down from the low cliff at the top of the slope, solid shot cracking off the armour, bolt-rounds exploding, las-beams scorching the paint round him. The number of gunshots increased as men were redeployed to face the Baneblade. Bannick saw their crouched forms lit up by the flares, hurrying along trench lines reinforced with tree trunks between rockcrete firing positions like beetles fleeing a disturbed log.

'Sir, come down. We're getting close,' urged Epperaliant.

A lascannon beam scored a glowing furrow in the side of Bannick's cupola. 'Negative, I've a better field of view up here.'

The forward heavy bolter turret came to life, tracking across a timber-and-earth revetment. Splinters of wood and clods of soil flew outwards. The trench behind flashed as bolts detonated. Firing from there ceased. The right-hand sponson opened up a second later to similar effect.

'Leo, take over on the forward turret,' said Kalligen. 'Permission to engage with the demolisher, sir?'

'Aye aye, fire at will,' said Bannick.

'Demolisher free!' reported Epperaliant.

The deafening *thwack-boom* of the short-barrelled demolisher shook the tank. Fire blasted from the ring of exhaust ports around its muzzle, putting Bannick in mind of the fire-breathing draco of ancient legend. The shell slammed into the scarp, burying itself in the hillside before detonating and blasting rock outwards.

Now Bannick did duck into the turret, the hatch held over his head. Rocks rattled off the top of the tank.

'Meggen,' said Bannick. 'We're clearing the line in a couple of seconds.'

'Positioning turret,' said Meggen. 'Preparing to fire.'

Bannick waited for a hail of heavy stubber bullets to pass, then stuck his head out of the hatch. The ridge in the hill they followed was dropping lower to the main body of the slope, bare stone breaking through the turf. Ahead, crags blocked themselves in onto the sky, periodically lit by discharges of las-fire and the wider flash of artillery. The ridge dropped. Bannick scanned for the Destroyer. There was no sign of it. Battle raged fiercely on the forward slope. Kenrick's men were well sheltered in the wrecks of their transports. Mortar fire thumped down relentlessly on the enemy emplacements, thickening the pounding rain. He picked out a target.

'Meggen, bunker, twelve degrees left.'

'Got it, sir.'

Magnesium rounds hissed out from the tank's coaxial autocannon, stitching the hillside closer and closer to the bunker, until three hit home and Meggen had the shot ranged.

'Fire!'

The main gun discharged, the shell's rocket burn shooting it rapidly across the open space. It impacted the bunker with a resounding boom, blasting it to pieces.

'Direct hit! Well done, Meggen.'

With some of the pressure off the main attack, Kenrick's men pressed forwards.

'Shoam, left, follow the scarp. We're going round the back.'

The tank tilted alarmingly sideways as Shoam spun it round without slowing. Meggen swung the turret right round so that it faced the rear, and loosed two further shots towards the main conflict. The slope at the top was steep. Ganlick cursed as a back-pack came loose from its straps and bounced across the command deck into his chair. It was now frighteningly obvious that a vehicle with a higher centre of gravity would have toppled, Bannick was almost standing on the side of his cupola. Turf wrinkled as the tank slid slightly, but the slope held, and the Baneblade rolled around the cliffs at the north-western end of the crags. Men were running along the top shooting. A grenade bounced close to hand, exploding as it rolled down the hill. Bannick returned fire with his pistol. The gunner's hatch clanged back and Meggen stood up, and grabbed the handles of the pintle-mounted heavy stubber.

'Take this, you yellow basdacks!' he shouted. A rocket round spanged off the main cannon, thrumming off high where it gave out in a brilliant white starburst.

'Lascannon team, right, right, right!' shouted Bannick.

Meggen swung the gun about, sending a stream of solid shot at the three-man team setting up the lascannon above them. One took a bullet through the head, the others leapt back.

'Scarp end approaching. Prepare to turn. Take it easy, Shoam. This is the steepest part.'

Sparks flew as the right sponson grated on rock. Using the contact as a guide, Shoam pushed the tank past the end of the ridge. The ground dropped away two hundred feet there into a small valley where a lazy brook ran, the source of the Drava. Scree slopes gathered in folds in the land above it. The tank shifted sideways.

'Come on!' said Bannick. 'Come on!'

Shoam gunned the engine. The smoke-stacks belched fumes, the treads bit into the thin soil, and the tank came round the northern side of the hill where the ground levelled. A rise blocked sight of their approach from the northern slope.

They crested it and came down all weapons firing.

'Full speed ahead!' shouted Bannick. The tank levelled out and accelerated. It could go no faster than a man could sprint. Their goal was a hundred yards away. Tank traps blocked the gap in the cliffs. The ground had been blasted to mud and loose rock. On the other side of that, the Destroyer surely waited.

Bannick scanned the ridge. The northern slope was shallower than the south, but the cliffs were twice the height. Great portions of the crest were a tangle of bomb-shattered trees and cracked rock formations. The approach was almost like a broad road, as Kenrick had described it. A ribbon of muddy earth led into the rock formations, but the terrain that flanked it offered ample opportunity for ambush.

'Emperor-forsaken thing could be anywhere,' said Bannick. 'All guns, lay down a suppressive pattern.'

All through the attack the enemy artillery had been firing, the beat of the guns picking up tempo as the Yellow Guard anticipated defeat. They would cast as much destruction at the Imperials as they were able before they fell. Bannick admired such determination.

The Baneblade was fifty yards from the beginning of the approach when the Destroyer struck. From a hiding place among the leaning stacks and frayed stone tables of the ridge, its blast took them all by surprise. Without warning, a blade of high-powered energy seared the sky, causing it to bang with pressure differential. It took the tank along the right side of the command deck, blasting a hole through the plasteel and causing havoc. *Cortein's Honour* rocked at the impact. Shouts and cries replaced the intense, noisy chatter of men at the job of war. The internal comms buzzed and died.

'Sir!' yelled Leonates from below. 'Sir! Ganlick is hurt bad! Epperaliant is down.'

Someone was screaming below, endlessly, horribly. Bannick ignored it. He could not afford to be distracted. 'Get Gollph to the foot of the ladder. We'll have to relay orders verbally. Meggen, target the source of that blast!'

'Aye, sir!' The turret shifted minutely to the right, and Bannick thanked the Emperor and Omnissiah both that its motive engines still functioned and the turret ring had not buckled. *Cortein's Honour* shot back, the shell's casting the roar of a wounded, furious beast. It impacted in a narrow crevasse between two giant boulders.

'Smoke! Smoke! Smoke!' he yelled. The launchers at the front made hollow popping noises. Tubular grenades went spinning through the air, landing at preset distances in front of the tank to pump out thick white vapour all along the ridge.

'Take us right, Shoam!' Bannick bellowed. The order passed along to Gollph who ran to the front. A second's delay. Too long, but just quick enough. Another Destroyer blast punched through the smoke, cooking off the vapours and leaving a long, clear tunnel that wound in on itself until it collapsed back into the smokescreen.

'Damn it! Faster!'

Again the order was relayed down. The tank accelerated,

treads squealing. The demolisher cannon barked, then the main armament, blasting again at the Destroyer's location. Both tanks were firing blind. Either one could emerge victorious.

Blinking after-images, Bannick traced the line of the laser destroyer back to its source. 'Barrel up, three degrees. We have to get it before they move,' ordered Bannick.

'Emperor, guide my hand!' shouted Meggen.

A third las-blast thrummed through the night, the boom of displaced air making Bannick's ears ring through the protection of his vox-set. It sheared off the right sponson lascannon turret. The severed power couplings fountained sparks.

Meggen kissed his hand and slapped the shell as the auto-loader slammed it home. He pressed his eye to the cannon's periscope.

'Fire!' shouted Bannick.

'No! Wait! Nearly, nearly... Got it!' he replied, and depressed the firing pedal.

One last time the cannon roared at the Destroyer. They were rewarded with an enormous explosion. Plates of metal pinwheeled high into the sky and came clattering down all over the rocks. Between two small rock formations, the square, blocky tank hull of the Destroyer was outlined by flames coloured by chemical burn. A burning man threw himself from the wreck, landed hard on the ground, rolled once, then was still.

'Got it? By the Emperor, Meggen, you got it all right! Shoam, hard right, hard right. All weapons, fire at will. Let's drive through these basdacks and show them the error of their ways.'

The Baneblade rode up the natural way onto the top

of the hill. A narrow plateau greeted them, studded with well-protected artillery pits. Their coming had not gone unnoticed, and a storm of fire blazed in.

'Meggen! Kalligen! Kill these guns.'

The turret whined back and forth, blasting shells at the artillery. Lesser, solid-shot anti-tank autocannons wheeled about to meet them, but such was the thickness of the Baneblade's armour that their rounds spanked off at high speed, whining into the night. *Cortein's Honour* fired back, blasting men into the air and shattering guns. Secondary explosions bloomed throughout the enemy positions as munitions cooked off. Hemispheres of earth and bodies were heaved high by the demolisher, and then the Baneblade roared up over the slight rise in the centre of the hill, and into the battered scrub on the south side. Pushing the remaining trees aside, *Cortein's Honour* rolled over burned stumps and foxhole alike, bolter fire blasting the men running from this embodiment of the Emperor's displeasure into bloody rags.

Multiple red flares went from below. Bannick ducked down into the turret. 'The Four Hundred and Seventy-Seventh are making their assault, cease forward fire. Hard left, Shoam. Let's finish this now.' He ducked down, crabbed over to the gunner's turret and re-emerged there. Legs either side of Meggen's back, he manned the heavy stubber. Adding its bullets to the firestorm kicked out by the super-heavy tank, Bannick took a full and active part in the slaughter, howling wordlessly as he killed.

CHAPTER FOURTEEN
THE SACRIFICE

IMPERIAL GOVERNOR'S PALACE, MAGOR'S SEAT
GERATOMRO
087298.M41

Dostain couldn't sleep any more. He didn't like to. His dreams excited and repelled him in equal measure. He feared that were he to sleep too much, and sink into that nocturnal netherworld too often, his disgust would melt away, leaving only a fearful longing for more depravity, more excess.

But sleep deprivation does things to the human mind almost as terrible as the worst of dreams. When he moved his head, it seemed his soul shifted within the box of his skull, imparting a delay to all sensation. His mouth was dry, no matter how much he drank, and he was maddeningly, insatiably hungry. At the edges of his vision small black shapes flowed over the objects in the room, new companions whose faithfulness he had not requested nor desired.

So it was that when Dib crept through his door, Dostain

took him at first for a hallucination. One of the sliding shapes given flesh, and he laughed at it in fear and
resignation.

'Heir the Second? My lord?' said Dib.

Dostain blinked stupidly. He had to swallow three times
before his tongue worked around the words his brain
commanded it to say.

'Get out,' he said. 'Leave me be. These dreams. They are
your doing. I know it.'

'Me? I give nothing that is not already there,' said Dib.

'Get out!'

'Are you sure, my lord? You are losing this war you
started, and you know that too,' said Dib. 'And that is not
my doing.' He was no longer a youth, but a glorious and
powerful man. He was naked except for a long, horizon-
tally pleated kilt that garbed his perfect legs. Armlets and
medallions of strange gold decorated his body, clinging
to his muscles in ways that accentuated them uncomfortably for Dostain, for it made Dib too beautiful to bear.
His second greatest fear was that Dib would seduce him,
his greatest that he would enjoy it. Dib sat at the end of
Dostain's bed and gave him a sad, understanding smile.

'I offered you a choice between slavery and power. You
have done nothing! Choices need tending as much as any
garden. They are not simple boxes to be filled on a form,
sealed away and forgotten, but living things! Your choice
requires attention, or it will turn and the outcome will
not be to your liking.'

Dostain peered closely at Dib. The youth wavered,
replaced by Pollein, beautiful Pollein, immodestly dressed
in Dib's strange clothes.

'You like this body, I know. I do not think you care much

for the soul that it clothes, but the flesh itself... Well, that has cast a deep and powerful spell on you.' When she spoke, she did so with Dib's voice. She leaned onto the bed and began to crawl up it, her eyes fixed on Dostain's. 'Do you know, the most powerful urge of any organism is to reproduce. Of course, there are individuals within a sentient species such as yours that try not to. They deny themselves the genetic continuation of offspring for one reason or another, but most of them still practise the act of coupling. Do you know why?'

Dostain moved backwards up the bed and fell into his pillows, undone by lust and lack of sleep.

Pollein leaned over him, her long hair brushing his sweating face, making it hard to think.

'Because it is nice,' said Pollein. She leaned down and kissed him passionately. He squirmed against it, but gave in, responding urgently. Then Pollein's head withdrew, and it was Dib's again. He sat back and laughed. Dostain wiped at his lips in disgust.

'Oh, poor boy,' said Dib, tousling his hair. 'Prefer the real thing? I can give her to you.'

'You'll make her want me?'

'I can't do *that*. Who has that kind of power? Not I. My lord has, but he is of a very rare sort.'

'What kind?'

'A god,' said Dib provocatively, then laughed again. 'I can't make her like you, but I can give her to you to do with as you like. You don't really like her anyway, so what does it matter if she likes you or not?'

'What do you mean?' gulped Dostain.

'Don't be so naive.'

'I won't be a party to seduction by force.'

'Oh, you have morals now – the boy who provoked rebellion.'

'It wasn't supposed to...'

'Then you are just greedy. Listen to me, foolish boy.' Dib leaned in. 'Their armies draw nearer and still you have not acted. I offer you the girl as a sweetener, but I shouldn't really. Call me generous, if you like. It's very easy, what you have to do. I don't know how much easier I can make it.'

'I don't want to know!' said Dostain.

'Too late!' sang Dib.

An image came into Dostain's head. His monstrous cousin in its crib, woven from forbidden science and Huratal's yearning for vicarious immortality. Dostain clutched at his skull.

'I can't!'

'It's not really alive! Why so squeamish? It's hardly even a person. Kill it, and as the next eldest heir, you shall be Lord of Geratomro.'

'Lord of nothing!'

'Then you will all be killed. This war is nearly done. The Imperial Guard are three days from the outskirts of the capital. Do this thing, and I shall provide the allies I promised as your coronation gift, and you shall have your aunt, the pretty one,' laughed Dib, 'as your bride the same day.'

'I won't!'

'Then you shall burn.'

Dib slid from the bed and walked towards the door. He pressed two fingers to his lips, kissed them, and blew the kiss to Dostain.

Dostain sat in his bed, so frightened his teeth chattered. Burned.

Pollein.

Burned.

'Wait!' he called. 'Wait! What must I do?'

In contrast to those of her treacherous nephew, Huratal's dream was a lovely thing, full of dancing and beautiful bodies. She rarely dreamed of carnal pleasure; she was past all but food and drink. Epicurean consumption had replaced the exercises of the night. But the dream was glorious, a sensuous infinity of writhing bodies that awoke in her desires she had not felt in a long time.

A terrified wail yanked her from sleep to wakefulness in one step.

The warm afterglow of her dreams dissipated in the dark of her room. She was soaked with sweat. The room was too hot. The fire, tended to by her handmaidens through the night, burned high. An overpowering musk cloyed at the back of her throat.

She sat up in bed, pushing her sheets aside. It was the depths of the night, dark as it ever became. Rain pattered against the window. Wind soughed its sorrowful way through the spires of her palace, shaking the edifice with its ethereal strength. Her senses strained, alive as they were at no other time. Her nightmaid had stepped out, and she was alone. For a vertiginous moment she felt as though she were the only person left alive on Geratomro, perhaps anywhere in the galaxy. There is no loneliness like that felt in the last watches of the night, no matter how rational a person may be.

'Joliandasa?' she said, too disquieted to feel fury at her nightmaid's absence.

She got out of bed with difficulty, her weight dragging

at her bones. Her feet sank into the fur of the rugs around her bed. She moved quietly, terrified for some inexplicable reason of making a noise. She could not see her canids either. 'Mikki? Gilli? Come my babies, where are you?'

The noise came again, a child's wailing echoing up the corridors of her palace.

'Missrine!' she gasped. A mother knows her babe's cry.

Joliandasa appeared at the door.

'Where have you been?'

'I... I went to fetch more wood, my lady. I came quickly when I heard you shouting. What has happened?'

'Do you hear the cries?'

'No, my lady.'

'Fool! Missrine! Someone has my child! Sound the alarm, fetch my soldiers!'

More ladies-in-waiting arrived at the door, covering their faces with their hands. The crying started again and didn't stop. 'Moooottthhhhherrr!'

'Do something! Do something, all of you, or I'll have your heads!' snapped Missrine. She heaved her way across the room, the short distance leaving her breathless.

The threat only worsened the matter, and the women panicked. They flapped their hands. One of them swooned into a dead faint. Missrine regretted now her practice of surrounding herself with the weak-minded.

'Get out of my way!' screamed Huratal. She bowled them aside by dint of her bulk, and burst from the door.

For the first time in decades, Missrine Huratal I broke into a lumbering run. Missrine II's nursery was her destination.

She arrived to find the crib upended, grav-motors spitting sparks. The tubes that fed Missrine II with the elixirs she required were unplugged and dribbling onto the floor, staining spilled satin sheets toxic colours.

The smell of musk was in the nursery too, and there it was overpowering. The wet nurses lay sprawled on the floor, dazed, unable to speak. At first she thought they were affected by drink, but they were too languorous, reaching out to stroke at her and smiling foolishly.

'Get up, get up! Where is Missrine? Where is she?' the Governatrice demanded. 'Where are my soldiers?' she yelled.

'Madame, madame?' said one of the girls woozily. 'It was Dostain. He has the Heir the First.'

'What, what?' Missrine said. She got down on her knees with a grunt to hear better, her vast stomach inhibiting her movement.

'Dostain! He was... He was with a youth, and Heir the Third Pollein. So beautiful,' giggled the girl. 'So beautiful.'

Missrine hauled the girl half upright and smacked her back and forth across the face, but although blood ran from her nose, she could not be roused. Her eyelids fluttered over eyes in which only the white could be seen.

'Mooooootther! Help me!' came Missrine II's cry, close by. Any other who heard it was discomfited by the heir's unnatural voice, for it was thin and whining. But to Missrine, it was everything.

'Mother's coming!' she cried, and lumbered back to her feet. The vat-born heir's wails increased in volume. She ran round a corner, bouncing off the wall in her haste. A door ahead lay open. Purplish light shone from inside. As she raced towards it, Dostain staggered out from the room, bloody to the elbows. He collapsed against the wall and ground the heels of his hands into his eyes as if he could rub out whatever he had just seen. Her ladies-in-waiting came running after their Governatrice, apparently having gathered their wits. Too little, too late; she would have them all killed if her heir had been harmed.

The cries had stopped. Her heart fell through her stomach. Missrine II was dead.

'What have you done? Where is my heir?'

Dostain's head came up, grinning wildly. He blinked as if the sight of his aunt were a completely novel and confusing experience. Slowly, his eyes focused within their rings of blood, and his smile turned into a frown. He reached up to wipe the sweat from his forehead, smearing more vitae over his eyes, like the war-paint of an island savage.

'We have new allies, aunt. The war will be won!'

'Where is my heir!' bellowed the Governatrice. Her ladies-in-waiting held back, weeping. None dared look into the room.

Dostain looked at her, his mouth slack. He pushed himself up the wall, smearing it with blood.

'I... I'm sorry,' he said. 'I didn't want to do it. She made me. Pollein. I mean, Dib did. It was him, wasn't it? I don't know any more!'

'Joliandasa, call the guard! Have them arrest my nephew.'

'They did not do this alone,' said another voice, smooth as silk. 'Will you arrest me too?'

A young man of radiant beauty, quite naked, stepped from the room. His skin glowed – literally, appearing so healthy and vital that a sheen clung to the curves of his muscles. His hair was blond as the morning sun. Absently, he brushed a tangle of it from his shoulder.

'Who... who are you?' asked the Governatrice.

'Someone of consequence,' the man said. He advanced on Huratal. 'He did you a favour, killing that thing. That was no child. A bundle of cloned organs and machine parts. How could you love it?' He shook his head disapprovingly.

The youth's eyes were brown, the deep brown of forest pools, full of motes of gold as lively as darting fish. Huratal felt herself being dragged towards them, and she staggered back.

'I know you,' she whispered. 'The Devil-in-the-bush!'

'No royal "we" today?' said the youth. 'No such thing exists as the Devil-in-the-bush. It is a story, as you so rightly pointed out to the corpse-god's lackeys before you had them killed.'

'Dostain, what have you done?' said Huratal.

'Your own laws do not permit such technomancy as created that "child". Indeed, I believe they are outlawed on most of the worlds of your petty Imperium. What your heir did is no worse, not in an absolute moral sense. He ended an abomination. Don't you think, Dostain?'

Dostain began to cry. Huratal stared at him in disgust. When she looked back at the man, she saw Pollein instead, the gauzy dress she wore stuck to her skin with blood. She moved with a sinuous sensuality to Dostain's side, and placed a tender hand upon his shoulder.

'She is quite talented, you know,' she said in the youth's voice. 'Very powerful. I'm surprised you didn't notice. Or is this your greatest crime? Did you keep her? Did you keep your sister from the Black Ships?'

Huratal's eyes bulged.

'Ha! That's it, isn't it? Stupid woman. I have you to thank for my presence then.' Pollein curtseyed. 'This world will be mine, thanks to you.'

'Pollein!' said Huratal. 'Pollein.'

'Sister?' said Pollein in her own voice. She smiled, but the purity it once exhibited, and that Huratal had always so despised, was tainted by something fell. 'Something wonderful is coming!'

Then she was gone, and the thing wore the man's shape and spoke again. 'Dib! Dib! Devil-in-the-bush!' It laughed. The sound was a peal of silver bells, but it made Huratal feel nauseous. 'I quite like it. It's not my name, of course, but you need some sort of label, shall we say.' The golden man ceased to smile. 'Can you guess my real name? If you do, I will let you live. But you never will.'

The thunder of booted feet rang up the corridor. A score of Yellow Guard approached the murder room from both ends of the corridor. Huratal's maids fled, shrieking as the soldiers took up double firing lines, their weapons upon the golden man.

'Mistress!' shouted Oravan.

'Oravan! Kill him, kill him now,' said Huratal, stepping back.

'My lady, kill him?' he replied in confusion. 'It is Pollein there, your sister. You wish us to kill the Heir the Third?'

'Now!'

'We may kill you!'

Dib, for it was Dib Huratal saw and not Pollein, cocked his head and pulled a face. 'They might. They really might.'

'Do it!' said Huratal.

Oravan needed no more convincing.

'Fire!'

Scores of las-bolts hammered into Dib's flesh, making the golden skin smoke and curl. He stood smiling sweetly, even when a beam of coherent light punched out his eye neatly as a needle. But he did not fall.

'Emperor's teeth!' yelled Oravan. The shooting dwindled away.

With his remaining eye, Dib looked himself over. Even as he did so his flesh rippled, and became whole again. A new eye pushed its way out of the back of the ruined socket, swelling like a fruiting fungus captured by pict-feed and sped up. His completed face changed, then back again. Now he was Pollein, now he was Dib.

'My turn,' he said.

He lifted his hand. There were no pyrotechnics, only a wall of invisible force that crushed men's souls. Twenty men fell, writhed on the floor making noises of unashamed pleasure, then as one twitched their last and died, their backs arching so hard in their spasms that they broke.

Dib stalked towards Huratal.

'Do you know, your subjects say you have no heart?' he said. 'What do you say we take a look?'

Drawing back his arm he punched forwards, smashing his fist through her ribcage with an awful crack. Huratal grunted as Dib rooted around in her chest cavity. She shook, eyes rolling back in her head, blood pouring from her mouth.

'Hm, I can't find it,' he said. 'Perhaps they are right?' He withdrew his arm, dripping with blood.

She fell to the floor. Dib licked at her vital fluids absently. 'That's that then,' he said. He walked to where Dostain sat against the wall, dripping red upon the marble.

Dib knelt before Dostain and bowed his head. 'My lord, you are Heir the Second no longer!'

Dostain drew in a snivelling breath.

'Don't be like that! You're the king of the world, my boy! Stand tall now.' Dib reached and grasped Dostain under the armpits. To an observer, had there been any left alive, it would have looked like an act of kindness, but Dostain felt a serpent's hooked fangs bury in his flesh.

'You are the Lord of Geratomro! And will be forever and ever, and ever. Your allies come. The first ones you'll like, the others you'll get used to. Well, eventually. They'll stop the dogs of Terra. But first,' Dib said, clapping his hands, 'we must arrange your coronation and wedding. It will be fun! I do so love parties. But oh, I suppose,' he said, looking down at Pollein's ruined dress, for he wore her shape again, 'someone really should fetch me some new clothes. These are quite ruined.'

'Girls,' Dib called, treading bloody footprints down the corridor. 'Oh, girls!'

CHAPTER FIFTEEN
THE MOORS

HILL SEVEN-BETA, RASTOR TERRITORY
GERATOMRO
087298.M41

Smoke drifted in lazy streamers across the battle-scarred ground of the ridge. Bannick sat shivering in the cupola of the tank, more from shock than the cold. The grey dawn revealed the extent of the carnage on the hill. The broken bodies of men lay tangled with blasted timber and metal. A hand grey with dust poked out from underneath the rubble of a shattered trench-line. Bannick stared at it as he smoked. He never smoked, but last night had shaken him. When Meggen offered him a cheroot it seemed like a good idea. He sucked in the foul-tasting smoke and blew it out mechanically.

Men moved all over the ridge. They spoke very little, numbed by exhaustion. Priests chanted somewhere out of sight, praising the Emperor for victory and commending the souls of the dead to His care. The scent of incense mixed with spilled promethium and residual fyceline.

The occasional gunshot cracked out as the 477th put the enemy wounded out of their misery. At least that killing masqueraded as mercy. The few Yellow Guard prisoners had been shown no forgiveness and were shot without compunction, but not immediately. Their screams still rang in Bannick's ears. Their bloodied bodies lay heaped with their fellows killed in the attack. Everyone was filthy. Huddles of men given no duty crouched in the lee of the escarpments not far away, all grey with mud but for pink holes where tired eyes peeked out. The rain and the attack had churned the slope into a slippery morass. From the hill-top, Bannick had a fine view over the mist-shrouded lands to the south. Where the fog had lifted, he saw large patches of terrain churned by warfare. On the western horizon pillars of black smoke climbed skywards, the glow of fire banishing the night early. Something like thunder sounded far away, that abrupt rumbling that spoke of lance strikes. In the near distance he could just about make out the line of the road. The tiny shapes of armoured vehicles moved alongside it, headlights winking in the early morning. They were free of bombardment; at least he could cling to that.

His eyes were drawn back to the dead hand. What had driven its owner to fight so fiercely against overwhelming odds? Would he do the same if his own planet were threatened? To rebel against the rule of the Imperium was unthinkable to Bannick, but it might well have been the same for this dead soldier until recently.

He thought of what the 477th had done to the captives. Nobody here could claim the moral high ground.

He turned away, and slid back down into the tank.

Ganlick's body was encased in a waxed canvas sack.

There was one for each of them in the tank's stores, names already stencilled upon them in anticipation of their inevitable deaths. Epperaliant had his arm bound up. His face was raw with burns. The morning breeze blew in through the breach the Destroyer shot had burned through the armour. The tank had been angled slightly down when it had hit, and the beam had continued into the comms and tac desk. Epperaliant's sliding seat had been at the far of the rail when his station had been destroyed – only that had saved him. Kolios worked underneath the desk, singing praises to the minor spirits of vox and cogitator, his box of tools open beside him.

Ganlick had not been so lucky. Molten plasteel was flung across the command deck by the blast, catching the third loader in the side of the head with force enough to crack his skull as well as burn his flesh from the bone. Bannick couldn't get the image of his wounds from his mind. His screams had blended into the clamour of battle, and when the fight was done, so was Ganlick. They said it had taken him minutes to die. Bannick had come close this time himself. Molten metal was splattered all up the back of his own seat, burned through the padding to the wirework beneath, heavy lumps of it resting on the deck-plating. If he hadn't have been in the turret–

'Sir!' Epperaliant saluted him, snapping Bannick out of his daze. 'Kolios has restored internal vox, but we've no long-range communications capabilities.'

'What's the rest of the damage?' asked Bannick.

Kolios slid himself out from under the tac desk. The red cowl he wore over his Astra Militarum fatigues was stained with oil. Bannick felt for men like him. He was neither of the Adeptus Mechanicus or the Astra Militarum. There were insufficient enginseers for one to be stationed on every super-heavy tank, but the vehicles' technical complexity meant a well-trained man was needed to effect battlefield repairs. Those chosen were not scions of Mars. They would never be accepted as tech-adepts. Because of their training they stood apart from the run of the men, scorned by the Adeptus Mechanicus and their former countrymen both. They were trapped between two worlds. The tech-adept aspirant bore these burdens with a solemn stoicism.

'The main logic engine has been destroyed, sir,' said Kolios. 'It is beyond my skills to repair. We have three of five cogitators operating at limited capacity, but machine shock has set in to them. They mourn their brothers' deaths and may well die in time. Our targeting aids and capacity to link into the army group noosphere have gone. Life support controls are inoperable. I might salvage the long-range vox, but other than that our communications capacity is limited on every front.'

'My chartdesk?'

'The device itself is functioning, but without the direction of the tactical cogitator array it is useless,' said Kolios.

'But our reactor, guns, all that. We can still function?'

'Yes, sir. The power feeds to the right sponson are severely damaged. The lascannon array will have to be replaced by the company fabricatum.'

'I saw it come off, Kolios. What's left of it is scattered across the north face. Of course we need a new one,' said Bannick tersely, and instantly regretted his tone. His men looked at him in surprise. 'I'm sorry. I'm... I'm tired.'

Kolios paused a moment before continuing. 'The bolters on that side are also affected. I can patch the lines, but the efficiency of motive force transference to their servo-motors will be lower, and the guns will be less responsive.'

'Can you work on this while we move?' Bannick asked, pointing at the tac desk.

'Yes, sir, I can.'

Bannick looked through the hole in the hull. 'Then patch this and fix the power lines to the sponson. I'll go find Kenrick, borrow his comms and get on the vox to Hannick. Meggen, Shoam, get Ganlick to the priests. At least here he'll be buried alongside his fellow Paragonians.'

Bannick climbed off the tank, his boots sinking halfway up his calves in the grey mud. Paragonian field engineers were already setting to work repairing the fortifications. He caught the arm of a passing sergeant, who directed Bannick towards the centre of the trench complex. There a squat bunker, crowned with camouflaged comms arrays, hid behind stubby columns of rock. Bannick passed between sentries on the main gate. Plasteel doors had been blown off their hinges. He descended steps into an unexpectedly extensive complex. Lumen strips flickered on emergency power. Blood was everywhere. The smell of weapons discharge and death was strong in the enclosed space.

Kenrick was in the enemy command centre. Like in Matua Superior's fort, the rebels had succeeded in destroying all their informational technologies before the Astra Militarum could take it. Wrecked machines and burned-out cabinets were being carried out by Kenrick's men, and Bannick waited to let them by. Inside, enginseers were at work setting up portable command units. The large chartdesk at the centre had been patched up and put back into the service of the Imperium.

'Bannick!' said Kenrick. He was elated. Victory had made him forget the concerns he had before the attack. 'I'm glad you're here.'

'Sir,' Bannick saluted.

'Without you, we'd still be at the bottom of this bloody hill. Thank you.' He held out a grubby hand. Bannick shook it.

'You suffered casualties, I hear?'

'One dead, one wounded. *Cortein's Honour* took a direct hit from the Destroyer. Only the Emperor's protection kept us all from the grave.'

'I am sorry. A terrible business this. I envy you your war on Kalidar. Ever since we were raised we've been fighting men. It still makes me sick to the stomach that they'd turn and that my soldiers must die when there are so many other threats to our kind out there. These people are so stupid, so short-sighted.'

Bannick swallowed, suddenly nauseous. He agreed completely, but his words stuck in his throat.

'My comms array is out. If I might, I wish to use your long-range vox to contact my company commander and refresh my orders, sir.'

'Be my guest. I'm rather tempted to order you to stay here – you're a fine asset to command, but I'd be overruled. We're to occupy this fort in case of enemy pushback. I doubt it will happen, but it is good to be ready. Good too to see that someone with foresight is up there, watching the war. Especially when it means my men are off the front line for a while.'

'That sounds like Iskhandrian,' said Bannick.

'Perhaps. It's hard to know who's really in charge at the moment. Jindilin, show the honoured lieutenant here to the vox-array. Take as long as you need, Bannick.'

It took five minutes of negotiating vox-relays and their various operators before Bannick was patched in to Hannick. Bannick passed on the news of the engagement and the damage to *Cortein's Honour*. Hannick gave him his orders.

Bannick pushed the chair back and got up.

'*Cortein's Honour* has been ordered to rejoin the rest of the company. We're moving on Magor's Seat.'

Kenrick gave him a sympathetic smile. 'If there's anything your men need, Bannick, let my quartermaster know. He's not bad for a Departmento puppet.'

Cortein's Honour was resupplied, and Ganlick's corpse removed. Kolios finished his makeshift repairs with help from Kenrick's two enginseers, although the long-range vox could not be saved. They took a brief few hours rest, and were on the move again by Geratomro's chilly noon.

Rather than head back to the road, Bannick opted to traverse the land to the north of hill seven-beta and meet up with the advance on the main highway to the north west.

They cut back across country. The elevation grew steadily higher until it became a moorland plateau cut with numerous ravines and dotted with stony tors.

The men put their tank in order, taking it in turn to rest, while Shoam drove them overland. The Savlar refused to relinquish his sticks, and Bannick did not have the energy to challenge him. Instead, Bannick kept a constant line open to Shoam's compartment. The hiss and click of his nitrochem inhaler provided a steady, soporific beat to the day. Bannick was dead tired, but would not rest. The high moors were colder still than the lower plains. No arable agricolae were there, but rough stone walls divided the landscape into huge tranches of land dotted with lumbering grazing beasts. They saw only one deserted village, a rough place whose crude dwellings collapsed when the tank rumbled through it. On a few occasions, Bannick spied men watching from the far side of ravines, but they made no move against them. Relying on their physical maps, Bannick directed the tank towards a railed transit way. Once on this, the Baneblade used its white rockcrete bridges to traverse several deep valleys.

This broken area of the moors was small in extent. In the first hours of night, the wrinkled nature of the terrain smoothed out, and they came again to an area that was flat, although the elevation of the land continued to increase. A cold mist fell, so thick they were forced to slow their advance, for without the tank's augur systems they had to rely on one of the crew scouting ahead for hazards on foot.

Bannick dozed in the turret as his men worked. He was so tired not even the opening and slamming of the gunnery hatch as the crew took it in turns to guide the tank woke him, and no one had the heart to disturb him. An hour before dawn bright flashing in the viewing panes of his cupola woke him up.

'Col?' said Meggen, who was sleeping in his gunner's chair. 'What was that?'

'What?' said Bannick. His mouth was furry with dehydration.

'The light!' said Meggen.

They both watched as the outside world blinked. The tank was moving very slowly.

Bannick got up and flung back the turret. Freezing mist greeted him. The tank's running lights and search-lights refracted in the mist, lighting up the space around them but limiting visibility as surely as if they were in a white-walled room.

'Kill the lights!' hissed Bannick into his vox.

Meggen switched off the search-light. A second later the headlights went out.

Grey dark engulfed Bannick suffocatingly.

Above, where the mist thinned, the flashes came again. Quiet sonic booms, muffled by the cloying fog, reached his ears. Meggen popped his head up.

'What's that? Orbital bombardment? There's nothing out here.'

'The highway's not far,' said Bannick.

'Why would we fire on our own men?'

Bannick was quiet, thinking. The rumble and squeaking of the tank was loud in the mist. 'We're one hundred and eighty minutes from our goal. Perhaps someone in the column has an idea what's happening.'

They hit a steep slope. Shoam pushed on. On the map the contour lines marked out the moors as a huge bulge that stopped suddenly at an escarpment, down which they now went. It levelled off quickly, and the rough pasture of the higher ground gave way once more to fields, hedges and small roads. The Baneblade rolled over them all. The mist thinned, but did not lift. When the sun rose it came as a blur in the east, becoming a pale circle as it climbed. In its light, the mist changed, taking on strange hues.

'Can anyone smell perfume? Ganlick said the air filter here was bust, didn't he?' said Kalligen.

'Probably some local phenomenon – plant pollen, something like that,' said Meggen.

'Put your respirators on, just the same,' Epperaliant ordered. 'Leonates, you distribute them.'

The crew groaned. Leonates got up from his station and pulled the respirators from the net slings around the tank's walls. One was passed up through the turret ring to Meggen and on to Bannick.

'We should be coming up to the road in a moment,' Bannick said.

Sure enough, the gantry of a road sign loomed flatly out of the fog. The road was significant, four lanes built onto an embankment that raised it over the level of the fields. It was empty of traffic.

With the sun finally burning off the last of the mist, Bannick scanned the revealed view with his magnoculars. A deserted, agricultural landscape spread out into the distance. The dome of the higher land stepped up almost imperceptibly to the southwest. There was a bombed-out factory complex off a slip road a mile away. Further still a small town squatted in the black soot of its own ruination. A few broken-down groundcars and personal possessions scattered all along the road indicated that a flood of refugees had passed by, but the land was devoid of human souls, military or civilian.

'Epperaliant, try the short-range vox. Keep me patched in.'

'*Cortein's Honour*, Seventh Paragonian super-heavy, requesting contact. Come in.' The vox clicked. Only a hiss replied.

The second lieutenant tried several times while Bannick ran the magnoculars all around them.

'The column should have been here by now,' said Bannick.

'Maybe we missed them,' said Kalligen. 'They may have moved on.'

'There's no sign of them at all,' said Meggen. 'Usually our boys make a bit of a mess. All this is civilian junk. Col, sir, can we take these respirators off now? I hate them.'

'No. Leave it on. There's something on the air, gas maybe.'

Bannick let his magnoculars fall to his chest. 'There's a bridge two miles back down the road. Maybe it fell. Let's check it out. Shoam, about one hundred and eighty degrees. The rest of you, weapons free. There's something about this that's not right.'

CHAPTER SIXTEEN
HUNTED

Cortein's Honour proceeded at cautious pace towards the river. According to the maps, this was the same valley that ran beneath the western edge of hill seven-beta, but it had grown large. Fed by the many small gullies cutting into the high moor, where the main highway to Magor's Seat crossed it, the Drava had become a shallow river three hundred yards wide on a gravel bed. The road ran straight over it on a level deck supported upon plascrete piles, the escarpment that marked the beginning of the moors brooding over it all.

'All halt!' called Bannick. They stopped at the edge of the bridge. He leaned forwards. 'The middle's gone.' At the far side he saw vehicles standing idle. A look through his field glasses revealed them to be wrecks surrounded by bodies.

'Back back!' he called. He looked for movement across the river. 'Ambush.'

'There might be survivors, sir,' said Epperaliant.

'Get *Cortein's Honour* off the bridge. We'll ford the river.'

Shoam guided the tank off the road, crushing its barriers, and down the embankment. The river was edged with rockcrete near the bridge, so they drove to where sandy banks took over, the tank jolting as it dropped down onto the gravel of the bed. 'Secure all lower hatches!' ordered Bannick. Shoam never cracked his so much as an inch, but Kalligen liked his open. It clanged shut.

Peaty water surged over the Baneblade's glacis in a blunt wave as it pushed on to the far side. The bridge had been blown in the middle, a neat job that had collapsed twenty yards of it into the water.

Meggen emerged from his hatch to look it over.

'Demo charges,' he said. 'That's too clean for a cannon hit.' He grasped the heavy stubber's handles lightly.

They emerged on the far side, the tank heaving itself up the bank and coming down hard.

'Halt!' said Bannick.

'Emperor's Throne,' said Kalligen.

Across the highway were hundreds of dead bodies, already beginning to swell in the warm sun. Black-feathered avians hopped and squabbled over the choicest morsels. Knocked-out tanks and personnel transports were all over the road.

'Forwards, Shoam, three hundred yards. Take us parallel to the highway.'

There was not one survivor. Many had been blown apart.

'Mass-reactives killed these men, not las-beams,' said Meggen.

'Gollph, Vaskigen, with me. Bring your small arms.'

Meggen ducked back into the tank. He came back a

moment later with a lascarbine that he handed to Bannick. Bannick unfolded its stock and checked the powercell.

Gollph and Vaskigen climbed out of the rear hatch.

'Now can we take our respirators off?' asked Meggen.

Bannick nodded. After the foul smell of the breathing mask, the air was gloriously sweet. There was no scent upon it, however.

'Keep your eyes open,' Bannick said. 'If you see anything suspicious, obliterate it.'

'Aye, sir,' said Meggen.

Bannick clambered off the tank. Its engine idled quietly behind them. The turret motors whined as the cannon tracked across the river and back. The three tankers ducked low and ran along in the shelter of the embankment. They stopped and risked looking over the barrier. The road surface was hidden by an unbroken slick of sticky blood. Flies rose in clouds at the tankers' movements.

'Ambush, for sure,' said Vaskigen. 'Look, lead and rear tanks taken out. Blocks the road. Then they killed the ones in the middle,' he said, pointing out the vehicles wrecked in the act of driving off down the embankment. 'I saw this a lot fighting the eldar back before Kalidar. You know, it wasn't that much different to fighting them on Agritha. Hit and run. I can't see any of theirs.'

'Who do this?' said Gollph. 'Geratomrans not fight well, except yellow men.'

'Could it be the eldar?' said Vaskigen. 'Word is they've been raiding this whole sub-sector, taking advantage of the crusade drawing off so many men and all. Agritha wasn't alone.'

Bannick looked over the dead men's cratered flesh. 'I don't know. These wounds look like bolt blasts, like

Meggen said. We're not going to know until we find an enemy corpse.'

'Maybe they took them all back. When eldar win, that's what they do.'

'Eldar bad men?' asked Gollph.

'Eldar aren't men at all,' said Vaskigen.

They went further. Bannick checked their distance to the tank. Sixty yards now. He was on the verge of ordering them back when Gollph touched his arm and pointed.

An outsized, armoured hand stretched out from behind a Chimera's hull.

Bannick put his fingers to his lips and beckoned them forwards.

They crept round the edge of the Chimera.

A giant lay slain on the far side. It was seven feet tall, clad in violently pink-and-purple armour, an archaic looking boltgun decorated with leering faces lying at its side. A ring of dead men surrounded it. Bannick raised his gun and pointed it at the giant's helm lens. Bolt casings tinkled across the road as his feet nudged them.

'Adeptus Astartes!' said Vaskigen. 'Have you ever seen one in such armour? What's he doing here?'

They looked around, fanning out without consultation.

'Here is another,' said Gollph quietly.

'And a third,' said Bannick. 'There, one of their transports, a Rhino.' He nodded towards a squat armoured personnel carrier, whose lurid paint had been stripped away by fire.

'That looks like it's been hit by a battle cannon,' said Vaskigen. 'I don't understand. Were they fighting our men? Is this some kind of mistake?'

'The fire of brother on brother. I have heard of it

happening,' said Bannick. He approached one of the corpses. 'I do not recognise these symbols. And look, this one bears a necklace of skulls.'

Gollph looked at them. 'We tell story on our world. Time when Sky Emperor make His mightiest son chief of all the others, and is rewarded by betrayal. Heaven shook for many years, and when it was done, the Emperor's son was dead and many worlds lost. Is why Bosovar alone for so long, so the elders say.'

'The legend of Horus,' breathed Bannick.

'Traitor Space Marines? Legiones Astartes?' said Vaskigen, his ordinarily bluff manner replaced by horror.

'Come on,' said Bannick. 'Let's get back. We should leave this place. Now.'

They jogged back, scaring up flocks of cawing avians from their meals.

'Listen!' said Gollph.

They halted. Bannick heard nothing but the chuckle of the river over its stony bed, laughing at the slaughter.

Gollph darted off towards a mound of dead men. He waved frantically. 'This one alive!'

They ran away from the road. A man lay close to death, his face bloody and all four limbs crooked at unnatural angles. He was saying something, but his lips were cracked and his words were so hoarse as to be inaudible.

Vaskigen leaned in close. Gollph's eyes widened and he grabbed his arm. 'No.'

'What?' said Vaskigen angrily. 'This man needs help! He's a son of our world. Let go.'

Gollph gripped him hard. 'On our world, bad men leave bad presents on bodies of captured braves. We be careful.'

'I thought you were changing, Gollph. I thought you

weren't such a savage feral basdack any more,' said Vaskigen harshly. 'Looks like I was wrong.'

He shook Gollph off.

'Vaskigen!' shouted Gollph.

Vaskigen stepped forwards. Gollph jumped back and
knocked Bannick off his feet as an explosion blasted the
first loader into pieces.

'No, no, no!' said Gollph.

Close by, Bannick heard engines revving.

'Come on, come on!'

'He was my friend!' said Gollph. 'Why did he not listen?'

'Come on!' said Bannick.

He grabbed the feral man's wrist and tugged him to his
feet. The engine noise grew louder.

'Run!' Meggen shouted from the top of the tank. 'They're
coming!'

'We're leaving!' said Bannick into the vox pick-up of
his headset.

Cortein's Honour's engines rumbled. Another engine
answered, then another.

Gollph and Bannick scrambled up onto the Baneblade
as three light tanks burst onto the road half a mile away,
moving at speed.

'Get in!' he shouted, throwing himself up onto the turret and diving head first into the cupola as bolter fire rang
off the front of the Baneblade. 'Three Predator-class Adeptus Astartes light battle tanks coming in fast. Shoam, full
reverse! All weapons, open fire! Keep them back.'

Bannick turned around awkwardly and put his head
up out of the turret. Bolts buzzed past, one blowing
apart on the open hatch and peppering his skin with
microshrapnel. He yanked the turret hatch down and

peered out of the glass viewing blocks set all around the hatch ring.

'Back up, back up!'

The Predators were smaller than *Cortein's Honour*, but they were much faster. They fired as they came, lascannons decorated with leering gargoyle mouths spitting ruby light. They were terrifyingly accurate, the las-fire scorching the armour of *Cortein's Honour* all around the turret. Two of the tanks split, heading for the wounded side of the Baneblade. The Paragonians' remaining lascannon turret fired, but went well wide. 'Calm down, Leonates! Take your time. They're trying to pull the tank's fangs and trying to flank us. Don't let them, Shoam.'

'No, sir,' said Shoam, the first Bannick had heard from him in a day and a half. 'Savlar like to die just about as much as you do.'

Beams pumped out from the enemy lascannon as Leonates tried to home in on the tanks, but he kept missing.

'Do not fire so wildly,' said Kolios. 'You risk the power shunts.'

Bannick could taste it, the fear on them. They were not facing other men, or orks, or eldar, but the Emperor's finest creations, creatures bred for war. To be in combat against them was a man's worst nightmare.

Bannick looked back. The river was a hundred yards away from them. The tank reversed as quickly as it could towards it. It shook as it barged a vehicle wreck out of the way.

'Right stick, right stick!' shouted Bannick. 'You're taking us up the embankment. If we get caught on the bridge we're dead. Get us in the river! Let the water slow them down and even things up.'

'I am disengaging the safety guard on the reactor. Diverting extra power to the engine. Be warned, this will anger the spirit of *Cortein's Honour*,' said Kolios. There was fear in him too, no matter how hard he attempted to mask it.

The metal of the tank vibrated. *Cortein's Honour* roared.

The *thwack-boom* of the demolisher sounded. A cone of soil burst in front of one of the Traitor Space Marine tanks.

'Basdack!' shouted Kalligen as the tank rolled neatly around it, guns unswervingly tracking the Baneblade. Besides the two lascannons mounted in their turrets, the tanks all had another pair in sponsons. They were dedicated tank hunters, outfitted to destroy enemy armour.

'Dammit,' growled Meggen. 'That's a lot of lascannons.'

'Heavy bolter! Take out their sensors! Aim for their targeting arrays,' yelled Bannick. 'Buy some time! Meggen! Hold fire! We're damaged, let's make them think our cannon is malfunctioning, draw them in. When we drop down the bank, they'll have to follow if they want to be sure of catching us. I want you ready to blast one of them apart.'

'Aye, sir! Gollph, send us up an AP shell, double quick.' He slammed the eject, shunting the unfired shell out of the breach. The shell lift wound up, bringing up a quartet of blue-tipped shells. Meggen helped the auto-loader slam the round home. Leonates shouted in triumph as his weapons hammered a Predator's sponson-mounted augur array. The soulless glass eye shattered in its housing, spewing sparks. The lascannon sagged in its cowl, caught on the ground and was ripped off.

Still the tanks had many teeth. Endless rounds of las-fire hissed into the front of the Baneblade, scoring the metal with molten furrows. The tanks' turrets smoothly tracked

Cortein's Honour as they split. Bannick ducked as one of the turret windows smashed and melted armourglass dripped into the cupola. The tank's armour was proof against the lascannons, but there were so many vulnerable areas. If they hit the treads or got behind the Baneblade and fired on the engine block, or managed to take out Shoam, they were dead.

'Damn it! Into the river!' When he looked again, the Predators were closing fast. One of the two on the right ran up the embankment onto the road. The other pursued them closely, while the third, on the left, came in wide, pummelling the side of the tank. Leonates yelled in fright as his left-hand sponson blew, the bolter ammunition inside spraying off in corkscrewing fireworks.

'I'm down to the heavy bolters in the right turret, sir. They're not responding well.'

'They're out of my fire arc, sir,' reported Kalligen.

The two Predators on the right were drawing near, the third a quarter of a mile away and coming parallel to their left flank. All of them were out of the demolisher's fire arc.

'Where's the river?' said Shoam, who was driving blind.

'Keep going! We're nearly there. Slow down on my mark, or we'll come down too hard and submerge the exhaust. Everyone brace!'

The tank's rear tracks hit the bank. A natural levee had built up there, and the Baneblade jounced over it. *Cortein's Honour* slithered down the bank into the water, the over-heated engine bringing forth clouds of steam. Bannick held his breath as the bow tilted up, exposing the tank's underbelly for a dangerous second. They slipped into the river unharmed.

'Now, Meggen, track thirty left!'

As *Cortein's Honour* levelled off, the lead Predator, the one on the left, cleared the levee, bouncing down after them. Meggen held his fire.

'Fire!' said Bannick.

'Not yet, not yet, not yet!'

The second Predator cleared the bank on the right, tipping forwards to expose its weaker top armour.

'That one!' shouted Meggen, putting the battle cannon shell through the turret. Fire flashed inside. The tank stopped dead, black smoke pouring from every aperture.

'One down!' yelled Meggen.

'Sir, the third tank is taking up position on the bridge overlooking the river,' called Epperaliant, who was rushing from viewing port to viewing port on the command deck.

'Bring us in closer to the piers, Shoam. Cut into its firing angle.'

'What about the third tank?' said Leonates. 'It's drawing alongside!'

'Kalligen, get on it. Shoam, fifteen degrees left. Keep Kalligen in line.'

At first the Predator pulled forwards, but as the water deepened, the more powerful engines of the Baneblade won out, and they began to make distance on it. As they moved by, it unleashed a furious fusillade against the left side of *Cortein's Honour*. Tocsins rang below. Lesser alarms peeped with infuriating insistence. A ruby las-beam scored the air from above.

'Meggen, put a round across that thing's bow.'

'Aye aye,' said Meggen. The main cannon boomed. The angle was hard and Meggen missed. A massive chunk of rockcrete blew out of the bridge.

'Again!' Bannick looked behind them. They were coming

in on a shallow oblique line at the bridge. 'Shoam, when I give the order, hard reverse left, full ninety degrees. Kalligen, get ready.'

Meggen's second round took the bridge underneath, putting a hole in the deck.

'Basdack! I cannot get a bead on it from here.'

'Stop firing,' said Bannick.

The third Predator was out of sight.

'I think it's falling back,' said Epperaliant.

'Keep eyes on it,' ordered Bannick. The shadow of the bridge moved over the turret.

'Now! Now, Shoam!'

Shoam yanked the left stick backwards and pushed the right forwards. The Baneblade moaned at the sudden change in direction. Water churned audibly against the hull as tracks spun on loose gravel, and it turned to the left.

'Full reverse!' yelled Bannick. Shoam drove it back into the shelter of the bridge. 'Meggen, bring the turret around, cover the rear, depress main gun full!'

'Turret around, depressing main gun full!' he shouted. The Baneblade retreated into the shelter of the bridge.

Whichever side the Predator came at them, it would be facing down the barrel of a main armament. Not even the Space Marines could survive that.

But they did not come. Seconds ticked by, becoming minutes.

'They're Space Marines. They're not going for this,' Bannick said to himself nervously. Noise in the tank died away. A tense silence reigned.

'They're coming from the rear!' shouted Epperaliant.

'And the front!' said Bannick, seeing the snarling muzzle

of a lascannon emerge around the pier. 'Kalligen! Meggen! Fire! Fire! Fire!'

The third Predator had come off the bridge and out-flanked them, coming in from the rear. The first attempted a dash to the left side of the tank, but Kalligen caught it square on.

The Predator exploded outwards, the force of the demol-isher blast enough to burst the armour asunder and shock the Baneblade itself. Red-hot shards of metal hissed into the water.

The battle cannon boomed half a second later. The shell glanced off the Predator's angled turret armour and went whooshing away over the river.

'Basdack! Armour's thick!'

Through the clouds of exhaust smoke and steam pour-ing up around the engine block, Bannick saw the Predator turning so it could bring all four of its weapons to bear on their vulnerable back end. Three of them were already hammering the Baneblade.

'Shoam! Full reverse, now!'

The engine roared. The Baneblade slammed back into the Predator's bow. It fired wildly, catching the Bane-blade's right-side auxiliary fuel drums and causing them to detonate. A ball of flame washed over both tanks. The Predator was pushed backwards towards deeper water. Tracks churning the river cloudy, it slipped down the edge of gravel bank. With a throaty, bellowing roar, the Bane-blade upended it, pushing it onto its side, then over onto its roof.

'Forwards!' yelled Bannick.

Still dripping burning promethium, the super-heavy pulled off from the Predator. Nosing the wreck of the other Space Marine vehicle out of the way, it pulled out into the river from under the bridge. The rear ramp of the Predator was being forced open from inside. A pair of bare-headed crewmen, trailing hard-wired interface cables, staggered out.

'Meggen! The crew are bailing. See to it they don't get far.'

'Already on it, Col,' said Meggen.

A final cannon shot rang, punching through side of the Predator. Hatches blew as it detonated. The rear ramp flipped off and flew free, skimming over the river's surface. The Space Marines were thrown forwards, disappearing into the water as fire rushed over them. Bannick doubted very much that it would be enough to finish them, but there would be little they could do to harm the Bane-blade without their tank.

'That's it, that's the last of them. Well done, crew,' said Bannick.

Whoops of relief sounded through the tank. As it pushed on back over the river, Bannick kissed his amulets, then placed his hand gently on the rim of his cupola in thanks.

'And praise to the Emperor and Omnissiah,' he said to *Cortein's Honour*.

CHAPTER SEVENTEEN
A NEW ENEMY

ASTRA MILITARUM CASTELLA, MAGOR'S FIELDS,
THE NORTA GREAT PLAIN
GERATOMRO
087398.M41

Cortein's Honour limped into camp some six hours later.
What should have been a stronghold to launch the final
subjugation of a world had become a fortress under siege.
Artillery fire fell sporadically around the perimeter. Overhead, the sky flashed with low-orbital burn up: debris
and munitions, the fall out of void war. The fleet was
under attack.

Bannick looked overhead at the flashing sky. Brilliant
stars fell, orbital bombardment shells keeping back the
enemy from the camp. Twenty kilometres away the capital city of Magor's Seat squatted darkly, its towering
spires spindly in the distance. The multiple rocket flares
of descending ships lit a trail from orbit to the planet's
main landing fields.

He directed the Baneblade up a river of mud masquerading

as a road to a gate in the prefabricated rockcrete walls. A gate was set there, flanked by two octagonal concrete bunkers hiding behind heaps of sandbags. The sergeant-at-arms, a Cadian, came out at their approach.

'You're with the Paragonian's Seventh super-heavy?' he called up.

Bannick looked at the man humourlessly. The company emblem, number and the tank's name were all emblazoned on the sides clearly enough that they showed through mud and battle damage.

'You can stare at me all you want, sir,' said the soldier. 'I'm asking because you're supposed to be dead.'

'We're not,' said Bannick

'I can see that. I'm glad, if you care.' He pointed through the gate. 'Your company's on road twenty-one, of the Principia.'

'I know where road twenty-one is,' said Bannick. Most Imperial Guard camps followed a standard pattern, as dictated by the Tactica Imperialis. The Baneblade growled, sharing his annoyance, and rolled into the camp.

It hadn't rained all day but the ground was saturated from the prior downpours, and churned to a sticky, viscous bog. Men ran along lightweight aluminium duckboards bordering the tents, but even these were sinking into the ooze. When the Baneblade turned onto road XXI, it pushed a slow wave of muck up onto the pavements. No shouts of annoyance followed them; instead cheers rang out as the news spread that the tank had survived. There were only seven super-heavy tanks in the whole of the Paragonian contingent. The loss of one had severely dented morale. The reappearance of *Cortein's Honour* brought forth jubilation among the harried Astra Militarum.

A hollow square delineated by tents was the temporary marshalling yard of the Seventh. Slender towers of tubular aluminium supported by tensioned hawsers and topped with floodlights stood at each corner. A large command tent occupied the south-eastern corner. Most of the usual support vehicles were absent, but all three of the other super-heavy tanks sat idle, side by side.

First Gunner Rollen of *Artemen Ultrus* was on guard, sitting glumly on a plastek barrel at the junction of the yard and road XXI. By the time Bannick ordered Shoam into the yard, Rollen was on his feet, craning his neck to watch the tank's turret sail through the sea of tents.

'You've not left us room to park!' shouted Bannick down to Rollen.

'We thought you were dead. Dead men don't need a spot.'

Crewmen were climbing from the other tanks and emerging from tents. Their cheers joined those of the men outside.

'Bannick! You're alive. We feared the worst,' said Marteken from the top of his own vehicle. He held a steaming mug of recaff in his hand, his shirt off and shaving foam all over his face. Bannick saluted him.

The tech-priests came out from behind *Artemen Ultrus*. Brasslock slogged his way through the mud, his robes already filthy with it.

'What have you done to my charge?' said Brasslock wheezily.

'Everything I could to keep it alive,' said Bannick. 'I opted to cut across country to rejoin the advance at the River Drava, but we arrived to find only the dead. Hundreds killed.'

'What happened to the tank?'

'A hit from a Destroyer, then an encounter with a hunting pack of tank killers. Don't worry, Marteken, you won't have to face them. We killed them all for you.'

'Now that's a relief,' shouted Marteken. 'I'll go back to my shave then.'

Bannick clambered out of his hatch and walked across the front of the tank, jumping down in front of Brasslock.

'A Destroyer?' said Brasslock, with as much excitement as Bannick had ever heard him exhibit. 'You secured it, I trust? Such vehicles are a rare prize.'

'I am sorry, Magos. It lies in pieces atop hill seven-beta.' He rested a hand on Brasslock's shoulder. Brasslock gave it a sidelong glance. 'Where is Hannick?'

'Hannick is here, honoured lieutenant. You're late!' said Hannick.

Bannick saluted the captain and walked over to join him. In daylight Hannick looked worse than ever, his skin was sallow, and he leaned heavily on a cane.

'Good to see you, Colaron,' he said.

'You likewise, sir.' He looked around nervously, sure what he was about to say was blasphemy. 'Our attackers. I have never seen anything like it. They were Space Marines.'

'The treachery of Geratomro grows daily. They have petitioned the oldest of the Imperium's foes for aid, and they have answered.'

'I thought such things were myths.'

Hannick spoke softly. 'They are not. A long war has been waged by them, millennia old, and we find ourselves caught up in it.' He looked up and smiled. 'Get yourself cleaned up as best you can. I've had orders from high command. Briefing in twenty minutes.'

'Where is our support group?' asked Bannick. He could not see their wheeled shrine, service vehicles and engin-seers in the yard.

'Lost. We must do what we can with what we have, Colaron.'

Honoured Lieutenants Marteken, Hurnigen and Bannick joined Honoured Captain Hannick in the Seventh's com-mand centre. Hannick had managed to secure a flat-pict tac table. A few flimsy folding tables and chairs made up the rest of the furnishings. The day had darkened with thick cloud that brought chill and gloom. A lone lumoglobe buzzed noisily at the apex of the tent, where bewildered bugs battered their faces against it. The sound of covering orbital fire was constant.

'I am sorry about the space, gentlemen,' said Hannick, gesturing at the open sides of their tent. 'I'll keep the briefing, well, brief. Our enemy has wasted no time.' He pushed a pile of papers to the side of the tac table and keyed its activation stud with his company signet. The pict screen embedded in the ornate surface ignited, showing blurry, low-definition imagery. 'High command relayed news of an incoming hostile fleet at twenty-three twelve last night to me. The enemy came in line of battle, direct from the sun and in the blindside of the planet, evad-ing augur detection until the last. They engaged the fleet shortly after, deploying simultaneously to the surface by drop pod and gunship in the teeth of our fire.'

'Emperor,' muttered Marteken.

'They are Space Marines, no matter what wicked mas-ter they might follow now,' said Hannick. 'They launched attacks immediately, cutting off our line of reinforcements coming from the south. That's what you saw, Bannick. From your experience we can deduce they've left ambush units behind to pick off stragglers, intelligence I have passed on to high command. We pushed on ahead of the advance as instructed. We missed the ambush, a shame, as our presence may have tipped the encounter in our favour. We can only assume that the majority of our on-planet supplies, the lower tech-adepts, recovery tanks, mobile manufactoria and the rest were caught up in the slaughter. That brings me to my first point – we must conserve our supplies. Spares and replacement parts, ammunition for our larger guns, these things will be hard to come by for the foreseeable future. There will be no resupply while the fleets are engaged. Their fleet is small, but fast. Ours holds station above us here.' He tapped the scratched glass of the table. A red circle pulsed over the castella. 'Theirs is here, over Magor's Seat. As you can appreciate, this is no distance at all when it comes to void war. The fleets are fighting at what is, for them, point-blank range. Our ships are taking something of a pounding. If they move, our camp here will be obliterated from orbit. However, we expect that as soon as the enemy fleet has deployed all ground force assets, they will withdraw. They are swift and cunning and heavily armed, but the size of their craft makes their fleet ill-suited to a protracted firefight.'

'How many are there on the ground?' said Bannick.

'The Emperor alone knows. High command does not know exactly what we're facing. Traitor Space Marines for sure. Maybe other assets. Are there one hundred, a thousand? Ten thousand? Our forces number in the region of five million in and around Geratomro, but Iskhandrian's lightning war, which had us so close to victory, has left us spread out and vulnerable. One of the Traitor Space Marines is worth fifty normal men in open battle, and they're not playing that game. They continue to employ hit-and-run attacks all over the continent. Our supply lines are being targeted, as are units on the march from the subdued cities. It is only a matter of time before they begin to isolate and retake the cities we have fought so far to reconquer.'

Hannick coughed, a short fit that the others politely waited through. They always began short, and became more severe. Hannick sped up his briefing before he was overcome.

'And there's worse. An Ark Mechanicus of some kind accompanies their fleet. Even a sizeable Space Marine fleet could have deployed in Magor's Seat and withdrawn in under a few hours. High command is certain they're in a holding pattern directly opposing our own fleet because they're landing something else, something big.'

The lieutenants looked at one another.

'Engines?' said Marteken. 'Traitor war engines? First, Traitor Space Marines, and now, Traitor Titans, Traitor Mechanicus?'

'There is a danger we'll be facing Traitor Titans.' Hannick coughed again, a worse fit. The lieutenants pretended not to see the blood on his handkerchief when he dabbed at his mouth. 'In fact, high command think this so likely that we've been ordered to reorganise. On this planet we have a grand total of two engines of our own – not a true force of the Titan Legions. A show to cow those Planetary Governors who haven't quite got the guts to go the whole way like Huratal has. The Warhound *War's Gift*, and the Reaver-class *Ultimate Sanction*. If there are enemy engines, they will need support. Therefore, with immediate effect, the Lucky Eights, the Eighteenth Atraxian and the Seventh Paragonian will be split and temporarily reorganised in group Epsilon and Ultra. Under my command, Epsilon will consist of *Ostrakhan's Rebirth*, *Artemen Ultrus* and the Atraxian Baneblade *Fidellius* and Stormsword *Refutation of Sin*. We will be supported by the Eighth's *War Forged* and *Saint Josef*. Our role will be to lead the spearhead into Magor's Seat in an attempt to cut the head off this rebellion.

'Group Ultra will comprise *Lux Imperator*. It is to join the Eighteenth Atraxian's Shadowswords *Indominus* and *World Burner* under Lieutenant Askelios – he's liaison with the Atraxians. Ultra will be led by Honoured Captain Parrigar and the *Righteous Vengeance* from the Eights. He's in overall charge, but Askelios is the man to listen to when it comes to shooting war engines. Ultra will begin the engagement concealed here to the east, well out of the line of attack, and is to work in close conjunction with Princeps Gonzar and Princeps Yolanedesh. Their plan is to draw the enemy engines from the city, where they might be flanked and brought down by our Shadowswords.'

'Titan hunting,' said Hurnigen, a gleam in his eye.

'And us, sir?' asked Marteken. 'Can you give us any more specifics at this time?'

'We're going right for the heart of Magor's Seat. There's a void shield up around the palace that has to come down. We're to lead the spearhead to take the generatoria. We need to finish this quickly. If we let the Traitor Space Marines establish themselves here, we'll be fighting this war for decades. It'll be a close fight, but it needs to be done.'

'What about *Cortein's Honour*, sir?' said Bannick with rising dismay. 'We can get it up and ready for battle again within five hours.'

'Not according to Brasslock.'

'Brasslock is wrong.'

'You will not be at full operational status,' said Hannick. 'Without full communications you'll be sitting kree birds ready for the poacher's gun. I won't send a wounded tank into battle just to lose it.'

'Sir!'

'Don't worry, Bannick. You'll get your fight.'

'Sir?'

Hannick took in a rasping breath and looked at the table. 'Bannick, I want you and whatever of your crew you see fit on *Lux*. You are to join group Ultra. Hurnigen, you are to remain here.'

'But, sir!' protested Hurnigen.

'Bannick has experience facing Titan-class engines, thanks to that scuffle back on Kalidar. You have not. He also has more experience working with the Atraxians. Furthermore, you are injured.'

'But I have the training. Bannick's never been in the–'

'Experience has the edge,' said Hannick. 'Bannick is a veteran super-heavy tanker of the war against the orks. As newest member of this company, you are not. I–' He lapsed into a coughing fit so severe that Marteken fetched a chair, folded it out and put it behind him. Hannick gratefully sat in it and doubled over. The coughs this time lasted more than a minute. 'Those are my orders, Hurnigen,' he gasped.

'I'll take Meggen, Epperaliant, Leonates and Shoam,' said Bannick.

'Epperaliant is injured too!' protested Hurnigen. 'And Meggen.'

'Neither of them are as badly hurt as you are,' said Bannick. 'Meggen's cut was shallow and is well on the way to mended. Epperaliant won't be left behind.'

'Sir!' said Hurnigen.

'I'll need Starstan, of course,' said Bannick.

'You'll not take one of my men apart from the tech-priest?' said Hurnigen. 'Are you trying to insult me?'

'No. Your men are good fighters,' said Bannick. 'But it is my crew's ability to work as a team that is paramount. To mix crews now when we do not have to would be foolhardy. However, a Shadowsword needs an enginseer.'

Hannick nodded, and slowly stood again, leaning for support on the tac table. 'If that's what Bannick wants, that's the way it has to be, Hurnigen. I'm inclined to agree with him. You're a main gunner down, and Shoam is a fine driver.'

Hurnigen's face went tight, but he nodded.

'You'll be here, Hurnigen. I need you to liaise with the Munitorum adepts, the Eighteenth's support units, whoever, to scrape together whatever you can to keep our tanks firing and in the field.'

'Yes, sir,' said Hurnigen, standing to attention and staring ahead, his jaw clenched.

'There's more you men need to be made aware of. An inquisitor arrived this morning on a sloop, a tiny little ship, but fast. Inquisitor Lord Militant Vesh, he's called. He's attached himself to Iskhandrian, which shores up the general's position, but he has begun issuing orders of his own. There will be commissars arriving to be attached to each unit for the duration of this war. I heard a rumour,

not that you should give credence to it, that they fear
corruption from the foe. Expect at least two or three per
squadron.'

'That's... unusual,' said Marteken.

'These are unusual times. Fighting men is one thing,
transhumans is another. The danger these traitors pose
goes beyond their martial power. You must be vigilant,
and you must be pure. Make no mistake, these are the
most terrible enemies we could face. You might think
them ogres from fairy tales, but what you might have
heard is one hundred times worse in reality.'

The tank commanders nodded gravely. 'Yes, sir,' they
said in unison.

Hannick looked them each in the eye, giving them a solemn look that imparted the seriousness of the situation
far more effectively than words could ever manage. 'You
have your orders, gentlemen. Prepare your crews. We are
to deploy at oh-six-hundred hours. You need to get some
food and rest. Get to it.'

The honoured lieutenants saluted.

'Bannick, a moment.'

Hurnigen walked out stiffly, then Marteken. Bannick
waited.

'Sir?'

'There is a further reason I have removed Hurnigen from
command of *Lux Imperator*. Sit.' He gestured to a chair.
Bannick took to it. Its back legs sank into the soft mud.
'Brasslock tells me that the machine-spirit of *Lux Imperator*
is unhappy. Some nonsense about its soul being stained
by the treatment it underwent at the hands of the orks
on Kalidar.'

'Sir...'

'Bannick, we're both from Paragon. We make machines on Paragon. And while I am willing to believe that there is perhaps a spark of life in the more sophisticated mechanisms, I do not believe that pistons and bolt-shell racks and so forth come together in spiritual union to form a gestalt entity with a will of its own. The Emperor is a god I know exists, but the Omnissiah? Let the tech-priests cling to their religion. We've enough experience back home to know a lasgun will fire just as well whether it was sung to during assembly or whether it was not.'

'Sir,' warned Bannick. His hand went unconsciously to his twin pendants.

'It's bad enough that we let the machines choose the crew,' he said with a speculative look at Bannick. 'Anyway,' Hannick said hoarsely. 'Brasslock believes there is a disconnect between Hurnigen and the tank, that *Lux* chose him while it was still shaken after Kalidar, and that they lack sympathetic resonance or something. Brasslock says *Lux* no longer trusts him. Maybe it would were it not so traumatised, as he puts it. But to regain its fire it needs someone of a different quality. According to Brasslock, that person is you.'

'What does Starstan say?'

'He beeped at me for a while. As far as I could tell, he was worried. I assume that means that Brasslock is right. Prove to the adepts that *Lux* will function in battle. Then Brasslock will be happy and Hurnigen can go back to his command. But I have to say I am glad that you are going to be there with the Atraxians rather than he, if I am completely honest. You'll be working on your own with non-Paragonians and forge-worlders. You're better suited to that than he is. He's stuck in his ways and can be prickly. Let the Emperor turn His face from me if I'm pleased to be bruising the man's pride because a machine said so. He's a good officer, just a little young.'

'He's older than me,' said Bannick.

'You know what I mean. A man's wisdom cannot always be measured in years.'

Hannick coughed again. There was a moment of silence when he finished, then came the boom of artillery, very close.

'They're firing the big guns.'

'From within the camp,' said Hannick. 'Not ideal but if they were out of the fleet's protective umbrella they'd be gone in seconds.'

'They're targeting the city?'

'The ones with the range. Forget about taking this planet with the minimum of human loss. All that's gone down the river. We're to take it as quickly as we can now. If we must smash it, so be it.'

The first shells and rockets were landing on Magor's Seat. The rumble of their explosions were just audible over the next salvo. The ground trembled.

Hannick's breath rattled in his chest. 'That'll be all, Bannick.'

Bannick stood and saluted. 'Sir?'

'Yes?'

'If you're so certain that the machines don't have spirits, then why do you make obeisance to them along with the tech-priests before battle?'

Hannick reached for a sheaf of paper covered in Astra Militarum and Departmento Munitorum symbols and began to flick through it. 'I'm a sceptic, Bannick. It doesn't mean I'm a bloody idiot. Always assume you could be wrong. Dismissed.'

The camp erupted into activity like a hive of social insects prodded by a stick. Men ran in all directions. Engines roared and grumbled. Orders were shouted, and platoons of soldiers marched in neat ranks down the sucking mud of the streets. Priests were everywhere, wailing and singing, processions of icon-bearing acolytes trailing in their wake. In the marshalling yard of the Seventh, men hurried about. Hurnigen might not have liked his orders, but he set to them after the briefing with a will. A steady trickle of invaluable supplies came into the yard. The clouds cleared before evening. Darkness fell and the spot-lumens atop their spindly towers came on, bathing the yard in hard light that threw the churned mud into stark relief, so that it resembled the scarred terrain of a battleground in miniature. The sky flashed with orbital weapons discharge.

Bannick was checking over the cannon on *Lux Imperator* when the latest batch of supplies arrived. Hurnigen rode a trailer pulled by a small, tracked tractor piloted by an integrated servitor. Another scrounged asset, borrowed from the enginseers attached to the 42nd. Meggen rode behind Hurnigen next to a pallet of battle cannon shells. Once, Bannick had had a crewmate who could find just about anything. He was from the same clan as Ganlick. Now they were both dead along with so many others.

The tractor pulled up alongside the Shadowsword. Hurnigen handed up a thick bundle of cabling.

'You'll need this,' he said. Bannick nodded his thanks and passed the cable up to Gollph. 'You will take care of *Lux* for me, Bannick?'

'Of course I will,' said Bannick.

Hurnigen gave a worried smile and ordered the servitor on. Meggen jumped down.

'Any news?'

'Nope,' said Meggen.

'You can go rest if you like, Meggen. We'll all need to be on our best tomorrow.'

'If it's all right with you, I'd like to go over the firing drill for the volcano cannon. It's been a while and this thing hasn't been playing nice with its operators recently.'

'Be my guest,' said Bannick. He followed Meggen into the tank through the main hatch on the roof of the hull, a large rectangle at the back. There were a few openings on the top, including a cupola hatch. The space where the gunner's hatch might go was occupied by a powerful ranging augur whose red glass eye shone with malevolent intent. A second, smaller augur unit was located over the cannon, into which it was directly plugged. There was only one other hatch on the body of the tank, over the driver's station. This lack of exit points made the marque unpopular with tank crews. If it was hit and caught fire, there was no way out.

The interior of the Shadowsword was even more closed than that of the Baneblade, being laid out across two cramped decks. Everything was built around the massive volcano cannon; much of the structure was taken up by the capacitors needed to power it. All this meant that there was little room available for the crew, which numbered seven to the Baneblade's ten. Upon the command deck were stations for the commander, commsman and third gunner. The Shadowsword was a design without a secondary armament. Paragonian sponson gunners all had the same rank

255

of third gunner no matter which vehicle they served on to equalise ranks. This custom was not employed by every world, but it was common enough. The communications and tactical desk was wrapped around the rear corner on the right-hand side, behind the commander, who had a dedicated, armoured viewing loop over his instruments. The cannon's huge refraction array took up most of the command floor. On the other side of that was the third gunner's station. Unlike on a Baneblade, the third gunner was expected to run both sponsons – and the bow gun if necessary – without the aid of a loader. To the rear was a square hatch that led into the bowels of the tank. Down in the centre of the hull were the powerful dynamo and giant capacitors that provided the energy to power the Titan-felling blasts of the volcano cannon.

The enginseer had a station behind the dynamo. His main duty was to control the switch between motive units and dynamo to charge the cannon. Unless the capacitors were already charged, the Shadowsword could either fire or move, but not both. In the bow was another compartment housing the driver and first gunner. The driver's station was raised up and at the opposite side to a Baneblade driver's, and he shared responsibilities with the third gunner and commander for the operation of the bow gun. As on a Baneblade, this was a twinned set of heavy bolters, although they were not mounted in a dedicated turret and therefore had a limited range of traversal. A Shadowsword was not expected to engage the enemy at close range, but still its array of supplementary weaponry was formidable. By the driver, the first gunner fought surrounded by specialised displays and ranging units, his seat set well below the level of the driver's chair.

The power feeds and tops of the capacitors could only be accessed via a number of removable plates in the command deck. These were currently up. Bannick and Meggen were therefore forced to brace themselves against the low ceiling as they stepped carefully from strut to strut, as one wrong move might result in electrocution. Bulky Adeptus Mechanicus diagnostic devices, plugged directly into the reactor couplings, provided further impediment to safe progress. A painful blue glow shone from the capacitor arrays. The interior was sharp with the tang of ozone.

Inside, Epperaliant manned the comms desk. Starstan and Brasslock worked side by side on the lower floor, their bulky, augmetic bodies an encumbrance in the tight spaces of the Shadowsword.

'Toggling quinternary auxiliary power bypass. Powering up augur arrays,' said Epperaliant. 'Sir,' he said when Bannick dropped through the commander's hatch.

'How are your wounds? If you wish to remain I will take Second Lieutenant Jinereen.'

'You wanted me, you shall have me, sir. My arm's a little sore, that's all. Skin's tight, but the medicae got some gel packs on there and the burns aren't too deep. I can use my arm. I was lucky. Not like Ganlick.'

'Good. I do need you, Epperaliant.'

'Ah, honoured lieutenant. You have come to gauge our progress?' Brasslock stood. His age and his odd, altered body should have made him the most uncomfortable of them all in the claustrophobic space, but he appeared more at ease inside the tank than out of it, despite the contortions he was obliged to adopt.

'I have.'

'Then I report that all is functioning as it should. The

rest is dependent on our prayers. Starstan and I go soon to begin the benedictions of rousing, to prepare the engines for war. Should we beseech *Lux Imperator* correctly, I judge we shall have no more problems, not with you at the helm.'

'I need to familiarise myself with *Lux*'s equipment,' said Bannick doubtfully.

'Trifling differences, honoured lieutenant. You will experience no difficulty.'

'I'd be more comfortable on *Cortein's Honour*.'

'*Lux* is grateful that you are aboard, and therefore so am I. You and it share a certain affinity. It will work for you.'

'Thank you. I am glad to have the tank's blessing. I would have thought the same of you, Brasslock, that you would work well with it, after what you both underwent. Why do you not serve aboard as the enginseer?'

'My position is higher than mere keeper of a single machine.' Bannick hid a smile. He had never heard Brasslock be so haughty. 'Even if it were permissible, the memory is too raw for both of us,' said Brasslock sadly. 'My presence only increases *Lux Imperator*'s sense of humiliation. Starstan is better suited. He and *Lux Imperator* have a long history together.'

Starstan twittered binaric, then remembered himself and switched to an ugly, machine-synthesised Gothic. 'We are both at your service, honoured lieutenant. May we together smite the enemies of mankind. Preferably at maximum range, where the weapons of this medium-weight tracked engine are best able to inflict damage without repercussion to continued functionality.'

'Indeed.' Bannick did not find Starstan's precise reply as amusing as he normally would, for the image of Brasslock pinned to a *Lux Imperator* mutilated by the orks flashed into his mind, and would not easily be banished. Bannick's face froze. Starstan was too far gone from the state of base humanity to notice the change in Bannick's expression, but Brasslock, who maintained a degree of empathy for men, did.

'Are you well, honoured lieutenant?' The movement of the enginseer's mechadendrites slowed, until they hung in the air and pointed at Bannick, giving him the uncomfortable sensation that they were watching him with eyes of their own.

'Yes, yes, too much to do. Always nervy before an engagement.'

'Cortein often was too,' said Brasslock kindly. 'Do you know what he used to do? He would go down to the Wall of Honour and–'

A deafening bang interrupted the conversation.

'What by the Emperor was that?' said Bannick. He went to the cupola and thrust his head out.

The night sky was ablaze. The storm of fire overhead between the two fleets had intensified. A number of booms and strange whooshing noises rolled out from the position of the fleet – atmospheric disturbance from falling munitions and debris. Bannick climbed out onto the tank roof, followed by Meggen and Epperaliant.

'That's it,' Hannick said from the centre of the marshalling yard. 'The enemy have finished their landing. The fleet is pulling back, as predicted. The situation should be a little easier for the rest of the night.'

They watched as tiny dots, no bigger than bright stars, retreated from geosynchronous orbit over the city. They flew towards the camp, and the exchange of orbital fire became more furious. Where stars should have shone was instead a riot of flashes and brilliant, intersecting hair-thin beams of the lance batteries. The short-lived blooms of atomic torpedoes and the brief stars of nova cannons brought instant dawns to the plains, then faded, leaving the men night-blind. The camp stopped what it was doing to watch the spectacular display.

'Like Zero Night back home,' said Kalligen.

'People don't die from fireworks,' said Epperaliant.

Balls of fire arced down from space.

'They're bombing us as they leave,' said Meggen.

'Our boys will get it,' said Epperaliant.

Heavy ordnance burst far above, intercepted by fleet cannon fire and interdiction missiles. They exploded prettily, showering burning debris into the atmosphere that burned up to nothing as it fell.

'They're coming in for an intercept in retreat,' said Hannick, walking over to *Lux*, his eyes fixed on the heavens. 'See, they're coming in for their close pass.' He pointed with his stick. 'Then they'll be pulling back into the void as they cross over our fleet.' Hannick sounded excited. 'This is a taste of victory to come. If the Traitor Space Marines are not numerous enough to tackle the fleet, then they will not prevail in a ground war either.'

But it was not over. The sky sheeted white, and men threw up their arms to cover their eyes. A globe of nuclear fire shone in the sky, brighter than a sun. Geratomro basked in a brief, violent noon.

'Ship death!' someone shouted. Bannick blinked, his eyes full of glaring dots.

'But whose side?' said Meggen.

The ship's remains fell out of the sky. A fiery trail bigger than any comet fall burned across the heavens. The ship had been broken into five or six major pieces, and they spread out as they plummeted. Smaller chunks of debris came loose, peeling off on their own parabolic trajectories as gravity and friction pulled at them. The ship fell rapidly, burning brighter. As it got halfway to the southern horizon, a mighty roaring emanated from it that drowned out all earthly sound. A series of booms crashed across the night as the ship burned its way onwards towards the horizon, and disappeared.

They watched. Two minutes, three. The blaze of fire in orbit was abating, the traitor fleet breaking off for interplanetary space. Bannick doubted there would be a pursuit. If the Navy gave chase, they would leave Geratomro wide open to bombardment.

The sky rumbled. There was a sound like thunder and a flash as the falling ship hit the planet a thousand miles away. The ground shook gently. The southern horizon shone with the fires of impact.

'And that is why the Navy will not fight close in to an inhabited world, given a choice,' said Hannick. 'Wherever that landed will be an inferno.' He looked southwards, where a giant column of smoke and dust was unfurling towards the heavens. 'Tomorrow will be a dark day.'

CHAPTER EIGHTEEN
TITAN HUNT

MAGOR'S FIELDS
GERATOMRO
087498.M41

The tanks of ad-hoc unit Ultra rumbled out of camp under dark and churning skies. A mixed unit from two worlds in three liveries. The Atraxian tanks were standard grey. *Lux Imperator* bore the angular tan-and-green camouflage pattern that it shared with the rest of the Seventh. The Stormlord *Righteous Vengeance* bore similar colours in a different pattern. All identification was obscured by the thick, black rain that poured from the sky, bringing with it the ejecta thrown up by the crashed spacecraft: a slurry of ash, earth and atomised bodies. Curtains of it cut down visibility to a few hundred yards, and the tanks could proceed only with the aid of their augur systems. Their headlamps were masked to prevent their detection, and the slitted covers lit only a slice of the rain. Upon the fighting deck of *Righteous Vengeance*, Bannick could just make out the shapes of huddled soldiers. They'd thrown up a tarpaulin to protect themselves from the toxic down-pour, but Bannick doubted it would do them much good. Jonas was up there, somewhere.

Further towards the front, the ground became a hellish, war-blasted wasteland. Their maps were useless. Orbital ordnance and artillery fire had ripped up the once flat plains into a miniature mountain range of heaped earth and broken stone. Metal fragments from downed projectiles smoked in their craters. Brittle glass paved the areas hit by lance fire.

'*We're approaching mission point,*' voxed Honoured Captain Parrigar. '*Anywhere you think appropriate to stage the ambush, Lieutenant Askelios?*'

'*The ground is broken here. We should proceed a further hundred yards. Augur scans suggest the pressure ridge of a crater. We can gain a good field of fire from there and establish a defensive position,*' replied Askelios.

'*Understood,*' said Parrigar.

Askelios' tank, *World Burner*, turned and began to climb up a slope of loose soil. The Shadowsword sank up to its guards in the soft material, but it dragged itself upwards, volcano cannon nosing at the sky.

'Shoam, twenty degrees left. Take the ridge to the left of *World Burner*'s tracks,' ordered Bannick.

'Yes, sir,' breathed Shoam.

Rain drummed on the roof, muted by armour but audible nevertheless. Between Bannick and Leonates, the volcano cannon's refraction unit buzzed threateningly. Thick bundles of cables snaked up from holes in the floor and plugged into units all over it, radiating a palpable static. Lights blinked all over monitoring panels affixed to the back. It dominated the cramped command floor.

Bannick kept knocking his elbow on it. The cannon put out a lot of heat, making the tank even hotter and stuffier than *Cortein's Honour*.

'Starstan, how is *Lux* holding up?' he asked, for no better reason than he wanted to hear a human voice. He got an electronic facsimile instead.

'The tank is belligerent, ready for war. All signs of previous spiritual trauma are minimal. Hail the Omnissiah.'

Bannick regretted his desire for conversation. The crew spoke infrequently. Three commissars watched over their efforts. Suliban was with Jonas as always – he had yet to get to the bottom of why – while two others had appeared as if from nowhere, and taken up silent station. One aboard his tank, the other aboard Askelios' *World Burner*. Theirs was called Chensormen, a little vulture of a man, who seemed to be composed solely of a beak-like nose and perpetual disapproval. He had set himself up at the back of the command deck, where he was jammed in behind the refractor. Bannick felt the man's gimlet stare boring into the back of his head when he spoke, so he kept his orders minimal, aware everyone was being scrutinised.

'*Here is a good spot,*' voxed Askelios. *World Burner* came to a halt on the rim of the crater. '*Lux Imperator, deploy to my left.* Indominus *to the right.*'

'*Looks good to me,*' voxed Parrigar. '*Support tanks, begin preparing positions. Everyone off,*' Parrigar ordered the Paragonians riding his tank.

Bannick imagined his cousin leaping down into the muck, ordering his men to fetch their shovels. When he thought of the filthy rain and he safe in his tank, he understood why Jonas might bear a grudge.

Lux Imperator came to a halt. Bannick toggled switches on his command station, altering the view projected by his tiny pict screen. The assault would not begin for a few hours, after dawn. He glanced out of the tank's vision slit and corrected himself. After when dawn was supposed to be. There would be no sunrise today.

Emperor's teeth, Chensormen's staring was beginning to grate. He turned his chair round. 'Are we ready?'

'Aye, sir,' replied Epperaliant. 'Not much to do but wait.'

'The capacitor is ready for charging, Starstan?'

'At your will, honoured lieutenant, I shall disengage the motive force from the reactor coupling and redirect its holy power through the focusing mechanisms of *Lux Imperator* so that it might wreak havoc upon the enemies of men and machines at safe yet optimal distance.'

Yes would have sufficed, thought Bannick. 'Well then,' he said with forced lightness. 'No point hanging around in here. I am going to help the others prepare the positions.'

Almost before he had finished speaking, Bannick was reaching to fetch his rain poncho from the netting hanging around the cabin.

'I'll come too, if I have your permission, sir,' said Meggen.

'I have little to do,' said the Savlar, clambering out from his driver's station.

'Me also,' said Leonates, giving the commissar a side-long look.

'Is this wise, honoured lieutenant?' said Chensormen, who showed no sign of going out into the rain.

'Why would it not be, commissar? We are all wearing our vox-sets. We will not be going far. It is in the further-ance of the Imperium's better interests that we go to show solidarity with our comrades.'

Meggen hid a smirk behind his hand.

'Very well,' said Chensormen. 'A good sentiment.'

'I'll stay here then, shall I, keep the commissar and Starstan company?' said Epperaliant. He said it sharply as if he felt he had no choice, but Bannick could tell he did not wish to go out and work in the dirt.

'Inform us if anything changes,' said Bannick.

He clambered out of his turret. The black raindrops that evaded him fell down the cupola to stain the decking and his seat. Meggen, Leonates and Shoam clambered out of the wide hatch at the back of the command floor, not-so-accidentally knocking the commissar with their boots and knees.

'Emperor, it is grim out here,' said Bannick, regretting leaving the tank. The rain had a heavy, chemical smell, and the air tasted of metal. Thunder vied with the rumble of the artillery bombardment. Strangely coloured lighting chased itself across the low clouds.

'Better be out here with this deluge than in there being judged for crimes we are yet to commit,' said Leonates.

'Officious basdack,' agreed Meggen.

Shoam slid down the front of *Lux Imperator* and began unclipping digging tools from the track guard top and handing them out.

Bannick pressed his vox-piece close to his mouth and shouted over the rain and the noises of war. 'Epperaliant, put me through to Jonas' platoon.'

'*Aye, sir. Done.*'

Bannick spoke with Jonas' commsman. A moment later his cousin spoke over the vox.

'*Yes?*'

'Jonas, it's Colaron. We're coming to help you.'

'That's a... surprise, but thanks,' replied his cousin. 'Fifty yards out, to your left.'

The crew waited for an Atlas tank fitted with a dozer blade to pass to *World Burner*'s front, where it began to heap up a protective berm. Two others worked around them, building defences around the perimeter.

'Thing about Titans,' said Meggen, 'is that they're tall. Aren't they just going to fire over this?'

'Do you have to be so facetious all of the time?' said Leonates.

'It's called being laconic. Dark humour in the face of danger. It cheers me up. Do you have to be so miserable?' said Meggen.

'Stop that, you two,' said Bannick.

They trudged through the rain. Somehow Shoam managed to pull ahead of the other three while they were pulling their boots from the sucking mud.

'He walks like a man born to this hell,' said Leonates.

'He is,' said Meggen. 'I'll bet this is pretty nice territory compared to Savlar.'

Jonas' platoon were suspicious of why the tankers would want to come out into the vile weather, but welcomed their help just the same. Alongside his cousin, Bannick and his men spent the next few hours digging foxholes and squaring off the berms pushed up by the Atlas tanks. Bannick found himself digging next to a man in a greatcoat, and was surprised to see it was Suliban, his immaculate uniform caked in filth. The rain never let up and soon penetrated their ponchos and chilled them to the bone. By the time Jonas called a halt, everyone was soaked, freezing cold and unhappy.

'And I thought it was wet on Genthus!' he said. The

men who had been with him there laughed. 'Thirty minutes until the assault commences,' said Jonas, looking at his chronometer. Bannick instinctively checked his own. 'Got time for a cup of gleece? I'll have it warmed, just like back home.'

'I'm surprised you've any left.'

'I didn't have, but your uncle's bar proved very generous to a man with quick hands. I bagged three bottles, all told.'

'I should get back,' he said, meaning to sound business-like, although his head was full of how warm and dry his tank was.

'Hey, I've spent the last eighteen months bad-mouthing you to anyone who will listen. I feel I owe you a drink, although I don't want you to think I'm not still angry – I'm just angrier with the Unified Clan Council now than I am with you.'

'I appreciate the sentiment.'

'Yeah, well, I thought I should voice it without your uncle staring me down and half the top brass of the army group standing behind us, just so you know it's sincere. Come on. I promise it's drier in here.'

They went into a newly built dugout roofed with a sheet of pressed plasteel scavenged from the battlefield. The rain drummed off it, running from the front to make a beaded current of black droplets over the firing slit. Jonas' men crammed inside, raising the temperature with their body heat. Bannick shuddered gratefully at the slight increase in warmth.

Jonas introduced his command squad to Colaron. 'This is my ensign Bosarain, vox-operator Anderick,' he said. 'Lin is my medic. This is Killek, who I basically pro-moted to my squad so I could keep an eye on him, and this sorry looking dog is Micz.' He pointed out a scarred, squash-nosed man hunched over a meltagun. 'Probably the most dangerous man in the whole of the Four Hundred and Seventy-Seventh.'

Micz gave an ironic salute.

'And Suliban, you already know.'

The commissar dipped his head. Bannick returned the gesture, still on his guard. He introduced his own men. Shoam and Micz appraised each other a little too long for comfort.

'Now, Bosarain, about that gleece?' said Jonas.

'Coming right up, sir,' said Bosarain. He put a pan so large it must have been purloined from the mess in front of Micz, then he pulled out a bottle from his pack and held it up. 'There's only one left after this.'

'Put them both in.'

'You sure, Jonas?'

'Go ahead,' said Jonas. 'I'd rather go into battle knowing I'd drunk it than die regretting I hadn't.'

Bosarain pulled out another bottle and uncorked them together. The bitter-sweet smell of the gleece brought memories of home back to them all as it glugged into the pan.

'This is the tricky part. Micz?'

Micz unfolded his arms from around his weapon, rested it on his knee, and pointed the slot end at the pan.

'What the–?' said Meggen.

'I know what it looks like,' said Jonas. 'But he's good at this.'

'You gotta get the setting right down,' explained Micz, twisting knobs on the gun's control panel. 'Get it right and we get nice warm gleece.'

'Get it wrong and you'll kill the lot of us! A fusion gun like that will turn us all to steam,' said Bannick. He glanced at Suliban, but the commissar was looking impassively out at the downpour.

Micz shrugged. 'I better get it right then, hadn't I?'

Shoam crouched down, right by the pan.

'Here goes,' said Micz.

The meltagun gave off a faint hiss. A warm draught rose from the end of its slotted muzzle. Heat shimmer rippled the air between gun and liquor.

'Steady!' said Jonas.

'Steady as she goes and no more, sir,' said Micz. 'That should do it.' He released the trigger and set the melta down. The muzzle radiated a warmth that relaxed them all. With so many men packed into the tiny dugout and the melta giving off heat, steam rose from their uniforms, and the chill retreated from their limbs.

Jonas poured the gleece and handed it out in enamelled mugs. Shoam unbuckled his rebreather, revealing a sly yellow grin. Bannick looked to Suliban.

'Is this...?' he ventured.

'Allowed? Do not look to me, honoured lieutenant. I see the virtue in these little vices. You will hear no complaints from me. These men serve the Emperor well. What do I care if brave men drink together and do not shine their buttons?' He took a mug from Jonas.

'But, you're a commissar...' said Bannick limply.

'Commissars can be fools as readily as other men. The efforts of Jonas' platoon are directed in the correct direction, at the enemy. That is all I ask.'

'But he will shoot you if you disobey an order,' said Jonas conversationally. 'I've seen him do it.'

'Ah, poor Captain Rannigen,' said Micz.

'But he's not so stiff as some of the other... stiffs,' said Jonas. 'No offence.'

'None taken,' said Suliban. 'Leading men has more to do with understanding them than a strict adherence to the rules.'

'Praise be to the Emperor to that,' said Jonas. 'Everyone got a drink? Very good.' He raised his mug. 'Here's to making it out the other side,' he said. They drank. Bannick shivered again as the gleece warmed him. The buzz the drink gave was enough to mask the apprehension of battle, and they spent ten minutes in pleasant conviviality.

Time ran out along with the gleece. Bannick looked at his chronometer.

'We need to go.' He saluted his cousin and the commissar. 'Until later.'

'I'll walk you back,' said Jonas.

'It's raining.'

'I had noticed.'

Outside the dugout Jonas took Bannick's elbow and leaned close, the hammering rain masking his voice.

'You be careful. I've a bad feeling about all this.'

'We're facing monsters out of the deep past. We're all scared.'

'No, no – think. They're Space Marines, but they are not invulnerable. There's not so many of them, or we'd be done already. What's worrying me is if they don't have the ability to take us out in one go, why bother fighting us at all?'

They walked slowly. *Lux Imperator* emerged from the rain. The two Bannicks paused at the access ladder while Shoam, Meggen and Leonates clambered up.

'What do you mean?'

'Emperor, Colaron! Think. Why are they here? As things stand, we're bound to win. Though it will be harder for us with them being here, they can't hope to overcome us. All this, these strikes and feints, they're delaying tactics. They'll slow us down, but they can't stop us. It's obvious they want to take this planet, otherwise they'd have hit us with an asteroid, or dropped virus bombs, or those planet crackers the Space Marines use. So my point is, cousin, what exactly are they waiting for?'

A chill ran down Bannick's back.

'Now, if I can see that, you can bet your last quart of gleece high command can too. Something bad is going to happen if this attack fails. Can't you see it? The sense of desperation here. This mad rush for Magor's Seat. It's not the careful strategy Iskhandrian's been following. Things have got a little sloppier, a little quicker, since the inquisitor arrived.'

Jonas nodded at Bannick, urging him to understand.

The vox-set chimed in Bannick's ear.

'Sir, Parrigar and Askelios are calling for all hands to prepare. The assault begins in two minutes.'

'I'll be right there.'

Jonas prodded Bannick gently in the chest. 'We'd best pray to the Emperor all this works out. The funny thing about stories is that they're no fun to be in, and the ones I've heard about Traitor Space Marines really are unpleasant.'

Bannick took his leave and clambered back aboard the tank. He tore off his poncho and hung it to dry on the back wall, closest to the reactor where Chensormen lurked. He ignored the commissar's arched eyebrow.

Parrigar and Askelios were conferring on open vox. Bannick half listened as he stripped down to his vest – even that was damp – and sat himself down in the Shadowsword's command chair.

'Everyone look sharp. The time for battle is upon us.'

The 18th's support tanks withdrew, heading back to the safety of the castella. The four super-heavy tanks powered down to a bare minimum. Hidden by the storm in their earthworks, their voxes restricted to short range and operating on low power with their capacitors drained, they were virtually invisible to augur detection, but as soon as they charged to fire, their position would become obvious. The majority of Jonas' thirty-strong platoon made a cordon around them, primarily either side of the tanks' position, as the front was protected by a murky lake at the bottom of the crater, and the rear by the Stormlord. Upon *Righteous Vengeance,* a five-man squad, equipped with two meltaguns and two plasma guns, waited, culled from across Jonas' platoon, weapons sure to crack the armour of the Space Marines where lasguns would fail. They were to act as a reaction force. Together with the vulcan mega-bolter on the front of the tank, they might deal with any major threat from the traitors.

From their positions the Shadowswords had a clear shot across the battlefield. The ground was much disturbed and offered plenty of cover, but their target would be the enemy's god-machines, and those were so tall nothing on the surrounding terrain could offer them protection.

They could see little of the advance. The black rain blinded them to anything more than a quarter of a mile away. Flashes occasionally lit up the storm from the direction of the city, still some thirty kilometres distant. Bannick pitied the men having to traverse the sea of mud, but the Titans had to be lured out. In the cover of the towering blocks of Magor's Seat, they would have a plenitude of cover to exploit, and so would be at their most dangerous. Tactical sense dictated that they be drawn into the open and dealt with from all sides. Ordinatum gunnery officers aboard the fleet and the Shadowswords awaited command from Princeps Yolanedesh as to the most opportune moment to strike. It was a bold strategy, three disparate elements working in concert. There was a lot of technology, a lot that could go wrong. There was no other choice.

Bannick watched the advance on his pict screen; there was no chartdesk as he had on *Cortein's Honour*. No room or power to spare. Red dots and chevrons crept slowly across the map. Flashing icons denoted orbital weapons fire aimed at the city. The two largest denoted the Warhound *War's Gift* and the Reaver *Ultimate Sanction*. They walked towards the eastern flank of the army, slightly ahead of the main body and moving away. They were the bait, acting the arrogant conquerors in a ploy to draw out the traitor god-engines. *War's Gift* paced its advance in zigzags, scouting ahead in front of its slower companion.

In the centre a huge formation of tanks led the way, Honoured Captain Hannick's amalgamated unit in the middle. A column of armoured personnel carriers came after it. Behind them marched hundreds of thousands of men, protected from air and orbital attack by the umbrella of the fleet. The column kinked slightly as it followed the route of the main highway into Magor's Seat. It had probably been bombed to ruin, thought Bannick, and would offer no easier a road than the land around it. Everything was reduced to slurry.

The bitten-off talk of a large force going to war rattled over the vox-net, a staccato racket of acronyms and call signs. It would take a dedicated strategos to make sense of the battle chatter for an entire army group at the height of a fight, but for the moment the messages going back and forth all reported the same thing – advance proceeding smoothly, no opposition.

'Range guns for focal points at five hundred feet, twenty-four hundred feet, thirty-seven hundred feet,' said Askelios over the vox. 'Test generatorum coupling efficacy – low motive force, let's not give ourselves away.'

'Testing focal points now,' responded Bannick. 'Meggen, Epperaliant.'

'Aye aye, sir,' said Epperaliant. 'Meggen, on my mark.'

On a tiny glass screen set into his station, Bannick watched Meggen press his eyes against the rubberised seal of his augur display. Fully operational, it piped in a constant stream of data. Everything from gross range to planetary curve and air pressure differentials. If the augur systems were knocked out, it could be used as a simple periscope. Meggen had taken to the more sophisticated targeting gear easily, impressing Bannick.

'Five hundred feet,' said Epperaliant.

'Marked and correcting. Corrected,' said Meggen.

'Twenty-four hundred feet,' said Epperaliant.

'Marked. Correct.'

At each adjustment, the small whining noises of shifting servo-motors sounded from the interior of the barrel as its lenses adjusted the focal point for the cannon's terrifying laser.

'Thirty-seven hundred feet.'

'Thirty-seven hundred feet...' Meggen sucked his lip. 'Way off. Correcting... Starstan, could I have a little more torque on the beam focus?'

'Most irregular, but I shall comply,' said Starstan in his grating machine voice. He twittered at the machine. Data screed flickered over Bannick's screens. Indicator lights performed a mysterious, flickering dance. Starstan touched nothing. 'It is done.'

'Thirty-seven hundred feet, corrected.'

'I shall now apply the minimum current of motive force to the power couplings in order to gauge the efficacy of their functioning twixt blessed dynamo and most sacred capacitor. Exeunt electricum, Omnissiah desiderat,' droned Starstan. 'All ways are clear. Hail the Omnissiah.'

'All Shadowswords present well, Parrigar. We shall now test the beam focus at steps of one hundred feet, beginning at three hundred. Begin.'

Everything on the Shadowsword was about the volcano cannon. No one armament on the Baneblade commanded so much diligent attention. The devices were millennia tested, and had a reputation for reliability that many of the old, half-forgotten creations of the Dark Age of Technology did not. But that only applied if they were handled well. The secrets of their construction were jealously guarded, and that did not help their maintenance or correct use. A Baneblade's weapons were easier, more forgiving to the application of an unsanctified wrench. A Baneblade could also, Bannick reflected, shoot its way out of a poor situation. Shadowswords, on the other hand, had that awkward choice between movement and destruction. They were inflexible, all or nothing. With such a powerful armament, they were high on any enemy's list of targets. He tripled the risk in his head because three were in close proximity. Then he doubled it again. They were to fight god-engines, whose own weaponry could annihilate a company such as theirs with a single blast.

'Meggen?' said Bannick.

'Sir?'

'Check the focusing ranges again.'

'Aye, sir.'

'And when the time comes to fire just... don't miss.'

Battlegroup Geratomro, Additional assets

Adeptus Mechanicus (Mechanicus Militarum assets only, see sheet #992 re. Adeptus Mechanicus support elements)
Titan Legion, Legio Crucis, 1/20th Legion
Commanding officer Princeps Yolanedesh
Ultimate Sanction – Reaver-class medium Titan, Princeps Yolanedesh
War's Messenger – Warhound-class Scout Titan, Princeps Almodovar [note, recorded destroyed, Agritha IV]
War's Gift – Warhound-class Scout Titan, Princeps Gonzar

Adeptus Astartes
Black Templars Chapter, Adeptus Astartes, Michaelus Crusade [note, probable name change from Kalidar Crusade]
Commanding officer Marshal Michaelus
Est. 90 battle-brothers and associated support

Non-Astra Militarum ground assets, Geratomro campaign, 398.M41

CHAPTER NINETEEN
GOD-ENGINE

MAGOR'S FIELDS
GERATOMRO
087498.M41

Thirty minutes can last an eternity. Time crawled by with excruciating sluggishness. Bannick lay back in his chair bathed in the red light of emergency lumens. He was finally drying off. The rumble of artillery had a symphonic quality, an orchestra of drums that swelled and dwindled, their rhythms taken up by other percussive instruments of destruction, so that the tune never died. Keeping time was a new, steady, metronomic beat, slow as a sleeping man's heart. Boom, boom, boom. One thump after another, regularly paced. A faint tremor passed through the tank as the noise grew louder.

Bannick sat bolt upright. The sound... 'Footsteps!'

'*God-engine!*' The alarm was given by Askelios' second, Xetrexes, before Bannick reached the company vox-button, and was taken up by the entire unit.

Princeps Gonzar was on the vox a second later, the

Shadowswords listening in but not daring to respond. *'Confirm three enemy engines, Titan-class. Emperor preserve us, what has been done to them? I see two Reavers, and a third. The augurs are uncooperative... The third is a Warlord. Repeat, the third Titan is a Warlord.'*

'Steady as she goes, Gonzar. See if you can draw one of them off. Ultimate Sanction *is moving to engage. Nominate enemy Titans prime, second and Warlord. Acknowledge.'*

'Battlesign nomenclature accepted and input. War's Gift *is ready.'*

Neither princeps mentioned the existence of the dug-in Shadowsword unit, though half of what they said was for the tank commanders' benefit. Bannick watched the two Titans pull further away from the Imperial column of advance. Large, menacing red dots appeared on his pict screen holo, indicating the position of the enemy engines, as telemetry gathered by the Titans' augurs was fed via the army group datasphere to all its constituent parts. They were coming out from the city, heading on an oblique line to intercept the Imperial advance. *War's Gift* picked up speed, the mess of the battlefield posing no more obstacle to it than a couple of inches of puddle does to a man in good boots.

'They've taken the bait,' voxed Askelios. *'All crews stand ready.'*

Yolanedesh continued speaking over an open vox. *'Set intercept course, we'll meet them halfway. Moderati, prepare turbo lasers for maximum burst fire, reactor ready for rapid recharge. Let's see if we can take down a couple of shields at range.'*

'Stand ready to prime volcano cannon, at my command,' said Askelios. Parrigar, nominally in charge, let the Atraxian get on with it.

'*Wake carapace rockets and bless,*' intoned the princeps of *Ultimate Sanction*, slipping into full communion with the spirit of his machine. '*Targeting enemy designate Prime.*'

Bannick looked out of the viewing slit. The bevelled edges of the armourglass refracted the meagre light from outside. All he could see was sheeting black rain.

'Makes you wonder how much of this planet is up in the air, and how much is on the ground,' said Epperaliant, catching Bannick's peering.

'Your comment is illogical. Although three hundred and seventy-eight megatonnes of soil, rock and various vapours were ejected–' began Starstan.

'It was a joke, coghead,' said Meggen.

'Really,' said Starstan, managing somehow to imbue his emotionless voice with offence.

Bannick returned to his pict screen, eagerly awaiting each update from high command. The two enemy Reavers broke off from their advance on the loyalist Reaver, and were peeling off together towards *War's Gift*, which was backtracking towards the armoured column, now only a few miles out from the city, leaving the Warlord to head right for Legio Crucis' *Ultimate Sanction* alone.

'They're overmatching,' Bannick said. 'Doubling down in firepower. Those Reavers will make short work of Gonzar then turn on Yolanedesh. Even without them, he is not going to last long against a Warlord.'

'*Stand easy, Bannick. Gonzar is drawing the Titans towards our columns of medium tanks. We wait to do our part. If we fire up our reactors to charge the capacitors now, then the Warlord will kill us first before finishing off Yolanedesh,*' said Askelios.

Bannick held his tongue. He did not agree. The Warlord was moving past their position. If they attracted its attention, they would buy Yolanedesh valuable time. *Ultimate Sanction* was also more mobile than they. They should switch places, becoming bait themselves and allowing Yolanedesh more freedom to do his work.

'*We await the princeps' order,*' said Askelios. '*Stand ready to charge.*'

'*Firing carapace rockets on three, two, one. Loose,*' came Yolanedesh's voice.

The rain flashed. Bannick saw neither the source nor the target. A series of explosions and further flashes marked the rockets' detonation. Purple flares followed – the light of reacting void shields. Other flashes blinked in the rain as the enemy Warlord returned fire. Again, Bannick could not see its source. On the pict screen, the Reaver circled the Warlord like a smaller man makes use of nimbleness to outwit a larger opponent. The dark day blinked with lightning and weapons discharge. Booming in the sky that could have been simple thunder or explosions that brought the death of hundreds of men rolled over the Shadowswords' emplacement.

On the display, a number of tanks had split off from the main advance and headed in full combat order towards Gonzar's Warhound and the advancing enemy Reavers. Bannick's headset filled with crackling orders, so many that they overlaid one another to become a rush of white noise. The two enemy Reavers split, trying to outflank the Warhound. The dark strobed again, this time to the discharge of hundreds of battle cannons.

Gonzar's voice surfaced from the ocean of noise. '*Second is losing its void shields. Keep it up.*'

Brilliant lines cut across the horizon. The vox pulsed with throbbing discharges of energy weaponry.

'Warlord's coming closer,' said Epperaliant. '*Ultimate Sanction* is leading it our way.'

Massive explosions drowned out the vox in a blizzard of interference.

'*–ative,*' Askelios was saying. '*Maintain engine quiet. Do not charge capacitors.*'

'Fifteen hundred yards and closing,' said Epperaliant.

'*Set beam focus for close range,*' said Askelios. '*Prepare to charge cannons on my command, maximum power. We will get one shot. It must count.*'

Bannick stood a little in his seat and leaned towards the viewing block. Through the gloom he spied a giant shape walking backwards towards them. He threw up his hand to shield his eyes as a roaring stream of plasma lit up the day where the sun could not, shining off the underside of the clouds of dust that masked the surface from the system's star. The shock wave from the plasma's heating of the atmosphere was visible to the naked eye, sketched by the black rain, which twisted in on itself and was flung outwards with ear-shattering force. The army group's comms became an indecipherable racket.

'Epperaliant, isolate *Ultimate Sanction*'s vox-feed. We need to hear this.'

'Aye, sir,' said Epperaliant. The roar of a thousand officers talking together vanished. A quiet hiss replaced it, cut through with the buzz of weapons-generated interference.

'*Armament dexter, you are firing wide. Moderatus, correct range and aim,*' came Yolanedesh's voice. '*Carapace mount, throw our last salvo at its feet. I want to see this monster dance. Force it away from the army.*'

A stuttering light flickered in the distance. An alarm sounded in the background of *Ultimate Sanction*'s feed. A burst of static cut the transmission for a moment, then it returned with a shout and the singing of Adeptus Mechanicus damage control teams. *'Fleet, that last hit winged us. Transmitting coordinates. Prepare lance strike. Target Warlord, repeat, target Warlord. Alpha one,'* Princeps Yolanedesh voxed.

'That's the signal,' said Bannick. 'Get ready!'

'All weapons prepare to fire,' ordered Askelios.

'Preparing,' said Epperaliant. 'Weapon safeties off.'

Large switches clunked home as they were thrown.

The enemy loomed out of the dark, lit by the light of collapsing void shields. It was huge, monstrously so, bigger than the ork gargants Bannick had seen on Kalidar and more terrifying for its greater grace. The gargants had been little more than rickety fortresses on tracked feet; this had arms and legs, a hunched back protected by a heavy armoured carapace. The details of it were hazed by the spread of its void shields, presenting a sinister silhouette that had more of the look of a giant than a machine. It moved like a man, with all a man's murderous intent. The orks knew no better; they were an enemy Bannick could understand. Bannick found that, as he could not forgive himself for killing Tuparillio, he could not forgive his species for the cruelty it inflicted upon itself. This iron god was all the hate and cruelty man had to offer the galaxy incarnate. It horrified him, more so because in its form he could see himself reflected.

'Range twelve hundred yards and closing,' said Epperaliant.

'All tank gunners, fix range and focus,' ordered Askelios. *'Enginseers stand ready to reactivate reactors and charge cannon capacitors.'*

The Warlord paced backwards, still unaware of the

ambush hunters lurking to its rear. Now both god-engines were visible through the storm. A furious exchange of fire flew between the Warlord and the Imperial Reaver. The Traitor Titan was heavier, and carried far more armament. This was not a fight *Ultimate Sanction* could win on its own. Void shields on both Titans blazed as they collapsed, flaring layers of protection stripped back one by one. For a second the Reaver lost all of its own field protection. Only its armour prevented it being laid low, and this absorbed a punishing amount of fire before the shields burst back into life. When the soapy shimmer of field protection encased it again, the carapace missile launcher was ablaze, struck by plasma weapons hot enough to set the metal on fire.

'*Stand ready. Fleet, fire on my coordinates, now,*' spoke Yolanedesh.

Columns of light as broad as city blocks punched down from the heavens, emanating from orbit over the army castella and coming in at an angle at the Warlord Titan. Three lance strikes, all went wide. They hammered the ground, sending up geysers of super-heated steam that obscured Bannick's limited view of the battle. Lance fire against a planet was imprecise, inappropriate for anything smaller than a city. To hit something as relatively small as a Titan from orbit was difficult without close-in observer direction. Any strike would have been a great boon, but it was not the first intention of the battlegroup.

'*Charge now!*' commanded Askelios, his voice blurred into vox-screech by the interference thrown out by the lances.

More lance strikes slammed down. The tremendous amount of energy they released blinded augur, auspex, eye and sensoria, masking the charging of the volcano cannons.

'Engaging reactor,' said Starstan, his prolixity truncated by combat. Banded metal tendrils snaked out from under his robes and plugged into the various ports and sockets that opened to receive him.

Lux Imperator trembled as the reactor was coaxed into full life. Machines whined as the motive force was applied to them.

'Charging capacitors,' said Starstan. He threw a huge lever switch mounted upon a section of wall painted in the holy yellow-and-black stripes of warning. It connected with an impressive crackle. Blue light shone through the cracks of the deck-plates, mixing uncomfortably with the red of the operations lumens. One after another, the tanks reported their capacitors charged, the vox-officers speaking in whispers, as though afraid that if they spoke too loudly, the Titan would hear them.

More lance strikes burned the air.

'Target left knee. Prepare to open fire.'

'Final safeties off,' ordered Bannick.

'Final safeties off,' repeated Epperaliant as he flicked half a dozen large toggle switches. The tension in the tank built.

'Meggen, the weapon is free and at your disposal,' said Bannick.

'Aye, sir,' said Meggen, placing his eyes against the seal of his rangefinder.

Another lance strike blazed down. The beam hit the Titan full on. Light as close to collimation as it was possible to get within an atmospheric envelope contacted void shields. The beam held on. The shields shone brighter and brighter as they displaced the energy of the lance into the immaterium. Shining a bright white at first, the outermost shield dimmed through red to blue and violet, then collapsed with a shower of writhing lightning. The lance shut off.

'Shield down,' said Yolanedesh. 'We shall take the last. Moderati, open fire, all weapons.'

Ultimate Sanction's blurry form, lit as much as it was obscured by its void shields, opened fire with all its weapons. A wall of energy a hundred feet in front of the enemy war machine shone like molten gold, and the last shield gave out.

The Titan stood revealed, naked of energy, streaming with rain, war-horns blaring hatred against all good things.

'Open fire!' yelled Askelios.

Three volcano beams intersected on the Warlord's knee. Scaled-down versions of lance technology, they could inflict terrible damage even on a god-machine. The Titan staggered, molten metal coursing down its leg. The machine stumbled to one side, joint locking. It swayed, but it did not fall.

'It's not down!' yelled Askelios with rising panic. 'Prepare to fire again!'

'It's registered us. Emperor, it's bringing weapons to bear!' said Epperaliant.

The Titan was stuck in place, the joint of its left knee spot-welded together. With the hazing effects of the shields gone its hideous decoration was clear. All over its curved armour plates gaped screaming, daemoniacal faces. The head was made in the likeness of a skull still clad in shrunken, corpse-white flesh. A helmet of antique style capped this face, from under whose louring brows glowered a pair of blood-red eye-lenses yards across, the occuli of the great machine. The torso swivelled, the god-machine contemptuous of the fire slamming into its side from the advancing *Ultimate Sanction.*

War-horns blew a polyphonic wail that struck dread into the tank crews. A weapon twice as long as the Shadowsword moved to target the tanks' position while those on the carapace and the right arm swivelled to continue tracking the Reaver.

'Emperor, it's locked on to our position!' shouted Epperaliant over the wailing of alarms.

'Brace! Brace! Brace!' shouted Bannick.

A point of light grew from the muzzle of the Titan's weapon and engulfed the world.

Bannick was thrown from his seat as *Lux Imperator* was blasted by massive discharge. Instruments shorted out, screens died in the wash of accompanying electromagnetic energy. Sparks shot from instruments. A surge of visible energy arced up from the engineering desk through Starstan's mechadendrites and crackled all over his body. Smoke rose from his robes, his eyes blazed and he gave a hideous metallic screech. The short-range vox was filled with agonised screams, abruptly cut off as the equipment failed. The red operations lumens went out, plunging them all into darkness lit by the read-outs of isolated functioning instruments. Bannick's hearing burred and lights danced before his eyes, the pulse strong enough to momentarily disrupt the proper functioning of his brain. When he came to himself, *Lux Imperator* was moving out of control, sliding forwards. It slipped a few degrees to the left and came to a slow halt, the potential to move again prominent in Bannick's thoughts.

Bannick pulled himself up. 'Sound off!'

The crew shouted out their names. No one was hurt, except Starstan.

The operations lights flickered back on.

'Damage report!'

'All hale,' replied Epperaliant. 'The pulse knocked out our instruments, but they are functional. Fail-safes operated accordingly. I'm putting them back online. We weren't hit.'

'Starstan! Epperaliant, is he alive?'

Epperaliant got half out of his seat to go check, but with a wheezing groan the tech-priest pulled himself upright. He responded with a burst of binaric, before switching to Gothic.

'Minor damage sustained. My organism is still operational. Praise be to the Omnissiah, who replaceth weak flesh with the permanence of steel.'

'Then re-engage reactor with the drive units. Shoam! Pull us back. We must have slipped part-way into the crater. I do not want us sliding any further in, and we can't get a shot from here. Epperaliant, give me augur views of the others.'

'All external augurs are non-functional, sir. We're half buried. But I'm not reading the Atraxians on the vox or on our datanet. They're gone.'

Bannick looked out of the viewing slit. Mud and debris covered the tank's glacis.

'A shock like that will delay the recoupling of reactor with motive units. Two minutes, maybe more,' said Starstan. 'First, I must pray.'

'You can pray afterwards. Do it now, and give my apologies to the Machine-God.'

'But that is unwise. To re-engage major power sources without the correct rites can only–'

'Tech-priest, the wishes of the Emperor are paramount here,' said Chensormen, speaking for the first time. 'Not your god.'

'I'll pray with you later,' said Bannick. 'Just do it. That is an order, if it makes you feel better. Meggen, can you make the shot? Can you take out the knee?'

'If someone gets up on the roof and scrapes all the dreck off the rangefinder, I'll not miss.'

'I'll do it,' said Bannick.

'Colaron? Colaron?' Jonas spoke over the formation vox-net. *'Are you still alive? I can see your tank.'*

'Jonas? We're still here.'

'Praise be to the Emperor! You're halfway down to the lake in the crater bottom. The rest of the tanks are dead.'

'We'll get a clear shot. We're going to bring that Titan down. Maybe you should fall back. When we begin powering the capacitors it'll see us again. We'll have to move, disconnect and charge. That will take us at least a minute, plenty of time to see us. Epperaliant, prepare to signal Princeps Gonzar and Yolanedesh, full encrypted data-squirt, no vox. We have to let them know we're alive.'

'Countermand that. They'll hear us, vox or not. Even if they don't know what we're saying, we'll draw the enemy engine's fire,' said Chensormen.

'You, sir, with all due respect, are here to ensure I follow my orders, not to question the methods I employ to do so. Or are you afraid?' Bannick gave Chensormen a challenging stare.

Chensormen's jaw tightened. 'A commissar fears nothing. Watch your tone, honoured lieutenant.'

'Then please hold your silence. Epperaliant, proceed as I instructed. The enemy engine will have plenty of time to kill us once our reactors spike for capacitor charge. If the Titans cannot hold its attention and keep fire off us, then it won't matter if it notices us ten seconds earlier or later. We will be just as dead. Epperaliant, relay the following message – Shadowsword *Lux Imperator* ready to re-engage. Distract enemy engine from the front. Draw fire. We shall take out the weakened knee.'

'Message sent,' said Epperaliant. Ten seconds later he spoke again. 'Reply incoming. Princeps Yolanedesh responds in the affirmative. *Ultimate Sanction* and *War's Gift* moving in for close engagement. Emperor's light guide you. Yolanedesh out.'

Bannick patted the rear of the massive volcano cannon. 'Do you hear that, *Lux*? You have proved that you can still fight. Now is your time to shine.'

Parrigar's voice cut in through the short-range vox. 'Maybe it is, but we have other problems. Traitor Space Marines, coming in fast.'

CHAPTER TWENTY
REVELRY AND REVELATION

IMPERIAL GOVERNOR'S PALACE, MAGOR'S SEAT
GERATOMRO
087498.M41

Dostain's coronation did not quite match his dream. There were the people, the lords and ladies of Geratomro – more in court than under his aunt's rule, as so many of them had fled their own demesnes to take refuge in the capital. And they were dressed as in his dream, resplendent with the gathered wealth of a world, clad in jewels and shining gowns. There were the women, there was the feast. But whereas his dreams had been full of glory and pomp, the reality was full of fear. The palace shook with the impact of artillery strikes. Every impact brought a crackling thrum from the void shield, audible through the thick stone walls, that threatened its collapse. Dostain stared ahead, determined not to look up every time a shell slammed into the shield.

As each lord or lady came to kneel at the foot of his throne dais and proclaim allegiance, their eyes could not

help but flick from Dostain's face to the creature stood
next to him – Dib, who had grown in stature and beauty
to rival the most glorious of men. Long, golden hair lay on
his shoulders. His smile held the promise of easy friend-
ship and joyous times. The gleam in his eye spoke of wit
and intelligence. His clothes were cut to accentuate his
cleanly muscled frame. And yet, although all these charac-
teristics should have marked him out as a friend or lover
any human would desire, the combined effect was to ter-
rify. Between he and Dostain's throne stood Pollein. She
held the hand of Dib on one side, and of Dostain on the
other. In this way, there was a connection directly between
Dostain and the Devil-in-the-bush, a greasy current that
appalled the flesh as much as thrilled it that he wished
dearly to be rid of. Pollein had no such reservations. She
stood there looking as beautiful as the stars themselves,
her eyes sparkling but focused on nothing, saying, 'How
wonderful,' over and over.

The next lord came. The lord-civil of Matua Inferior.
Dostain bristled. The city had fallen not long after Matua
Superior.

'My lord, my planetary commander, I pledge the allegiance of Matua Inferior to your rule and through you
the... the...' The man stumbled over his words, a look of
horror creeping across his face as he realised he was about
to repeat the old oath to the Imperium. 'And through you
to your descendants,' he said, saving himself. 'Long may
they ever rule over us in blessed isolation and freedom
from the depredations of the most vicious Imperium.'
Bowed by the weight of Dib's glowing smile, the lord-civil
of Matua Inferior lowered his head and raised a fist. 'Long
live Lord Dostain!'

The cry that answered him was insipid. Too many eyes were on Dib. Dostain yanked his hand from Pollein's. Her brow creased a second, but the idiotic smile remained.

'How wonderful,' she said.

Dostain wiped his hands on his coronation robe. They were slick with scented oil. The strange sensation of Dib's presence grew even though Dostain was free of that indirect contact. He filled the room with his being, like a sickly perfume that crept down the back of a man's nose and choked him.

Dostain was angry, and anger yearns to be vented.

'You!' he shouted at the lord-civil. 'How dare you. How dare all of you! You come creeping into my throne-room and kiss my hand, demanding I look favourably upon you. But where were you when the Imperium came? Where?'

'I... I..' said the lord-civil. 'My lord.'

'Crawling out of your palaces like serpents fleeing a fire in the dead of night. Matua Inferior fell without a single shot being fired. And yet you come here protesting its loyalty? How dare you!'

'What is to be done, my lord?' said Dib insinuatingly.

'I... I should punish him. Punish him for cowardice! Yes!' Dostain's moral sense warned him against pursuing this argument. He ignored it. He was too hot. Sweat dribbled from under his ornamental helm and down his pudgy face. Someone would pay for his discomfort.

'And how are cowards punished?' said Dib.

'Death! Death!' said Dostain feverishly. He fumbled at the gold-plated bolt pistol at his belt. With a shaking hand, clumsy in its flared glove, he pulled the weapon out of its holster and pointed it at the lord-civil's head. It was a small calibre, but would kill with a single shot.

'Coward!' shouted Dostain.

'My lord!' said the lord-civil.

'My lord, Dostain, reconsider,' said the Lord-Fiduciary Ando. 'This is not you. You are a good man, my lord.'

'The old Dostain is dead! I was forced to kill my aunt to prevent our defeat. I will show no mercy to cowards who flee their cities.' Dostain levelled the gun at Ando. 'You wish to take his place?'

Ando raised his hands and stepped back. 'No, no, my lord. I merely seek to advise.' He disappeared back into the crowd.

The lord-civil of Matua Inferior began a scream that was cut off by a wet bang as Dostain put a bolt into his face. His head exploded into a cloud of red mist, and his body toppled onto the dais steps, hitting the floor before the heavy report of the bolt pistol had ceased to echo around the hall.

A horrified crowd stared up at him.

'How wonderful,' murmured Pollein.

'A very fine shot, Dostain,' said Dib, clapping his hands. 'Bravo.'

Their gold-dusted skin and enticing garments splashed with blood, the concubines screamed and shrank back from the corpse. A spreading wash of crimson trickled down the steps, carrying white pieces of the lord-civil's brain away. They looked like pleasure boats on a red river, recklessly daring cataracts.

'You!' shouted Dostain, jabbing a finger at a concubine. 'Come sit on my lap.'

Biting her lip to stifle her tears, the girl came and placed herself on her planetary governor's knee.

'Is there more need for this tedious charade?' said Dostain. 'I wish to feast, and sate my appetites.'

He patted the girl's behind.

Dib smiled. Something inside Dostain curled in disgust. The perfume on the air mingled with blood, each scent strengthening the other until he felt dizzy with the stink. He longed for the sweet wine from his dream to wash away the flavour. Part of him shrilled inside. He could stop it now. He could. He knew it.

But he could not. There was a feast of flesh, wine and meat to be enjoyed. The perfume intoxicated him. His scruples melted under its influence. His body, always large, called out for excess. He had everything. He wanted more.

'Not quite yet, my lord,' said Dib. 'There is one more lord who wishes to pay his respects, and he is no coward, I assure you.'

Dostain swept an increasingly drunken gaze around his court. He could see none missing. As a boy raised in the most paranoid of circumstances, he had a honed ability to detect unexplained absences.

'Who is he, this lord? Where is he?'

'One you will like very much.'

'Send him in!' Dostain was beginning to enjoy himself again. The perfume lost its forbidding edge.

Dib clapped his hands and waved them encouragingly. The court trumpeters blew their long horns. 'Open the gates!'

Trembling servants drew open the doors to the hall. In strode a man of titanic proportions, flanked by two others of only marginally lesser size.

The court herald looked at them dumbfounded.

'I give you Damien Trastoon the Pleasure Seeker, Lord of Space Marines!' Dib called.

Trastoon towered head and shoulders over the courtiers

who crowded Magor's Hall. Heavy ceramite boots clanged on the stone floor. He wore power armour of brilliant, lurid pink, finely worked with grimacing faces. The jets of his back-pack, antiqued bronze orbs held in beast claws and spread like wings behind him, leaked a purple vapour. Upon his face was a brazen mask, wrought to resemble a snarling maw. The helm swept up from glowing lenses into a crest of horns, also of bronze. Upon his pauldron was a symbol a little like those used to denote the sexes in ancient alchemical texts, those circles with lines coming off their sides – arrow for male, an addition sign for female, but upon his armour blended and decorated with ornate curlicues.

Trastoon came to the foot of the steps. His men put their boltguns at rest with a perfect display of synchronised movement. Trastoon reached up to his helm. The members of the court gasped and murmured. The crowd shimmered in Dostain's vision. The individuals in it seemed to melt together so that to Dostain's eyes it was one gaudily clad beast. Someone was weeping. Dostain's head spun.

With a hiss, Trastoon disengaged the upper part of his helm and pulled it free. With a soft touch, he pressed at the side of his vox-grille mask and detached it from his gorget and the soft seals at his neck. Putting the mask into the upturned bowl of his helm, he stood revealed, the most perfect and repulsive creature Dostain had ever seen. His skin was a flawless, pearlescent white. One eye was a pure emerald green. The other was golden, slitted like a felid's. Above the golden eye, two delicate horns, pink and smooth as the lip of a seashell, curled up from his forehead.

'Hail, Dostain!' he shouted, clashing his arm against his chest. 'Free Lord of Geratomro!' His voice was pure and clear, but his words dripped with venom. His lips curved into a cruel smile. 'You have shown wisdom beyond your years in rejecting the False Emperor and claiming this world for your own. For was it not always yours, and did not the lords of Terra, the lickspittles of the corpse-god, impose themselves upon you and usurp your rightful rule? You are a true heir of Magor, my lord.'

With long, smooth strides he walked up the steps to the top of the dais, his feet further mangling the remains of the lord-civil's head. The weight of Trastoon must have been immense, for the boot squashed flesh flat and crunched bone on its way to meet the marble of the stair without hindrance.

'I am Lord Damien Trastoon of the Emperor's Children. Well met.'

'Em-em-emperor's children?' stuttered Dostain.

'Yes, we are all children of the Emperor here, are we not? Isn't that what He would like you to think, that He looks on you as a father?' Trastoon leaned close and hissed through pointed teeth. 'Lies. He is a mutant, like those He oppresses on every world. A psyker, like the many thousands He slaughters every day to maintain His unnatural life. I name Him hypocrite. False.' He stood erect again, imprisoning Dostain in his shadow as surely as if it were a cell in a tower. 'The name He gave us we keep. An irony. Humour is pleasurable, all the better when its sweetness is laced with the bitterness of the sardonic. Who does not like to laugh?' he shouted, and Dostain flinched. 'Pleasure, satisfaction, fulfilment. The Emperor offers none of these things, only slavery! To Him, we were merely tools. To Him, we of the

Legiones Astartes were expendable weapons. Thanks to our true lord, we are masters of all we survey.' He bowed, that awful smile chasing itself across his face again. 'Except here, of course... This is your world, my lord.'

He turned to Dib and bowed more deeply. 'My lord. It is pleasure unbounded to stand before you.' This time there was no irony in what he said.

'Our master is pleased that you came,' said Dib.

'How could I not, when the opportunity for such divine entertainment presents itself?' He turned to Pollein. 'This is the gateway? How charming.' He ran an inhumanly large, armoured finger along Pollein's jaw-line. She shuddered, whether from pleasure or horror, or a mix of both, Dostain could not tell.

'How wonderful,' she said.

'Who-who is your master?' said Dostain. Trastoon swivelled smoothly, returning his attention to the new Lord of Geratomro.

'Why! The lord of excess! The prince of pleasure! The lord of beauty and of abandon. Do you not know him?' he said in arch surprise.

'I have never heard of such a person.'

'No. You are the slave of the dusty corpse-king. How awful. Count yourself among the blind and the impoverished. But rejoice! We bring news of a fair prince who will treat you as you should be treated, with kindness and rewards of piquant sensation never to be bested.'

'You said nothing about a prince,' said Dostain to Dib. 'Am I not king?'

'I said nothing about a great many things. But all is to your benefit, my lord.' Dib and the Space Marine lord shared a smile.

'Bring in the feast!' called Trastoon.

'But we have a feast!' said Dostain, rousing himself from his stupor. He pointed at the long banqueting tables lining the hall.

Trastoon paid him no mind. The doors swung open again. Lines of human servants entered, some carrying tall ewers, others trays of goblets. They were dressed to preserve only the smallest part of their modesty, and often not even that. They were heavily tattooed, their eyes caked with make-up, spiked collars around their necks, and their hair styled into extravagant spikes and crests of every colour. They passed into the crowd, and began to pour wine. A heavy smell blew into the room, an unpleasant odour masquerading as something fine.

The lords and ladies reluctantly drank of the wine, but the instant it touched their lips their unease melted away. Gaiety replaced fear. An excited chattering set up in the hall.

'My lord,' said Trastoon, taking a goblet from one of the slaves and holding it out to Dostain. A clear, viscous wine clung to the inside, giving off a sweet pungency.

'Drink.'

'I–'

'Drink! You must drink, then you must eat. You must have your strength for your wedding night,' he said lecherously.

'I have my strength,' Dostain said weakly.

Trastoon looked meaningfully at Pollein. 'You require more.'

Dostain took the goblet. The scent masked the perfumed air and made his mouth water. With the Space Marine staring at him, he had no choice but to sip.

As soon as he did, his mouth tingled with pleasure. It was the wine he had supped while sleeping, but the flavour when tasted for real transcended that of his dreams. It was the sweetest he had ever had. Before it had a chance to travel down his gullet, he was suffused with a giddy euphoria. He began to smile.

'Yes, yes?' nodded Trastoon enthusiastically. 'Is it fitting to your palate, my lord?'

'It is very fine!' shouted Dostain.

The transhuman took a mighty goblet appropriate to his size and raised it in salutation.

'Your health!'

Dostain, laughing uncontrollably, forced some wine into the girl on his lap. Her sullenness vanished instantly upon tasting it, and her warm body relaxed into his.

Trastoon held up his goblet to the room and shouted out, 'My lord demands a tribute, a celebration of carnality and excess! To Planetary Commander Dostain! Eat, drink, abandon yourselves to revelry and revelation!'

Halt the tank, and thank the machine-spirit for its indulgence.

Let first the primary safety catch be released, and praise given unto the Omnissiah, who is the lord of the light of knowledge.

Let the engine main switch be disengaged from its alpha setting, thus freeing it from the sacred duties of the motive unit that propels the armoured servant of the Emperor and Omnissiah into battle. Give praise to Mars, and the majesty thereof.

Let the engine main switch be engaged with the beta setting. All glory to the domains of Mars, which protecteth the wisdom of the past.

Let the engine be activated, so that its might may be harnessed by the most holy dynamo, and so call forth the motive force unto the shell of the tank, and catch it gently within the capacitors.

Sing the praises of the motive force, so that it might quickly fill the energy reservoir.

Ensure capacitor charge is at the one hundredth of one hundred per cent.

Bless the refractor array.

Petition the ranging unit for a truthful refraction index.

Set refraction index.

Sing the praises of the motive force made light, the photonic sword of the Omnissiah.

Fire.

> – The Prayer of the Volcano Cannon,
> from an Adeptus Mechanicus primer
> for the novice enginseer.

CHAPTER TWENTY-ONE
SHADOWSWORD

MAGOR'S FIELDS
GERATOMRO
087498.M41

Jonas strained his eyes peering out into the gloom. 'Can't see anything!' he said. His nerves were ragged. Space Marines. Gods in man's form, and they were coming for him.

'Be brave, Jonas,' said Suliban. 'The enemy are men still, and can be killed. Think of your warriors. Do not dishearten them before the fight comes. It is bad enough that they might die – do not make cowards of them through your own fear.'

There were a dozen men in the dugout. His command group – Micz, Turneric, Bosarain, Suliban, Killek – and his sole support unit, a heavy group of two heavy bolters and a light autocannon. The wheels of the guns' carriages had been levered off the ground by the legs of their static mounts. The dugout was well constructed. His men were competent and bold. Against any other foe he would have rated their chances well.

Jonas shook his head. 'I'm sorry,' he breathed. He was soaking wet. Emperor alone knew what was in that rain. His world had become a small stage, curtained by rain and lit blindingly with short-lived red-and-orange flashes of the Titan battle. Lance beams slammed down from orbit intermittently. Further off, the noise of hundreds of tanks firing at once rumbled like thunder arrested at the peak of its sounding, never dying away as it should. The light of the weapons pulled the world in tighter rather than expanding it, making him feel more trapped. Right in front of him, the Titans continued to exchange volleys of fire fit to level cities. The power on display was beautiful in a terrifying way.

His vox-bead bleeped in his ear. *'Targets advancing. Four hundred yards and closing,'* said Gulinar, Parrigar's second in command and vox-operator.

'I still can't see anything!' hissed Jonas, more quietly this time, quiet enough that his words were inaudible under the clamour of war.

Jonas watched the god-machines. What he was seeing was almost incomprehensible. The Warhound had come in from the enemy Titan's right, and was weaving back and forth in tight zigzags faster than the towering enemy's carapace weapons could track. The huge cannons were obscured by the rain and the Warlord Titan's armoured shell from over whose lip their discharge stabbed out like thunderbolts. His vox-bead pulsed with every shot. The Reaver circled further out to the right. Itself a towering monstrosity, in comparison to the enemy Titan it seemed like a child. The infantry were all reduced to insects by this quarrel of metal gods. Far off, the continued rumble and flash of cannons lit up the stalking shapes of the lesser enemy Titans, whose own weapons swept from side to side like the scythe of a farmer.

Both of the Imperial Titans were closing in on the crippled enemy Warlord, firing as they approached. Having attained a position out of the firing arc of the right arm, the Reaver marched straight at its foe. The whining grind of monstrous motors penetrated the racket of their fire as the left arm and both top mounts locked on to the Reaver. The Reaver's void shields had been up and down throughout the fight, and once more they flared at the immense amount of punishment they absorbed. Quickly the first collapsed with a dull, purple flash.

Jonas' cousin's tank was dragging itself very slowly back up the slope into a better firing position. The Shadowswords' emplacement was unrecognisable. The crater edge had given out where *Lux Imperator* had been stationed. A deep, smoking furrow, patches of it still glowing with heat, marked the position of Askelios' tank. That had been completely obliterated. The other Atraxian Shadowsword was a dark hull leaning away from Jonas' position.

'I never thought to be fighting them. Space Marines. They are supposed to be all that is good in the Imperium,' he said.

'As I said, they are men, and men can be corrupted.'

Jonas smiled and gave a sidelong look to Suliban.

'I did not mean that it were a matter of levity,' said Suliban.

'It's not that,' said Jonas. 'I'm smiling because you, commissar, are dirty, for the first time since I have known you.'

Suliban adjusted his filthy poncho. His high-peaked cap had collected a layer of silt, deposited by the rain.

'You look so uncomfortable, it's comic–' Jonas was

interrupted by a sudden and unexpected noise from the vox-bead: not a signal, but a pulse of raw electromagnetic energy. The sky out towards the main advance filled with a growing ball of fire, followed seconds later by a blast of hot wind that whipped the black rain under the roof of their shelter.

'Engine death!' said Bosarain.

A triumphant, army-wide broadcast a moment later confirmed the kill: one of the enemy Reavers, pummelled to its end by concerted battle cannon fire.

'One down, three to go,' said Jonas.

'Look!' said one of his men, leaning out of the shelter and pointing down the rough slope of the crater.

Jonas peered over the edge of the dugout. Emerging directly from the black water collected at the bottom of the crater were huge, armoured figures. The first walked straight at the steep slope below. They mag-locked their bolters to their chests then propelled themselves up the mud slope on all fours with horrifying speed.

'Emperor,' said Suliban. He raged at seeing their god's finest servants turned traitor, but there was fear there, too.

Jonas swore. The Space Marines were coming up under them. The angle was too steep for his heavy team to target.

The blazing light of the dying reactor blinked out, plunging Jonas' environs into blackness.

'*Hostiles! Hostiles!*' voxed one of his sergeants out on the left flank, away from the crater. The snapping reports of lasguns came swiftly on the heels of his words, then the terrible bangs of bolters, their clean, triple barks clear under the booming of the Titans' war.

'Heavy team, pan left,' said Jonas shakily. 'Open fire.

The rest of us, grenades and lasguns. Micz, get your melta ready.'

The men quickly rearranged themselves to the right of the heavy squad. Huddled together, they leaned into the damp bank of the dugout, knuckles white.

'Ready?' said Jonas.

His men nodded. Suliban disengaged the safety on his pistol with an audible snap.

'Raise Parrigar.'

'I can't,' said Anderick.

'Then we're on our own.'

The heavy weapons took aim on half-seen figures attacking the left flank.

'Now,' mouthed Jonas.

Lit by the wrath of heaven, Jonas and his men leaned over the edge of the dugout and opened fire on the monsters climbing up to kill them.

'Steady, steady!' said Bannick.

Through the brief day of the dying war machine, the Shadowsword crept backwards up the hill. Every few feet, the tracks slipped on mud so soft it was little better than slurry. For those moments, they held their breaths as Shoam delicately manoeuvred until the tracks bit again.

He was standing inside the hatch, feet braced against his seat's reinforced armrests, exposed to the foul air, hands caked in the mud he had scooped off the ranging augur. Rain ran off his greatcoat, streaking it with its load of dirt and ash. More mud rolled off the Shadowsword in ripples as thick as dough. Flashes and bangs, almost lost under the ongoing roar of the god-machines' conflict, drew nearer to their position. Frantic bursts of short-range vox told him the story. Traitor Space Marines in hideous armour were attacking the left where Jonas was stationed. Out of sight on the other side of the pressure ridge, *Righteous Vengeance* roared into action, heading to where the fighting was fiercest.

None of that could concern Bannick. Not even if the enemy were feet from his tank. 'Mute my vox, Epperaliant, but keep me informed if anything important happens. We've one shot. We need to concentrate.'

The tank rolled further up. The flashed reflections of explosions playing on the black water in the crater receded. Flickering lights like sideways candles were bolts streaking through the air, betraying the Space Marines' positions. The brightest of the weapon's discharge lit them up in stark whites, running giants in horned helmets and armour adorned with leering gargoyles and cruel barbs. Their attention seemed to be on his cousin's position, not on the tank inching its way backwards. The orbital strikes had ceased. Only rain fell from the sky. Far away, at the heart of a concentration of flashing detonations, he thought he saw the second enemy Reaver marching through the lead echelon of tanks seemingly without harm towards the heart of the Imperial advance. The damage it could do there...

He checked himself. He could not think like that. The first Titan had fallen to the concentrated firepower of an Imperial tank regiment. They could do it again. He could not consider how many had died in stopping the first.

Slowly, slowly, *Lux Imperator* crawled out of the crater. Bannick upended his full canteen over the glass of the ranging eye and scrubbed at it with his sleeve.

'Meggen?' he voxed.

'I can see fine now, Colaron,' he said. 'But we're three degrees off getting a clear shot.'

The volcano cannon had a very limited range of elevation and traversal. In some of the more primitive patterns of the tank, the weapon had none at all.

'Come on!' he growled. Filthy water ran down his face, its acrid taste polluting his lips. They drew level with the empty shell of *Indominus.* Its paint was scorched around every aperture. Melted armourglass had reset in cloudy pools around its sightless viewing slits. The main cannon hung limply, bent to one side.

'Nearly there,' voxed Meggen.

The three Titans were firing mercilessly on each other at point-blank range, like wooden ships from a primitive world unleashing cascades of shot at their enemy, regardless of the damage inflicted on themselves. The Warhound was agile, evading the ponderous swings of the Warlord's right arm, and harrying its right with blazing spears of tracer shot from its vulcan mega-bolter and the blinding flash-blast of its plasma cannon. Despite the awesome destructive potential of these weapons, they posed little threat to the Warlord on their own. Perhaps for this reason, the enemy princeps spared only the right arm for the task of keeping the Warhound at bay, and perhaps only because the Reaver was out of the fire arc for that arm. Its other three armaments, twin carapace lasers and the terrible focused energy weapon that made up its left arm, concentrated fire on the Reaver. The energy unleashed was awful, enough power to fuel a city for a year expended in moments. The Reaver responded in kind. The amount of effort the Imperium could spare for destruction was boundless, when there seemed so little for peace.

The Reaver's final shield was close to failing, its displacement aura very low in the spectrum, a flickering violet he could only just perceive. Princeps Yolanedesh edged further and further to the left of the immobilised Titan, hoping to get behind it. This would have been the best way of ensuring the Reaver's long-term survival, had they more time, for there was a blind spot to the very rear and the torso could not turn further than sixty degrees. With the Warlord's knee crippled, Yolanedesh could destroy the enemy engine at leisure. In reality, it was too far to go. Without bringing down the enemy Titan's void shields again soon, the Shadowsword's shot would be wasted, and they would all perish. Yolanedesh evidently knew this, for he went slowly, all weapons firing, rather than making a dash for the rear. It was a ploy, one designed to give Bannick a chance.

'There!' shouted Meggen.

'Halt!' commanded Bannick. The tank lurched to a stop.

'Charge capacitors. Engage cannon charge,' commanded Bannick. 'Set refraction index for minimum range. Prepare to fire.' He could go back down, he would be safer there. But the spectacle of the machines warring kept him where he was. A series of clunks came from beneath his feet as the engine reactor's drive was engaged with the tank's dynamo. A whine built.

A streak of light burned itself onto his eyes. Lascannon burst, right to the glacis. The score of its impact glowed redly.

'Traitor Space Marines to the front! Shoam, man the bolter. Leonates, sponson bolters and lascannon on roving fire. Put a spread out, keep them back.' Even Space Marines would keep away from such firepower. Little else would stop them.

'Cannon fifty-five per cent charged,' said Starstan.

The last void shield on *Ultimate Sanction* flickered out, low and blue as burning brandy. It staggered as the full force of the Warlord's fire tore into it. Glowing chambers on the Warlord's left arm lit in sequence, and it spat a lightning-white shaft of light at the smaller engine, smashing its right arm off in a spray of molten metal. The Reaver's war-horns let out an anguished wail, and it staggered to its left, bringing it into the fire arcs of all four of the Warlord's weapons.

'How close?'

'Ninety per cent,' said Starstan emotionlessly.

'Can you not pray more or something?' said Meggen. 'Our Titan is getting torn to pieces.'

The second arm cannon came around to target the Reaver, showing the enemy princeps' disdain for the Warhound nipping at its heels. Four beams of light intersected on the Reaver's midriff, burning through its chest armour and burrowing into the reactor behind. The cannons snapped off. Bannick threw up his arm just in time to prevent himself being blinded as *Ultimate Sanction*'s reactor detonated.

A hemisphere of energy engulfed an area five hundred yards in radius, annihilating everything it touched. Blinding light seared the battlefield. Static discharge earthed itself in metallic objects hundreds of yards further out. Clouds of billowing steam boiled skywards. Scorching shock wind buffeted Bannick.

He lowered his hand as the bubble of energy sank in on itself and vanished, leaving a broad, glowing circle of glassed earth as the Titan's grave marker.

'One hundred per cent,' said Starstan.

'I'm ready. Should I take the shot?'

'Epperaliant. Is the last shield down?'

'I can't tell! All my instruments are scrambled.'

Bannick blinked. *War's Gift* still darted about, miraculously evading the larger Titan's blows. Ponderously, the Warlord's torso swung about, carapace weapons angling down. Defiantly, the Warhound opened fire. A stream of glowing mega-bolter shells spattered off the big Titan's armour.

'The shield! The last shield has come down. *Ultimate Sanction* did it! Meggen, open fire!'

A thrumming burr preceded the volcano cannon's discharge. Bannick averted his eyes from the muzzle as it spat white light at the Titan, bright plasma exhaust bursting from the sleeve vents as its beam shot out in a perfect ray of super-aligned photons.

The shot hit home on the weakened knee, shearing right through. For a second the Titan stood tall, and Bannick thought their last effort had been in vain, but then, as its torso continued to track the Warhound, it fell to the right. The severed lower left leg stood a moment longer, then toppled backwards.

The Warlord fell face-first into the mud. Sluggishly, it tried to move, but could not.

War's Gift jogged to the front, levelled its guns at the command deck, and sent a stream of mega-bolt-rounds into the head. The Warlord shuddered, and lay still. Execution done, *War's Gift* let out a triumphant howling from its war-horns, turned and ran back towards the main advance.

'They're leaving it?' said Leonates.

'They will attempt to capture it, purify it and resanctify the engine in the name of the Emperor and Omnissiah,' said Epperaliant. 'A Warlord for a Reaver, not a bad exchange.'

'Omnis sancta omnia,' intoned Starstan.

'Meggen, get on the heavy bolters. Let's keep the enemy back while we drag ourselves out of this mire,' said Bannick. He bent to lower himself down into the tank, but a hand grasped him hard by the back of his coat and hauled him into the air.

'It is a little late for that,' said a silky voice.

Bannick looked up into the respirator grille of a Space Marine. Casually, the warrior tossed a grenade down the open hatch. Bannick had time to see the yellow flash and dull crump of detonation before the warrior threw Bannick off the top of the tank, and jumped down after him.

The warrior locked his bolter to his thigh and advanced upon Bannick.

Jonas and his men fired downwards, the beams from their lasguns doing little more than scorching the enemy's battleplate. Jonas' mouth ran dry. As soon as the Traitor Space Marines made it to the top of the slope, they would kill everyone in the dugout. There was nothing that could prevent that.

To their left, giants appeared in the storm, their bolters flashing with muzzle flare as they gunned down Jonas' men in the slit trenches yards from his position.

'They're coming! They're coming!' shouted Bosarain, right before a bolt took him in the chest. The explosion took the entirety of his left side and his head with it. The banner of Jonas' platoon fell bloody into the earth. The man next to him screamed, turned and ran, abandoning his heavy bolter.

'Halt! You defy the will of the Emperor!' shouted Suliban, but his gun was already levelled, and the round left the barrel microseconds after the words left his lips. The soldier sprawled forwards, a crater in his back. Other men close to flight returned to their weapons. The autocannon coughed twice and one of the monsters staggered back at the impact. Cheers died on men's lips as the monster righted himself, drew his pistol and recommenced the slaughter.

'It's no use,' said Jonas, lowering his gun.

'Stand firm, Lieutenant Bannick,' said Suliban.

'I am standing, commissar, but it is still no use.'

Lin Coass Lo Turneric, dressing the stump of a man whose arm had been blasted off at the elbow, caught Suliban's expression and gave Jonas a warning look. Jonas ignored it.

'Look! We can't hurt them. We can't...'

A terrifying screaming filled the dugout.

'Down!' yelled Suliban, tackling Jonas around his midriff. He bore the lieutenant into the mud as the thunderous noise of a heavy bolter loosing shot at close range obliterated every other vestige of sound in the dugout. Jonas rolled onto his back to see a giant standing on the edge of the dugout. Rain poured down in streams through the shattered plastek roof.

There was a bolt lodged in the Space Marine's torso, the last few seconds of its propellant charge fizzing to nothing. The Space Marine gurgled out a laugh, raised his outlandish axe. The bolt exploded. Stinging shards of ceramite peppered Jonas' skin. The Space Marine fell forwards, smoke pouring from his neck seal and the black hole in his chest. Jonas scrambled out of the way of the falling body just in time. It landed hard in the mud, sinking under its own weight.

'Suliban! We have to fall back.'

Another Space Marine clambered over the lip of the trench. Micz caught him full in the face with a blast from his meltagun, and he tumbled backwards, headless.

'We're not going to stay this lucky. We need Parrigar.'

Suliban's eyes narrowed. Then he nodded. 'Very well.'

Jonas grabbed at his vox-bead. 'Parrigar, come in. We require immediate extraction. We're being overrun.'

'I still can't raise him,' said Anderick.

'He can't be dead!' said Jonas. If *Righteous Vengeance* was gone, they had nowhere else to run.

From the ridge some yards to their right and above them, the glaring blast of *Lux Imperator*'s cannon bathed the hellish scene in bright light. For a second, the world seemed to stop. Moments later, the Titan collapsed, and the howling confusion of combat swept back into the void left by the Titan's fall. Jonas' men were too occupied to cheer the engine's death.

The vox crackled.

'*I'm inbound*,' said Parrigar. '*Coming right up behind you. Stand ready for extraction.*'

'Fall back!' ordered Jonas. 'Mission accomplished!' he shouted. 'Platoon, fall back!'

Jonas had not expected an orderly retreat, and he did not get one. In a scrambling run the tattered remnants of Jonas' platoon fled their trenches and dugouts, abandoning their heavy weapons. Bolters barked as the Space Marines crested the ridge in numbers. Burning bolts buzzed past Jonas' head, burying themselves in the earth and exploding. Clods of mud blew into the air, further obscuring sight. He and Suliban sprinted side by side. Men fell all around them. Then searchlights were stabbing through the gloom, and the black shadow of *Righteous Vengeance* roared out of the night, streaming filthy rain from its plating.

'Part either side of the tank! Stand clear of the weapons!' ordered Parrigar through the tank's vox-hailer. It was as if the tank itself gave voice. 'Stand clear!'

The barrels of the mega-bolter began to turn, burring as they built up to firing speed. Jonas threw himself to the side, then ducked low as he saw the heavy bolters mounted in *Righteous Vengeance*'s sponsons tracking targets behind him. They opened fire, blades of flame stabbing from the muzzles. He ran on, the space between his shoulder blades itching in anticipation at the explosive death he was certain was coming. Bolts whistled overhead in both directions, their rocket trails crisscrossing the sky. Then he was past the sponsons, following in the footsteps of exhausted, terrified men up the access ladders to the fighting deck of the great tank. Men pushed each other up from below, while others leaned down, hands grasping for the slippery arms of their comrades. Rain hissed in the beams of the meltagunners. Streams of plasma lit the scene more brightly than flares.

He had been wary of the order to concentrate his special weapons in one squad, but now he whispered silent thanks to the Emperor for Parrigar's insistence. Space Marines were closing in from the sides. Bolts spanked off the thick armour of the tank, but the men scrambling to get aboard were torn apart, and it was through chunks of their flesh and their spilled entrails that Jonas scrambled upwards.

Hands reached for him. From below someone pushed, and he hauled himself over the armoured parapet encircling the fighting deck. He leaned back out, reaching for Suliban. The commissar shook his head, instead taking charge of the men below, who were panicking as more Space Marines came out of the downpour.

'There!' shouted Jonas, slapping one the meltagunners on the shoulder and directing his fire at a Space Marine advancing with his bolter tucked into his shoulder, methodically shooting Jonas' men. The first roaring fusion discharge missed, but the second was good, obliterating the Space Marine's torso. The reactor in his back-pack exploded, and the traitor fell into the mud as a collection of smoking limbs.

'Well d–' began Jonas. The mega-bolter opened up, rendering speech pointless. His ears rang at the fury of the weapon. Men were still running for the tank. A couple fell, one shot from behind, one caught by the tank's secondary weapons as he ran at it in blind fear. The mega-bolter cut out, leaving a cone of shattered enemy before it. *Lux Imperator* was coming down from the top of the crater ridge towards the Stormlord, bolters blazing. A score of huge, armoured figures were illuminated by its spotlights advancing towards the tanks. Flames and explosions were everywhere. Rain glittered in the light.

'Jonas Bannick, this is Parrigar. We are going to have to leave. Augur scans indicate dozens more of the enemy closing in on our position.'

'My men–'

'Are good as dead. I am sorry. I cannot risk Righteous Vengeance. *I have tarried longer than I should.'*

The engines growled, and the tank began to roll

backwards. Those men not already aboard stumbled onwards after it. The machine went at no great pace, but soon it was up to a man's running speed, and none of them could run well in that mud.

'Suliban! Suliban! Take my hand!' shouted Jonas, leaning down over the parapet. The commissar looked around, and abandoned his efforts reluctantly. He pulled himself up onto the track guard, other men grasping at his ankles. Jonas grabbed him by both hands and dragged him into the back.

The tank was firing constantly now. Bolter fire came in from all sides, rattling off the tank's thick hide. When one of his men firing over the side took a bolt in the chest, he ordered the rest to get down.

'Sound off!' he bellowed over the roaring chug of the mega-bolter.

Fourteen men replied. He had set out into this war with forty. Around half of them were veterans from Gulem. Once again, his platoon had been savaged.

'We live to fight another day,' said Suliban, and patted Jonas with one dirty glove. Then he stood tall, ignoring bolt-shells whistling by.

'Men of the Imperium!' he shouted, his voice pitched perfectly to cut through battle's roar. 'Today you fought well against a foe that would best most warriors. We have many dead, but out there, in the dark, lie the shattered bodies of dozens of traitors, traitors of the blackest sort, the very sons of the Emperor Himself, who, despite the gifts given them by their father, our God, chose to betray Him. For each of the dead lying there, the Emperor thanks you, and be sure that now He sheds tears upon His Golden Throne for every one of His loyal servants who have perished today upon this dire field.' The men were intent on him. 'Think and be satisfied that, through your efforts directly, one of the great god-machines of the enemy has been brought low into the dirt. Few men can claim such an act of valour. Hold your heads up high, sons of Paragon. You have performed your duty well.'

Suliban sat against the fighting deck wall. Jonas tipped his head back and stared at the black clouds.

'A nice speech, commissar.'

Suliban stared ahead dourly. 'I meant every word. I believe every word.'

'I know,' said Jonas quietly. 'So do I.'

Suliban gave him a grateful look. It struck Jonas then how young he was, this commissar with the power of life and death over them all. A hand of the Emperor, barely old enough to be called a man.

The throaty roar of engines broke his train of thought. Jonas stood and put his head over the parapet.

Headlights were speeding through the storm in close formation towards the rear of the Stormlord.

'Emperor save us,' he said. 'There are more.'

Lux Imperator pulled away. Spouting blue smoke, it shuddered forwards, took a hard left turn and drove towards the sounds of combat, anti-personnel weaponry barking, leaving Bannick sprawled in the mud. They had left him for dead.

With long strides that seemed nightmarishly slow, the Space Marine paced across the torn ground to where Bannick lay.

Bannick's heart froze, but his hand did not. His fingers closed around the wet, gritty hilt of his power sword, still scabbarded and belted to his waist. He got unsteadily to his feet. His head spun from the impact, his ribs were bruised and every breath hurt. The Space Marine drew nearer, unaware of the blade Bannick held hidden behind his back. As he came within thrusting distance, Bannick flicked the activation stud on his sword. The scabbard disintegrated around the weapon. He pulled it free. Ignoring the ache in his chest, he executed a perfect duellist's thrust. The disruptive field flared as it encountered the Traitor Space Marine's plastron, piercing one eye of the brazen face cast upon it with a crack. The blade point slid after, into the Space Marine's heart.

A back-handed blow sent Bannick back down and skidding through the sloppy mud. The Space Marine stood transfixed by Bannick's blade. His shoulders moved in convulsively, as if he would catch the sword by the movement. He let out a gasp of surprise, and gripped the sword blade in his hand. The field banged again as the Traitor Space Marine's fingers closed around it. The other hand groped for the hilt's activation stud.

Bannick scrambled backwards, half swimming in the mud. The Space Marine hunched over the sword for a moment, not moving. He dared not think he had killed it, but hope undid his best intentions.

It was not to be. The Space Marine's fingers found the stud and deactivated the disruption field. With a grunt, he drew out the power sword. In his grip, it seemed the smallest of things, a child's toy. He threw it aside into the mud and stood erect painfully.

The Space Marine came to stand over Bannick, reached his hands to his helm and undid clasps there. Small jets of air hissed from uncoupled seals, heavy with a perfume strong enough for Bannick to smell in the rain.

Bannick blinked gritty water from his eyes. The man revealed beneath the helmet was beautiful, more perfect than the most exquisitely carved statue in a cathedral, more finely formed than those artworks that purported to show the inherent superiority of the human form over all others in the galaxy.

Stark, purple tattoos marked his face. His lips were full, nose strong, cheekbones perfect in their angle and sharpness, and he held himself with a bearing more refined than the highest Paragonian aristocrat. His skin was flawless, bright, and his blue-white hair was cropped close to his skull. Bannick's breath caught in his throat. For all his perfection, there was an air of ineffable sorrow about the man. He looked down at Bannick with bright eyes that wept quicksilver tears into the rain.

'That was a good thrust. You are a fine swordsman, for a mortal. For the first time in a thousand years, I am wounded,' he said. 'For the first time in ten thousand, I came close to death.' The language he used was almost incomprehensible. It was a form of Gothic, but full of strange stresses and archaic grammatical forms. The Space Marine took a step forwards. He was as solid as a tower, clad in heavy armour covered in soft leather. Bannick shrank back when he made out the outlines of a flattened human face, eyes and mouth stitched shut, wrapped around his greave. 'Never in all the years of the long war has a mere man caused me harm. You have destroyed my birth heart. I shall never have another.' The Space Marine's eyes closed and he tilted his face into the downpour. 'The feeling of loss is... exquisite. I remember times I thought

325

never to recall as I contemplate its destruction. I have memories of a time that was lost brought out by the pain. Such *pain*. It is a blessing. I thank you.' He looked down at Bannick and smiled. The lips were perfect, the teeth behind them perfect, and the malice behind them the most perfectly formed of all. 'I should not wish you to miss out on such experience. I shall repay your gift. You are blessed. We shall travel the roads of agony together.'

He snatched out a long, silver blade from a scabbard at his belt, and knelt, licking his lips in anticipation. Bannick tried to scramble backwards, but the Space Marine slammed down the heel of his hand into Bannick's forearm, pinning him fast. Were it not for the softness of the ground beneath, his arm would surely have been broken. The knife slid into his sleeve and parted it with no resistance.

'I shall find you a fine nerve to pluck. You shall sing the song of pain, and we shall rejoice, for no sensation is wasted, and my master, Slaanesh, will be most gratified.' He looked Bannick dead in the eye. 'Be joyful. There is no purer form of offering than gratification.'

The knife tip pricked his skin. Bannick felt nothing as it opened his flesh, it was so sharp. But then the point bit into some vital pathway, and he sang indeed.

There was a roaring through the pain. Yellow light fell onto the pair in the mud. The rapid report of a bolt-gun on full auto rang out, riddling the traitor's body. The Space Marine fell away with a sigh of pleasure. The knife slipped agonisingly out of Bannick's flesh. He sat. Agony coursed up his arm and he nearly fainted. The deafening rumble of *Righteous Vengeance*'s mega-bolter sounded sporadically. *Lux Imperator*'s bolters chattered away almost meekly by comparison. Both tanks were away from him, lumbering silhouettes in the rain whose angles were lit sporadically and confusingly by the battle. The shouts and screams of frightened men competed with the fire of automatic weaponry.

A huge, blocky combat bike came to a sliding halt. A figure dismounted and strode towards him, tall and imposing as the dead traitor, framed by the headlamp of his steed. Another Space Marine, armoured and girded for war. His armour was black and trimmed in red, bedecked with skulls, bones and other talismans of grisly aspect. This new monster stood over the injured Bannick, eye-lenses glaring. The figure moved his bolter, and Bannick expected it to point at his head, and awaited the hammer-blow detonation in his skull. But the Space Marine only shifted his weapon so that he might hold it one-handed. He leaned forwards, and offered his left gauntlet to Bannick, fingers spread wide.

'Hail to you, though poorly met on this day of torrents and of treachery. You have survived one of the worst creatures this galaxy has to offer, son of holy Terra, and you yet live. The Emperor of Mankind watches over you. Take my hand and be risen from the earth. Your struggles for the Imperium are not yet done.'

Bannick clutched the warrior's arm. His shock subsided. A small force of Space Marines had been with them since Kalidar. He recognised the armour now, the emblem of the gothic cross blazoned on the pauldrons and chest. He was suddenly cold, and his teeth chattered with the same insistency as the bolters in the distance. 'You are not going to kill me. You are of the Black Templars.'

'I am not going to kill you, I swear. I am Adelard,' said

the warrior, 'sword brother of the Michaelus Crusade of the Black Templars Chapter, Adeptus Astartes, and loyal son of Rogal Dorn. You have nothing to fear. We are brothers, you and I. Warriors in the never-ending war. Come with me, and be safe.'

CHAPTER TWENTY-TWO
DAEMONGATE

IMPERIAL GOVERNOR'S PALACE, MAGOR'S SEAT
GERATOMRO
087798.M41

Dostain's wedding and coronation passed in a blur. It was certain the wine was of no normal vintage, but he did not care. It heightened his senses and dulled something important inside his mind. Upon his throne, he indulged in heroic acts of gluttony while his court threw off its inhibitions and sank into sybaritic indulgence. Coy whispers became discreet liaisons. Laughter rang out from every corner. They sipped wine to begin with, but only to begin with. Soon they were guzzling it, and cavorting openly with one another and the servants of the Space Marines, dancing, singing, feasting and shouting, until all in the hall were drawn into a grand display of excess. Trastoon cheered to see such abandon. Dib wandered the hall, fingers trailing along backs, whispering things into ears that either horrified or delighted them.

Music struck up. Drums beat out a rhythm to quicken

the oldest heart, flutes played unearthly melodies. The beat became wilder as the wine flowed quicker.

There were moments when Dostain's attention shifted somehow, and he saw scenes of bloodshed and horror. Faces stained red with vitae, the flesh of living victims consumed by laughing courtiers, and the music became screams torn from the throats of tortured men. At those moments, the servants of the Emperor's Children took on a different form, and the golden cauldron they served their wine from became a hideous creature that mewled in agony. Then he would blink, and he would see none of this, just unrestrained revelry as practised in the old days of Geratomro. Unease would linger a few moments, soon to fade under a sense of triumph and joy as he took another sip of the delightful wine.

'How wonderful,' said Pollein leadenly. Trastoon massaged the back of her neck possessively. Dostain thought this odd one moment, and not at all the next.

The evening wore on. Dostain's sense of time collapsed like a shattered mirror. Temporality became flashing images falling past his mind's eye without any sense of order or relative importance. The tiny sounds of cutlery on plates or the glint of candlelight on a diamond facet of the chandeliers had as much weight as the loudest horn or the most beautiful woman. Trastoon's face became the only constant. Always he was by his side, scrutinising him, as if there were some meat Dostain might provide to satisfy an unknowable hunger. The new governor's pleasure was shot through with discomfort at this regard, though only when he groggily remembered it. All the while, the shattered impressions of the revel piled one atop the other until Dostain's mind was overwhelmed with sensation.

Then there was only Trastoon's eyes, burning into his, and a short darkness fell. Only the eyes. One gold, one green.

A strong hand lifted his head. A warm goblet was pressed to his lips.

'Drink, my lord! Soon you must be away to your marriage bed. A little more sweet wine to awaken the senses.'

'Whu?' he said blearily. The girl had gone from his lap. Pollein had gone from his side. 'Where is my wife?' he said clumsily.

'Why, she enjoys the marriage feast, my lord, as a bride in the gaze of Slaanesh should.'

The Space Marine restricted his view to a small triangle caught in the crook of Trastoon's elbow. Dostain could not see Pollein through this small window, and while he looked there the scene flickered back and forth from white-lit pleasure to carmine-illuminated bloodshed. Neither remained long. Both the transition between the two and what he saw in the latter made him ill, and he vomited copiously. Trastoon stepped smoothly back to prevent the vomit splashing his boots.

'Oh, my lord!' the Space Marine tutted. He nodded behind him at one of his helmeted fellows, who shoved his way roughly into the crowd. He plucked Pollein from a mass of bodies entwined in the remains of the food atop a banqueting table. The Space Marine was none too gentle, and the revellers made odd cries at the pain inflicted on them.

'Why is she naked?' he said.

'What was that, my lord?' asked Trastoon.

'She has no clothes. Why?'

'How will she love you otherwise?' said Trastoon, hauling

Dostain from his chair and carrying him like a child in his arms. 'They are ready,' said Trastoon to his brother, who had Pollein slung over one shoulder.

Dostain snuggled into the hard armour of the warrior. His misgivings gave way again to satisfaction. His aunt was his, by marriage, by right. He had wanted her for so long. It was wrong to deprive someone of physical bliss.

Next thing he knew, he was in his bed and she beside him. Surely, he thought, it should be day? But day never came, darkness reigned, and black water fell in sheets from the sky. Far away there was a rumbling noise punctuated by dazzling flashes and world-shaking booms. Her touch drove it from his mind.

The spell upon Pollein seemed to melt away, and she came to shuddering life. Experiences were his to know that he had never expected to feel. All the while he had the impression of something vast watching him, sharing the sensations, something that seemed benevolent on the surface, but within which strong currents of evil ran.

Dostain did not care. He did not care that Trastoon and his warrior companion stood guard by the door. He did not care that the day never came.

'Pollein, Pollein!' he cried.

'Dib, Dib, Dib,' she murmured.

He did not care about that either. Only the feeling of her next to him. He was a lord of the world, and the lord of the woman he had long desired. No better fate could he wish for.

Nothing lasts. At the end, they fell drunken and exhausted. Dostain's eyes slid shut. Before he drifted into a troubled sleep, he felt Trastoon move to his side and lean down. He whispered into his ear so closely that his lips brushed his sweat-beaded skin.

'And so the Prince of Pleasure rewards you for your sacrifice.'

What sacrifice, he wondered. There was none. He had done nothing but gain. Not the way he had expected, but he had won.

Weight shifted from the bed next to him, and he passed out.

Dostain awoke alone. He stank of excess, of vomit, of sweat and of stale wine. His head throbbed with intolerable pain. He sat gingerly at first, then threw back the covers and rose in a panic at what he saw.

His room was in disorder, all his furniture upended, the curtains torn down, his wash-bowl and mirrors smashed. The lumens were out, and as he groped around for a source of light, he trod on jagged glass, injuring his feet. His own cries sickened him, and he was forced to lean against one of his dressers, whose drawers had all been ripped out and their contents scattered. He found a mismatched pair of slippers and pulled them on, moaning at the swimming of his head as he bent over.

'What happened?' he croaked. 'Pollein?'

He knew what he was going to find before he turned back to the bed.

The sheets were twisted up into damp knots, blood-stained and wine-soaked. He shuffled towards it. Every breath acted as a pump to force the acid up from his stomach into his gullet. What was left in his gut roiled. His breath stank, his nostrils felt hot and dry when he breathed. His forehead too was overly hot, and free of sweat. He had a terrible thirst, but his ewers of water had been upset, spilling their contents upon the marble floor. Rarely had he paid so badly for a night's indulgence.

'Pollein?' he said in a small voice. She was nowhere to be seen. He roamed pathetically to all four corners of his large chamber searching for her, his feet crunching on broken ceramics and glass. He went to the small garde-robe behind its folding screen. There was a tap there. He turned it on and sucked greedily at the water pouring from it until a foul taste polluted it, and he yanked his head back, spitting mightily.

The tap sputtered bloody filth into the basin. With a shaking hand, he shut it off.

The water he had managed to drink sat uneasily in his stomach, but he forced himself to hold it down. He gave an acid burp. Outside it was still dark, and though the rain had eased it had not stopped. A strange glow shone from the sky, shifting and green as polar aurorae. That rumbling he had heard the night before was closer, and now he was sober he recognised it for weapons fire.

He called his servants. None came. Fighting down nausea, he threw on the first clothes he could find, and abandoned his wrecked chamber for the darkness of his palace.

No one answered his calls. He went looking in servants' chambers and the quarters of the lords and ladies who lodged at the palace. Each one was turned over as his had been. In many were traces of blood, smeared handprints on the walls, pools of it glinting darkly in the corners. The first he encountered he slipped in, barely avoiding a fall. There was a heavy scent in every room, the perfume of the night before mixed with the stink of blood and sweat. These smells the perfume accentuated rather than masked, and in the worst rooms he had to cover his face. He wished he had a weapon.

All the while the sound of cannon fire grew closer. He could not yet hear the sound of small arms, but he felt in his gut that it would not be long. Anguish clawed at him. Where were his new allies?

It was not long before he found the first of the bodies. A man, lying on his back. His robes and gut had been slit open, the stomach emptied out so that there was a bloody cavity where his organs had once nestled. There was a look of bliss on his open-eyed face. His dead stare troubled Dostain so that he knelt and closed the man's eyes.

In another room he found a couple, their flesh run together, their faces joined by a long tube of skin at the mouth. From the look of the wounds all over their bodies, they had clawed at each other before the end, though their fingers too were buried deep and seamlessly into each other's skin. More horrors awaited him. The nearer he drew to the banqueting hall, the more he found: people dead in the most horrific of ways, many with expressions of pleasure plastered across their faces.

Towards Magor's Hall the floors were covered with blood. Isolated pools at first, then as he drew nearer, a continuous slick that stretched from wall to wall. Steeling himself, he paddled through it, ignoring the screamed pleadings of his heart that he flee and never look back. He had nowhere to go. He had been duped. There were dark stories, read in forbidden books and passed on by word of mouth among the elite, of such happenings as this – things that made the legend of the Devil-in-the-bush seem positively benevolent; tales of gods and their servants, treachery on a galactic scale in the distant past of the Imperium.

He had been a fool. Blinded by love. And it was love

he felt for Pollein. Now he had sated his baser desires, his affection for her had blossomed, but because of his shame, he found it hard to attribute his search to pure motives. All he could be certain of was that he had to find her. Conflicted, he pressed on.

The approach to Magor's Hall was silent, empty of the servants, Yellow Guard, petitioners and others who would throng its length on a normal day. Through their blood he approached the hall that was supposedly the seat of his power. He had no right to it; he had bought the throne with blood. Dostain suspected there would never be such a thing as a normal day on Geratomro ever again.

The golden gates were ajar. He slipped through to find a scene of such awfulness his knees gave out and he collapsed to the floor.

His court had never gone home. All remained at the feast. All were dead. Most were in a state of undress. Many had been partially devoured, human bite marks all over their skin. Musicians had been strangled with the strings of their instruments. His courtesans lay piled naked and bloody atop each other all over his dais.

For this, he had slain his Aunt Missrine. For several minutes he wept, now smirched with blood himself, until he heard chanting. It drifted in and out of hearing, and he held his breath to catch it. Feeling weak, he pulled himself from the lake of blood on the floor, and headed for the rear of the hall, past the gory banqueting tables and his charnel throne. The serving doors at the back were open. From there the sound came.

Dostain hurried through low, mean servants' corridors. These places he had not ventured into since he was a child, when he had run wild through areas supposedly too lowly for a man of his blood to tread. As he had grown, he had disdained them and the people within upon whom he had once looked well. Not one of his servants was present. He remembered them now without the filter of privilege, how they had indulged him not because of his high birth, but in spite of it. He hoped they had got away.

He came to a servant's staircase that led all the way down to the kitchens in the bowels of the palace. The smell of roasting meat rose on the draught. Dostain had no desire to find what flesh cooked in his ovens, and exited via a hidden doorway into the grand lobby of his palace. Again, there was not a living soul. The body of a Yellow Guard lay across the open doors. Dostain glanced down. It seemed the man had shot himself in the head. His laspistol lay a few feet from his outstretched hand. Dostain plucked it up.

Beyond the doors was the Founders' Plaza. With a shaking hand he pushed against the ornately carved wood of the gate.

They swung wide upon a vision of hell.

The statues of the Founders – Magor and his thirteen companions – were obscured by piles of bodies stacked around them. Blood covered the mosaics of the plaza. Piles of burning heads lit the square under the dark skies. Heavy drops of rain pattered down to hiss in the fires, striking slow ripples from the blood underfoot. A ring of Space Marines surrounded something in the centre of the square that gave out an impure light. Dostain slipped through the gap, trying not to look at the dead faces staring out from the piles of corpses. There must have been hundreds of them, thousands, the people of the city slaughtered like livestock.

He approached the circle of monsters unseen, skulking between the piles of burning dead. A tall being led their chant, shouting out phrases that they thunderously repeated. Their high priest was not human, but a serpentine being with a four-armed torso and pale pink skin. Four horns crowned a head set with three blood-red eyes above a hooked nose and a mouth overfull with diamond teeth.

Dostain barely recognised Dib, but Dib it was. Beside the beast was his wife. He could barely recognise her either.

Pollein's body had split and stretched, becoming a fleshy arch. Her limbs hung limply from either side. From the top dangled her arms, from the bottom her legs. Her head was set into the apex between crushed-up shoulders, the obscene keystone to a hellish portal. Dostain choked back a cry. When her eyes opened and her mouth formed soundless words, he almost lost his mind.

He took aim to end her misery, but Dostain had never been a competent shot; he had never needed to be. The las-bolt sparked off the head of Magor's wife peering out from her mound of corpses with blind marble eyes.

Naturally, he was seen.

Dib, or the thing that Dib had become, or the thing that Dib had always been, threw up his hands in greeting.

'The master returns to us! Our Lord of Geratomro. Come to me, Dostain. I bring allies who will ensure your rule forever.'

Dostain backed away, the laspistol up but uselessly shaking in his hand. A pair of Space Marines detached themselves from the circle and came stalking after him, enormous armoured hands held out ready to grab and rend. He fired one more shot, and this one did hit. It struck a groove in a massive pauldron with no greater effect than if he had cast a pebble at the warrior. The Space Marine took the weapon and crushed it to broken components in a mighty fist, then he was seized and dragged before Dib. The creature's tail lashed back and forth. It rose up over Dostain. With a horrible smile, Dib followed his anguished eyes to the doorway of flesh that had been Pollein. She mouthed at him still. Her eyes were dreamy, and he saw with utmost horror that she was still saying 'How wonderful' over and over again.

'Yes, a pretty sight,' said Dib. He lowered himself down to Dostain's eye level, his serpent's body circling him. 'Behold, your wife, the witch! Of all the very many foolish things your Aunt Missrine did, not handing her sister over to the Black Ships of the thrice-cursed corpse-god was perhaps the most reckless. Mercy. Affection. Weaknesses. She has a powerful mind, Pollein, and a soul that burns in the warp like a beacon to those such as I. Great enough to allow me through. A charming legend that of the Devil-in-the-bush, don't you think? And so easy to slip into. Why, I think perhaps I might have been him before. I forget. Time does rush on so.'

Dib swayed for a moment, then said, 'In more fortuitous eras, this unguarded mind of your dear wife would be gateway enough for many of my lord's servants. But not far from here, Macharius brings the lies of your Emperor to hundreds of new worlds, and the vile light of Terra waxes strong. No matter. A tide of blood shall be the key to fit the lock. When the soldiers of Terra come marching in here with their songs and their desperate courage they will slaughter your men, and slaughter your citizens, and they themselves will be slaughtered. Their deaths are all I need, and they are inevitable. There will be soulfire enough not just for me, but for many! A daemonic legion will pour through this portal into this universe of ash and fire, and remake it in a fashion more pleasing to my Dark Prince!' He bent low again and caressed Dostain's cheek. His touch burned. 'You and I are going to have a lot of fun together, Dostain,' he whispered, 'and we shall have all eternity to enjoy it.' Dib cocked his horned head. 'It begins soon! Hearken! They approach. Those whose souls shall provide the final pry and fling the door wide! The Black Templars are coming.'

Dib's voice gave way to the guttering of flames and the sizzle of rain on hot fat. Dostain heard guns large and small only streets away. There was defiance in him still, and he attempted to stand, but the metal-clad hands of the Emperor's ungrateful children held him fast. He might as well have been pinned by a mountain. The chanting began again.

So ensnared, Dostain awaited the end of the world.

CHAPTER TWENTY-THREE
MAGOR'S SEAT

SUBURBS, MAGOR'S SEAT
GERATOMRO
087798.M41

Bannick was aboard *Righteous Vengeance* having his wounds seen to when Meggen caught up with him. The first gunner greeted Bannick with a manner as close to joy as he ever exhibited, but all was not well. Most of Jonas' platoon had been wiped out alongside the two Atraxian Shadowswords, and Bannick's hopes that *Lux Imperator*'s crew had survived the grenade were soon dashed.

'Leonates is dead,' said Meggen as Turneric, Jonas' medicae, patched up Bannick's arm. He scrubbed inside the cut with a stiff brush covered in powdered disinfectant.

'Hold still!' said Turneric as Bannick winced. 'I have to get all the mud out of this wound or you'll lose it to infection.'

'It's more painful than the wound,' he said.

'You'll thank me for it,' murmured Turneric. 'Please hold still. There are others that need my attention. The sooner I am done with you, the more lives might be saved.'

Bannick shut up, gritted his teeth and took the pain. When he was done bandaging up Bannick's arm, Turn-eric gave him a stimm-shot from a hypospray and rushed off. Bannick got up groggily.

'I don't see why he couldn't have done that before the cleansing,' said Meggen as he clambered down the Stormsword's access ladder. He offered his arm to the honoured lieutenant. Bannick waved it away.

'Leonates?'

'Threw himself on the grenade. Brave boy.'

'We're getting short on crew,' said Bannick. He reached the ground and sank mid-calf in the mud. Meggen gave him a strange look.

'I'm sorry, I don't mean to be callous,' said Bannick.

Meggen nodded. 'Yeah. I'm sure,' he said uneasily.

The downpour had petered out to something approaching normal for Geratomro. The raindrops were cleaner. The sky, however, remained thick with cloud that reduced the day to a grim twilight. *Lux Imperator* waited a dozen feet from the Stormsword, lights blazing and engine idling. Bannick was grateful for the heat put out by the big machine. Under a tarpaulin drooping with collected rain, Parrigar, Suliban, Chensormen and Jonas waited for him. Sword Brother Adelard stood outside, being too tall for the rough shelter.

'All fixed up and ready to fight?' said Parrigar.

'Aye, sir,' said Bannick. Three Space Marines were gathering their dead. Two giant, armoured corpses were laid in the dirt and covered with shrouds written all over with scripture. Another pair of Black Templars wheeled bullet-holed combat bikes into place beside them. A sixth bearing a massive sword and clad in ornate black armour watched on in silence. The Space Marines retrieved a beacon from the saddle packs of a bike, rammed its spike into the ground and extended its antennae. A signum light began blinking, and the Space Marines dipped their heads a moment.

'They gave their lives for the permanence of humanity,' intoned Adelard.

'Praise be,' the great warriors responded.

'Honour the legacy of the Chapter.'

'Praise be.'

'Honour the legacy of Rogal Dorn and of Sigismund.'

'Praise be.'

'Honour the gifts of the Emperor,' continued Adelard.

'Praise be.'

'Honour the battlegear of the dead.'

'Praise be!' the six Space Marines shouted, clashing their forearms on their breastplates.

'To your bikes, the time is at hand,' said Adelard. The Space Marines dispersed.

'There is no harder fight than that against our erstwhile brothers,' said Adelard. The shrouds of the dead flapped mournfully in the gathering wind. 'The beacon will draw in our Apothecary and Techmarines to recover their gene-seeds and wargear. All is not lost, and many traitors died at the hand of my two brothers here. I am satisfied.'

'Your beacon might also draw the enemy,' said Jonas. Bannick couldn't speak. He had been in the presence of Space Marines before, but they had not been armoured and he'd had other things to worry about that night aboard the command Leviathan on Kalidar. Power armour added so much more mass to the warriors. It was like conversing with monuments heavy with history. They were on his side. He knew that. He was still afraid of them.

Adelard regarded Jonas with the blank face of his helmet. 'Your position is already known. They will not come here. It is not their intention to push forwards. This group came here to disable the tanks so that they might remove the threat to their blasphemous engine.'

'Then what is their strategy?' asked Bannick.

'This planet is to be claimed in the name of old, dark gods.' He pointed to the sky over Magor's Seat. 'There. The discolouration of the clouds. It is already beginning. Daemon sign. Only faith and fury might save this world now.'

'You're not serious, are you?' said Jonas. 'Daemons? They're myths.'

'There are things in this galaxy many men would rather be kept secret,' said Adelard, turning to the commissars. 'Our order do not hold with this... *opinion.* How is faith to be tested, if the greatest evils are obscured? So say we.'

'My lord,' warned Suliban.

'Do not become concerned at my words, commissar. I will say no more lest I endanger these warriors to no good cause.'

'I don't like where this is going,' said Jonas.

'And you should not,' said Adelard. 'To know more would risk your lives from the actions of men less faithful than I.' By that he clearly meant the two commissars. Adelard rested a hand on Jonas' shoulder. 'Faith, brother. That is the only armour a warrior of the Imperium requires. Remember that, in the hours ahead.'

Chensormen and Suliban glanced at each other.

'What now then?' asked Bannick. 'Are we to return to our units?'

Parrigar cleared his throat. He looked haggard. They all did. 'No.'

'Just why exactly are you here, my lord?' asked Jonas suspiciously. 'It was pretty convenient you showing up like that moments before we were, well, all killed.'

'We came looking for this tank, *Lux Imperator*, the light of the Emperor,' said Adelard.

'Why?' asked Bannick. 'Who sent you?'

Blood-red eye-lenses turned towards him. 'Prophecy.' He pointed at the warrior armoured solely in black. 'Our brother has been chosen as the Emperor's Champion. His visions tell of great evil. You were in this vision, you and this vehicle. Our task cannot be completed without it. Now you must come with us.'

Adelard looked down at Bannick, who suddenly felt very small and very frightened. 'You have been chosen by the Emperor Himself.'

They came into Magor's Seat through the sparse suburbs climbing the lowermost slopes of Magor's Peak. Above the towering palace spires, green and red lights danced in the cloud, playing havoc with the vox. Soon after passing into the first district, they lost contact altogether.

'Magor's Peak, Magor's Park, Magor's Seat... Who is this damn Magor anyway?' muttered Meggen, reading a placard by the road.

'The founder of this world. A mercantile guildsman who stumbled across the planet some seven thousand years ago. Did none of your men read the prescribed intelligence, lieutenant?' asked Chensormen.

'No,' said Meggen with a certain insolent satisfaction. 'They did not.'

'That is a minor offence, but an offence nonetheless.'

'And when do you suppose I should read these reports?' said Meggen, his voice testy over the internal vox. 'In battle? While I am in training?'

'In your leave,' said Chensormen.

'I've had two hours leave in the last three years. There's nowhere to leave *to* in the Guard,' said Meggen.

'Have the rest of you read the material? Speak up, I say!' demanded Chensormen.

Nobody answered him.

Nominal amounts of resistance were swept aside by the Space Marines, acting as outriders to the depleted tank unit. Bannick aided them for a while, firing the secondary weapons systems out into the gloom from his own station. The Space Marines did not seem to need the help, and he gave up after a while to conserve ammunition. They encountered only reserve troops, old men and pressed youths, many of whom surrendered as soon as their officers were dealt with.

The Traitor Space Marines were missing from the battlefield, a cause of some irritation to the Black Templars, if the change in tone to their incomprehensible battle cant was anything to go by. They spoke infrequently to the unmodified humans, and when they did their exchanges were shot through with religious aphorisms and snippets of catechism. Bannick began to feel less than devout in the face of their unshakeable belief.

Occasionally, the Space Marines shared dark jests, shocking simply because Bannick had not thought them capable of humour. Of them all, the warrior with the black sword fascinated Bannick the most. He spoke only to say 'this way' when questioned by Adelard as to the direction they should go. He lent the fire of the boltguns mounted on his bike to their lightning plunges through street barricades, but his sword remained in its scabbard.

'Who is he?' asked Bannick of Chensormen. The commissar, who had been sulking at the back of the tank, brightened and came round the blocky refraction array of the cannon to share his knowledge. Chensormen was that type of man who thought he knew a lot and has an overwhelming desire to share it. The station of his office prevented him from doing so – Bannick thought he did 'hang back and glower' exceptionally well – but when prompted, he was only too happy to speak.

'A champion of the Emperor,' he said, the light of wonder igniting in his eyes. 'We learned of the Chapter in the schola progenium. Many of the Space Marines are blasphemers, who hold that the Emperor is only a man, not a god. Not so the Black Templars. They worship Him more fervently than any, and are rewarded by Him for it. Their order is mercifully free of the taint of witchery, thanks to His intervention. They are visionaries, master warriors and indomitable crusaders whose wrath cannot be deflected once provoked.'

'That's great,' said Meggen. 'Still doesn't tell us who he is.'

'I was getting to that!' said Chensormen, his mood souring. 'On rare occasions, one of their number is visited by visions sent by the Emperor. He will see himself as a great warrior, sometimes even the time of his own death. Undaunted, he will take up one of their black swords, and be anointed as the Emperor's Champion.'

'So, what you're telling us,' said Meggen, 'is that the tall, silent warrior knows he is about to die?'

'Possibly, yes,' said Chensormen. 'Imagine, the glory of serving the Emperor in such a way!'

'Imagine,' responded Meggen, 'following him into a fight even a Space Marine can't win.'

They fell silent at that, leaving Shoam's dry chuckling to compete with the soft rumble of *Lux Imperator*'s engines.

Adelard called a halt not long after and summoned the officers to his side. Bannick and Chensormen dropped down from *Lux*'s skirts into a street that was probably pleasant not so long ago, but was now scarred by days of bombardment and crusted with black ash. Adelard sat astride his combat bike as his warriors searched side streets and the few open spaces between the buildings. The area was affluent, housing hundred-storey habitation blocks fit for the middling-rich. Glimpsed through shell-punched holes, fires burned out of control in their interiors. The air reeked of hot metal and scorched plascrete.

'Ahead,' said Adelard. 'Steel yourselves.' He pointed around a corner. Bannick walked past the Space Marine and came to a horrified, staggering halt. In a small public space furnished with a fountain was a pile of bodies so high and wide it was jammed hard against the two buildings framing it, their limbs hanging down in such profusion as to provide the illusion of fur or cilia.

Chensormen made the sign of the aquila.

Jonas joined them, followed closely by Parrigar and Suliban.

'Emperor preserve us,' whispered Parrigar.

'Now you understand where the populace has gone,' said Adelard.

'I've never seen anything like this,' said Chensormen. He put his fist up to his mouth.

'I have,' said Bannick. 'On Agritha. Work of the eldar.'

'As have I, many times. Never does it fail to ignite my

outrage,' said Adelard. 'There will be more such sights, and worse. But this is the work of men, not xenos.'

From over the city, they could hear the sounds of battle. 'And the Geratomrans, do they know what they are fighting for?' asked Bannick. 'How could they be duped so?'

'The ones that yet fight on are most probably insane. The agents of the Dark Gods have their means. Come, we must not delay, or the unspeakable shall be unleashed upon this world. Prepare your men. They will see things that they will not easily put from their minds. Whatever it is you witnessed on Agritha, honoured lieutenant, I promise you the traitors have worse in store.'

As the tanks drove by, the men goggled at the charnel scene, the tankers glued to their vision blocks and pict screens. The few remaining men of Jonas' platoon stood to stare over their parapet, too shocked to keep in cover.

They pressed on towards the city centre. The noise of battle echoed down empty streets where the Imperial forces penetrated the city. Aircraft screamed overhead. But Bannick's group met no resistance. Augurs and sensoriums picked up enemy forces, but these melted away. Cowardice, they put it down to, but after the fifth withdrawal, Bannick suspected otherwise.

'My lord Adelard,' he voxed.

'*Speak*,' the Space Marine replied.

'The enemy are presenting no resistance. They are allowing us through. Does this not worry you, my lord?'

'*It does not*,' said Adelard. '*You are correct, however. We are being directed to the central plaza of this city, by the palace.*'

'We're being shepherded?'

'*We wish to go there. They wish us to go there. Our goals*

accord. It is not shepherding,' said Adelard. *'Fate, honoured lieutenant. It drives us all, whether we are blind to it or not.'*

'Then the main battlegroup, they do not wish to let them through?'

'They do not. This engagement hangs upon the fulcrum of possibility. They seek to draw us in for their diabolical purpose. We seek to end their vile sorcery. Force of arms will determine the matter. Be not afraid. The Emperor is on our side. We cannot lose.'

The vox clicked off.

They passed more mounds of bodies, some arranged into complex, interlocking patterns. Adelard was right: this was on a much greater and more terrible scale than the atrocities meted out upon the miners of Agritha. That humans were doing this to other humans made it all far worse. Bannick focused on his work, but every time they passed another corpse mound, his attention was drawn morbidly to it. The streets closer to the palace were undamaged by cannon fire. Bunting and decorations, dirtied by the rain, were strung across streets and from lumen posts.

'They were having a party?' said Meggen. 'What insanity is this?'

Bodies had been added to the displays, and other, wetter additions taken from the innards of dead men. Revellers lay here in less structured piles.

'They look like they killed each other,' voxed Jonas. *'Are you seeing this?'*

'Keep your eyes off the road, lieutenant,' said Parrigar. *'For your own sake.'*

The sky overhead was twisting in on itself, forming a vortex darker than a black hole. Colourful plasma flickered around its lip that were painful to the eye.

'*And off the sky,*' the honoured captain added.

The small group broke onto the Founder's Avenue, the main road of Magor's Seat, a huge processional way lined with columns supporting statues of past worthies. A mile away, it ended in a square before the monumental palace. Adelard called a halt.

'*Hearken to me now, men of the Imperium. We approach our final goal,*' the sword brother voxed. '*Parrigar, you must remain here. Take up station on that street. Cover our rear.*' Adelard indicated a crossroads.

'*Understood,*' said Parrigar.

'*Honoured Lieutenant Bannick, I require your tank. You will follow me. This is what we must do...*'

'No pity! No remorse! No fear!'

– Black Templars war-cry

CHAPTER TWENTY-FOUR
THE END OF MAGOR'S LINE

FOUNDER'S SQUARE, MAGOR'S SEAT
GERATOMRO
087898.M41

A throaty roaring intruded into the nearing sounds of gunfire. Dostain looked up Magor's Way to see Space Marines on huge combat bikes burst into the square and open fire. A number of the Emperor's Children fell, but the traitors spread out unhurriedly, unslinging their weapons and returning fire upon the Adeptus Astartes. Several of the traitors carried devices more akin to musical instruments than guns, and they played twanging cacophonies of destruction that burst apart the piles of bodies around Magor's companions and shattered the stone beneath. Dostain's captor remained still besides the rearing Dib, who laughed long and loud.

'They are here – the Black Templars! The final guests at our celebration!'

Between the spread parts of Pollein's body, the membrane of energy glowed kaleidoscopically and began to throb, bulging outwards in time to the Emperor's Children's war-instruments.

One of the Black Templars was brought low, his bike shattered into scrap by sonic pulses. The Space Marine skidded free, sparks flying from his armour. He rolled and pushed himself to his feet, drawing his sword.

'For Dorn! For the Emperor!' he shouted, and ran at the Traitor Space Marines, only to die in a hail of bolt-rounds.

Dostain watched dispassionately, shocked out of his fear. They could not all be bent on attempting such a suicidal dash, he thought.

The Black Templars drove full tilt into the Emperor's Children, the mass of their steeds bowling over those who got in their way. Boltguns blazed. As they reached the centre of the square they leapt off their bikes, allowing them to slide away, wheels still spinning, to crash into the followers of the Dark Prince. Their legs aided by their armour, they leapt improbably far, cracking the paving when they landed. There they drew blades and axes attached by steel chains to their wrists, and charged without delay, yelling praise to the Emperor and damning the traitors for their treachery. Slender power swords met heavy axes in showers of sparks. The Black Templars were furious warriors, moving with smooth grace despite their size and armour's mass. Impelled by the momentum of their bikes, they cut several of Trastoon's followers down before they were slowed.

'Impressive, aren't they?' hissed Dib to Dostain. 'But these sons of Dorn face the sons of Fulgrim. They are the Emperor's Children, for whom perfection was once a byword. Each one of these warriors has fought for thousands of years, and their mastery of blade-craft is unsurpassed, even by the so-called Knights of Dorn. Watch, and see the dogs of the Emperor die.'

Trastoon moved into the melee towards a Black Templar whose armour was trimmed in red. This one fought ferociously, bolt pistol in one hand, a power axe in the other. He hooked his axe-head behind the knee of a traitor, whipping him off his feet and bringing him down hard, ending his unnatural life with three bolt shots to the brain. Before the first had died, he pivoted on one foot, coming in low, his axe sweeping around to cleave another traitor through the chest. Lightning burst around the impact point, there was the almighty bang of annihilated atoms, and blood welled unstoppably from the shattered chest. Another died, riddled with shots from the red-and-black warrior's pistol, then another, and another. All the time the warrior moved faster, sang louder, his axe hewing down traitors. His blows became frenzied, and his battle-song throbbed the very stones of the square.

Dib winced. 'Prayers to their god. None of that will work here.'

Trastoon decapitated a Black Templar, sending his helmeted head rattling among the feet of the fighting Space Marines. Seeing the red warrior occupied, he charged, only for his sword to be met with the reinforced haft of the warrior's axe. Trastoon pushed down hard on his foe, but the Black Templar threw him back, and the two staggered away from each other.

The square filled with the ringing of weapons, the crackling of disruption fields and the banging of shattering matter. The combatants moved too fast for Dostain to make sense of. A space formed around the warrior in red and black and Trastoon, warriors from both sides having the sense not to intervene, and they circled each other warily.

'I am Sword Brother Adelard of the Black Templars,' said Adelard, brandishing his axe. 'I challenge you! May your death be as clean as your life has not.'

Trastoon saluted, holding his blue-steel sword in front of his face, the power field making his fanged mask jump and quiver.

'I am Damien Trastoon, and I have been killing the sons of Dorn since Horus declared war on the falsehoods of the Emperor. It is I who shall be your death, knight.'

'Let it be seen,' said Adelard. He came in with a devastating overhand swing of his axe that Trastoon caught on his own blade and flung wide. He thrust at Adelard, but leapt back as Adelard levelled his gun and loosed a pair of swift bolts. Incredibly, Trastoon deflected one with his blade and dodge the second. It buried itself in the thigh of another traitor so that he fell with a cry, and was finished by another Black Templar.

The Black Templars were hard pressed, outnumbered several times over. A third fell, cut down from behind and run through by two swords from the front. Only four remained. But one of those was a warrior like no other.

'The Emperor's Champion. It is his death that will lead to the opening of the gate,' said Dib.

'You expected them?' said Dostain.

'Of course. We let them through! Time has no meaning to my master. They rush to confront us for pride. He has foreseen it. The death of one of such exquisite purity has value in the working of magicks. For his blood, the warp will obey me. Watch him, marvel at his skill. Martial prowess such as his is rarely witnessed.'

This warrior fought his way forwards with insane power, smashing aside all who came against him. The Emperor's Champion's armour was marked by tiny script and fluttering parchments. A wreath circled his helm, and he bore in his hands a sword of purest black that he swung without tiring. Each blow felled multiple opponents, cleaving through ceramite armour and flinging back their bodies. A nimbus of light surrounded him, so pure that it was painful to look at, though it was by no means bright. When it settled on him, Dostain was filled with shame, made aware of all he had done wrong these last months. In that light was the truth of his treachery, and it was more than he could bear, but the Traitor Space Marine held him in place, and he could do little more than cringe from it.

Weapons clashed and songs vied with blasphemous war-cries as a hundred centuries of hatred was vented on both sides. A third Black Templar fell. Knowing what the loyal warriors of the Emperor would do to him if they prevailed, still Dostain found himself urging them to win. The sound of the greater battle had halted some distance away, near where his best troops were stationed, reinforced by more of Trastoon's warriors. The Imperial Guard would be too late to save him, only the Black Templars could, and he realised now that it was not his life in the balance – he could never keep that after what he had done – but his soul.

'Fiend! Fiend!' called the Emperor's Champion to Dib as he smashed his way through the melee towards the daemon. He barged aside a warrior in pink and gold, reversed his sword and drove it backwards. It pierced back-pack, back and chest, emerging from the front of the traitor and steaming with blood cooking in its disruption field.

He withdrew his sword and flourished it at Dib. 'In my dreams I have seen you. The Emperor has sent me to bring about your end. Stand forwards, and fight!'

Dib smiled. 'Who could possibly ignore an invitation like that?' he said, and darted at the Champion with the speed of a striking serpent. From each of Dib's hands a sword sprouted, exotic alloys gleaming bright colours and dripping with exquisite poisons. He duelled with the Champion, Trastoon with Adelard. The numbers of the traitors had been reduced to a dozen, but the two other remaining Black Templars were isolated, heavily beset by them. One more went down, knocked onto his back. A blade was driven through his breastplate with a sickening crack.

Before he died, he looked at Dostain. His bolter came up, and he fired. Dostain expected the end.

There was a bang directly behind the planetary governor. The giant holding Dostain crumpled, his helmet hollowed out. His hand spasmed on Dostain's shoulder as he fell, crushing Dostain's collarbone.

Screaming at the pain, Dostain fell down with the warrior over him. In panicked agony, he pulled himself out from beneath unnoticed and crawled away.

'Damn it, Shoam, get us closer,' said Bannick. 'There's no way we can get a clear shot.'

He checked the ranging augur again. The view from its eye was obscured by the massive statues of the square and the corpse mounds heaped around them.

Lux Imperator nosed its way down the long way to Founder's Square, hugging the shadows of the buildings. The imperious countenance of the statues looked out over a sea of corpses. Shoam drove over them. There was no way to avoid the dead carpeting the street.

'That light there! Do you see it, Meggen?'

Meggen looked out through the same instrument as Bannick. 'What is that light. And is that a...? It looks like a body...'

Bannick pulled his face away from the eyepiece and wiped his face. 'Ignore it. That is our target. Get a good range on it, but avoid looking at it if you can. Epperaliant, what news from the battlegroup?'

'I've managed contact only intermittently with high command, sir. But as far as I can tell, the advance has stalled five hundred yards back. We're on our own. I'm getting some strange readings from that square. I... I don't understand them.'

'Think not on them. You witness the diabolical arts of the traitors. These things are not for men such as we to witness,' said Chensormen. His hand tapped at his bolt pistol. Bannick wished he would shut up; he was putting the crew on edge. He tried to focus on the melee in the square, where giants from legend clashed surrounded by the worst evil humanity had to offer. He caught a glimpse of Adelard duelling a massive champion of the Dark Gods, then he was swallowed up again by the battle.

'Shall I ask Parrigar to come up and support?' said Epperaliant. 'The Black Templars are outnumbered.'

'Negative. With two super-heavies we're likely to be spotted, then the game is up. We have one shot at this, do you hear that *Lux*?' he said, and rapped his knuckles on plasteel. The sound of the engine hitched.

'*Lux Imperator* is aware of the gravity of the situation and wishes wholeheartedly to bring it to a satisfactory conclusion,' said Starstan. 'It will not fail you, Honoured Lieutenant Bannick.'

Bannick squinted down the rangefinder again. He bit his lip.

'Shoam, bring us another hundred yards closer.'

'Then we'll be only one hundred and fifty yards away from the gateway, sir,' said Epperaliant. 'We'll be seen.'

'And I really don't want us to miss,' said Bannick. 'Get us closer. Starstan, prepare to charge volcano cannon capacitors the second we halt.'

Dib and the Champion duelled. Unholy blades clashed upon the edge of the sacred black sword. Dib whirled and darted faster than Dostain's eyes could follow, but every strike in his flurry of blows was met by the black sword. One by one the other Traitor Space Marines fell around the combatants, dispatched by the Champion when they strayed too near. Soon, there was only Trastoon fighting Adelard, and Dib fighting the champion.

Behind them the unnatural gate pulsed. Dostain peered at it, though it hurt his eyes. On the other side of the membrane of light he saw images of creatures gathering, lovely yet terrible, pressing hard against the glow. For now they appeared unfinished, flat, like uncompleted sketches drawn by a madman.

Dostain crawled faster, his wounded shoulder hunched and left arm drawn up like a wounded dog's leg. He dared not stand, but cowered, watching men far better than he fight because of his actions.

Adelard whirled and chopped without slowing. His battle-hymn was loud and pure after many minutes of fighting, but his enhanced metabolism was more than

matched by that of Trastoon, who was further strengthened by the unholy power of the warp. Trastoon leapt
high and drove down at the sword brother, the sorcer-
ous energies sheathing his blade colliding with the purer
power fields of Adelard's axe in eruptions of light and
sound. Adelard staggered back. Dostain watched, his heart
in his mouth, as Trastoon drove at him again, his sword
blurring arcs of painful fire before him. Again the axe and
the sword met. Again the combatants parted. Adelard was
being pushed away from the gate, back towards the ring
of Founders' statues and the piles of corpses. Dostain felt
sick. This was what he had brought on his world. Suffering and death. He looked around for a weapon, anything.
His eyes lit upon the boltgun of the dead Space Marine,
but even with both arms he would not have been able to
defy its magnetic lock and pull it away from the armour.

Then he saw the pistol, holstered at the Space Marine's
side. His injured arm held awkwardly, he crawled over.
Nervously, he looked up, but neither Dib nor Trastoon
saw him.

Dostain reached for the bolt pistol with his right hand.
It slipped free from its holster easily enough, but he nearly
dropped it when he lifted it up. Sized for a Space Marine,
the bolt pistol was too massive for a normal man to wield
comfortably. With difficulty he sat back, rested it on his
knee and aimed it at Trastoon. His finger felt inadequate
for the task of pulling the trigger.

'You should join me, you are a good warrior,' Trastoon
shouted over the buzz and crackle of locked power fields.

'Never!' said Adelard.

'Reconsider. The Emperor is intolerant of those who call
Him a god. You are ignorant of the lessons of the past.'

'Lies!' cried Adelard, and flung the Chaos champion's blade aside.

'Then you shall die,' said Trastoon. He thrust with his blade at Adelard, both hands on the hilt. The axe came down to force it aside, but there was too much impetus behind the blow, and it slammed into Adelard's torso. Adelard spun with the hit, but the blade scored a deep smoking gash across the gothic cross moulded into his chest. The power cables underneath parted and spat. Adelard let out a metallic cry through his vox-grille and fell sideways, his armour dying on him.

'So many have fallen to me. You are but the latest,' said Trastoon. He raised his sword.

Somehow, Dostain pulled the trigger without yanking the gun off target. The shot rang out. The bolt flew true, smashing through Trastoon's power armour and exploding inside his wrist.

Trastoon staggered, his left hand hanging by its tendons from the ruin of his arm. His ugly helmet turned to find his assassin. When he saw Dostain, the stolen bolt pistol propped upon his knee, Trastoon laughed.

'You? You dare to defy me?'

'I am Planetary Governor. This is my world,' said Dostain, and fired again. The second bolt hit Trastoon in the side, and his sword fell from nerveless fingers. The champion tottered. With a growl of effort, Adelard thrust upwards from the ground, the spike atop his power axe slamming up through Trastoon's gorget and into his brain.

Trastoon collapsed to the ground and Adelard fell back. The fight between Dib and the Champion was reaching its climax. The Black Templar's armour smoked from a dozen rents. His blade slowed. With a triumphant screech, Dib fell upon him, all four swords plunging into the Champion. He covered the warrior in an obscene embrace, snake-like body coiling around the Black Templar.

At this blow the membrane dividing the material realm from the warp pushed outwards and did not rebound. In this new extrusion, thousands of pairs of hungry eyes looked out into the universe.

'The way is open!' screeched Dib triumphantly. 'The way is–' Dib made a clicking noise in his throat and arched backwards. The Black Sword burst from his spine, thick blue ichor running over his serpentine body. The sword ground round, opening the wound wide, then cut outwards, almost cleaving Dib in two. The daemon herald fell gurgling, and the Champion staggered free, his armour shattered and blood pooling around his feet.

He raised his sword to the heavens and tilted back his head. 'Emperor, hear me! I am Brother Bastoigne of the Black Templars! I have served you! I have served you! Witness me! No pity! No remorse! No fear!' He reversed his sword and plunged it point first into the stone. Then he knelt. Head bowed in prayer and hands clasped around the hilt of the black sword, he died.

The membrane quivered. Pollein's head mouthed, 'How wonderful.' Dib's top half lay still, his nearly severed tail squirming beside him.

Adelard rolled onto his side and laughed, his mirth growing in volume until it encompassed the whole square. 'You lose, daemon! There shall be no horror upon Geratomro this day.'

Dib roused himself, his torso curling in upon itself like a dying insect's. A wet tearing saw his tail come free, and he crawled away from the gate.

'There is but... one more death needed here, Templar... and I have found it. The last of the house of Magor.'

With the last of his ebbing strength he plucked a dagger from his belt and cast it out.

'No!' shouted Adelard.

The blade buried itself in Dostain's forehead. His eyes rolled backwards, and he fell dead.

'It... is... you... who... loses,' hissed Dib. Before he had finished speaking, his body was already collapsing into bubbling, black filth.

The membrane swelled and thinned. The faces pressed against it lost their flatness, becoming more real as the colour drained from the energy field. Then it popped, prosaically, like a child's burst balloon.

A hideous laughing filled the square, and the numberless brides of Slaanesh spilled into the world.

'Emperor!' said Bannick. Through the rangefinder he saw a thousand nightmares pouring into the square.

'Sir, this is like nothing I've ever seen,' said Epperaliant. 'I can make no sense of these augur readings.'

'We should open fire. Now,' said Meggen.

'Not yet! Look, Adelard is alive,' said Bannick.

They watched through their scopes as the Space Marine pulled himself inch by painful inch away from the gateway as the square behind him filled with its unholy crowd. The beings were all colours, and a shimmering light surrounded them. They fought each other and danced, and leapt upon the bodies of the fallen to tear at their flesh.

'We should do it now!' shouted Meggen.

'Wait for his signal!'

Adelard crawled on as more and more of the beings flooded the square.

'He's going to make it!'

'Col! Give the order, Colaron! Do it!'

Chensormen crept forwards, staring out of Bannick's viewing block in dismay.

'He is right. Fire now!'

'Back off!' shouted Bannick. 'He's still alive. We await his signal.'

The Black Templar reached a lumen where Founders' Way entered Founders' Square and wrapped both hands around it. A group of creatures noticed him and approached. Their backward-jointed legs gave them a strutting, predatory walk. They were hideous yet beautiful, parodies of the human form, androgynous things that blended male and female anatomy to disturbing effect. Long tongues slid out from between pointed teeth. Many of them had slender, chitinous claws in the place of hands.

'*Now,*' voxed Adelard. '*Do it now!*'

Bannick was frozen by the sight of the creatures. Slowly, one turned to regard him. He could swear it was looking right into his soul with its round, black eyes, right through the ranging equipment.

'Sir!' shouted Epperaliant. 'He has given the order.'

Something bigger was trying to come through, bull-headed and mighty. The gate shook with its roaring.

'Sir!' shouted Epperaliant again.

Bannick blinked and looked away. His head was full of horrific imagery. His own memories of Tuparillio dead and Brasslock mutilated were bad enough, but they had been perverted, made obscene and they squirmed in his mind. 'M... Meggen, open fire. Open fire!' he yelled, mastering himself.

Lux Imperator's volcano cannon vomited the light of the Emperor into the heart of darkness. It incinerated daemonic flesh, and slammed into the unholy gateway. The result was a titanic blast of violet unlight. For a second, the square teetered on the brink of the warp, and the crew of *Lux Imperator* had a veiled view of the horror that awaited them on the other side of death.

The gate swelled, leaving Adelard to sit upon its edge. Then, with a thrumming boom, it imploded. Daemon creatures were sucked howling back from whence they came. A wash of energy blasted outwards, sending Adelard bouncing up the street and clearing the sky above the square to reveal the blue sky of noon.

Echoes died. After-images died. What did not die and never could was the memory of what Bannick witnessed in that square.

Silence fell.

'We... we did it,' said Meggen.

'No. *Lux Imperator* did,' said Bannick.

'Emperor protect us all,' said Epperaliant.

'Lux Imperator! Lux Imperator, *come in!*' Cholo's voice crackled out of the vox.

'The vox is working,' said Epperaliant in a daze. 'Erm, Bannick, I've clear signals across all channels.'

Bannick rested a shaking hand on the refraction array. His wounded left arm pulsed. In his head, Tuparillio danced with the creatures in an eternal hell of purple fire.

'Sir?'

'Respond on my behalf. *Lux Imperator* to...'

'Stop!' said Chensormen. He had his gun out, causing Epperaliant to give out a strangled cry of surprise. 'You are all under arrest. Hand over your arms.' Bannick turned in his chair, this new development driving back the horrific images tormenting him. 'Slowly, honoured lieutenant. I am relieving you of command. This vehicle is under my control. You, commsman, do not answer those hailing you. Lock the hatches. Nobody is to leave this tank.'

He waved Epperaliant out of his chair. Epperaliant obeyed in baffled consternation.

'We've done nothing wrong,' said Bannick. 'We have ended the rebellion. The war is won.'

'This war is never won,' said Chensormen, 'and regrettably you have seen the truth of the war behind the war. You have done well, and fought with honour and courage for our lord the Emperor of Terra. You should be proud. But it is over now. This is a situation that can only be handled in one way. I–'

Chensormen gave out a bubbling moan and fell to the deck, blood frothing at his lips, eyes wide, revealing Shoam crouched in the ladder well behind him, a bloody shiv in his hand.

Bannick's good hand went to his sidearm, Epperaliant stared at Shoam, mouth still agape. The Savlar coolly ignored them, climbed up onto the command floor, sat across the dying commissar and calmly stabbed him through heart. The commissar's head lolled, his eyes dulling.

'What have you done, you basdacking Savlar murderer?' yelled Epperaliant.

'Mute the vox,' said Shoam.

'What?'

'Lux Imperator, *respond. This is Cholo aboard* Ostrakhan's Rebirth. *We're breaking through. The enemy are fleeing. What is your position and status, over?*'

The crackle as Cholo waited for a reply sounded like an accusation. Epperaliant's hand hovered over the response button.

'Mute the vox, Epperaliant,' said Bannick.

'Sir, we've got to report this. It'll see us all–'

'Do as he says,' said Bannick. 'Let's hear Shoam out.' His hand stayed upon his pistol butt.

'Yeah, you know, don't you, honoured lieutenant,' said Shoam with a yellow-toothed grin. He slipped his make-shift knife back into his boot. 'You understand, else I'd be dead already. What I have done,' he said to Epperaliant, 'is saved you all.' He wiped his shiv on the commissar's uniform. 'This one here, he was going to kill you for what you saw.'

'What the... Shoam? What the basdack have you done?' said Meggen, who had come forwards to investigate the ruckus.

'You best listen to this, Meggen man,' said Shoam. 'You too, coghead. We're all in this together.'

'In what?' said Meggen.

'What do you mean, what we have seen? The xenos?' said Epperaliant.

'You know those weren't xenos,' said Shoam. 'Leastways, not in the normal sense.'

'Explain yourself. I think we've only a few minutes before people get suspicious,' said Bannick.

'Nah, you got longer. There's a war on. Shoam lifted his respirator to his mouth and took a long draught of nitro-chem. 'We Savlar are sent everywhere, to the worst places, places where people like you don't go. We are scum – nobody cares about the scum. Thing is, when you're scum, you learn to survive. We can survive anything.

You survive Savlar itself, it gives you the knack to keep from death until it can't be kept no more. When I was a boy, I hear tales of places my kind fight, places filled with things like what we saw. Things that aren't xenos, noble boy, things that are worse by far. There was this one regiment. It wasn't the first, and it ain't gonna be the last. It fought these things, and it won. And they were all making with the celebration at the end, when some high-born dog gives the order, and they were gunned down. Them that ran were hunted, and then the hunters were shot too.'

'How can you know, if they're all dead?'

'I didn't say they were all dead. Like I say, Savlar survive. Not all of them died. Savlar are everywhere. One or two got word out to other Savlar, and Savlar talk to Savlar wherever they are, because we don't trust no one else. This here, the Imperium doesn't want anyone to know about it. They will kill and kill to keep the secret. Men like this stuffed jacket.' He prodded the dead commissar with his toe. 'He'd kill you all then kill himself for what we seen. You wait to see what happens to this world now. If we breathe a word of this, then we all die.'

'But why?' said Epperaliant.

'Because we know the truth,' said Shoam. 'We know the truth that the Emperor ain't the only god in the universe. Them things we see, they're the servants of the Dark Gods. Things from the warp. Things I ain't supposed to know about, things you ain't supposed to know about.'

'Lux Imperator, *come in. We are reading your ident beacon. We have a fix on your position. Is anyone alive in there?*' came Cholo's voice.

'We're going to have to dump the commissar somewhere.

They see shiv marks in him, it won't matter what I say,' said Shoam.

'Get his body below,' said Bannick.

'You basdacking kree bird, what have you done!' shouted Meggen.

'Do it,' said Bannick. 'Hide him.'

'Col!'

'Just do it!' shouted Bannick. 'Best to have options, right, Shoam?'

Shoam nodded in acknowledgement. Roughly he bundled the dead commissar below.

Bannick looked to them all. 'What do you say, are we going to keep this between ourselves?'

'What basdacking choice do we have?' said Meggen.

'I mean, we can tell absolutely no one, not even the others on *Cortein's Honour.*'

Meggen nodded hesitantly. 'Sure. If the other option's death. I'm in.'

'Starstan?'

'I do not care for the policies of the Imperium, but those of the Adeptus Mechanicus are hardly less stringent. Should it be known what occurred here, I would be in danger myself – although not in the same way as you, the result would be the same. I shall keep my silence, if I can be assured that you shall keep yours.'

'Epperaliant?'

'Sir, I... I can't. I... If this is supposed to be secret, maybe there's a reason. Maybe we shouldn't know. Maybe–'

'Epperaliant, if we do speak, we'll all die. Shoam has it right.'

'He's a *criminal*. What he did is wrong,' said Epperaliant pleadingly.

'Fine. See me swing,' said Shoam, clambering back up the ladder. 'Then you bleed out your last in an Inquisitorial interrogation chamber. We'll all die one way or another, nobleman,' said Shoam.

'Sir...'

'Lux Imperator, *we are approaching. We'll be with you shortly. Scout elements have you sighted. What happened down there?*' said Cholo.

'Epperaliant, I need to know you won't talk,' said Bannick desperately.

'I cannot promise that,' said Epperaliant. 'He's lying. We could have valuable intelligence. A new threat...'

Shoam chuckled and shook his head. 'That threat is as old as time, and then some. You know nothing they don't already. You heard what Chensormen said.'

'Sir! Please.'

Bannick's gun rasped from its holster. He held it unwaveringly at the commsman.

'Epperaliant, I respect you greatly as a second in command and as a soldier. But if you do not swear to hold your tongue, then I will shoot you myself. All our lives are in danger, do you understand?'

Engines sounded outside then stopped. Muffled shouts came closer.

Epperaliant sat up straight, and pulled down his jacket to smooth away some of its wrinkles. 'Then shoot. I will not lie. The commissar must have had his reasons. I cannot perjure myself, not on the say so of Shoam.'

Footsteps clanked on the ladder at the rear.

'Damn your pride!' said Bannick desperately.

'It's not pride, sir.'

'Epperaliant, please.'

Epperaliant shook his head. 'You will not kill me. I know you Colaron Vor Artem Lo Bannick. You are a good man, an upstanding man. You know what Shoam suggests is wrong. We must go to a higher authority. You will see I am right and he is wrong.'

Bannick thumbed the catch back on his laspistol. Charge lights blinked from red to green. The sound of men scrabbling at the roof hatches penetrated thick metal.

Epperaliant's eyes widened. Maybe, at the last, he was surprised that Bannick would go through with it. 'Sir, I...'

Bannick discharged his pistol. A sharp crack heralded murder. Epperaliant slumped over his desk, smoke rising from either side of his torso.

Bannick let his gun clatter to the floor. The blood drained from his face and he fell into his chair. 'What have I done?'

'The right thing,' said Shoam.

The hatch opened. Weak sunlight filtered into the command deck, making the crew screw up their eyes.

'Get word back to high command, they're still alive.' A trooper's face poked through the hatch. 'You won the war!' he said, then his face wrinkled as he took in Epperaliant. 'What happened here?'

'Some enemy witchcraft turned him against us,' said Bannick.

'Where are the others?'

'Dead. In combat,' said Bannick. 'They were heroes.'

The man withdrew, shouting for medicae and stretcher-bearers. More engines and voices approached.

CHAPTER TWENTY-FIVE
THERE IS ONLY WAR

MEDICAE FRIGATE *MERCIFUL SISTER*
GERATOMRO ORBIT
088298.M41

Rank bought many things in the Astra Militarum, but all of them started small. A little extra food, a few luxuries, incrementally more until one reached the highest echelons, where a man might live like a lord. But for one such as Honoured Captain Kandar Ostrakhan Lo Hannick, rank afforded little consideration. He had a little space to himself in the medicae frigate, partitioned from the rest of the ward by plastek screens, and no more than that.

Bannick sat in the cramped space by the captain's cot, his dress uniform immaculate and boots polished to a mirror shine, a rack of new medals pinned to his chest. Propped up on hard pillows Hannick looked shrunken by comparison. Lank, untrimmed hair framed a pale face.

'It is secondary silicosis, a delayed effect of the environment on Kalidar,' he said to Bannick.

'Dust Lung,' said Bannick.

Hannick sighed. 'A delayed and pernicious kind, yes. I performed all my rituals properly, from my personal cleansing to petitioning the spirit of my respirator for safety,' he smiled. 'Yes, Bannick, I know what you're thinking. Maybe I wasn't enthusiastic enough, but it's more likely the equipment wasn't good. Emperor knows how many others have got it waiting inside them to push their lungs out of their windpipes. I have been informed a screening programme of the Kalidar veterans is being undertaken, but it is a little late for me.

'I thought one day I'd complete my fifty subjective years' service and take the Emperor's gift, get a patch of land somewhere. It's a hard life, but better than a quick death.'

'Be a farmer? Why by Terra would you want to do that?'

Hannick's laughter at Bannick's expression set off another round of coughing. He feebly dabbed the blood away from his lips. 'Why not? Do you remember what it was like to be a Vor back home, Bannick? We remember Paragon as perfect, but it rarely lived up to its name. I just wanted to go somewhere quiet, where I'd be left alone for a handful of years.'

'You retire with honour, sir.'

'I'll be dead in four months if I can't find someone to fit me with augmetics,' said Hannick plainly. 'Good quality lungs that'll leave me still able to move about are expensive. The Hannick clan has the funds, if I can get them across thirty light years, into a warzone and find a sympathetic medicae. And even if I could get replacements as good as my originals were, what will they mean? Twenty-eight more years of war.' He spoke now to himself more than Bannick. 'I don't think I can do it.'

'That's it, you're giving up?'

'No, no, I'm not giving up,' said Hannick 'I've only got one life. If the Departmento Munitorum want to squander it for me in battle, that's their business, but I'm not lying down and letting night fall on me without putting up a fight. What use is the Emperor's protection...'

'...if we choose not to protect ourselves?' said Bannick, finishing the saying along with the captain.

'Right. So I'll do my best. I'll probably die. If I don't, and I'm lucky, I'll be able to walk but I'll be discharged on medical grounds. New lungs aren't like a new eye or arm. They can limit a man. If I'm a little less than lucky, I'll be put behind a desk and forgotten about. If I'm really unlucky, I'll be back in that basdacking tank.'

Bannick was taken aback. Hannick rarely swore.

'Don't look at me like that. I've seen too much. You know what I mean. You've been in service now for three years subjective, seven actual. How many men have died by your side?'

'A lot,' Bannick answered. He knew the number, but would not speak it.

'One hundred and ninety-nine, Bannick. I've lost one hundred and ninety-nine men. How fitting that I might make the two hundredth?'

'What will happen to the company?'

'We'll be out of commission for several weeks. So much of our armour took a beating down there, and the Arks Mechanicus have a backlog that'd stretch all the way to the next star system. There's the pacification of course...' said Hannick, his voice trailing off. 'After that, well. *Ostrakhan's Rebirth* will probably require a new master, as will the Seventh. I'm recommending you.'

'Marteken has seniority. He's served far longer than me.'

GUY HALEY

'Marteken is not ready, and never will be. He's a good enough commander, but lacks the foresight to manage a full company in battle as well as his own tank. Besides, he's getting nervy. Most importantly he does not want to do it.'

'He'd have no choice if ordered.'

'You know men do not work that way. Another reason you're fit for the post, and he is not.'

'What about Hurnigen? He's served barely less time than me.'

'Well, he is a better prospect, or he will be, one day. The master of a Shadowsword requires different skills to those of the other tank roles, skills he's only now acquiring. He is best where he is, for the time being at least. No, it is your name I am putting forward as my replacement. I am sorry.'

'There is no need to apologise. I am honoured, sir.'

'Is the appropriate response, but there is every reason for me to apologise. It might not happen. My recommendation is only that. The appointment is the army group's to make, and that means, ultimately, the Departmento Munitorum's, with a big helping, meddlesome hand from the Martians. But, but...' Hannick coughed again; his chest twitched with the effort of keeping the coughs shallow, but he failed. Soon he was bent double, Bannick holding a kidney bowl beneath his lips as red mucus dribbled out. Finished, he sank back into his pillow with a long groan.

'Emperor, this is tedious. I half wish I could just get on and die.'

'Don't say that, sir.'

'It bloody hurts.'

'I have experience.'

'Ah yes, I remember. You had the lung wash.'

'Also deeply unpleasant.'

'Well, that won't help me. Not now.' His eyes closed a moment, and he breathed raggedly. His face had sunk in on itself, the skin waxy and sallow. Bannick sat there until Hannick roused himself a little. 'I'm tired, Bannick. Leave me.'

'Sir.' Bannick stood to attention and gave the honoured captain a crisp salute. 'Thank you, sir. For everything.'

'If you ever get the chance to live out the last years of your life in peace, remember me. Light a candle or something. It's the little things like that which keep us human. Without remembrance, loss, grief, mercy... we're nothing. We're just killers.'

'I will, sir.'

Hannick smiled at that. He turned his pallid face, now sheened with sweat, to look at Bannick.

'It was a good last battle though, wasn't it, Bannick? While you were waiting for that one shot, I led those tanks right into the teeth of the enemy. I wish you could have been there to see it.'

'I hear it was a charge worthy of a song, sir.'

Hannick nodded. Still smiling, he fell into an exhausted sleep.

Three days later, he died.

Bannick walked quickly along the portway of the medicae frigate. In his pocket, his crumpled order papers rustled. Geratomro was not done with him yet. On the surface were three hundred million civilians the Inquisition had declared as traitoros in extremis. The planet was to be depopulated and resettled. It looked like Bannick's uncle and the others would get their wish. A new Paragon was to be born from the bone and blood of an alien world. Every man, woman and child below was being assessed and vetted. Many would die in the penal legions. Others would be sent to provide slave labour on other worlds. Bannick had his part to play in this awful task.

Bannick halted by an observation cupola and stepped inside. Blue light reflected from the planet made it feel colder than it actually was.

The first of the ships bearing the new slaves rose from the surface to the fleet. The funeral pyres of those deemed unsuitable for servitude were visible from orbit.

He would do his duty, though he did not relish it. The thought that he could defy his orders crossed his mind. He had done so already, and it had cost a man his life so that Bannick might spare his own. Cravenly, he still wished to live.

Sword Brother Adelard had sought him out some days after the battle, striding into the Imperial castella where Bannick was overseeing repairs to the Seventh's tanks. His armour had been repaired and repainted so well it appeared that he had not been in combat at all.

'You need not worry,' he had said. 'I told the Inquisition that you saw nothing. By datapacket, naturally.'

'They would have executed you?'

'With warriors such as myself, they prefer a full mind-wipe. But that is a form of death in itself. My Chapter would never allow that to happen. It is wasteful of experience and time. While I was being remade, many wars would go unfought.'

'Then maybe you better leave. You are vulnerable here.'

'They will not take me. We Space Marines are nearly

autonomous in our actions for the Imperium, but even we must obey the Inquisition. However, if they were to attempt to come against me in violence, my crusade would retaliate. So the Inquisition will not ask, and thus the delicate balance of power is maintained, and every agency may keep face. That we work to protect mankind and the Inquisition does also is all that matters, in the end.'

'But they would kill me.'

'Without hesitation,' Adelard said bluntly. 'My Chapter teaches that this is wrong, that the bravest souls can bear the weight of the truth, and that without it they cannot be properly tested and forged into weapons for the Emperor. You are one of those brave men, Honoured Lieutenant Bannick. If you were not, I would kill you myself.'

'I see.'

'Take heart. Do not be sorry that you live. There are men who strive for their own goals without thought to the consequence. You are not one of those men. In you, the Emperor has a worthy servant. Praise be.' The Black Templar clashed his arms in a cross over his chest.

'Praise be,' said Bannick, and saluted back.

Adelard left him then. Bannick realised he had never seen him without his helmet.

Bannick could not fully agree with Adelard about his worthiness. Dark dreams plagued him. Only constant occupation kept the images of the square from his head, and sleep brought terror. In light of this he saw his own desire to survive not as the Emperor's judgement, but as a selfish urge that made him no better than the Paragonian clan lords now lining up to take control of Geratomro. These lesser sons had been sent to join the military by families to whom they were surplus, but their desire for power never left them, and privileged men will always seek to take more to themselves, and carve out their own little empires. They wanted the good life, Bannick wanted to live. The impulses were not so different. Once more, others had suffered for Bannick's motives.

Trying not to think about what awaited him in the transit camps and cleansing centres on the surface, Bannick headed for his shuttle.

ABOUT THE AUTHOR

Guy Haley is the author of *The Devastation of Baal, Dante, Baneblade* and *Shadowsword,* for Warhammer 40,000, and *Throneworld* and *The Beheading* for The Beast Arises series. For The Horus Heresy he has written *Pharos* and The Primarchs novel *Perturabo: Hammer of Olympia.* His enthusiasm for all things greenskin has also led him to pen the eponymous Warhammer novel *Skarsnik,* as well as the End Times novel *The Rise of the Horned Rat.* He has also written stories set in the Age of Sigmar, included in *War Storm, Ghal Maraz* and *Call of Archaon.* He lives in Yorkshire with his wife and son.

WARHAMMER
40,000

CALGAR'S
FURY

PAUL KEARNEY